ONCE UPON THE TIME IN LIBERIA

A Collection of Short Fictional Stories

Dr. Peter Z.M. Nehsahn

No part of this book may be reproduced in any manner, stored in a retrieval system or transmitted in any way by any means—electronic, mechanical, photocopy, recording or otherwise without written permission from the copyright holder except in the case of brief quotation embodied in critical articles and reviews.

Copyright © 2020 by Dr. Peter Z.M. Nehsahn
All rights reserved. Printed in the United States of America

DEDICATION

To All Liberian Pupils Who Hunger for Literature to read

TABLE OF CONTENT

FORWARD

"A dog enjoys playing by repeatedly falling down."
Meaning: If you want to be a part of any group
or organization, you cannot stand on the sideline
and complain of being left out, rather you fully participate.

This book is borne out of the author's passion and desire for reading. He grew up on his maternal grandparents' farm and had no access to public or private education. His parents later took him to a rubber plantation when they sought treatment for his maternal grandma's ailing heart. There, he grew up some more. When the plantation introduced free education for workers' children, he wanted to go to school, but his grandmother advised his mother against the idea. He was the only son and she could not afford to lose him to education. His Mom's three other sons had died young. According to grandma, education would take her daughter's son away, never to be seen again.

Before he started working as a water-boy on the plantation, he went early in the morning and stood by the warehouse used as a single classroom and recited the alphabets just like the students inside. His outside classroom days ended abruptly when his Daddy got sick. He, his Mom, younger sister and grandma left the plantation, though grandma was never cured of her illness. Shortly after they returned home, grandma died. Several weeks later his Daddy also died. His younger sister was barely two years old.

After the deaths of his grandma and Daddy, the author asked his Mom if he could go to school. With grandma dead and gone, his Mom accepted his request and promised to help in every way possible. The folks in his hometown, headed by the chief had started a school because they lovededucation. The chief did not have children when he started the school, but he wanted other kids in the town to have an education. The author can record the chief pleading with parents to send their children, boys and girls to school. Back then, parents did not send their girls to school. They gave them up into marriages. This was a major source of income, especially for a father who had three or four daughters.

The school had one teacher with no textbooks. He taught all subjects. He prepared the lessons from his previous notes and taught whatever he could teach. The parents paid the tuition; one dollar (US) and fifty-cents per month. It was later raised to two dollars and fifty-cents.

For a farming town of less than 300 people in the 1960's, that was a huge sum of money. Most parents, including the author's Mom worked tirelessly to provide money for tuition every month. They carried a fifty or sixty-pound bag of kola nuts, called *kinjah* for a measly fifty cents to a commercial town almost three miles away. His Mom had to make at least two trips a day to raise a dollar.

When it was time to read, each student was called to the front of the class to read. Grades two through four had the same reading textbook. Once he learned to read, the author was hooked. He read all kinds of books; short and long story books. He also read novels. He did not understand some of the words, but he read them anyway. As time went on, family members would gather around him to retell the stories he had read. His favorites were *Alibaba and the Forty Thieves*, *Pegasus the Winged Horse*, *The Shepherd Boy and the Wolf*, and *Hansel and Gretel*. By the time he entered high school, the author was reading the *Perry Mason Series*. He was fascinated with the names of the characters; Perry Mason, the defense lawyer assisted by his detective Paul Drake and secretary Della Street, and of course, Mr. Mason's adversary, Mr. Hamilton Burger the District Attorney (DA).

The author will never forget his first big novel in high school; *Henderson The Rain King*. It was about a white man who went to the jungle of Africa, and was forced to marry the daughter of the Chief of the clan. He became the *Rain King* after marrying the Chief's daughter.

The author's grandma was right about one thing. The quest for education took the author away from home to a school at a local mission station all year, and saw his Mom only during the Dry Season vacation from mid-December to March. He later left and went to Sanniquellie City, the seat of the local county government almost forty miles away. But Mom was glad that her only son was eager to get an education, and she supported him with the little money she earned from weaving baskets and making gardens. By the time he graduated from high school, the author's Mom had lost both of her parents. Grandma would have been proud of him though it was against her wishes to go to school.

To top it all, education took the author away from his extended families and friends to the great United States of America. Before her death on August 23, 2014, his Mom visited the United States to see him graduate from seminary with a doctorate degree in ministry.

The dream she began in a small farming town decades earlier came true on that day. She was blessed and proud to live to see it happened in her lifetime.

As he was writing this book, the author said to himself, "Perhaps other children from towns and villages who may read this book, will have big dreams; dreams of getting an education with the help of their poor, but hardworking parents. They too could write for other kids to read. A kid like him who never owned a textbook while growing up, even in high school."

ONCE UPON THE TIME IN LIBERIAN is a fictional book with real life lessons for people from diverse cultural backgrounds. There are words and phrases in this book that are common to Liberians. They have been marked **bold** and *italic* here in the **FORWARD** and throughout the book so as not to create confusion for non-Liberians. Yes, there is such a thing as a ***Liberian English*** (bold and italic the author's). Travelers to Liberia may hear these words and phrases when they engage Liberians in conversations in churches, public places, and on both high school and college campuses.

Here are some of the words and phrases. ***Bounce grumble***, meaning to start an argument or commotion. It may also mean to protest depending on the circumstances (e.g. elections, debates, rallies, competitions, etc.). ***Oldman/pappy***, or ***oldma***, the former is used to address an older man, and the latter for an older woman. ***My men***, used in arguments, fights or friendly conversations to address a man. ***You boy***, used generally to address a young man of any age, especially if you didn't know his name. And ***you girl*** is used for a girl.

Borrow, recruiting players outside of one's school, or team to play. ***The game ended in confusion***, meaning one of the teams walked off the field, or a fight broke out due to bad or poor officiating. ***Dirty your news***, when a player is beaten or dribbled cleanly by another player, especially if the ball went between both legs of the player beaten or dribbled. ***Spectator***s, generally refer to fans, whether home fans or visitors. ***Witness the game or movie***, meaning to watch a game physically in person, or watch it on television.

Men like me, meaning one has a reputation and status and should not be disrespected. ***Do you know who I am***? Used by government or high ranking officials in the society, including their children, family members, relatives, friends and associates to assert their superiority over others. ***Someone played or ran politics on me***, meaning the speaker was undermined by nother person. ***My men move from here men***, meaning beat it or get off or out of my face, or when what one hears is too good to be true.

Cane Juice, locally brewed liquor or "moonshine" made from sugar cane. *Cut the grass*, meaning to mow the lawn. *Throwing the Eye-Right*, a special salute presented at annual parades of primary, middle and high schools in the country in celebration of Independence Day, National Flag Day and the United Nations Day.

Mamiewatta/Mommywater, a mermaid, used in reference to a beautiful woman. Any beautiful woman is likened onto a *Mamiewatta* or *Mommywate*r. *A grownaboy-grownaman* or *grownagirl-grownawoman,* a boy or a man, and a girl or a woman who roams the streets and lives or survives by stealing, committing petty crimes such as picking pockets. *Whorepojoe or wayoo,* a prostitute or anyone without loyalty to an individual, an organization, a school, a town or village.

They say, falsehood or rumors; *Spoil my name*, meaning someone tries to ruin or tarnish your reputation, or when no appreciation is shown for good deeds done to or for someone. Many Liberians of all ages will end a sentence or statement with the letter "*O.*" For example, a Liberian might say, "I am not going with *you-O*," or "I will not do *it-O*!"

God-ma, an older lady, single or married who is in a sexual relationship with a younger man. She helps to support the younger man to maintain the relationship. The opposite of *god-ma* is *god-pa* with the same meaning, except the older man is taking care of a younger woman.

The word *"embarrass" or "embarrassing"* may be used in all circumstances, contexts and cases. Liberians with or without formal education will use it instantaneously in speeches, conversations, etc., or when offended.

Again, *ONCE UPON THE TIME IN LIBERIA* is purely fictional based on the author's imaginations, therefore, characters in the book are fictional. Any reference or resemblance to a person, or persons, a group or groups of individuals is purely coincidental. And for the purpose of this book, football and soccer are used interchangeably. Football is the universal name of the sport, and soccer is the name used primarily in the United States of America.

This edition has been revised to include applicable Liberian Gio ethnic parables at the beginning of each chapter. The meaning of each parable is printed after the parable, taking into consideration that this particular meaning may differ depending on where the Gio ethnic group resides in Liberia, whether in lower or upper Nimba County.

ONCE UPON THE TIME IN LIBERIA is not strictly for laughs, but it will make you laugh, cry and chuckle, and may even make you wonder what in the world you just read. Some of the cities are actual cities in Liberia, and others are fictional cities created by the author.

PROLOGUE

"What you took time off to do, you cannot be lazy doing it."
Meaning: If you took time off to complete a
specific task, you cannot be lazy completing it."
Or anything you aspire to become in this life, you must give it your best.

March 1971

It was a glorious Friday afternoon, a day in the last few weeks of the Dry Season. The commercial parking lots or stations in Sanniquellie City were packed with students rushing to their hometowns and villages to get away from the neverending hunger of the city. Students despised this city because of its hunger, but nothing would keep them away. Around those stations, students from the same towns and villages stood together with their meager belongings in hands or by their sides. Those who could afford a bottle of soft drinks at the price of twenty-five cents stood under tin roof shops manned by Lebanese merchants. Back then, a bottle of soft drink cost twenty-five cents, but only a few people could afford it. A quarter would cook a day's meal so most students did not spend it on a bottle of coke. As they sipped their drinks, they were glad that they would be away from this city for at least ten days.

Sanniquellie had two of the best high schools in the county. Graduates from Sanniquellie Central High School, a government run high school, and Saint Mary's High School, run by the Catholic Church did extremely well in writing the National Examinations or the West African Examination Council (WAEC) and went on to attend a university or a college in Liberia. There was a lesser third one run by a local church. Unlike the former two, classes were conducted within the church. Students who failed at the two main high schools ended up at the third high school and graduated. It was a dumping ground for struggling students. Students who failed at this high school went home and forgot about completing high school.

This isolated city sat between a mining town and another commercial city. Gompa City to the south was approximately tweleve miles away. And Yekepa, the mining town on the northeast was about the same distance from Sanniquellie. A railway from the mining town ran parallel to the city on the northeast side, just a few hundred yards from Sanniquellie Central High School. The railway also divided the city from the main grassy dormant airport.

A plane landed there maybe once or twice a year. The country or county did not have commercial flights. When the iron ore train went by, the entire campus shook like earthquake tremors or aftershocks. And the noise was deafening. Teachers always stopped teaching when the train went by.

There was never a quiet or dull weekend in Sanniquellie. If a national music band was not in town playing, one of the high schools was playing a soccer game or some type of sporting events such as a basketball, volleyball or women's kickball tournament.

And there were troublemakers too; three boys who picked fights with everyone, especially strangers. The one who picked the fights was lazy, but the other two were strong. The two strong ones would send him to the market square to pick a fight. He would take someone's goods without paying. When he was confronted, he would be the first to strike, and then run back to his friends. And when he was pursued, all hell broke loose. This was an all-day fight! If police were called, they would run away, and then return as soon as the police left. They fought people in the day, at night, in nightclubs, bars, restaurants, in the alleyways, byways, parking stations, in the streets, and in buses. They did not fight on campuses because they were not students. If they fought on campuses the principals would ask their students to beat them up. One cherished the days when principals took the laws into their own hands to protect their students.

The original inhabitants of Sanniquellie lived in a small community in the center, barely the size of an apartment complex. They were concentrated around a small local church whose elder was reportedly hundred years old. He was a tall slender man who wore no dentures or corrective lenses for a man of his age. His head and beard were completely white as snow. He sat in a rocking chairs all day in front of the church.

It was Easter Vacation! The two major high schools in the city would close within in three days. The students were about to scatter throughout the surrounding towns and villages in search of foods and return to schools ahead of the Raining Season. It began in mid-April to mid-October every year. This was the time in Liberia when all roads became impassible. The muds on the roads would be almost waist deep, and become impossible for motorists to travel. A few government employees with Land Rovers and four-wheel-drive Jeeps would drive through to the nearest town or village.

Many daredevil drivers would travel in the rain from one mud to another. This was a season of "mud to mud." One would get into a car and arrive at the first mud. Then, he or she would get off the first car, take off shoes, walk in the mud, and get over on the other side of the mud to a waiting car. He or she would board the car praying and hoping to reach his or her destination before nightfall without the next rainfall. Raining Season was always a nightmare for travelers, especially students. It took days and weeks to travel during the Raining Season.

Three days arrived quickly! Zac Kolah and Sam Gbaar raced to the parking station to get on a commercial vehicle bound for home. They were glad Easter Vacation was in March this year rather than the usual late April every year. As they walked briskly, they couldn't help, but expressed excitement for the chances their high school had that year. The year stood out because many students from Tappita Memorial Junior High School transferred to their school. In the boys' high school, football, basketball, volleyball, and women's kickball were considered all sports. In other words, that year their high school looked stronger in all sports. The rival school up the hill did not stand a chance against them. In fact, the chances of the rival high school challenging their high school in all sports competition was remote that year.

They arrived at the designated parking station to find it almost deserted. Parking lots or stations were specific depending on where one was traveling. This particular one was designated for those traveling to towns and villages north and south of the city. Many of the vehicles were gone because they were full quickly with other students from various elementary, junior and high schools in the city. They, too [other students] were rushing to their homes to bring back foods before the Raining Season begins.

They waited for at least forty-five minutes before one commercial pickup truck showed up. This time of the year, commercial drivers were bluffing because they had more passengers than they normally carried. They tended to overcharge or refuse to carry passengers. Zac and Sam were lucky. This driver was going their direction, although not their hometown. He would stop in Gompa City, then Zac and Sam would find another commercial vehicle traveling to their home. That was no problem because Gompa City sits on a major highway that crisscrosses the country. They would have no problem finding a vehicle going their direction.

The driver agreed to carry them although the boys had no fares. They have always depended on their feet on arrival. They would run away as soon as the driver stopped the vehicle to collect his fares. Zac and Sam had loaded suitcases with rocks and newspapers before leaving the house for the parking station. They would use the suitcases as decoys to get away from the driver while collecting his fares from other passengers. It was a risk, but they had done it before, and gotten away or were never caught.

If they were caught and taken to the police, they would be set free. After all, they were students, and students were supposed to take such risk because they did not have incomes. Sometimes students were fortunate to meet former classmates or teammates in the police stations in uniforms.

The roads were in fairly good conditions because the rain has not begun in earnest. There were potholes everywhere, but not deep enough to hamper smooth travel. It was a bumpy ride, but there was no mud, and the driver knew how to dodge the potholes. It took them approximately one hour to arrive in the city. The car was full so they did not have to stop to pick up additional passengers on the way. When they arrived, they asked the drive to watch their suitcases while they went to a friend nearby to get their fares. That was the last time the driver saw them.

The driver thinking that they left important suitcases behind, hurriedly brought them down and opened them with haste. To his dismay, he found rocks and newspapers in the suitcases. He was furious, but the boys were gone. They have run as fast as possible towards the highway leading to their hometown to wait for another vehicle.

It did not take long for the next vehicle to arrive. In those days a passenger on a lorry or a taxi did not pay the fare until he or she reached the destination. One must arrive safely at his or her destination before paying the fare. From Gompa City to the boys' hometown costs only seventy-five cents. It was a lot of money back then when the boys were in high school.

No matter how packed or full the lorry was, the conductor or carboy would find anyone a seat. He went around the lorry and shouted "Let's dress, let's dress!" Sometimes he grabbed a passenger by the waistline through a window or an opening and dragged him or her forward. A passenger who refused to cooperate was yanked off the car, period.

It was a practice for commercial drivers or car owners to write special slogans on their vehicles. They lived and operated their vehicles by those slogans. The slogans were like rules that governed them in their daily activities. Some of the slogans were; "Cow Way Nor Get Tail, That God Go Drive Naw Flies" (God helps to drive away flies from a cow with no tail); "No Condition Is Permanent;" "Poor No Friend;" "Everyone For Himself, God For All;" "Heaven Helps Those Who Help Themselves," and many more. Some used their nicknames such as "Sugar Boy," or "Lucky Boy" on their vehicles. The red lorry that Zac and Sam got on next had written on the both sides, "No Condition is Permanent" in gold letters.

There was barely any seat on the lorry, but Zac and Sam agreed to ride on the top of the lorry or hang onto it just like the carboy. The distance was barely two-hour drive. If the road was paved, it would probably take forty-five minutes. Hanging or riding on top of the lorry was a golden opportunity for the boys. In fact, this was exactly what they anticipated all along. This would allow them to jump off into their communities when they arrived home. As they left, they began to strategize how to pull this trick off. This was quite easy since they were heading home. The easterly wind blew their nostrils almost dried as the lorry raced down the dusty narrow road with its horn blaring to warn pedestrians or animals of oncoming lorry.

It has always been a taboo in Liberia for cars to blow their horns to warn pedestrians or animals to leave the roadways. They see the cars coming, but unless the driver blows the horns, they will not leave the roadways. An angry pedestrian might shout at the driver, "Driver, your car ain't get horn eh, try and hit me, you will see what will happen to you." Of course, in reality he or she would not know what would happen to the driver if he or she [pedestrian] was struck and killed. But then wait a minute, in a village on the road, villagers would descend on the driver and his carboy and beat them to death.

This has always been the relationships between motorists and ordinary Liberians as far as one can remember. And both sides have gladly accepted their lots without qualms. It was understood by all drivers that they would blow their horns before the pedestrians would leave the roadways. And there were very few civilians who voluntarily left the roadways when they saw oncoming cars. Without crosswalks, the pedestrians made or set their own traffic rules.

Half a mile before they arrived, Sam and Zac came down around the side of the lorry to ensure a smooth landing after jumping off. Somehow the conductor knew they were up to something. Throughout the ride, they have been discussing their escape plan. The conductor did not understand them because they spoke their local Ethnic Gio dialect, but from the look on their faces and how they constantly glanced at him during their discussion, the conductor knew something odd was in the making. An experienced conductor knew these things. He would alert his boss about troublemakers and those who may not be able to pay correct fares or no fares at all. Of course, the driver had the final decision because he was the boss.

Back then, there was no designated or special parking lot or station on the highways. Passengers were dropped off along the way whenever and wherever they called out to the drive. In fact, they told the conductor where (what farms, villages, towns, junctions, etc.) they would get off, and the conductor shouted to his boss, "Hold it," when they arrived at the destination or location.

The boys' plan was to jump off the lorry and run as fast they could go at the first stop or "Hold it" when they arrived at home. The conductor bent over the moving car and whispered something to his boss to alert him about an impending trouble.

The boys did not pay attention to him. This was home and no one dared, not even a conductor, a stranger and his boss would come after them in the narrow ways in this densely populated city.

Students from all over the towns and villages surrounding this city were also here for school. If the conductor and his boss came after them, all hell would break loose. All they had to do was to shout for help in their native tongues, and the crowd would descend on the conductor and his boss like locusts. Again, an experienced conductor and his boss did not risk their lives and futures for a dollar and fifty cents. They would rather live and drive overtime to make up for the loss than lose their lives.

The boys decided to make their get-away jump and run halfway to the center of the city where there were many pedestrians; not hundreds, or thousands, but many enough to confuse the conductor and his boss into identifying them among the crowd. The timing had to be perfect. Both of them would jump off at the same time and run into opposite directions to confuse the conductor and the driver. They did not have fake suitcases like on the first trip from Sanniquellie to Gompa City, but these boys were two of the top football players in this city. They were known and their parents were important people. These were desperate times so they had to take these risks. In any case, boys had to be boys by doing some daring, but bravely stupid and dumb things.

As the car headed down the main street, the driver had to reduce his speed for fear of hitting a pedestrian or an animal; sheep, goats, chickens, or cats. These were everywhere crossing the streets along with the pedestrians. As the driver came to a crawl in the city center, Zac and Sam jump off the lorry and ran in opposite directions as planned. The carboy shouted to his boss, "Hold it,' as he came down swinging back and dragged his feet to stop as most conductors did.

He, too jumped off the lorry and took off after Sam. But the few minutes it took for his boss to stop the car gave Zac and Sam added advantages to dash into the narrow ways between cluster of mud huts and disappeared. The conductor could not catch up with Sam. He was nowhere to be found.

These boys were footballers and knew how to run. As he raced after Sam, the conductor came across two boys who looked like Sam. He stopped abruptly and almost out of breath enquired if they had seen a boy in a white T-shirt and blue pants go by them. They too looked at him and asked, "What happened"? The conductor replied, "My bossman and me brought them from Ganta (a popular name for Gompa City), but they can't pay.

They jump from the car and run." The boys broke out into laugher and said to him, "And you think you will find him again, the man is from here!" They walked past him still laughing. They said to each other, "Boy, Zac and Sam pulled another fast one again"!
They would meet Zac and Sam later on or the following day at football practice and joke them about it. And Zac and Sam would not be offended at all. Again, this was not unusual. Students did them all of the time!

The conductor returned to his boss almost out of breath. His boss was standing by the car waiting after he had collected his fares from the other passengers who did not run away. He made no attempt to go after Zac. As an experienced driver he knew that these things always happened in this country. This kind of problem was always associated with picking up student passengers. When you picked up students going on vacation, you were likely to lose on collecting fares. Students who lived in towns and villages along highways were notorious offenders. The driver told his carboy, "Get in the car, let's go. We will catch them one day. All days for rogues and one day for master." In other words, a thief may break in and steal all the time. But one day, he will break in when the home owner may be home and he will be caught.

They parked for a few minutes, picked up some passengers and headed back to Gompa City. They did not want to wait around until nightfall. They did not know anyone in this city, and couldn't afford to wait here to collect a measly one dollar and fifty cents. It was a lot of money, but not enough to make a driver and his conductor to spend a night in a city.

Zac and Sam kept a low profile all evening for fear of being spotted or caught. They thought the driver and his conductor would stick around searching for them. They did not show up at football practice. They wanted to go to practice because other friends would be expecting them to show up. Well, they had eight days left for Easter Vacation before returning to school. They had at least six days for football practice.

As the night fell, Sam thought about going to Zac's house to visit, but he changed his mind. There was no need to go anyway. After all, he would meet Zac tomorrow on the practice ground. Sam went to bed earlier than usual. This was a long bumpy ride and he needed to rest and be ready for football practice the next day. That night Sam slept soundly and woke up refreshed in the morning. By eleven o'clock in the morning, Zac was waiting for Sam outside. The danger has passed. Now they would walk around the city to let friends know that they were back in town on vacation.

As they walked to the market square, they laughed to themselves about the event the day before. Anyway, they did not have to worry about it when returning to school. Their parents would make the fares available to them to travel.

When they turned up for football practice the following evening, their friends were glad to see them again. For the next several days Zac and Sam practiced hard with the home boys sharpening their dribbling skills. They would return to school in six days, and the interclass football tournament would begin the first week of April. They were in different classes because of their last names. Sam Gbaar was in grade eight section B and Zac Kolah was in Grade eight section C. Maybe their classes would meet in the final. Maybe, no one knew! For the past two years, grade eight section B had won the trophy.

Easter vacation ended quickly. On Sunday, the boys packed their belongings, including food items and headed to the parking station. As they said their final goodbyes to families, friends and girlfriends, Zac and Sam could not wait to return to school where they would meet friends again. There, they would focus on school and sports until December when they would attempt another daring ride and escape from another moving lorry during the Christmas vacation. Zac and Sam looked at each other, smiled and said, Sanniquellie, here we come!

ONCE UPON THE TIME IN Liberia, two young men from a local high school had the audacity to challenge the norms of the silent Drivers' Union of Liberia; "you ride a car, you pay," and got away with it. They were never caught in their adventures and went on to complete their high school education.

CHAPTER 1

DEBUTANTE ANNIE KERN, THE FEMALE FOOTBALLER

"A woman can never perform as a traditional masked dancer" (Devil). Meaning: There are some tasks in this life that a woman cannot be allowed to perfom. But this story shows that was then, but this is now!

It was Monday morning in Grae, and everything looked bright as usual. It was the Dry Season in Liberia. The population of the town had jumped to at least a thousand people because of incoming students from villages, towns and cities near and far from Grae. One could hear footsteps and giggling as the students hurried to school. School started earlier this year in the first week of March. The mango trees along the road to Grae Junior High School were beginning to bear. By the end of May, one would only find leaves, but no fruits. My God, mangoes were the only meals some students ever had after schools.

Because school started in March, Easter Vacation would come at the beginning of May. At Grae Junior High School (GJHS), every year was different. Some years were worse than others if the Raining Season came early and Grae was cut off from the rest of the surrounding villages and towns due to bad roads.

This year was unusual, too. The girls were more than the boys were on campus. There was no need to be alarmed. By July, many students would drop out of school due to various reasons, with hunger being number one. To students who were not residents of Grae, they were on their own.

Annie Kern, a bubbly and vivacious young lady, had just transferred from Kpaytuo Elementary School to Grae. She was the only sister of three boys. Two of her older brothers lived in the big city. Annie did not know which one of the big cities. The third one was working at Cocopa Rubber Plantation thirty-five miles away. He often came home on leave to see his parents. Evans Dahn had dropped out of high school and gone to work to help his parents. Annie did not like her brother dropping out of high school, but Evans was a grown man, and, he would do whatever he wanted with his life. Annie was always glad when Evans came home on leave. He always brought her a gift from the plantation.

Annie's cousin, Yarwoan and her husband Julius Kpan lived in the town. Annie had come to live with them while in school. She was fortunate to have her Daddy's sister living here with her husband. My God, Raining Season would easily be described as a hunger season in Grae, perhaps in greater Liberia.

Grae was a small farming town on the highway leading to southeast Liberia. The main highway divided the town in the middle. The town's people raised their livestock in the town. Chickens, ducks, goats, pigs and sheep were everywhere.

Here, motorists did not break for animals, and animals knew it. One would see a rooster or a chicken flying when a car went by. The pigs and goats stayed off the road completely. Of course, some motorists had to break for a few sheep. They would lie on the main road and refuse to move. Motorists believed killing sheep with a car would bring curse on them, especially if you were driving a commercial car. My God, anything that happened to anyone in Grae, perhaps in Liberia was attributed to witchcraft or voodoo.

There were two merchant shops in the town, one owned and operated by a Lebanese merchant and the other by Julius Kpan, the husband of Annie's cousin Yarwoan. During the farming season (March through November), the town was deserted, except for students. Some students who lived in villages and towns at least two or three miles from Grae, walked to school every morning, and walked back home after school. It cost fifty cents or seventy-five cents to get to some of the villages. But, my God, it was impossible for students to earn that kind of money in Grae. Of course, unless you were Julius Kpan or the Lebanese Merchant Hadda Mahmoud.

Annie Kern has been different since birth. She was one of those girls whom you called a "Tomboy." She did things boys did. She climbed trees, raced with other boys, kept her hair short and wore pains. That was unusual for a West African girl born in a village. Daddy Kern did not mind too much about Annie's behavior. But her mother cared so much about her and did not want Annie to grow up like a boy. Mom Narleay Kern always screamed at her; "Annie, stop dressing for school like a boy. Boys will be afraid of you!" Annie would smile at her mom and run out of the house for school. By age ten, Annie had long-legged for a girl her age. At school she ran faster than some of the boys.

Grae Junior High School was short on everything, especially athletic equipment for girls, so the only ball on campus went to the boys. It had eleven shorts-less, nameless and numberless red T-shirts for the boys' football team. It did not have boots or socks. The boys played in their Baamen Pumas provided by their parents. Baamen Pumas were black worn by members of the Baamen Football Club, a national team in the country. The poorest kids played in their bare feet or wore see-through plastic sandals known locally as 'Sankpas." To prolong the lives of their sneakers, some of the kids wore their Pumas only to school and for games.

Grae High School's volleyball net was stored in a box on the floor of the assistant principal's office. The net was older than some of the kids in the school. The school had a net, but there was no volleyball. As usual the assistant principal had pledged to buy a volleyball for the last five years. He had promised to travel to the city to buy one. But whenever he traveled, he was always short on money. My God, you did not blame the man. He spent his money buying stuff on credit;" known locally as "Limited Power of Attorney" (LPA) to meet his family's needs.

He and other teachers had to chase the paymaster around the country to get paid. LPA cut down expenses and trips teachers had to make chasing the paymaster. The LPA Merchant became the middleman between the working teachers and the government.

So to survive, the teachers had to mortgage their salaries before they got them. And when the Lebanese Merchant in the city or town got the checks, he took out what was owned to him and gave to the teachers whatever was left of their paychecks. My God, every teacher hated the system, but they could not do anything to change it.

If the girls started out playing with the football, it was sure to end up in the hands of the boys on the football team. The older boys always came and took the ball away from the girls. The girls would end up hanging around, playing hopscotch or jumping ropes until recess was over.

Like most schools in the district and county, Grae Junior High School did not have a lunchroom or eating place for students. Whatever the World Food Program provided through Care Program barely met the demands of the growing student population. The bulk of the food items, including cornmeal, brown rice, cooking oils and flours were distributed among starving teachers and their families. The little left for students was prepared on Fridays and distributed. Students ate in the classrooms at their desks or in the open fields outside.

Those who ate outside fought large green flies for every bite in their bowls or on their plates. Those who failed to carry their eating utensils to school ate on sheets of papers or in their hands.

Principal Jerry Gaye had promised every year to provide plates and spoons to students for the past fifteen years, even if it came out of his pockets. Well, in a Liberian town like Grae, principal always talked big talks, but never walked the walks. The students knew his promises were lies.

Onetime last year, Annie followed the boys and kicked the ball around with them. Thereafter, she was hooked. She became regular at the boys' football practices. Instead of hanging around her friends and talking or jumping ropes after the boys had taken the ball away, she decided there and then that she would follow the ball wherever it went. When she became regular at the boys' football practices, they began to like her.

Tormen Sahn, a talkative on the team said it would be a surprise if Annie learned to play with them. That was unusual for such a statement coming out of his nostrils. He was the one always breathing fire like an aggravated bull in a ring. When everyone turned and looked at him, he quizzed back, "Are you surprise"? Of course, everyone was shocked that Tormen of all the boys on the team would welcome a girl with an open arm, especially to play on the team. He always talked about girls being this and that. My God, that boy was always fuming about something.

But Annie smiled and said to herself, "If Sahn's son welcomed me, I am truly welcomed. Annie had seen him on campus getting into fights with other boys over nothing. At last month's practice, he was suspended for two days from school for taking the ball and putting it under his arm and would not let it go. He felt he was fouled and the referee did not blow his whistle. And the referee was the assistant principal of the school. My God, the boy had the nerve to stand up to the assistant principal on the football field!

Johnny Dahn kicked the anthill right in front of him in frustration and jogged to the other side of the small football field. He picked his T-shirt up from where it had been discarded earlier. The boys never played with their shirts on. The school did not bother to provide practice jerseys for the boys. The football jerseys were worn only on game days. The team had eleven red T-shirts, the color of the school. When a substitution was made, the outgoing player took off his sweaty jersey and handed it over to the incoming player. Every player was always ready and prepared to smell or endure someone else's stinks. The players didn't do anything or care about it.

For the last fifteen years the principal had promised to buy them practice jerseys at the beginning of the school year. Just like the promise about the plates and spoons. The boys had grown tired of hearing his empty promises like a politician.

This was Johnny's year to shine for Grae Junior High School. He had trained hard during the Dry Season when school was out, preparing for this year. And now this, a girl was going to steal his spotlight. My God, to Johnny the fun days of playing football were over with a girl on the team.

"Hey Johnny," James Luah said as he ran after him. "Don't tell me you are afraid of a girl?" "I just don't want her spoiling our practice," Johnny said between his teeth. No, Annie did not hear him. The coach did not pay any attention to the boys. He shouted to them to get back quickly for warmups. Johnny walked briskly to the coach and inquired sarcastically, "Are you sure you want a girl playing on the school's football team?" Coach Harry Kahn straightened himself up. "Sure, why not?" "You are afraid to let a girl play alongside you on the football field, and she might outshine you, Johnny?"

This was Coach Harry Kahn's opportunity to make history in the county, if not in the whole country. It would attract other schools in the county, perhaps in the nation. My God, he cherished the moment when Annie would take the field one day at home or away to the surprise of everyone. He couldn't wait! At this moment, he wasn't thinking about Johnny's dribbling skills and the fact that he netted ten goals for the school last year.

The boy kept to himself often, but he would skillfully hold, control and handle the leather unlike any kid his age. At sixteen Johnny would dribble any man on earth if he got the ball first. Coach Kahn was proud of him, but Annie was a history in the making for Grae Junior High School. He did not want this opportunity to slip through his fingers. He envisioned Annie playing in big cities like Bahn, Gompa, Sanniquellie or Gbarnga. My God, his hands were beginning to sweat. Coach Kahn's hands always sweated when he was excited about football.

He played amateur football after high school. He had dreamed of playing for Lone Star, the national team of the country, but his parents had advised him against the idea. Rather, they had encouraged him to become a teacher to help other kids in the town. After mauling over it for a year, he had gone and completed the Teacher's Training College. He had returned to his hometown to help the kids. He loved the kids. He and his wife Stella have two, a boy and a girl. They just turned six and nine years old respectively.

This was what his parents wanted him to do. And they were proud of him, especially Daddy Kahn. He always boasted to his friends about the great services his son was rendering to the people of Grae. My God,

African Dads always boasted about these things to their friends and neighbors.

After the first two years of teaching, Harry had fallen in love with the profession. He was one of the best teachers at Grae Junior High School. Of course, football was his passion. He did not have the opportunity to play for the national team, but he hoped to train some of these boys to fulfill such dream for themselves, and not for him.

The boys respected and admired him. They had seen him played as a young man for his school and for his town. My God, he was good! He would bounce the ball on his head for at least five minutes without the ball touching the ground. Then he would trap it at the back of his neck, roll it over his head and trap it over his right instep and lift it almost to his chest level. He could bend, flex and stretch like a rubber band. My God, how in the world could Harry do that? Some of the kids had dream of learning some of his tricks. He had always told them, "It was not magic. It took hard work and long hours of practice."

Johnny respected the coach. After all, he was a role model and seemed like a big brother to him. Johnny's older brother, Francis Dahn had killed himself in a hunting accident ten years earlier. At times Johnny saw Coach Kahn as the replacement of his big brother who was taken away so suddenly in a freak accident with his own single-barrel shotgun. While trying to remove a piece of wood from the barrel of the shotgun, he had inadvertently pressed the trigger.

It was a horrible sight to see. Francis had almost blown his face off. He was barely recognizable at burial. If Coach Kahn said it was all right, then it was all right with Johnny. To him, Coach Kahn knew everything about football. As far as he was concerned, he never met anybody who played football better than Coach Harry Kahn. To Johnny, Coach Kahn was a legend.

Tualie Kahn, Coach Kahn's nephew and the team's captain volunteered to help Annie with trapping, controlling, and dribbling skills. Heading was a piece of cake since she kept her hair short. Those who resented her at first when she started began to like her. They began kicking the ball around with her. Annie wanted to feel and be like one them. But it was early for her to celebrate being accepted as a member of the boys' union. That was what the football team seemed like. They hung together. They went to recess together.

Those who were in the same class sat in the same row. They walked together after school. They even protested unfair treatment of one their members together.

They did everything together. It was like a bread and sandwich union where nobody got a taste unless you brought in fillings. My God, these boys were more than a union. But with Coach Kahn's help, there was a chance for Annie. He would have his ways when it came to football matters. He would live or die for these moments.

Ever since she was promoted to the seventh grade, Annie had been crazy about soccer. So when the boys came and took the ball, it was an opportunity for her to follow them in order to touch and kick the ball. Kids on campus began to notice her. At Grae, it was unusual for a girl to play soccer. Sarah Woanbeah, one of her best friends had begun to joke and call her funny names; "The woman footballer;" or "Lady Wannibo Toe" (Wannibo Toe was one of the best footballers to ever play in Liberia). Annie would smile and only ask her friend for support and encouragement.

Transferring from Kpaytuo Elementary School to Grae Junior High School was a dream come true for Annie. She had heard so much good things about Grae, especially the reputation of Coach Kahn. Though she never saw him played, she liked him the first time she met him. He had come to be one of her secrets. She felt in love with him. Not the kind of silly stuff boys and girls giggled about to each other on campus. This was special to talk about, even to her best friend like Sarah Woanbeah.

His neatly combed Afro hairdo and dark brown eyes were evenly matched. He did not wear a beard, but his mustache was perfectly trimmed above his upper lips. His lips were nice and evenly dark for a man of his age. His wife Stella was the luckiest woman in the world, Annie thought to herself. He would demonstrate ball trapping and passing skills so perfectly, and he had such a way of kicking the ball so lightly to the right person. My God, the man was good and handsome. She was glad he was her coach.

Annie was improving fast. Coach Kahn had told her that she would play her first game in three to four months if she kept improving at her current pace. She was excited beyond words for the prospect of playing with the boys in a football game. She could not wait to tell Uncle Julius and Cousin Yarwoan after school.

When Annie arrived at home, she was dead tired and her legs hurt. She has to change her clothes and hurried up to help cousin Yarwoan Kpan prepare for dinner. It was a long day because she had to stay after school and practice with the team. The end of the third month was fast approaching. And she did not want to miss out on the opportunity of playing her first game.

One day at practice Coach Kahn had asked Annie to take the penalty kick. For the past practices he had taught her the best techniques in taking penalty kicks. He had stressed to her, "Never paid too much attention to the goalkeeper, and don't ever let him intimidate you no matter how good he may be." He had told her repeatedly to step up calmly to the ball, just a few feet away and concentrate on the ball and where she would kick it. That had worked well for Annie because the goal posts were empty when they practiced.

During practice on this day, the team was separated into two teams; the substitutes against the eleven members of the starting team. When a handball was committed in the penalty box, Coach Kahn asked Annie to take the penalty kick. Johnny did not like the idea of a girl taking a penalty kick in an important practice. If they lost, the substitute players would boast all week. But it was his words against the coach's words which did not matter.

Annie stepped up to the plate with both legs separated from each other with her eyes on the ball as if the ball would fly away. Coach Kahn shouted to her, "You can do it, Annie! Remember what we practiced." Annie forgot one important lesson the coach had taught her, "Lift your head to see where you are kicking the ball." The substitute goalkeeper Meawon Mianway was jumping around making funny faces to distract Annie, but she kept her eyes on the ball. With her head bowed and zeroed in on the ball, she kicked the ball to the far right of the goalposts.

To Johnny Dahn, Annie had committed an unpardonable sin. She missed a penalty kick intended to give them a boost in this important practice. He wondered why the coach did not ask him to take the penalty kick. He was the superstar on this team, and in the school. Today, Johnny had forgotten the penalty kick he missed when Zuatuo Junior High School defeated Grae one goal to nothing two years ago. The penalty would have tied the game had he scored.

Annie turned to face the boys and Coach Kahn with a frown on her face. She almost stumbled and without a word went and hugged the coach. This was the day to make her coach proud for selecting her to play with the boys, and she blew it. There was nothing to cheer about at either end of the field. The rest of the boys felt disappointed, except for Tualie and his uncle. The teasing would come later tomorrow in class and on the campus, but at least for the moment none of them dared to say a word with Coach Kahn standing there.

Coach Kahn told her it was all right to miss a penalty kick. "Great players of all generations missed penalty kicks," he had said without mentioning names. Of course, he had
Johnny in mind when he looked over at him. My God, he had consoling words for kids when they felt bad about certain things.

The opposing team seemed clumsy in ball handling. Jack Kruah, the left defender deliberately grabbed the ball with his hands when he was beaten cleanly by Johnny.

Before Coach Kahn would say a word, Johnny immediately took over. He tried to appear very much that he was the coach. "All right guys, I am taking this penalty kick." He walked over to Annie. "Girl, you had your chance, and you blew it. You can watch me and I will teach you how to take a penalty kick." "If I ever get another chance, I will score," Annie said as she took a few steps away from Johnny.

When it came to taking penalty kicks at practice, it was no sweat for Johnny Dahn. The kid was indeed the superstar at Grae and everyone knew it. And Coach Kahn had respect for him as well. But he tried not to make Johnny become overconfident or cocky.

Coach Kahn was once a superstar for his school and his town. He himself had to battle the problem of overconfidence. His own coach had warned him to be the best he could without being overconfident or cocky. Goalkeeper Meawon Mianway was no match for Johnny's skills. He collapsed on the right side of the goalposts and the ball went to his left. Goal!

Practice was intense. The substitute team scored a goal from a corner kick headed home by Sammy Whimpeah. It did not take long for the starting team to score three more goals. It was getting dark so Coach

Kahn called the practice off. The boys and Annie were tired. They had practiced for two hours without breaks. Unlike real games, practices did not have halftime breaks. You played until the referee blew his whistle when it was getting dark.

There was no watch to keep time. The sun light was the referee's watch. When the sunlight was gone, the practice was over. My God, those were exhausting two hours for both teams without a drink of water or any type of liquid. The boys would drink out of bowls when they got home. They were thirsty like wildebeests in the Serengeti National Park in Tanzania, East Africa. Each of the boys would gobble down at least two cups of water when he got home.

Both teams gathered with Coach Kahn for his final words. He told Annie, "You did real good today. Keep it up." He told the boys to congratulate Annie. Everyone did, except for Johnny. Annie has missed the first penalty kick. She assisted on the second goal Johnny scored. It did not matter to him.

As they started on the way to their various homes, Annie turned to Coach Kahn and Tualie and said, "Thanks Coach, and thanks to you Tualie. You are the only boy on the team who like me. Tualie was not sure. He thought her voice was quivering, but he was not going to feel sorry for her. My God, this was football and not girls' kickball. Some of the boys on the team did not care if you were a girl or not. If you came to play, they would tackle, slide, drag you down or do whatever it took to win, even at practices. And Johnny was notorious for that kind of play. Good thing he was Annie's teammate.

Annie ran and got home quickly in time to help her cousin get ready for dinner. Cousin Yarwoan Kpan did not object to Annie playing like Mom had. It was Mr. Julius Kpan who warned Annie to be careful not to break her legs because he felt football was too rough for a girl.

But he never told Annie to quit football.

Julius Kpan did not play as a kid or a young man, but he was an avid fan of the game. Nothing in the world would stop him from watching a football game. It did not matter what team was playing. When the national team played, he stayed in his shop on his small shortwave radio to listen to the commentary. My God, He knew everything there was to know about football though he never learned to play the game. He could not wait to see Annie play her first game with the boys. He promised her that he would not leave town no matter what the occasion. He would stay just to see her play. And Annie had accepted his support by saying, "Thank you Uncle Julius." That's how she called him.

At the beginning of May, Grae Junior High School accepted an invitation from Zuatuo Junior High School for a soccer game. Both principals agreed to cut down the number of sporting events that day since Grae had a volleyball net, but no ball. GJHS students had not practiced volleyball so they were in no shape or form to challenge Zuatuo in a volleyball game. Instead the girls would play kickball first, follow by football. This would be Grae's first major sporting event immediately following the Easter Vacation.

Zuatuo was their arch rivalry ten miles southeast of the town. Grae lost to Zuatuo two years ago. Thereafter Coach Kahn had vowed to take revenge no matter how long it took. My God, he couldn't wait because he had a surprise for Zuatuo that would shock the nation.

Annie was attracting a lot of attention on campus. Within three months, she had become the most popular girl on campus. Her teammates did not take special interest in her. She was rough for a girl. They did not even look at her when she passed by them. She was ateammate, and not feminine enough to be a boy's girlfriend. It did not really matter to Johnny.

He knew he would never be the center of attention anymore. Playing soccer for GJHS wasn't fun any longer. It was all Annie's fault.

There was a boy on campus who took special interest in Annie. Boyd Dennis was a showoff because his father was the local magistrate in the town. He behaved as if his father owned the town. But Boyd Dennis was nice in spite of his penchant for showing off.

One Friday after practice, he had followed Annie and introduced himself. He had smiled at her and she had smiled back. What on earth would go wrong? There was no reason she could not be friends with him. What was she afraid of anyhow? Boys on her team were not interested in her anyway. Sometimes she acted like some of the village girls on campus.

Annie felt that today was the beginning of new friendship with someone other than her best friend Sarah Woanbeah. She did not have to make any announcement to her teammates or Coach Kahn that she had found a friend who was interested in all she did.

Boyd Dennis and his parents had moved from a rubber plantation about thirty-five miles away. He did not have a girlfriend at GJHS other than his two younger sisters. My God, girls hated his gut for showing off all the time. He talked about the plantation, the nice school building he used to go to with its lunch program and his rides on the school trucks and wonderful sports program. But Boyd was not interested in any sports. He was a bluffer, a showman who loved to dress sharp so girls would notice him. He was not a sportsman. He did not have a trace of sportsmanship in his blood. When it came to buying snacks for other kids to impress girls that his parents were rich, Boyd was the man.

"You rode a truck to school everyday?" Annie asked. "Yeah, all the divisions had trucks for students." "I missed riding to school." "Do you like it here?" "Not a chance." "Why did you come here?" "My Dad was reassigned in this town." My God, adults did not consider the feelings of their children in a small town like Grae, perhaps in the whole nation. It did not matter anyway. Mr. Johnson Dennis was a government employee, and had no say in wherever he was sent.

Boyd had become a regular *spectator* at Annie's practices. She had invited him to come and watch her play. He was amazed and proud of her. He never saw a girl play football before until he met Annie. After practice, Boyd had stared at her with his mouth open. He just could not believe it. My God, she was pretty good at handling and passing the ball. Frankly, she was getting better than some of the boys.

Zuatuo High School arrived in Grae on a bright sunny Saturday afternoon, one of the few remaining dry days in May before the Raining Season took off in earnest. They arrived singing their usual football song. "If you play we will play, and if we play we will win." The song was repeatedly interrupted by the familiar chants popular with schools, villages, towns, cities and football teams across the nation. "Amen, men, Amen, men. What's wrong with everybody? It's all right. Who says so? Everybody. Who's everybody? Zuatuo Junior High School." The chant was meant to instill fears in the hearts of the opposing teams.

The yellow pick truck with the inscription, "No one knows tomorrow," written on both sides encircled Grae as the visitors sang and chanted. The driver of the truck and his conductor joined them in their song and chants. Crowds were beginning to gather to take a glimpse at the visitors. As they went around, dust settled over Grae like mushroom clouds. At the end of the third encirclement, the truck headed to GJHS campus with bare feet and shirtless kids following in pursue. My God, it was a perfect day for a football game. The truck stopped directly in the front yard of GJHS. Zuatuo's girls disembarked first and were led to one of the classrooms by the kickball coach and Home Economic Teacher Zaylay Tete Tiah.

Zuatuo's girls dressed up and took the field first in their kickball game. Zuatuo was no match for Grae. Zuatuo did not know that Annie was also on the kickball team. Girls of Zuatuo never met a girl who would kick a football farther and harder than Annie Kern. Before it got worse, both principals and coaches decided to end the carnage early to allow an ample time for the football game. By the time the game was called off, Grae was leading Zuatuo fifteen runs to one. My God, it was a bad day for the girls of Zuatuo. They could not find anyone to counter Annie in running, kicking and catching the ball.

While the kickball game was going on, GJHS Football Team was in the auditorium of the school building dressing up for the game. The ninth-grade classroom was given to the visitors to dress up. Grade nine was the senior class at GJHS. So out of respect for the visitors, their classroom was given to them. They sang and as they dressed. They had beaten Grae two years ago at home in Zuatuo. They came to repeat what they did two years ago, but this time on Grae's home turf.

It was almost a ritual that the home team took the field first, followed by the visitors. Coaches and school officials who claimed to have medicine for football always told visitors, "Never be the first to touch their field. If they made medicine, it would backfire if they stepped on their own field first." Some of the players had contacted an oldman who lived a few yards across the street from the main road. He had told them to stay off the field though it did not matter. He had guaranteed upon his mother's grave that GJHS would win the game.

However, Coach Kahn had told them to warm up outside the field until Annie arrived. This they did as they waited for her.

By four-thirty o'clock in the afternoon, Greyson had come out for warmups. They came out dressed in their usual red nameless and numberless short-sleeve red T-shirts, the color of GJHS.

They did not take the field first. They lined up outside the field as they jumped around in circle. Annie was the last to come out and join the team. After the kickball game, it took her a few minutes to get ready. As she jogged to join her teammates, Coach Kahn was right behind her waving a red handkerchief. My God, the whole town went crazy! For some of the older folks in Grae, this was unbelievable, to see a girl played football with the boys. It was just impossible!

Harry Kahn had dazzled this town and surrounding villages with his foot works and brilliant scoring skills, but this was shockingly awesome. As the GJHS cheerleaders, students and **spectators** shouted, "An---nie, An---nie, An---nie," the boys of Zuatuo came out running, some of them halfway dressed, to see what the commotions were all about. To their shock and disbelief, a girl was warming up with GJHS Team. The school and coaching staff from Zuatuo were surprised too.

But Coach Kahn cherished every moment of it. After all, he had anticipated this day and knew that it would come sooner than later. He was excited to the point of not controlling himself as he went around the field shouting, "Yes, yes, yes, yes, I say yes." My God, he wished the entire nation was here to see Debutant Annie, The Female Footballer!

Annie was tense and nervous. She could hear her own heart beats. She had practiced with the boys on her team. But how would the boys from Zuatuo react to her? Would they deliberately try to hurt her when they find out that she is good? She tried to suppress the thought and focus on a pleasant outcome of the game. But my God injury was a part of the game of football. How could she forget that?

She was at home and no player on Zuatuo's team would deliberately try to injure her. My God, a game in a small town like Grae, all hell would break lose. Zuatuo's students and officials would be beaten, and no one would intervene. Visiting teams knew these risks and advised their players to refrain from any act or conduct that would lead to fights. In fact, Uncle Julius told Annie, "If any boy from Zuatuo intentionally fouls you, I will get him." She remembered those comforting words from Uncle Julius. When she lifted her head, her eyes caught Boyd Dennis'. He smiled at her and shouted, "Don't be afraid, I am here!" She was glad to hear those words from Boyd, and that he was at the game.

All players from Zuatuo finally came out dressed in their yellow long-sleeve T-shirts with faded numbers. My God, you did not tell whether the color of the numbers was red or purple. The jerseys were numbered from one to eleven with no names. They did not have matching shorts, boots, or socks. They all came out running, and stopped short of the football field. If the home team did not take the field first, they would not. The coach has stressed this to them in the classroom while they were dressing. They hurdled up behind the southeast goalposts and repeated the usual chants. "Amen, men, Amen, men. What's wrong with everybody? It's all right. Who says so? Everybody. Who's everybody? Zuatuo Junior High School!"

At five-fifteen o'clock, both coaches could no longer tolerate the standoff. Coach Kahn and Coach Martin Zaahn of Zuatuo went in the middle of the field accompanied by referee Joe Kolie and the two line judges and reached a compromise. GJHS would take the field first at the beginning of the game and Zuatuo would take the field first at the beginning of the second half. Case closed. My God, let the game begin!

The standoff had almost killed the spirit of the game. Grae was set to make history in the county, perhaps in the country, but the football medicine man almost ruined it. The visitors grew ever more confident when they saw Annie Kern dressed up and warming up with the boys to play. Some of the players shouted, "Coach you think we are so lazy that you brought a woman to play against us? We will show you."

How could Annie Kern, the bubbly and vivacious beautiful young girl become a no-nonsense hard hitting, sliding and tackling female gladiator for ninety minutes? Zuatuo was about to find out. She had traded the soft sneakers she used for the kickball game for a Baamen Pumas. This was her first game, the greatest challenge of her young high school football career. She was not going to disappoint Coach Kahn, Cousin Yarwoan, Uncle Julius and of course, Boyd Dennis. She had overheard him bragging to Zuatuo boys and girls that they would be beaten by a woman today. They did not understand what he meant. They all thought Boyd Dennis was talking about the kickball game. As usual, he was dressed to impress. My God, Boyd always looked neat when he got dressed up. And Annie was glad that he was her boyfriend.

As they continued to warm up, Johnny came to Annie, "Don't try to force anything out there today." Annie sarcastically replied, "Don't you worry, Coach Johnny, I won't." Though Annie was glad that Johnny was on her team, she did not like his constant corrections. Sometimes, it was annoying to listen to him nag forever about every bad play. But Coach Kahn had always told Annie, "Don't pay much attention to him. Good players often did that."

And a girl, My God, Johnny would not have permitted it without Coach Kahn's approval. And he would not dare to disrespect the coach without being kicked off the team.

GJHS finally took the field, followed by Zuatuo. Someone in the stand shouted, "My people you'll play the ball now so people can see Annie play." Fans were growing impatience with both schools, especially with the officials for delaying the game unnecessarily based on the advice of a medicine man. Some of the fans knew these things. They have had to cope or deal with this medicine issue when they too played as young people. My God, some of them hated their failure to prepare themselves for games because the medicine man said they would win, but they lost the games.

The game started five-thirty o'clock local time. It got dark faster at the beginning of the Raining Season. Annie lined up at right forward position to the right of Johnny Dahn. Tualie Kahn lined up at left forward, left of Johnny. For the first time since Annie joined the boys' football team, Johnny smiled at her said between his teeth, "Girl, let's do it," as he passed the ball to Tualie. Tualie took a few steps forward, stopped, turned around and passed the ball to Annie. She trapped the ball and waited for Johnny to race toward Zuatuo's goal. When Annie trapped the ball, everyone went wild, including the visitors. Coach Kahn dropped down on both knees as though he was saying his final prayers before a guillotine came down separating his neck from the rest of the body. My God, this was his glorious moment. And no one was going to take it away from him.

It was too risky to pass the ball to Johnny and he knew that. He was being chased by three Zuatuo's defenders. Annie also remembered his words, "Don't force anything." So, Annie turned around and passed the ball back to Tualie. He beat two Zuatuo's forward who had come behind to help and hung the ball over to Tormen. When it came to stretching the wings, Tormen Sahn was one of the best. He attempted to race the left Zuatuo's defender to the goal, but the defender kicked the ball outside, giving Grae a corner kick into the thirty fifth minute of the game.

If Grae defeated Zuatuo by one goal to nothing, it would be a great payback for one nail defeat at Zuatuo two years ago. The first half ended in a draw. Referee Joe Kolie announced that he would grant only five minutes for halftime break because it was getting dark. Soon it would too dark to play.

Zuatuo's boys had come here boasting that they would beat Grae five goals to nail. For the first half of the game, they had managed a measly two shorts at the goal. Annie Kern had proven to be too much for them. At times they were confused as to who marked her. To be beaten cleanly by another boy during a football game was normal, but to be beaten by a girl was a disgrace. No player from Zuatuo was willing to be the first Guinea pig. Such a player would be the laughingstock of Zuatuo Junior High School.

Zuatuo took the field first at the beginning of the second half as stipulated before the game began. In the 75th minute Annie got a pass from Johnny. As he raced towards the goal, he was closely marked, nearly covered by two Zuatuo's defenders and another forward who had retreated to help. It did not matter to Johnny. He expected a return pass from Annie, but she had a different idea.

She dribbled the midfield defender cleanly. When she got by the left defender, Annie was already in the penalty box. When she beat the defender; a short slightly heavyset boy nicknamed "Bob, The Slide King," brought her down hard from behind. All hell almost broke loose. Coach Kahn ran on to the field accompanied by six other town folks, including Uncle Julius Kpan and Boyd Dennis. Uncle Julius had come to see Annie play as he promised her. They all shouted in unison, "You short boy, you want to hurt the girl, eh?" Boyd Dennis ran to Slide King and tried to shove him, but he was stopped by one of the line judges or referee's assistant.

Coach Kahn confronted referee Joe Kolie demanding that Bob be sent off the field. But Referee Joe Kolie refused. Annie was slow getting up in the midst of the near chaos. Johnny helped pulled her back to her feet. "Annie, remember this is football," Johnny said as he held her hand. Somehow Annie knew Johnny would say that. She did not take an offense at him because she knew it too.

The last thing Zuatuo wanted on this day was a fight. Many of the men who accompanied Zuatuo Juinor High School, including Principal Ayi

Tarpeh knew the reputation of Julius Kpan. His nickname was "Hardhead man." On many occasions, and in market grounds, towns and villages, he had fought three or four men at one time and beaten them all. He was a nice and quiet man, but when it came to fights, he had no match in the district. The man would head-butt anything that stood at his chest level. He would grab a man and head-butt him into unconsciousness.

Zuatuo don't do it! This was a friendly game, and no one from Grae or Zuatuo wanted it to **end in confusion.**

Referee Kolie blew his whistle for a penalty kick and warned "Slide King" that another foul like that would send him off the field. Bob "Slide King" did not mind or pay attention to the referee. But there was no way under the sun he would allow a girl to **dirty his news.** My God, back then somebody mocked you of dirtying your news if he dribbled you cleanly.

Johnny took the ball and put it under his arm. That meant he was going to take the penalty kick. The referee took the ball from him and pointed to the penalty spot. As he stepped forward, Johnny fought hard to suppress flashbacks from two years ago when he missed the penalty kick that would have tied the game when both teams played at Zuatuo. But Johnny Dahn was too good to make those kinds of mistakes twice in his junior high school football career. He counted four steps backward from the ball.

When the referee blew his whistle, he took three steps forward and stopped, thinking he was going to kick the ball, Zuatuo's goalkeeper sprang to the left of the goalposts, and Johnny netted the ball on the right side. The referee almost lost control of the game. **Spectators** took to the field to celebrate. Johnny's teammates lifted him up three times and brought him down. The line judges and the referee managed to get the **spectators** off the field after what seemed almost like an eternity.

In those days, time wasted or injury time was never added. When Referee Joe Kolie sounded his final whistle, the invisible scoreboard (no school had one) read, Grae Junior High School 1, and Zuatuo Junior High School 0.

At the sound of the final whistle, the ten boys on Grae's team lifted Annie up on their shoulders. They had to be careful to carry her like a log because she was a girl. They raced to the other end of the field singing, "Play la ball, Annie play la ball. Score la goal, Annie score la goal." Coach Kahn met them in the middle of the field with a chant of his own.

"Amen, men, Amen, men. What's wrong with Annie? She is all right. Who says so? Everybody. Who's everybody? Grae Junior High School." When he repeated the chant, the boys lowered Annie slowly to the ground. And then Annie and the boys lifted Coach Kahn up in their palms. By this time the folks in the town had joined the celebration. They carried the coach as they sang, "Seolaylay, seolaylay, seolaylay kpaoo, kpamu kpaoo"! They took Coach Kahn to the end of the field and brought him back. By this time, it was getting dark and everyone, including the visitors was leaving to get home.

There was no autograph session or news conference, but Annie was glad this game was over. She was met halfway from the center of the field by Boyd Dennis. He lifted her up and kissed her on the forehead. This was a junior high school. No kissing in public or monkey business here. Though some of the older boys and girls were sexually active, Annie Laykarnue Kern was not interested. She wanted a boy as a friend, and she found that in Boyd Dennis. He understood and respected her wishes.

Boyd Dennis accompanied Annie to her cousin's house. He chatted with cousin Yarwoan briefly and left for home. He knew Annie needed to rest after the game, and was happy to give her chance to rest.

Tomorrow was Sunday, and Annie would be at church. They would meet at school on Monday.

Uncle Julius came out, lifted Annie and said to her, "I am proud of you Annie. I never knew a girl would play football like that. If you keep it up, I will buy you a football boots." "Thanks, so much Uncle Julius," Annie replied as she headed to her bedroom to change out of the soiled jersey. She felt relaxed and at peace with herself that she had done her best, especially in her first game. She had finally gained the respect of the boys, including Johnny Dahn. The butterfly she felt before the game was gone. She did not score, but her dribbling skills had awarded a penalty kick to GJHS. And Coach Kahn was proud of her and what she had accomplished in a very short time. She went to bed that night feeling good because she had helped GJHS to win the game.

Mr. Saye Johnnie, the founder and proprietor of Naaman High School (NHS) in Gompa City was on his way back from Tappita to Gompa when he stopped in Grae to watch the game. Today he saw history unfolded right before his eyes. He would never forget this day as long as he lived. He saw a girl played football on boys' team.

Mr. Johnnie was a guitarist and a part-time musician. He and a group of men had released an album in the early 1980's. The music had become quite popular in rural northeastern Liberia. He was always searching for something big. My God, he was a headline grabbing freak. He spent the night in Grae.

He got up early in the morning and went to the school to meet Coach Harry Kahn and top school officials. The purpose of the meeting was to extend an invitation to Grae Junior High School to travel to Gompa City for sporting events with his school. Coach Kahn and the school official gladly accepted the invitation to travel to Gompa City before the Raining Season would begin. He wanted to showcase what he saw at Grae Junior High School to a larger audience in the city.

Mr. Johnnie arrived back in Gompa City late Sunday evening. Early Monday morning he called his school officials and coaching staff to a hastily arranged meeting and told them about his adventures, and how he had seen Annie played and had extended an invitation to Grae Junior High School thereafter. Coach Amos Saye did not take him seriously. He inquired further from Mr. Johnnie. "While on your way from Tappita to Gompa City in the early 1980's in rural northeastern Liberia, you watched a girl played on boys' football team? "What was her name again?" Mr. Johnnie repeated, "I said her name is Annie." Coach wanted to burst out into laughter, but he managed a chuckle because he did not want to get into trouble with his boss.

Coach Saye was not impressed at all. He had his eyes on big city schools, and not on a smalltown school with a girl on its football team. "Coach, I am telling you, this Annie Girl can play," Mr. Johnnie tried hard to persuade his coach with those words. Mr. Johnnie also added, "By the way, we need funds to buy athletic equipment for the school. Moneys generated from this game will be used for that purpose."

Back in those days, schools did not have athletic equipment. Exceptions were private schools operated by religious and charitable organizations and churches. The fortunate ones got their athletic equipment, mainly basketball, football, boots, jerseys, shorts, socks, and volleyball, including net from the West through missionaries or Peace Corps Volunteers.

Coach Saye had his eyes on big city schools, but he did not have the team and the players. NHS has been in operation for a short time. They were getting to attract students, especially players from some of the schools within the city. An eighteen year-boy, Absalom Gondon had transferred from a local mission school to NHS on a football scholarship. My God, Absalom was good, but he could not make a football team by himself.

Mr. Johnnie and Coach Saye had their work cut out for them. Both men had two weeks to assemble a football team to face Annie and Grae Junior High School. And to build a fence around the public high school with palm branches.

Mr. Johnnie was born and raised in Gompa City. He knew his way around. When it came to contacting players, he knew exactly where to go to find players. He met the boys on practice grounds on the government school campus and asked them to come and help. They gladly accepted his request.

Back then, boys who played football in the city did not have allegiances to their schools. As long as there was a chance to play a football game, they played. They were always eager to show their talents and skills hoping to be spotted by teams and other schools in the city or by recruiters from other cities or various football and national teams in the country.

A school **borrowing** players from other schools within the city was common practice and was acceptable. If a school did not mind being called **"borrow, borrow** school," it b**orrowed** for every sporting event. Of course, in rare cases coaching staff threatened their players with expulsion, if they played for any school other than their own. My God, it never worked. Boys would be boys.

Wherever there was a football game, boys volunteered their services. Sometimes they were not called or invited. They heard about a football game, and showed up ready to play. Of course, every player who showed up did not get a jersey, only the best one. Back then, there was a common saying; "experience players don't fight for jersey. Jerseys are handed over to them."

Mr. Johnnie and Coach Saye prepared hand written flyers and placed them on doors of shops, electric light poles, market places and campuses within the city. Annie Laykarnue Kern was a household name in Grae. No one knew her in the city until now. But suddenly she had set Gompa City abuzz and was becoming the talk of students on campuses across the city. It was not an April Fools' Day joke as students thought it was. After all this was the first week of June, and not April. Mr. Johnnie would only say "wait and see" to those who did not believe him that a girl would play on men's football team. He was a cheerful man who made everyone laughed. People thought the idea of a girl playing football was one his practical jokes. My God, Mr. Johnnie was good at telling jokes. He would make you laugh even if you were mad at the whole world.

NHS started preparation for Annie Kern and Grae Junior High School earlier than usual. Mr. Johnnie was an African man, yes, a Liberian. He knew girls would play kickball, but football, especially with boys, impossible. He had not gotten over the shock and awe of seeing or watching Annie played. He watched the young lady dribbled boys, some of whom were older than she was, for the fun of it.

Mr. Johnnie played as a young man for his school, and no more. He never had passion or love for the game. He abandoned it after high school to concentrate on his guitar lessons and teacher's education. He turned out to be a Liberian folk singer and a teacher. He was very good at both. He later founded his own high school.

Education was important to him. He started the high school as an alternative to students whose parents were not interested in sending their children to a public school. He made the tuition affordable for poor students of the city to complete their high school education. Mr. Johnnie was a generous man who would help anyone in trouble. Most students, even outside of his high school knew him. He was a people's person and had special ways with kids of all ages. But there was no way in the world he would allow a junior high school football team from a small town as Grae with a female player to beat his high school. His high school would lose respect and credibility among the sister schools within the city.

Gompa City lies in central Nimba County. It is a commercial city with a population of 41,106, (2008 census). But who did the counting? The main highway from Monrovia intercepts at a crossroad in the city center at a filling station. As far as anyone can recall, this filling station has always been there. Before the war, Gompa was a vibrant city with booming economy. Many Liberians and other internationals, especially Africans sought employment or business opportunities in the city. It had a motel. In her glory days, the motel brought a popular Liberian singer to town to perform. It shut down following the military coup of 1980. It later resumed operations in the late 1980's with a new name, Paradise.

The city also had several bars and night clubs, including the famous Dark Forest, Frog Island Bar and Restaurant, and the Roundtable Bar. My God, back in those days everyone came in to dance when "Sweet Mother" played at the Dark Forest. Gompa was a city always alive, drinking, and dancing.

Both sides of the main street were lined with shops operated by Lebanese, East and North African merchants. It had two dilapidated cinemas or movie theaters. When one went in to see a movie, he or she came out smelling like someone from a smoke sale. Movie goers were always angry because the movie projectors were old and worn out. Films would break in the middle of the movies, leading to near riot outside the theaters. Occasionally movie goers demanded and got refunds for failed movies. The historic Chief Gbatu's Quarter sits on the left side of the highway leading to southeastern Counties. Residents with taste for **King Juice,** Palm Wine and cassava dough frequented the Chief Quarter.

The city had several elementary, middle and high schools, both private and public, including the famous government high school, making it an ideal city for young people across the country. The annual inter-high school football tournaments from the months of March to May were the best times to be alive in Gompa City.

The City borders Guinea on the Northeast at the Saint John River. The Liberian-Guinea border is approximately forty-five minute-walk away from the city center. The most historic attractions or landmarks are the George W. Harley United Methodist Hospital and the United Methodist Church.

The hospital has a nursing school, and the church runs a school from Kindergarten to high school. The paved highway from Monrovia to Sanniquellie, the seat of local county government stops two miles outside the city at the National Hansen's Disease Hospital.

The city was undergoing a major transformation shortly before President Tolbert's assassination. During the redevelopment, streets were laid, making Gompa a paradise for avid joggers. Joggers used to wake up early in the morning and jog around the city. The sudden death of the president brought everything to a halt. Thursday is the official "Market Day" in Gompa City. On this day farmers and Liberians in various villages, towns and cities bring their produce and other commodities to the market. Every Thursday, Gompa City becomes a city outside the capital city, Monrovia.

Again, the news or rumors of a girl playing on boys' football team was too good to believe. In those days, no one heard of a girl playing football. Yes, a girl played kickball and, on rare occasions, played volleyball, but a girl playing soccer with boys, impossible! Maybe, but not possible!

Preparations for the trip to meet Naaman High School was intense. Unlike Zuatuo, NHS was in a large city. When it came to football, boys in a large city were different. They practiced daily and had the conditioning and stamina. And when a school faced an opponent and the school was not sure of defeating the opponent, the school requested and got players from sister

schools around the city. For NHS it was a no brainer because it had been in operation for less than five years.

Coach Harry Kahn was not taking any chances. He did not know much about NHS and its football team. He was willing to take a scouting trip to Gompa to find out the strength of their football team. He would watch them practice, then come home and prepare his football team accordingly. This would also help him to come up with his starting lineup.

Coach Kahn slipped into Gompa City Friday evening unannounced. He did not live in Gompa, but he knew a lot about the city than most of its transient inhabitants. He played one or two football games here during his playing days. He came here frequently to purchase school supplies for Grae, mainly papers, chalks, pencils, notebooks, crayons and ink pens. But he did not know much about Naaman High School. It was a new school.

He headed to the northeast side of the city and was met on the way by his friend DeQuincy Elliott. "Hey my Liberian brother, what's the occasion?" DeQuincy said. Before Coach Kahn would reply, DeQuincy added, "By the way, I read a poster this week that your junior high school is coming to town to play against Naaman High School and you have a girl on the football team?" He began to laugh so hard almost to the point of **embarrassing** Coach Kahn. When he finally stopped, the coach calmly said to him, "Annie can really play." DeQuincy looked at the coach up and down and said, "***Men, move from here men.***" My God, back then that's how you brushed people off if you thought they were not serious. Sometimes you simply said, "I fear you O," and walked away.

Coach Kahn did not tell DeQuincy that he had come to scout Naaman High School. After what seemed like a mockery session, the conversation turned to good old days when the two men met at the teacher's training institute. They could not believe that it has been fifteen years since they sat in class together. It was great to see each other again. They walked the rest of the way without saying a word about football or school.

When they arrived at Mr. Elliot's house, his wife was still at the market shopping for dinner. It was getting close to dinner time and Mrs. Comfort Elliot was not home yet to prepare dinner. DeQuincy sent one of his nephews living with him to the market to look for Aunt Comfort. That's how the kids called her. The couple did not have children of their own at the time, but Mr. Elliot's two nephews and his wife's cousin were living with them and going to school.

The boy ran to the market and found Aunt Comfort buying dried fish and palm oil. He told her that they had a guest and Uncle DeQuincy wanted her to come home and prepare dinner. She hurriedly bought the rest of her dinner supplies and rushed home with her husband's nephew. Mr. Elliot quickly introduced his wife as she came through the front door. They have been married for two years. Coach Kahn was not invited to the wedding. "Man, you got married and did not invite me to the wedding?" "My parents wanted me to get married so they can see their grandchildren. Mama said she was not getting any younger. It happened so fast, I am sorry." Coach Kahn brushed his excuse aside by saying, "I am glad you are married. And your wife is beautiful." Dinner was ready at eight-thirty in the evening. Comfort was a terrific cook. The cassava leaf and dried fish with a flavor of seasoned palm oil was simply beyond words. The two men started their conversation after dinner. They were busy enjoying their meals.

My God, back then, Liberians did not talk much at dinner. When it was time to eat, you ate and talked later. Coach Kahn said, "Thank you Madame Comfort for cooking," as the children removed the dishes.

The conversation resumed after dinner. Mr. Elliot wanted to know what it was like coaching a men's football team with a girl. Coach Kahn did not hesitate to tell his friend that he enjoyed every moment of it. In fact, he hoped that one day Annie would play on the national level. This had caused DeQuincy to laugh again.

Without invitation Comfort Elliot injected, "Thanks Harry for giving this young lady a chance. Liberian men think only they can do anything. But a woman is supposed to get married, stayed home and have their children." "What's wrong with that?" Her husband replied. Coach Kahn did not want to get involved in a dispute between a husband and wife over any topic. My God, he wished he would change the perception of the men in the country that a woman could do anything a man could do. Annie Laykarnue Kern has shown it to the boys at GJHS.

Coach Kahn stood up and walked towards the door. He told DeQuincy and Comfort that he was walking down the streets to search for school supplies. Since his last trip to Gompa, he had inquired about the general location of Naaman High School. He would visit the campus Saturday morning, and then return to watch the boys' football team at practice.

Coach Kahn returned to the Elliot's home about ten thirty at night and was shown his stranger's room. He went to sleep immediately. Whatever the thoughts were about Naaman, he would sleep over them until in the morning. There was no need to worry over the unknown. The possibility that Naaman would recruit players from other schools within the city did not bother him or cross his mind. He saw it first hand as a player across the district and county. My God, nearly all schools did, if they wanted to win football games. But on rare occasions it backfired because the recruited players did not do so well. They did not know each other's styles of play or because they did not train together as a team. Sometimes they refused outright to do their best because the schools were not their schools. If they lost, their schools did not lose.

Coach Kahn woke up Saturday morning about eight thirty to a breakfast of boiled cassava and eddoes with fried fish. He enjoyed every moment of it. He just fell in love with Comfort Elliot's cooking. He thanked Comfort and told DeQuincy that he was walking down to the store.

About midday Coach Kahn walked to the only self-service filling station in the city. He stood there for an hour looking around as motorists and pedestrians raced across the streets dodging each other like watching a car chase in a detective movie. He felt dizzy just looking at cars and people moving. He finally headed up on the southside of the city towards Naaman High School. Mr. Saye Johnnie had described the location, and then given him the direction to his school.

He was not impressed with NHS. The school met in a residential building, barely the size of a local community center. It had a small football field under development. The boys' volleyball and girls' kickball teams practiced on the field. The boys had their football practice on the campus of the public school on the northwest side of the city. He almost shouted out, "We can beat them," but kept that to himself. He did not want passersby to hear him talking to himself.

Coach Kahn returned to Naaman campus around five o'clock in the afternoon and waited for the various teams to show up for practice. About thirty minutes later, the volleyball and the girls' kickball teams showed up. Very few students. He inquired from one of the volleyball players about the boys' football team. He was told that they practice on the government school football field. The coach also inquired and got the direction of the shortest route to the campus. He jogged and arrived there at six o'clock. He stood there and watched the boys practiced for thirty minutes. He wanted to leave, but something prompted him to remain until after the practice.

He observed their dribbling and passing skills and took special note of Absalom Gondon. After the practice, he approached the older gentleman who had also come to watch the kids practice. He inquired about Absalom Gondon. Lemuel Reeves told him that the boy was from Naaman High School, and that he was one of the rising football stars in the city. He took note of some of the boys too.

As a former player, he knew the good, the bad and the ugly. The latter was called "a **Gbugor**," or a dummy footballer in Liberia. A **Gbugor** did whatever the coach told him to do. A **Gbugor** was a nightmare for any player no matter how skillful or talented the player was. My God, did GJHS had one! His name was Samson Guanue. He was a nineteen year-boy and stood six foot tall. He was taller than all the football players at Grae. Coach Kahn smiled to himself because he found the answer to the skills and talent of Absalom Gondon. Samson would run as though it was his nature. And when he kicked, he did it to clear the ball out of his goal area as taught by his coach. He was not dumb, but he just did not have the skills to play football. He just kicked, period. If you stood in his way, he kicked you and the football.

Early Sunday morning, Coach Kahn said his farewell to DeQuincy and Comfort as they prepared for church. Harry Kahn was not a religious man. He knew there was a higher power who controlled the universe, but going to church was another thing. All the noise of choirs singing and preachers shouting about God they could not see and the constant talks of money, especially the preachers' special love offerings irritated him. My God, he felt people stayed too long in church doing nothing.

He walked briskly to the parking station and got on a lorry bound for Grae. He had seen enough of Gompa City. He got his school supplies and saw Absalom Gondon played. Mission accomplished. Now he needed to get back and prepare for Naaman High School Football Team. Within one and half hours, Coach Kahn was back home in Grae. His wife Stella met him at the door. "We were worried sick about you. You should have sent words that you were all right." Stella complained.

Back in those days, there were no telephones. People sent messages by folks they knew. Many people from Grae traveled back and forth to Gompa City to conduct businesses. Harry should have sent a message by them to his wife that he was well. He forgot because his mind was on Naaman High School. He had been busy strategizing how to counter the skills of Absalom Gondon.

Monday morning at recess on Grae campus, Coach Kahn hurriedly assembled members of the football team to brief them on his scouting mission. He personally invited Samson Guanue to the meeting. "Lady Annie and the gentlemen of Grae Eagle." For the first time, in a long time, Coach Kahn mentioned the mascot of Grae. And when he said it, there was an urgency in the tune of his voice. "I visited Naaman High School in Gompa this gone weekend. Their campus is nothing compared to ours. They did not seem to have the players, but they would recruit players from various schools within the city, but don't be afraid." When he used the word, *afraid,* Annie and Johnny looked at each other. They wanted to come out say, "Coach, let's go and possess the land." But the coach had not asked for anyone's opinion yet. He had some important details to tell the team.

Samson Guanue! Do not say it coach. These kids know Samson Guanue, but it was too late. The hissing sounds of disbelief were already building into a rumbling of contempt and sinister laughter. Coach looked at everyone with a stern face. "I have invited Samson to be a member of this team, no comment. Period!" Samson smiled at everyone, and said, "Thank you so much, Coach. I will learn hard and fast. You will not be disappointed."

Samson Guanue was a nineteen-year-old eighth grader. My God, what a tribute to his family that he was young and in grade eight. He was six feet tall with crude haircut. His mother had been his barber since birth. She did not do a good of it, but who cared about Samson's hair. Most kids were afraid of him because of his height.

And back then, it was not unusual for nineteen years old men to be in grade eight. Throughout the district, county, and perhaps in the country men and women in their forties and fifties were enrolled in high school. My God, some were determined to get high school diplomas and become teachers. They left husbands, wives and children at homes in pursue of their dreams. Nearly half of them succeeded. Graduation days were nothing short of miracles for these old folks.

Members of the football team thought Coach Kahn must had gone mad. They were going to the city to make a name for Grae Junior High School, and the coach had selected a *"gbugor"* or a dummy footballer to come along and play.

The team returned to practice that Monday afternoon. Practice was intense. At times it was funny, watching Samson trying to kick the ball with all his might. Sometimes, he missed when the coach rolled the ball to him. Other times it was aggravating to watch a grown man learn to play football.

Johnny and Tormen wanted to know why Samson had not played in all these years until now. Samson knew better. Nobody got paid for playing football in Liberia. Those who played did so for the love of the game. Players who got hurt playing were left in the hands of traditional bone doctors and "quacks," or bag doctors. Players paid their own medical bills. If Samson got hurt, who would help his aging parents at home and on the farm?

Samson was the only child of his parents. Mrs. Sunny Guanue had been told she would not have children because of her age. But she and husband Matthew Guanue did not give up. They traveled across the district seeking fertility herbalist. They met and consulted an older woman herbalist and fortune teller in Karltuo. She told them they would have one boy, and then no more children thereafter.

When Mrs. Guanue was pregnant with Samson, rumors spread that she had drunk poisonous herbs from an unknown herbalist and gotten sick. She was going to die. She hid herself for the last three months of her pregnancy. Samson was delivered on the family's farm by a traditional or empirical midwife and brought to Greyson to the surprise of everyone. His mother had always warned him, "Go to school, but don't play ball and break your legs. You are the only child. You will take care of us when we are old."

On this special occasion, and for this game only, Coach Kahn promised Mr. and Mrs. Guanue that Samson would never play football for Grae after this game. After all, Samson had one year remaining at Grae. In a year he would graduate and transfer to a high school of his choice. Mr. Guanue did not mind about his son playing football. He only told him to be careful and not get hurt.

Samson was sored following his first day of workout and practice in many years. He went home almost limping. He went through the back door and got in the house. His mother heard him pouring water into a bucket and asked what was going on. "I am trying to take a hot bath," Samson replied. "In this heat?" His mother shouted back. But he was already in the bathroom outside the building.

In rural towns and villages, people bathed outside in bathrooms built with bamboo, and sometimes with palm branches. There were no concrete floors on the inside. People stood on gravel or planks and bathed. He massaged his aching feet, ankles and muscles with hot towel. They felt good!

The next day Samson was ready for practice. He kept progressing as the practices continued. By the end of the week, he could kick the ball with no problem. To test his theory of Samson guarding Absalom Gondon at Naaman High School, Coach Kahn divided his football team into two teams; six players on each side. Coach Kahn instructed Samson to guard Johnny Dahn, and never to leave him alone. Johnny was five feet and six inches tall. It was impossible to hide from the six-foot frame of Samson. Fortunate for Annie, she played on Samson's team. She did not have to content with him. Samson marked Johnny so tight he barely got the football. Johnny asked the coach if he would take a breather. Coach halted the practice so everyone would rest. My God, Coach Kahn was a football genius. Would Samson duplicate the same performance at Naaman High School within a week?

The kids looked forward to the trip to Gompa City. Some of them had never been there, except for Johnny and a few other boys, including Annie's boyfriend Boyd Dennis. Mr. Robertson Dahn, Johnny Dahn's father had a drugstore in Grae. And when he went to Gompa City to purchase drugs, he took Johnny along. Mr. Dahn had promised to send Johnny to Gompa City after his Grae days were over. With the talent and skills of Johnny, a school would be glad to have him.

Annie was glad that she would get the chance to play before a larger audience than her first game. Though nervous, she did not dread the moment. With Boyd Dennis, Uncle Julius Kpan and Coach Kahn on the sideline, she would give it all that she had in her arsenal. Aunt Yarwoan would not take the trip. She stayed behind to take care of the family business.

Coach Kahn had emphasized to Annie that great players of all times lived for moments when they would play before hundreds, perhaps thousands of *spectators*. He mentioned the great Wannibo Toe of Liberia, including John "Monkey Brown, Mar Saar, Santos Nyanatee Maria, Anthony Grey, Borbor Gaye, Josiah "JJ" Johnson, John "Black Jesus" DeShield, Garrison and George Sacko, Jackson Weah, David Momo, Solomon Sipley and others. He even mentioned the best footballer of all times, Pele of Brazil. Annie would be her best, even if not the likes of these players. She had something to prove; a woman would not play football among men. Perhaps Annie would be the first female on the face of the earth, though in a rural small town in a small country on the West Coast of Africa called Liberia to do it. From that moment on, Annie dreamt of her glorious moment.

Time came for Grae Junior High School to travel to Gompa City to meet Naaman High School. It was an unusual Saturday in the middle of June. It was bright and sunny. It seemed as though Coach Kahn had spoken or prayed to the high power, he believed in to hold on to the clouds. There was not a single cloud in the sky. It was just beautiful for a football game. On Friday, it was announced that students interested in traveling to Gompa City for the game would pay a dollar. Players would pay fifty cents, and the cheerleaders would pay seventy-five cents. GJHS rented two pickup trucks or lorries; one for the players, coaches and school officials, and the second one for cheerleaders and *spectators*.

The first pickup truck or lorry was red in color, rented from Mr. Musa Bility, a local vender from Grae. He was an interesting man. He did not own a shop or store. He sold his goods in the front of his house and in the marketplace on Saturday, Grae's official market day. He also traveled around the district on designated market days selling his goods.

He had three wives with nine children. He traveled to Gompa City every Thursday (official market day) to sell his goods. On Fridays, he rested because he was a Muslim. The white inscription written on his pickup read, "Only God knows tomorrow."

The other pickup truck or lorry was rented from Selekie Kromah, a friend of Mr. Bility from Zuatuo. They were not business partners, but their religion and ethnicity brought them together. Mr. Kromah's pickup truck was yellow with red the inscription "Poor no friend."

My God, every commercial vehicle had some types of inscription, some catchy phrase with special meanings to the owner. The two pickup trucks were to leave Grae at twelve o'clock midday. Any students not on campus by eleven o'clock that morning forfeited whatever fees she or he paid for the trip.

As the students were juggling for space on the lorry, Boyd Dennis arrived, dressed in all red, including red shoes. He said to one of the officials in charge of placing students on the lorry, "Teacher, Annie is playing in Gompa today, I am going to see her." Again, Boyd Dennis was dressed to impress. He had been the first student to pay his fee of one dollar for the trip. The official paid him no attention. He only said he was placing students on the truck in alphabetical order, except adult *spectators* like Mr. Julius Kpan. They were seated first before the students. Boyd had to wait until the official got to the letter "D."

For publicity, Coach Kahn prepared two white posters with the inscriptions, "Here comes Annie" and tied them to the front bumpers of both trucks. Both trucks left the campus little past twelve midday for Gompa City. Coach Kahn started with the usual chant; "Amen, men, Amen, men. What's wrong with Grae? All right. Who says so? Everybody. Who's everybody? Grae Junior High School." "Amen, men, Amen, men. What's wrong with Annie? She is all right. Who says so? Everybody. Who's everybody? Grae Junior High School." Both trucks took off from the campus and did two circular rounds in the center of Grae before heading northeast to Gompa City.

As they went, they sang those football songs familiar to nearly all rural Liberians. "If we play, we will win. If you score, we will score." "Play la ball, Annie play la ball. Score la goal, Annie score la goal."

Grae arrived in Gompa City a little past three O'clock in the afternoon. It was still a beautiful day, even in the city. Both trucks drove on the Main Street of the city all the way up the hill near the grounds of the United Methodist Hospital, and then back and very close to the public high school campus.

The singings brought many onlookers into the streets. The city was almost on the edge. A young woman called Annie was playing on the men's football team and had traveled to this city so the world could see her. Unbelievable! Many residents thought it was a trick by Naaman High School to generate funds for the school. Who ever heard of woman playing on men's football team? Some were willing to go and see for themselves, but others thought of something else to do than to fall for a scam like that by Naaman. They had read the flyers, but to see it physically, it was impossible.

On the completion of their third trips on Main Street, the trucks headed to Naaman High School campus up the hill on the southwest side of the city. They sang as they drove up the hill with the cheerleaders' truck ahead this time. When they arrived on Naaman's campus, residents came out to see Annie. She was in the red truck with the players. She mixed with the cheerleaders so no one would recognize her. There were rumors that Naaman had contacted a voodoo chief to make sure that it did not lose to Grae Junior High School. It would be a terrible shame on the city.

Whatever you did back in those days, you never got dropped by a girl. If it ever happened, you would be ridiculed until death.

Grae disembarked from both vehicles. They were not impressed. Grae School had talked so much about Naaman High School as if it were a junior college with an elaborate campus located in the suburb of the city. In comparison to Grae, Grae was a paradise. It was built by the government in the late 1970's. It was not equipped with lots of things, but Grae had a beautiful campus and was well kept and maintained by the students.

Coach Kahn and Grae officials met with their counterparts from Naaman. As Mr. Johnnie had indicated in his followed invitation letter, the volleyball and kickball games would be played on Naaman's campus and the football game would be played on the campus of the public school. Case closed, and let the games begin! No, not so fast!

Naaman's subtle recruitment of players from various schools within the city was almost exposed. Yes, they **borrowe**d to the teeth. Naaman got Tina Tee from a Ganta Mission School within the city. She stood five feet and three inches and weighed less than 100 pounds, and known to her friends as "TT." But she could kick and run. Coach Kahn grew suspicious when spectators who knew Tina were inquiring if she had transferred to Naaman Academy. She refused to answer. She was busy putting on her sneakers for the kickball game. Coach Kahn wanted to **bounce grumble**, or dig deeply into the matter, but he changed his mind. As a former player and now a coach, he knew these things happened all over the country. The kickball game started first, to be followed by the volleyball and the football games. The kickball game was a battle between "TT" and Annie. But "TT" alone could not make a team. No matter how hard she kicked, it was caught by Annie, or retrieved quickly to prevent a run. The game was kept close. But at the end, GJHS edged Naaman fifteen runs to fourteen.

In the volleyball game, GJHS was no match for the recruited talents from the city. GJHS was beaten three straight sets. My God, the scores were horrible to count. GJHS had a volleyball net, but no ball. No students played volleyball at GJHS.

Everyone hurriedly made his or her way to the government school field approximately one and half miles from Naaman High School depending on the route one took. There were shortcuts in the bushes, but you have to watch out for West African Green Mamba snakes.

The officials, coaches, cheerleaders, spectators and players from GJHS got back their on trucks and headed to the public school. They sang as they went. To them this was a victory to cherish. Naaman recruited heavily, yet could not defeat them in both games.

Yes, yes, the kickball, and the volleyball games, they were fine with girls dashing across the field and sliding to steal first, second or third base. In Liberia back then, football was the real game. When your school lost a kickball or a volleyball game to another school, you never talked about losing. You said the girls lost their game as if they did not represent the school. Volleyball was at times considered women's sport and not taken seriously. Did both schools have basket teams? My God, some of the students from GJHS had never heard of basketball. If they did, it was perhaps from kids who came from big schools in the cities or looking through a textbook.

The players from Naaman remained on their campus to dress up. The visitors arrived on the government school campus and went into one of the classrooms to get dressed. My God, most public school classrooms were never locked. Anyone went in there on the weekend and did some stuff people shouldn't do on public property. In small town and villages, goats and sheep slept in classrooms for comfort and warmth. GJHS found a classroom that was cleaner than the rest and went inside to get ready.

Naaman's students had built a fence around the field with palm branches. This was a fundraising game. It had two entrances, one on the south side adjacent to the goalposts, and another one on the northeast side of the field. To enter the field, an adult paid a dollar and students paid seventy-five cents. Teachers were placed at both entrances to weed out stowed-ways or those attempting to enter without paying a fee.

Back then, those who attempted to ride a car, train, or enter public arena without paying fees were called stowed-ways. My God, no one knew the exact meaning of the word, but everyone was quick to throw the word at anything that moved. There were stowed-ways chickens, goats, or sheep. And students who showed up late for school, but were never caught and sent to the principal's office were called stowed-ways.

Naaman High School arrived earlier than anticipated. Mr. Johnnie rented a truck for the short distance to the public school. Of course, they had to do a roundabout on Main Street before heading to the ball field. This was intended to attract more **spectators** to the game. Back then, when you heard, "Sarteah hey, "Laymah, Laymah Sarteah Laymah, Laymah, Laymah Sarteah Laymah," it was time to play football. In those days, my God, no matter what you were doing, you dropped it and ran to the ball field when you heard the song.

As they headed to the ball field, a few **spectators** hurriedly followed. They wanted to see a woman playing with men in a football game in Liberia. To many of these **spectators** seeing was believing. They had read the flyers and had come to see and believe.

Naaman's boys were dropped off on a dusty basketball court just outside south of the field. They stood there for at least five minutes singing "Naaman O, O, O, Naaman O, O, O, Naaman O, O!" After the usual chant, they finally entered the field through the entrance near the goalposts.

Yes, this public school had a basketball court, but with one wooden pole with the ring mounted on a square piece of wood as a back board. No one practice basket on the dusty court. It was frequently used for football ("Freetown Ball") practices. In this game, there was no offside or onside. You played wherever the ball went or landed. From the minimum of three players to the maximum number of five players against each other. The team that scored first, stayed on the court to play another incoming team. You get scored on; you are out. But today was not Freetown Ball. This was a real football game with far more important implications than Naaman High School. Naaman was representing Gompa City against a visiting school with a girl on its football team. Gompa's reputation was on the line.

Naaman's boys were dressed in their school color; blue jerseys with white numbers on the backs. The jerseys had no names written on them, and there were no matching shorts, boots, or socks.

But wait a minute there were two men who had their own matching shorts, boots and socks. Titus Versele and Tokpa Dunbar were two boys from Monrovia. They had been in the city barely a year. They grew up playing football in the sand on the beach at Coconut Plantation. When these boys trapped the football, you would hear a pin dropped. Again, Mr. Johnnie and Naaman had **borrowed** to the teeth.

This was somebody else's ball field so there was no reason to second guess which team would take the field first. Naaman took the field first while GJHS was still getting ready in one of the classrooms. Coach Kahn had a simple game plan. Samson Guanue would mark the best player on Naaman's team. If the game ended scoreless at the end of the first half, all GJHS players would retreat to the defense at the start of the second half to clog the goal mouth.

As usual Greyson came out dressed in their red jerseys. The boys came out first followed by Annie and Coach Kahn jogging slowly behind them and waving his red handkerchief as usual. Coach Kahn was jumping as if warming up to play. This was his moment he had wished for all year since Annie Laykarnue Kern joined Grae Junior High School Football Team. Gompa City, perhaps Nimba County and Liberia were in for a special treat.

Annie entered the ball field with thunderous applauds anyone had ever heard on this ball field. Everyone went crazy, almost knocking one side of the fence over. Everyone wanted to take a look at Annie. My God, Gompa City would never be the same after this game.

Coach Kahn and Annie joined Greyson players near the south goalposts. As soon as he joined them, he chanted. "Amen, men. Amen, men. What's wrong with Annie? All right. Who says so? Everybody. Who's everybody? Grae Junior High School." "Amen, men. Amen, men. What's wrong with Grae Junior High School? All right. Who says so? Everybody. Who's everybody? Grae Junior High School."

Coach Kahn and his staff hurdled around the players to discuss what they saw on Naaman's team. Two men who dressed differently. They did not appear local. Coach Kahn was not going to let this one slip by. He called Mr. Saye Johnnie and Coach Amos Saye and expressed concern about the two men dressed differently from the rest of Naaman's players. Coach Saye and Mr. Johnnie insisted that they were students at Naaman. When he was pressed further, Mr. Johnnie said the men would enroll next week for school. Therefore, they had the rights to play on the school's team.

The coaches and school officials almost got into a shouting match. Referee D.D. Carson and Mr. Jack Danzo, a prominent businessman in city went to the rescue. He called Mr. Johnnie aside and advised him that *borrowing* or recruiting players from schools around the city was bad enough, but recruiting men who were not even students of Naaman was going overboard. "But, Jack we have to defend the name and reputation of our city." "You can't do it by cheating," Jack replied.

Coach Kahn declared, "If Titus Versele and Tokpa Dunbar played, we would leave and go home." Fans and *spectators* who had paid their money to see or *witness* Annie play were getting jittery. Some of them were shouting, "If no game, we want our money back." The last thing Naaman wanted on this campus was rioting by fans. There was a soldier barrack or military base just three hundred yards away. Of course, they would not intervene because some of them were already on the ball field as *spectators.* They too would be entitled to refunds.

Players on both teams sat in the field a few hundred feet from each other. No one said a word from either team to each other. Time was running out and they too were getting frustrated.

Mr. Johnnie bowed to the pressure and asked Coach Saye to leave the two men off the team. Titus and Tokpa took off their jerseys and handed them over to Coach Saye. After all, this was a fundraising event. Mr. Johnnie and Coach Saye would not risk any trouble from the fans or *spectators*. Someone in the stand shouted, Naaman likes *borrow, borrow* too much. That's their medicine right there. Let's see what they will do here today."

Referee D.D. Carson was notorious for awarding penalty kicks to home teams in injury or extra time that had led to violence in Gompa City. He had built a bad reputation for himself. My God, back then they said, the *game ended in confusion*. There was not a game that D.D. Carson officiated that did not end in confusion. He was deliberately picked by the founder and proprietor of Naaman High School. He was desperate to win, and did everything imaginable to win. But many prominent citizens of Gompa City, including Mr. Jack Danzo cautioned D.D. Carson against cheating in this particular game. They had paid their money and come to see Annie Laykarnue Kern play, and Mr. Carson was not going to rob them of that opportunity. My God, he would bring the city on himself if he did anything other than what was advised.

All right, let the game begin! Fans were getting nervous and threatening to break down the fence and allow other *spectators* onto the field. But Coach Kahn had one more problem to solve. Mr. Koffa Jones, a noted voodoo man known in Gompa City was standing behind Naaman's goalposts. With his presence there, no one would score. That's what Naaman officials and players believed.

The game finally started at five O'clock. The coin toss was won by the visitors. They took the southern goalposts because Voodoo Man Koffa was standing behind the northern goalposts. Was it a fate or coincidence? It did not matter because Grae brought their own voodoo man too.

Today, Greyson had to be at their best. Annie stood at center forward position with Johnny Dahn to her left and Tormen Sahn to the right. They would switch positions during the game. Their positions were not permanent throughout the game, except for Samson Guanue. He was placed at right center back position to police and harass Absalom Gondon. Before centering the ball, Captain Tualie Kahn said to everyone, "Remember the game plan." They all nodded in agreement.

Hundreds of fans had come to *witness* the game and watch Annie play. She felt the butterfly crawling in her stomach and coming to her throat as she got ready to center the ball or put it into play. "I hope you are not afraid. We are here to protect you." Johnny reassured her. She put the ball in play by passing it to Johnny, followed again by another thunderous applauds. Oh my God, the girls on the field were excited to see one their own playing with men. Johnny turned around and passed the ball to Tualie Kahn, the team captain. Tualie passed the ball to Tormen

Sahn. Tormen got by one Naaman's play and passed the ball to Annie. She beat the first man that came running at her. Mr. Jack Danzo pulled a five-dollar bill and waved it at Annie and said, "Annie this is for you after the game." He was a businessman and a football fanatic. Coach Kahn was pacing the sideline as he had never done before.

The next pass from Johnny to Annie was intercepted by Absalom Gondon. But he made a terrible mistake by attempting to dribble Samson. Absalom did not know what hit him. Samson kicked him and the ball at least three two feet off the ground. Foul. Absalom got up slowly and said to Samson, "I am coming at you again." "I will be waiting for you," Samson replied.

The free kick awarded to Naaman was wasted. They had a chance to take the lead, A.B. Sayon kicked the ball over the crossbar. My God, A.B. did not know that football was a team sport. Every time he got the ball, he attempted to dribble at least six players from Grae. And when he lost the ball, he did not give chase.

By the fortieth minute into the first half, a third corner kick was awarded to Greyson. Coach Kahn had taught his nephew to be the best corner kicker there was. From the right flank of the ball, Tualie hung the ball like a kite in midair. Annie was standing around the penalty spot. When she spotted the ball in the air, she flew over everyone and headed the ball over the crossbar. She missed the goal by just a few inches. Coach Kahn fell to the ground face down. He had never seen Annie in such a form before. He got up quickly and smiled at those who were wondering if he was all right. Yes!

My God, men standing on the sideline were speechless. One of them shouted, "Annie after the game, I will marry you." While the men were speechless, the women on the sidlelines began singing a popular Christmas song in June with a different twist. "You like her, she will show you, you don't like her, she will show you."

Five minutes later Referee D.D. Carson blew his whistle. End of the first half. Coach Kahn's plan "A" worked. At half time, GJHS players sat in the middle of the field. They were surrounded by a large crowd. Everyone wanted to glance at Annie. This young lady had defiled the Liberian culture and was living the dream.

After ten minutes, both players were whistled back to the ball field. This time Naaman would put the ball into play. D.D. Carson and his two line judges did an excellent job during the first half. But what would happen in the second half was anybody's guess knowing Mr. Carson's reputation as a referee.

As the second half began, Naaman's cheerleaders and fans tried to get under Samson's skin to take his mind off his game. No, not Samson Guanue. "Hey Goliath, can you play football?' They tried to taunt him. Samson paid no heed to them. He came here on a mission; kick anything in your path. Period. Nothing was going to deter him, and he was not going to disappoint Coach Kahn and his school.

As instructed by Coach Kahn, every player, except Grandpa Doe came back to defend. He was barely five feet and four inches tall. So all his friends called him Grandpa. He was a good winger and could run. He was moved to play center forward position. This was a gate Naaman could not break through despite the talents they collected from various schools around the city. When nine men are defending a goal, no player can get by them no matter how talented the player is. They were given simple instructions by the coach. "Just kick or clear the ball out of your goal area." That's what Grae did the entire second half. They were not particularly interested in scoring or winning the game.

Mark Sackor, John Tarpeh and Matthew Joe and the talents from other schools were frustrated by the defense all afternoon. They could not get by Samson's long legs. Every position was doubled and at times tripled. Annie also did her part. She frustrated them no matter how hard they tried to intimidate her.

Mr. Johnnie had warned every player before the game that this was a special event to raise money for his school. No fights! Those responsible would be kicked out or expelled from school. That warning was also for D.D. Carson.

The second half of the game was what those who played the sport used to call "boom boom ball." Players did not trap or break the ball and make passes. They just kicked the ball any direction. Depending on the location of the field, sometimes it took forever to retrieve the ball. There were no nets behind goalposts in those days. So, after forty-five minutes of boom, boom ball, Referee Carson blew his final whistle. Game's over. For the first time in his life as a referee, D.D. Carson did not award a penalty kick to the home team in the dying minutes of the game. The invisible scoreboard read: Naaman 0 and Grae 0.

Uncle Julius Kpan was the first person on the field. He lifted Annie up and put her on his shoulders. Coach Kahn and his players joined him including several fans. Boyd Dennis was in the midst of it all. They danced with Annie around the field. They stopped in the center of the field and chanted; "Amen, men. Amen, men. What's wrong with Annie? All right. Who says so? Everybody. Who's everybody? Grae Junior High School." "Amen, men. Amen, men. What's wrong with Grae Junior High School? All right. Who says so? Everybody. Who's everybody? Grae Junior High School."

Mr. Johnnie and Coach saye came to Coach Kahn and his players and also chanted first about Naaman, and then about Grae and Annie. Naaman's school officials had no words to describe what they saw on the field. Unlike Zuatuo, they had recruited heavily to defeat GJHS. But Coach

Kahn countered with a simple game plan that neutralized the talents that Naaman assembled. It was a moral victory for GJHS. After all, this was Gompa City with all the talents one could find in a rural city.

As Coach Kahn and his players were leaving to get on their trucks, Mr. Danzo showed up and handed Annie a brand new five-dollar bill, and said to her, "I would like to see you back in Gompa City." As he left, he was shaking his head, "I can't believe it, a girl playing on boys' football team."

Naaman did not prepare meals for GJHS as it was the usual practices in most towns and villages. A big city school preparing meals for a smalltown middle school, no way. Mr. Johnnie and Naaman had made their money. They did not anticipate visiting Grae anytime in the near future. The prospect of retaliation did not cross their minds. Mr. Johnnie was satisfied that a middle school with a girl on its football team did not put his school and the city to shame. He wouldn't have been able to live with himself if Naaman had lost the game. As a Liberian man, such thought made him sick to his stomach. But for now, he would bash in the glory of bringing Annie Laykarnue Kern to Gompa City, the young talented lady that turned the football world of this city upside down, even to this day.

By seven thirty o'clock everyone from GJHS began boarding, ready to return home. Coach Kahn and his school officials were proud of their kids. They would leave singing as they had come.

As the players boarded their truck, what Annie Kern had always hoped for came true. Coach Kahn allowed Boyd Dennis to ride with the players. As he entered, everyone shouted, "Annie's husband, Annie's husband!" He sat on the right side of Annie, and said calmly, "Hey guys, hey guys, we are just special friends that's all." But Annie was glad that the coach had allowed Boyd to sit by her side on the way home. As they left, Annie Laykarnue Kern laid her tired body across Boyd Dennis' laps. He did not mind. In fact, he loved it.

As they sang on their way home, Boyd Dennis thought to himself, "Maybe one day a best dressed man and a female footballer would get married. What a team would that be!"

What a dream for Coach Kahn! He did it as he had anticipated several months ago; taking Annie to a bigger city to showcase her talents. She made him proud as a coach. In those days, there was no postgame show, interview or news conference. After the game fans and players mingled and then disappeared into their various homes.

Annie did not have an interview or postgame news conference, but several men of the city came to smile at her and shake her hands. She did something never seen in Liberia, perhaps in the world in the early 1980's. From this day forth, the boys finally embraced and accepted her as one of their own.

ONCE UPON THE TIME IN LIBERIA, a young lady came out of obscurity and changed the perception Liberian men had about Liberian women in general. She proved pundits and doubters wrong that a girl was not physically fit to play on a men's football team. Today, Annie Laykarnue Kern, wherever she may be, if she was fortunate to survive the Liberian Civil War, she is training many little Annies to change the world of football that indeed, let it be heard that a girl can play on a men's football team.

CHAPTER 2

THE BOY WHO LIED TO PROTECT AND KEEP HIS FRIENDS

"When a dog is stuck, it may let out a grunt."
Meaning: When you are hardpressed or forced into an
uncomfortable situation, you may do or say something
you may not otherwise do or say in a normal circumstance.

Twice a week, the boys in the dormitory met for Bible study in the dining room or Mess Hall. It was a Mess Hall all right! It was messy, a long table made with rough wood. It had two long planks attached parallel to both sides for seating. Most of the boys ate outside or standing up. The floor was a rough concrete that had to be swept constantly. A student had to splash cold water on the floor when sweeping to keep the dust down, and from settling on him. If he did not, he appeared like someone who had just climbed down a chimney.

The midweek Bible study was on Wednesdays, and the weekend Bible study was on Saturdays. Bible study was fun time. "James chapter four, and verse ten, Humble yourself in the sight of the Lord, and He shall lift you up; James chapter four and verse ten." Charles menlor just murdered Pete Lorlue. That was the only verse in the entire Bible that Pete knew. Everyone knew and left it alone for Pete. But on this particular Wednesday night, Charles decided to take away Pete's Bible life. What would he do now? Africanus Levingston had already recited John chapter eleven and verse thirty-five; "Jesus wept." What a horrible night for Pete! Well, for the rest of the night, Pete kept quiet until the Bible study was over.

It was not much of a Bible study. One of the older boys led by asking everyone to give a testimony about the goodness of God. It was fun singing and praising God in their ethnic tongues.

Those songs made the Bible come alive in those days because one knew the meaning of every word in the songs.

At the end of the Bible study, the boys would go to bed on hardwood bunkbeds. There were no mattresses. The boys spread their blankets on the planks and slept. They woke up in morning feeling as if they had been beaten with a rod.

Bedbugs feasted on everyone all night. To get rid of them, the boys had to boil water and pour it on the planks, and then leave the planks out for at least eight hours to air dry. The beds were too heavy to be brought outside. Back in those days one thought the houses were built around those bunkbeds.

The meals were horrible. There was no cook. Two boys were selected to cook meals for everyone for one month on rotational basis. The boys ate two meals a day; rice for lunch and cassava for dinner. For meat, fifteen men ate one can of salmon soup with the rice and another with the cassava at dinner.

Each student was required to bring a one hundred-pound bag of rice in addition to tuition of sixteen dollars. Those whose parents did not have them were rejected or denied admissions into the school. Of course, a student's parents had to be active members of the denomination. My God, being a Christian was not enough, but members of that particular denomination.

To gather or dig the cassava, student cooks had to travel at least three miles one way. My God, imagine a boy between the ages of fifteen and twenty-five with a fifty-pound bag of cassava on his head six days a week with sweats dripping from every pore in his body.

The cassava had to be fresh, so the cooks left immediately after school to make haste and have dinner ready at seven o'clock before the evening devotional. It was always a day of rejoicing when the cooks' terms were up. My God, they were happy that they did not have to make those six miles trip back and forth each day after school. And they had survived the onslaught of criticisms about their cooking and what terrible cooks they were, and they would have killed a boy with their recipe and all the bla-bla-bla-bla!

When it came to criticism about the food, Joe Boy Kollie was notorious. He would take one look at the food and slide the bowl to the cooks and say, "I can't eat this thing. What are you trying to do, kill me?" But when his turn came, he cried if a boy criticized his cooking. My God, it was almost like revenge of the nerds. You hated and criticized my cooking, I would do the same to you when you cooked.

Loud-Mouth Harry and his brother Lester Tay were the worse cooks. The rice was cooked hard and the cassava was never soft when it was made into dough or dumboy. No one would attempt to swallow it. He would tell those who complained, "If you don't eat it, I will eat it."

Any student who refused meals was sent to the hill to see Miss Missy, one of the meanest missionary ladies on the mission station. He had to answer to Miss Missy why he was wasteful with God and the mission station's money. My God, those grown men were treated like kids.

To stay alive and graduate, the students resorted to hunting and setting traps for small animals; rats, raccoon, possums and chipmunks. There was no fishing because the nearest body of water was almost ten miles away on foot. Forget the rights of these animals. These boys were starving to death. They did not eat breakfast seven days a week and were living on two cans of fish per day. Fifteen boys. My God, why wouldn't the missionaries shut the dormitory down and send the boys home to their parents? Why did grown men in their late twenties and early thirties not given a chance to eat what they wanted to eat rather than missionary slim fast diet?

There was no dormitory for girls on the mission station. They lived with their parents on the mission station or within the big city below and commuted to school daily. Good for them.

Depending on where one lived within the city, the mission station was at least three miles from the city.

The missionaries came here in the late 1930's and established the mission station. It never expanded beyond elementary or middle school. It had a small clinic that catered to Christians, Muslims, and non-religious people of the city. The clinic also catered to the surrounding towns and villages. The clinic was run by an old nurse who wore spectacles. She barely spoke louder than an earshot away. She always needed an interpreter to treat the people. And she did it through a student or nurse assistant.

Devotions were held in the clinic six days a week. They were mandatory for all male students living on the station. The first thing in the morning was devotional led by a pastor on the mission station. The singing in the morning at devotions was wonderful. My God, it was like hearing the choral of angels.

Several years later, the missionaries saw the need for a Bible school. They started one to train local pastors and evangelists. They did a pretty good job of it. My God, those older men and women knew the Bible from front to back upon graduation. Listening to them preach in their ethnic tongues was like listening to the great preachers of the twentieth century. They were literally walking Bibles.

All students were required to *cut the grass* or mow the lawn six days a week. First year students spent all afternoon cutting the lawn immediately after school, including maintaining the small airfield for a small plane on the mission. Students got out of school at twelve noon and went to work two hours later until six-thirty in the evening. And then, on Saturdays, they worked from sunup to sundown. There was not a single lawn mower on the mission station. Students used long sickled machetes to *cut the grass.* Students called those long blades grass-cutters or "blister blades." After working with those monsters for several hours, the students' hands were bloodied with blisters.

Students graduated to housekeeping after a year on the mission station. That was the place where students' prestige lay, in the homes of the missionaries. No more blisters from those monstrous blades. Students' hands became soft from washing dishes, doing laundry, mopping the floor and preparing meals. Of course, if the missionaries did not like a student's attitudes, he got demoted a lot faster than when he went in. My God, the student became the laughingstock in the dormitory if he got demoted.

It took nearly a year to accept Neil Mass into the mission school. His parents were not members of the denomination. In fact, his parents were not Christians. To add insult to injury, his father was a dreaded tax collector in the district like Zacchaeus in the Bible (Luke 10.-1-10). My God, how would angels allow the son of a tax collector to enroll in their school?

How could they? The parents went to the church and became members. Neil Mass, welcome to the mission school.

One Dry Season morning at the beginning of the semester, Neil Mass arrived with three big suitcases; black steel belted suitcases full of clothes. When he arrived in his father's car, the boys ran out to see. They thought a government official had dropped by to visit the mission. Neil was a dark-skin kid who stood barely taller than five feet and three inches tall. His hair was nicely cut, something that was about to change.

On this mission station, if a boy did not keep his hair low, he got a haircut from one of the missionaries. The haircut dreaded by all the boys on the mission; a white man cutting a black man's hair in rural Liberia in the 1960's. My God, the student looked ridiculous after the haircut. Neil had a wristwatch on the right hand. My God, the boys thought the son of the president of the country had just arrived. Most of the kids in the school had not even seen a wristwatch, and Neil, a kid barely seventeen years old wearing one. He was transferred here because the government school down the hill in the city could not handle him anymore.

He was beyond discipline and the principal and teachers could no longer deal with him. His father was the only tax collector in the city and had the money, but his money could not buy discipline for his son. At the advice of the principal, Mr. Mass transferred his son to the mission station so the missionaries would straighten him out. My God, they had canning ways of doing it.

Neil's father was educated, may be, otherwise he wouldn't have been employed as a tax collector. Or at least, he knew how to count money, though he counted more for himself and less for the government.

Since knowing one's birthday was the luxuries of the educated, the elites, the rich and famous by Liberian standard, the boys were curious to know Neil's birthday. But he [Neil] did not know how old he was. On arrival, he said he was fifteen. Two weeks later, he was turning sixteen. And three months later, he said, he was seventeen. And when he was in a good mood, he was fourteen.

But who cared about birthdays in those days anyway? A child was born and if he or she was fortunate to survive the onslaught of Malaria, Typhoid Fever, diarrheas, Meningitis, Whooping Cough, Measles, or Tetanus, he or she lived year after year hardly thinking about birthday. Why remember a birthday when the kid or the parents did not have any means to celebrate it? So in the life of a rural Liberian kid in the 1960's, a birthday was just another day. Neil's father was wealthy, but he did not know his birthday. The other kids did not hold it against him.

As mentioned earlier when Neil Mass arrived in his father's car, it happened often in those days. A government official would stop by unannounced at any school, at any time of the day, and all the students would be hurriedly assembled to do a performance for him or her. Students did not practice or rehearse, but they were always ready to sing a song, do trick drilling, say a poem, or any act to entertain the official. In the end, he or she [the government official] would leave without saying a word.

The students wished an elder of the town would say, "Hey government official how was the performance? Did you enjoy it or what? Say something to the students. Don't just walk away as if nothing happened here. The students just sang their hearts out without prior preparation." And the students also wished the principal and the school officials would shout at the top of their voices, "You corrupt government jive Liberian, say something to the kids." Not a chance because they were all in it together. They were the masters and the students were the slaves. Neil's father, Mr. Nelson Mass was one of them.

The epitome of it all came at the Annual Flag Day Parade on August 24th, and the Annual United Nations Day's Parade on October 24th. Kids were dragged out of their mud beds at the crack of dawn without breakfast and forced into kakis uniforms to parade before bunch of government officials. Government school students wore kakis and private school students had their choices of uniforms. Some schools wore interesting uniforms sewn by themselves. Some looked like Puss in Boots.

This was the gathering of schools within the district. They came with their good, their bad and their ugly. Some schools did trick drilling. Don't ask what they were. The students themselves did not know. They were taught to jump left or right and knock their dumbbells together in unison, and they did it perfectly after several weeks, perhaps months of practices.

And then came the ***Eye-right Salute***. This was the most prestigious and attractive. All schools lived and died on the ***Eye-Right Salute***. Students led by another student designated as a drill instructor led them in the rituals day after day for this special salute. The student selected to do the special salute had to be the brightest, cutest and well-dressed in the school. His or her parents, especially the father had to be a town, clan, or a paramount chief. If not, he must be someone known as the justice of the peace, magistrate or the owner of a diamond mine. My God, if the ***Eye-Right Salute*** kid's father didn't know the principal of the provincial government high school where the events were held, the school did not have a chance. No matter how well the school did, it did not even come close to third or fourth place

My God, the chosen student had to know his or her left hand from the right hand. At the command of the drill instructor; ***Eye-Right***, the lead student lifted his or her right arm, stiffened it at the elbow, positioned at right angle with four fingers, and the thumb bent inward, and brought it just over the right eyebrow. The head had to be turned exactly at the line of demarcation where the **_Eye-Right Salute_** was presented. Government and school officials waited at the demarcation line for the **_Eye-Right Salute_**. Those who got it, received a standing ovation. Those who failed barely got a hand clap. It was stressful and nerve wrecking for some kids who had never seen so many faces focused on them before.

Cousin William Willie did not have the slightest chance to throw the **_Eye-Right Salute_** though his father was known as a traditional boxer in the district. Cousin William did not know his right hand from left hand. When the drill instructor gave the command, William always saluted with his left hand. The instructor would tell him to raise both hands. When he did, the instructor would say, "William, this is your right hand, and that is your left hand.

Let's try again. Eye-right!" After the third attempt, William would still salute with his left hand. He had to be sent to the principal's office for saluting with his left hand. He would be given five lashes in his bare hands. And when the teacher said, "Show me your right hand for the lashes," William would show both hands. He got many of those lashes in his school days because either he deliberately refused to salute with his right hand or he did not have enough brain to know the difference between his left and right hands.

At the end of the parades, students assembled in the large auditorium of the high school for certain types of performances. They did skits, recitations, poems and singing. It was here one actually saw the good, the bad, and the ugly the schools brought. The winners were determined by the various school and government officials in attendance. Mr. Nelson Mass would attend on special invitation from the principal. Winners were not based on performances, but rather how well the principal of the big high school knew the winning school's principal or teacher as a friend, or if he received a nanny or Billy goat from him.

One Flag Day morning, Yeatown showed up for the annual parade with a boy who had the biggest head in the world, a medical condition called hydrocephalus, meaning accumulation of water in the head or brain. All these years Tim Bush had avoided going into public arenas in towns and villages. In those days, public arenas were marketplaces, courtyards and school campuses.

Yeatown was a small town with the population of less than two hundred people. Tim was born on the farm and hidden by his mother until he was a grown man. How he survived with such a head on the farm without medical care was another story all by itself. It was a miracle for Tim to grow up to be a man with that head.

According to Tim, his mother sought all traditional healers and fortune tellers, but they could not help him. Tim first entered kindergarten when he was a grown man. Since he was a citizen of Yeatown, every student was given a stern warning by the teacher, "You laughed at Tim, you are expelled." No one did, except in his absence and when the teacher was not around.

Morrison Kanneh, an outlaw and overgrown boy in the school constantly bullied Tim and called him "Big Head." The only teacher in the school was afraid of him because he was big and fought students all the time. A single teacher in the entire school would not do a thing to him. My God, Morrison' father was also the chief of Yeatown. A teacher wouldn't dare to take on the son of a chief if he wanted to keep his job.

Why did the principal make Tim to come to the annual Flag Day parade was anybody's guess. He knew the boy would attract a whole lot of unnecessary attention. Maybe he wanted to show to the principal of the big government high school that his school had an unusual student. My God, the pubic did not see it that way.

So, when Yeatown entered the city everyone came to see this student with an unusually big head. Tim was taller than nearly all the boys in the school. He couldn't hide. But how does a boy hide his head? Back then, students were never permitted to wear a hat or cap. It was disrespectful to school officials that got a student twenty-five lashes on his or her bare back or suspended from school. Repeat violators were expelled.

The onlookers couldn't keep their eyes off Yeatown Private School. It was terrifying. It was almost like a mob. The entire city nearly followed Yeatown talking and pointing at Tim's head all the way to the parade ground. When it got really annoying, the principal of the big government high school asked student military police (MP's) to drive the *spectators* away. Back then, every school had a group of men and women designated as MP's.

At the end of the parade, Tim Bush was the first boy to leave. No one could blame him. The poor boy just had the most horrible day of his life. He was just paraded as a gazing stock or a sheep being led to a slaughter house.

His mother was angry when he got home and told her what had happened to him that day. The only thing the teacher would do or say to her was, "Sorry, but all students had to go because it was required by the government of the country." What government? Yeatown was a private school in a small town. Government did not know if there was a Yeatown Private School. He, the teacher was paid by the parents of the students. He got fifty-cents per student at the end of every month. Students whose parents did not have fifty-cents worked on his rice, coffee, or cocoa farm for twelve hours.

In those days, school MP's were also used when it was time for a student to receive his or her twenty-five lashes. They would come and held the student down on a whipping table so the principal would not get hurt while administering his punishment of lashes. My God, some principals and teachers were notoriously free-spirit or liberal in awarding twenty-five lashes. Some went as far as getting the nickname, "Teacher Pepper," or "Teacher Smoky."

Students got twenty-five lashes for passing gas in class or coming late to school. A student got forty lashes if and when the parents came and complained to the principal that he or she had not been a good boy or girl at home. There were no inquiries or explanations as to what the child did. My God, MP's were called right away to the whipping table.

Some MP's enjoyed holding other students down to be whipped. They would be laughing and giggling while the student cried for help.

Pierre Nah was a fourth grader from Yeatown. He, too was almost a teenager when he entered kindergarten. But he was a smart kid. He learned faster than other kids who were at Yeatown. When he was promoted to the fourth grade, his uncle decided that it would be good for Pierre to attend the mission school.

Uncle J.K. Nah was a church planter and a founding pastor of Yeatown only church. Elders in the denomination knew him, including the missionary Miss Missy. Pierre had lost his father when he was thirteen years old. He was one of two surviving children of his parents. His mother was not a Christian. Pierre rode his uncle's coattail up the hill to the mission station.

The station was probably 500 feet off the ground on top of a hill. When one got on the top of the hill, it flattened. On top of the hill adjacent to the boys' dormitory laid a small airfield. The mission organization back in the West owned and operated a small Cessna Plane for emergencies and spreading the good news of Jesus Christ. At the southwest end of the airfield was a soccer field for boys.

Pierre's mother was a hardworking woman. She provided the sixteen dollars needed for tuition and the one hundred-pound bag of rice required at admissions. For the first time in his life, Pierre saw an airplane on the ground. It looked so big on the ground, but so small in the sky.

Pierre had to learn a lot of new things and ways on the mission. He had to learn to be punctual at school, learn to read, new pronunciations and new conduct. The missionaries did not like kids who talk a lot. When they were resting up the hill, one would hear a pin dropped. Their residents were a few hundred yards from the boys' dormitory. When they heard the boys talking while they were trying to sleep, there were some whippings when they came down to the dormitory.

Pierre had to learn to be quiet, too. That was the trademark of a mission boy. He just sat there like a dummy all day without saying a word until he was asked or spoken to, and then he spilled out some mission words because he had learned to speak like the missionaries.

When Miss Missy came down to the boys dormitory unannounced and said good morning, the boys answered in unison; "Good morning Missy." Those who did not answer, she slapped the hell out of them. They were sinners and children of the devil so they needed to be slapped them into repentance. That was part of the mission training. The parents did not object to it. In fact, the parents encouraged and approved of it.

Remember Neil Mass? He did not last. At the end of the first semester, he was shipped to Monrovia, the capital to live with his paternal grandmother. He refused to be spanked, so he was expelled.

Sam Barker, a 5th grader was another student who was expelled because he refused spanking. He was a man, six feet tall, and probably in his late thirties. He was older than all the boys on the mission. One morning, Sam showed up late for devotion. And when the headmaster,

Mr. John Kingston inquired as to why he was late for devotion, he simply replied, "I was getting dressed." Mr. Kingston said to him, "On this mission showing up ten minutes late for devotion would cost you ten lashes in the hand of your choice." Lashes were comparable to the number of minutes a student showed up late for school. No exceptions! The man did not have a watch. How would he know he was ten minutes late? Fortunately for the boys on the mission, there were no MP's. A student obeyed or got kicked out of school for disobeying.

Expulsion was a curse on a student's Christian character and those of his or her parents. They too were ridiculed as parents who could not discipline their own children. Sam did not mind. He was nobody's child anymore. He was a grown man, and no missionary dared put a hand on him.

Immediately, Mr. Kingston ordered Sam to go to the dormitory, pack his belongings and leave. Sam went to the dormitory just a few hundred feet from the school, packed his meager belongings and headed home. He did not get a refund for his sixteen dollars because tuitions were nonrefundable, but he at least got fifty pounds of his rice back. Students were still on line at devotion outside in the school yard when Sam left the mission. It was a sad day for many of the boys as they watched Sam leaving with his fifty-pound bag of rice balanced on his head and his little light brown suitcase in his right hand.

Sam and Pierre had been accepted on the same day. Pierre had considered him like an older brother he did not have. Pierre could not hold back tears. But Jay Glew, another older boy stepped forward to be a big brother to Pierre. Jay got to like Pierre even more when he discovered that Pierre played soccer well just as himself. From that day on, they were never separated.

Pierre's second day in class was not a pleasant one. Mr. Kingston threw an eraser at him and missed his head by inches. On his second day at school, he did not understand Mr. Kingston's English. He was an English missionary who spoke with heavy British accent. Students who had been on the mission for at least one to two years understood him, or claimed to understand him. At the end of the Arithmetic Period, Pierre was still working on his numbers rather than switching to Reading Period. For that Mr. Kingston threw an eraser at him as a reminder. The school had four periods; from eight o'clock in the morning until twelve noon.

Back then, the students called an eraser a duster because it was used to dust the chalkboard or blackboard. No matter what the color of the chalkboard, it was always called the blackboard. From that point on, Pierre was always alert about switching between periods. He felt that Mr. Kingston's next volley of erasers or dusters would not miss their mark; his forehead.

One day Loud-Mouth Harry Tay got his teeth knocked out when he climbed on top of a chicken house. He was barely five feet and five inches tall, but he was closed to 190 pounds, unusual for a Liberian kid eating only twice a day. Come to think of it, he ate extra because of all the reject meals from students who did not like his cooking. He was one of the boys who had graduated to working in the homes of the missionaries.

One morning when he finished the missionary's laundry, he was told to climb on top of the chicken house and rake the leaves off the roof. The roof was probably older than he was. When he got in the middle, the roof collapsed and he landed on his mouth on the concrete floor below. There was blood all over the place! His lower teeth went through his upper lip. He was flown in the mission plane to another mission station that had a registered nurse on duty. Harry was a horrible sight. He lost two of his lower teeth. His mouth was bandaged for weeks. He also missed school for several days. The boy would not come class with his mouth bandaged shut. How would he ask any teacher a question?

When he was completely healed, he was demoted from working in the homes of the missionaries. One of the Missies denied that she told Harry to climb over the chicken house. This was something he decided to do on his own. My God, what student in his right mind would climb on top of a roof, especially a chicken house without being told by the missionaries? He would be expelled.

The boys in the dormitory, including Harry's brother Lester kept their mouths shut. It wouldn't help to try to defend Harry against the missionaries for their unjust and hypocritical treatment of him. Besides, he was just a kid trying hard to please the missionaries and make his parents proud.

The boys knew they were all alike despite their different ethnic groups. "Maybe we don't belong here," they said as they talked about what had happened to Harry. If it happened to Harry, it could happen to another boy on the mission and the missionaries would say they were not responsible or accountable. Lucky for Neil and Sam, they were gone, out of this semi-slave camp. How much do students have to suffer to get an education? After the expulsion of Neil Mass and Sam Barker, the number of boys in the dormitory was reduced from fifteen to thirteen.

During Easter vacation in April of that year, Pierre decided to remain on the mission station and work. During vacations, students who remained and worked on the mission station got paid with clothes, not money. Pierre got nice used kakis shorts and a nice light blue long-sleeve shirt. Since leaving his parents' home, these were the best clothes he ever got. He only wore them to church on Sundays. By June of that year, he was getting used to mission life. In a very short time, Pierre had been promoted to work in the homes of the missionaries. He, too was glad that he had been taken away from the dreaded monstrous blade used to cut the lawn.

When it came to cooking, Pierre was one of the best cooks. He had learned it at home helping his mother after his father's death. When it was his turn to cook, he sent words to his mother to send him some nice seasoning, salt and pepper. The boys were happy when it was his turn to cook. Joe Boy Kollie was always his assistant. Pierre tried to help Joe since some of the boys picked on him because of his bad cooking.

Midyear vacation in July of that year, Pierre went back home to Yeatown to see his mother and Uncle J.K. Nah. It was great to see mother and uncle again. But everyone in the town, including the boys and girls began to laugh at Pierre. They asked about his type of education where he had to send words to his mother repeatedly for seasonings, salt and pepper. In Yeatown men did not do the cooking. That was a woman's job. On the mission, Pierre had learned to be quiet, so he did not answer his critics or get at those who were laughing at him. His mother and uncle did not care. They only encouraged him to try harder and succeed.

Mission life was tough, but it was a good learning environment. Unlike Yeatown and many other government schools, the mission school had textbooks, educational activities, good teachers, libraries, and much more. They taught good English too.

When a student from the mission school spoke, people paid attention. He or she sounded different rather than kids who went to other schools. At home Pierre would be with his friends and not say a word while everyone else talked and laughed. Sometimes, the boys would joke him, "After the mission life, we will put public life into you." Pierre would laugh and shake his head.

Vacation came and went, and Pierre returned to the mission station. It was good to be back at school. The annual Flag Day Parade on August 24th was fast approaching. The mission school had to participate.

Again, the school officials, especially the Liberians said it was government's requirement for all schools to attend the Flag Day Parade.

The mission school did not learn anything special to be presented at the parade, or after in the auditorium. The missionaries did not really care about what was happening down the hill in the city. They were comfortable sitting up the hill minding their own business. They rarely went to town to shop or mingle with the people. They used the small plane on the station to bring their supplies from Monrovia. Their supplies actually came from the United States and Europe and were transported to the station via the small plane.

Pierre woke up Saturday morning with a pounding headache. He got up early because he had to be at work in the missionary home on time. No student showed up late for work on Saturdays. It was a beautiful morning, unusual for the Raining Season. Outside was wet from overnight rains. Pierre wished he was not going to work, or today was Sunday since the church did not allow anyone to work on Sundays. He could not shake off the upcoming Flag Day Parade off his mind. He knew what it was like when he was at Yeatown Private School. He remembered the embarrassment and shame Tim Bush had endured during the parade. Everyone had looked at him as if he were the Humpback of Notre Dame.

He hurriedly brushed his teeth and stepped out the door. In the building next door Jay Glew was practicing the Liberian National Anthem; "All Hail, Liberia Hail." Pierre did not care much about the national anthem. Until now, he did not know the words though he sang it along with other students.

There were rumors, and they turned out to be true that the mission school was sewing uniforms for the parade. But to cut down on cost, one of the Missionary Missies would sew the uniforms for the boys in the dormitory. Students living in the Bible Camp for pastors with their parents, and those living off the campus would sew their own uniforms. But to avoid mismatch, Miss Missy got the cloths and students and their parents bought them from her. For the top, a shirt for a boy and a blouse for a girl. The top was a club flowery green piece. The pants and skirts were brown in color.

Pierre did not know that a woman would sew a man's clothes. Weird. One afternoon after school, all the boys gathered at the home of one of the Missies for measurements. Forget the measurements, Miss Missy sewed the uniforms as she saw them fit. For some of the boys, the shirts were too tight, the pants were too large and longer than they were. But the students' complaints fell on death ears. Miss Missy did not care. She just said, "What I have done, it's done."

Pierre's pants were one of the worse. The boys in the dormitory laughed so hard when they saw the pants and how baggy they were. Pierre wanted to take a drastic step like going on a hunger strike for baggy pants. Jay Glew advised him against it. After all, this was going to be a one-day parade. And after the parade, Pierre would cut the pants into shorts. End of the story? No, Pierre was determined to get an answer to his baggy pants dilemma.

At the beginning of August that year, a Liberian instructor was hired to replace the Headmaster, Mr. John Kingston. This was one of the greatest moments for Pierre Nah since his enrollment. J.J. Gunner was a brilliant man in his late twenties. He had just graduated from one of the prestigious government high schools in the county capital far away.

He came along with his fiancé. They were introduced to the jubilation of all the boys. At least they had someone they could identify with, and complain to without fear of being whipped. He, too was a product of another mission station within the denomination. He has had to endure similar treatment at the hands of the missionaries as a student.

He was sympathetic to the students' complaints. He promised the boys that he would introduce reforms in the school including boycotting the Flag Day Parade, better sleeping conditions and better meals for students in the dormitory.

Of course, he had to get married before he would become a fully-fledged employee. That he did quickly and was announced later that he had gone to get married. He returned a week later, and within a few days, he was gone, this time forever. He found a better opportunity than what the mission was paying him; sixty dollars a month as a full-time teacher. He taught fourth and fifth graders, Miss Missy taught second and third graders, and another Liberian pastor taught kindergarten and first graders.

Pierre was devastated when he heard that J.J. Gunner had left the mission school. What would he do now about his baggy pants with Flag Day only weeks away? He went to Jay again for another advice. Jay told him to let it go and that everything would be all right. There would so many students and schools, no one would pay much attention to his baggy pants.

My God, good thing Pierre did not have a girlfriend in the school. That was forbidden. Boys did not talk to girls. It was sin in God's sight for an unmarried man to talk to an unmarried woman, so the missionaries said. Girls or women were never allowed to visit the boys' dormitory unless accompanied by one of the Missies. Of course, there had to be a legitimate reason for the visit; such as a girl visiting her brother or a woman visiting her son. Boys and girls sat in the same classrooms, but never talked to each other in the class, or at recess or anywhere else on the mission station. My God, if a boy was caught talking to a girl, he would be whipped so bad that he would pray to God to heal his behind to sit down. The same fate also awaited a girl caught talking to a boy.

Meanwhile, it was a fun day when one of the missionary pilots decided to give all the boys in the dormitory a free plane ride on the plane. This was Pierre's first plane ride and probably his last. The pilot took four boys at a time; one with him in the front, and three in the back seats. There was a story that Mr. Dale Vern was an air force pilot for the United States during World War II. He would take off and hang over the city down the hill like a leaf or a bird. Then, he would nosedive the small plane as if he was about to hit the ground, and then he would lift off. Pierre and some of the boys who never flew on a plane before were crying like babies.

They thought that the plane would crash. But Mr. Vern managed to fly all the boys safely without any incident. He was a nice man. He and his wife had three teenage children; two boys and a girl.

In spite of all that was going on, the plane ride, preparation for the Flag Day Parade, volleyball and soccer practices, Pierre did not take his mind off the baggy pants awaiting him on that fateful Flag Day. Sometimes he wished the day did not come, or it would rain so heavily that the parade would be cancelled. Of course, that was an illusion or a wishful thinking on the part of a young man. Rained or shined, the Flag Day Parade had always taken place.

The Annual Flag Day Parade was not actually about the various schools and their students. It was about boosting the morale and prestige of J. Sand Karma, the principal of the government high school down in the city. The city was the capital of the district. To all teachers from the various towns and villages, Mr. Karma was the guru of education. He knew everything about education there was to know. All schools assembling on his campus and saluting him showed that he had influence in the district. No one actually knew his level of education. From the time this high school was founded, he had been the only principal. And no teacher from school around the district ignored him and got away wit it. A teacher who ignored

J. Sand Karma got fired. My God, all teachers were afraid of him.

Pierre Nah saw Principal J. Sand Karma's influence firsthand when he paid several unannounced visits to Yeatown. Yeatown was just three miles away from the big city. He would be accompanied by one or two of his teachers. When he arrived, a student ran and rang the school bell. Everything inYeatown would come to a halt. The students would be assembled to drill and sing songs. Oh, yes, they sang out of keys, too. A song like "Before the Heaven door closed, Oh Lord, I want to get to Heaven, the sun shine." What did that actually mean? The students did not know the meaning. They were asked to sing, and they sang.

Some of the songs were taught by traveling teachers. They appeared in Yeatown and taught for one week, and then they disappeared never to be found or seen again.

One of the students' favorites was, "Everywhere I go, Tete Palm Wine will follow me." Maybe where the teacher went, Tete Palm Wine followed him.

The biggest Billy goat in the town would be dragged before Mr. Karma and his guests. You are talking about chickens, ducks, and Guinea fowls? Please, those were freebies and giveaways. My God, men whose ears were trained to identify the calls of female Guinea fowls when laying eggs were sent into the bushes to search for eggs. Mr. Karma did not like duck eggs. They were too large. He preferred chicken and Guinea fowl eggs. The best cooks among the women of Yeatown were assembled to prepare the best meals. In addition, the town's folks would provide a big gourd filled with palm wine. Where there were no gourds, they brought three-liter bottles.

Ordinarily, the people of Yeatown never killed their livestock unless someone important died. But for Mr. Karma, they would kill a cow if they had one. After the lunch-dinner, the Co-Chief would show up and hand them fine broomsticks or bamboo sticks as toothpicks. That was his job assignment. If Principal Karma's ears were itching, he would pluck out a feather from one of the chickens and scratch his ears right there in solidarity with the ordinary folks. Yes, even as a big *Kwi* he would scratch his ears with a chicken feather as they do.

While they ate and laughed, usually in the Chief's house, the students stood outside in the one-hundred-degree heat. This was done so Principal J. Sand Karma would grant public school status to Yeatown Private School. At the end, he would rise up thank the elders of the town through an interpreter, usually the teacher. He wouldn't say a word to the students who had asked God in their song not to close His Heaven door on him. He had made these people believed that he had connections in the county capital to change things on their behalf or in their interests. My God, the mendacity of the man was glaring, but the people did not see it.

One day, Principal J. Sand Karma showed up in Yeatown with two Peace Corps Volunteers, and the town's folks went nuts. It was more than the president of the country visit. The town crier or announcer went around the town announcing that Teacher Karma had come with some *Kwi*-White Men. If the white persons were females, he would say *Kwi*-White Women. There was nothing fictitious or racial about it. An educated person was known to ordinary folks as *Kwi.* To impress the volunteers that he had influence in the towns and villages, he would make various demands in order to grant their wishes.

Elders who had gone on their farms to work were assembled to welcome Teacher Karma and his guests. That was how he was known to regular town folks and some teachers.

Of course, the students were the first on line to drill in their uniforms. Then came the poems or recitations. Pierre recited the entire story of Joseph in the Bible without catching his breath. And the students sang, "Teacher Karma you are welcome, Oh, welcome, Oh, welcome, Teacher Karma you are welcome here today." The elders and volunteers clapped their hands for Pierre and the students. But Mr. Karma only said, "Good, you'll keep trying."

"You'll keep trying," that's all? Do you know how long it took this boy to memorize an entire story in the Bible? Do you know how many chapters that covered? He did not really care. He had only come here to collect his goat and eggs because he had run out of meat and eggs from Yeatown on his last visit.

The big city had stores, shops and supermarkets, but it cost money to shop in them. But in Yeatown, it was always free. All he had to do was to tell the folks that he would change their school to a public school, and they would give him a beautiful girl to marry, and much more. Maybe he did not have children, so he did not know how children felt when they were not appreciated. On all his visits, he never brought his wife. My God, the mendacity of it all was palpable!

"Why do students had to go and parade themselves before grownups who did not care about them?" Pierre thought to himself. Within weeks Pierre Nah would be a laughingstock of the entire population of students in the district. He had never worn pants since birth. He had always been in shorts, and now he would debut in baggy pants. The thought made him sick to eat or sleep. Why did Miss Missy pick on him? After all, he was working in her home as a maid.

Maybe she did it on purpose to make him look bad to his friends. My God, Pierre was afraid to do anything that would bring shame on Uncle J.K. Nah and his mother.

The weeks went faster than anticipated. On August 23rd, the boys went to the home of Miss Missy to collect their uniforms. When they arrived back at the dormitory, each boy took turns trying out his uniforms.

Everyone's uniforms fitted perfectly. The boys were happy, except Pierre Nah. He was the last student to pick up his uniforms.

Wait a minute, what about Pierre? He was sitting on his bunkbed with his head buried in both hands. He was almost in tears. Jay Glew told him to put on his pants so everyone would see. Pierre hesitated, then got up slowly and put on his pants. Everyone almost cried out in unison, "It's big, but not bad!" They knew the pants were big, made for a grown man, and not for a boy like Pierre. They did not want Pierre to feel bad, except for Loud-Mouth Harry Tay. "I wouldn't wear them," he said and walked outside the door. At least he told the truth.

Pierre had hoped that J.J. Gunner would remain to help him with his baggy pants issue. Maybe, he would had written a special excuse on his behalf to Headmaster John Kingston so as not to attend the parade. But Mr. Gunner was nowhere to be found. He was gone, never to be seen on this mission station again. Why did he come here if he knew he wouldn't stay longer? Why did he raise Pierre's hope? Pierre had really liked Mr. Gunner. He felt betrayed. When Pierre needed him the most, he was not there. He would probably show up on Flag Day and laugh at his baggy pants. Mr. Gunner had even believed in him as a student. Pierre felt alone with his baggy pants on his mind. Alone in this world where adults, especially Principal J. Sand Karma and his lynching teachers down the hill in the city did not care about how a boy felt about his uniforms.

On August 24th, the boys were assembled at the crack of dawn, ready to march two miles down to the campus of the government high school in the city. Pierre was the first student to arrive in front of the school where all students met, including those who commuted to school and those living in the Bible camp with their parents. Pierre sat on a tree trunk when he arrived.

He did not want anyone to see him with those horrible baggy pants. Pierre had to stand up when it was time to march to the city. And when he did, at least forty pairs of eyes were focused on him. They were all standing there in their Flag Day best. Even Jay Glew had a necktie on since he was the tallest boy and served as a drill instructor.

Pierre was shocked at the reaction of the students. He stood there in their midst with his eyes wide opened saying, "Ok, students I am here for the parade. Just laugh your heads off." Just then, the Headmaster John Kingston appeared to give his final instructions. "Stay together, and don't cause any trouble," he said. Pierre wanted to say, "What about my baggy pants? Don't you see, I look ridiculous? You are the Headmaster, do something." But the mendacity of this day made it impossible for him to act.

Pierre did not utter a word from the mission station to the public school. Principal J. Sand Karma stood halfway to the campus to take inventories of all the schools. He wanted to make sure every school in the district turned out. He would stand there to take records of each school; their names, the names of their teachers, the color of their uniforms, the number of students in each school, and what was written on their banners. In this parade, every student had to participate unless he or she was on his or her death bed. The teachers marched in front of their schools followed closely by student drill instructors.

Pierre had prayed for rain shortly before they left, but it did not come. As usual all the schools did what they had to do. The usual rituals of **Eye-Right Salute**, poems, skits, dances, songs, and recitations went on in the large auditorium. After the parade, Pierre went into the auditorium and sat down until all the programs were over. Some friends from Yeatown came over to him and tried to make him to stand up, but he refused. They sat and talked after everyone had left. When majority of the students were gone, Pierre got up and went to the mission station. As soon as he arrived, he took a pair of scissors and cut the pants into shorts as Jay Glew had previously suggested. The Annual Flag Day Parade was over. My God, Pierre was happy!

When Pierre went to work the following Monday, Miss Missy asked if the parade was good. The missionaries never attended the parade. Pierre wanted to say to her, "I hate you for making me look ridiculous among my friends." But something inside him told him the battle was over. The pants were now shorts laying at the bottom of his little red suitcase. Case closed.

The second semester started with the thirteen boys. No other student had gotten into trouble that would lead to expulsion. And no students had been accepted into the school. The boys managed on two cans of salmon a day until the Raining Season was almost over. When it rained, it poured in those days in Liberia. By the middle of October, the rain began to give way to the Dry Season. It would rain heavily for at least two or three hours, and then it would stop and give way to the sun.

Before the end of the year, the boys decided to play a soccer game against the big government high school in the city down the hill. The idea was ridiculous because the mission school had only four soccer players and no goalkeeper. A goalkeeper was the most important piece on any soccer team. The rest of boys practiced occasionally whenever they had plenty to eat. Pierre and some of the boys were against it. The invitation was accepted with a warning from Principal Karma. "You will be whipped badly." No one, including the mission school officials took him seriously. In fact, the first-grade teacher said that this was a case of David versus Goliath in the Bible. The mission school was David and the public school was the Goliath. But David did not face Goliath without preparation. He had trained himself using his sling as a weapon, and he had killed a lion and a bear.

The mission school had not played a game all year, even against another weaker mission station. And now they were to play against a government high school with more than a thousand students. The government school had some of the best soccer players from the various districts.

The day arrived for the mission school to face the public school. The boys were brought from the mission station in a van driven by Headmaster John Kingston. Since the invitation, he had served as a coach for the soccer team. He played soccer in England as a young man. He was good, but couldn't play in student game. The mission boys came singing, "Never disappointed one day, since I joined the army of the Lord, never disappointed one day." Pierre wanted to find out if God actually cared about soccer. But the thought did not come to him again.

He was nervous because he had seen some of the boys from the public school played before. It was no joke. These boys would push the leather until one ran out of breath chasing them. They did not work on a daily basis like the boys on the mission station. The mission boys' team practiced only on Saturdays after work. The government school boys practiced twice daily, at recess and then in the evening.

Before Pierre and the mission's boys took the field, Mr. Kingston prayed for victory and protection against all injuries. As Pierre's heart jumped to hundred twenty beats per minute, he wished Mr. Kingston would pray forever until the referee blows his final whistle. When he finally said, "Amen," the government school soccer team was already on the field warming up.

In sympathy to the plight of the mission boys' team, the public school decided that the first-grade teacher, Mr. Davies Daniels from the mission school would serve as a referee assisted by two teachers from the public school. Pierre and the boys were delighted. After all, it was Mr. Daniels who encouraged the mission boys that this game was a battle between David and Goliath. Of course, he wouldn't cheat and get away with it. He was not just the first-grade teacher, but he also taught in the Bible school. My God, that would assassinate his character.

It did not take long for the mission school to capitalize on a defensive blunder by the public school. Jay Glew scored the first goal when two defenders collided in an attempt to pass the ball back to the goalkeeper. Jay intercepted the pass and blew past the goalkeeper. Jay was fast, and he could kick harder too.

Somehow, Pierre knew the public school was just playing to make them feel comfortable. Eventually they would come out smoking, and the mission boys' team would not have a chance. This they did at will. The mission boys' team did not have a goalkeeper to stop the volley of shots directed at their goal. Midway through the second half, it was five goals to one, in favor of the public school. When Mr. Davies Daniels blew his final whistle, the scoreboard read, Public school 6, and the mission school 1.

It was terrible to see Pierre and Jay chasing ten men around the field for ninety minutes. Pete Lorlue would play, but he was a bad soccer player with no dribbling or passing skills. He was always trying to cause injuries to other players, even at practices. His bizarre tackling in the penalty box caused the first three goals when penalty kicks were awarded to the public school. He would jump up like a goat and sit on the shoulders of government school players and bring him down. He did not pay attention when he played. He would deliberately kick another player in front of his own goal. Talking about goalkeeping, Loud-Mouth Harry Tay mounted no efforts to stop any shots directed at the mission school's goal.

After the game, Mr. Kingston suspended soccer for the rest of the year. The mission school was ***embarrassed*** in front of hundreds of fans.

My God, you did not blame Mr. Kingston for his action. A coach is a human being, too, even a missionary coach like Headmaster John Kingston. But Principal Karma tried to sooth the pain by saying, "I told you so. Remember you are a mission school, for Christ's sake! You don't have a football team."

But Jay and Pierre knew that the David Jesse from the mission station did not have the strength to fight against the government school Goliath. God is indeed faithful, but He also requires preparation by His people before going into battle. The boys were glad that this game was over and no one got hurt, even Jumping Jack Pete Lorlue did not hurt any player on either side with his reckless abandon style of playing soccer. God did answer Mr. Kingston's prayer for an injury-free game. Amen.

Dry Season was good time for hunting. The boys hunted in the bushes surrounding the mission station. That was how they supplemented their diet with extra meat, rice, and cassava. Hunting was not forbidden by the missionaries, but it was discouraged. The boys were not allowed to keep extra food rations under their beds or elsewhere in the dormitory. That would attract rats and roaches. My God whether there were foods in the dormitory or not, rats and roaches came. Of course, rats were good meat if caught by the boys. But telling Liberian boys not to hunt was like telling American children not to go out and play in the snow when it snowed heavily and schools were closed. Even if one of the boys did not hunt, he would not be a snitcher taking the matter to the missionaries. If he did, they would do anything to protect each other, even if it meant lying.

Before Pierre enrolled in the mission school, there had been a story locally that a gang of thieves had tried to invade the mission several years earlier. And when they were confronted by the security guard on duty on the mission at the time, they had murdered him in cold blood.

Therefore, the generator on the mission ran twenty-four hours on weekends. On weekdays, it ran for twelve hours, and then it was turned off until six o'clock in the morning.

Another security guard was hired. He was an evangelist and had gone to the mission Bible school. He was a nice man who loved all the boys in the dormitory. He and J.K. Nah, Pierre's uncle were friends. When the lights were turned off at night, he patrolled the mission grounds with a flashlight searching for intruders or thieves. It was rumored that Big Jimmie was a good fighter. Before he became Christian, no man messed with him and got away with it. Pierre was glad that a strong security guard or watchman like Big Jimmie was on the mission on duty.

One night, Pete Lorlue stayed out late until the lights were turned off. He may had gone to the big city down the hill to visit some relatives. On his way back to the dormitory, he took the short cut in the bushes behind the dormitory. When Big Jimmie pinpointed his flashlight at Pete and said "Who's there?" Pete did not answer the question. He just took off running with Big Jimmie in pursue.

Pierre was in the same dorm house as Pete. There were four students assigned to each building, two sleeping on each bunkbed. Pierre, Jay, Joe Boy Kollie, and another boy were housed in the same dormitory. At midnight the doors were shut. There was no curfew, but the boys had to be in their bunkbeds by twelve mid-night. That was the mission school rule.

No one knew until it happened, and so suddenly. Pete came running and with all his might and strength cleared the door completely off its hinges and fell in the center of the house with the door under him. It was so loud it woke everyone up in all the buildings. The boys ran to Pierre's dormitory to enquire what had happened. Big Jimmie followed and came to the dormitory. He was really mad that Pete did not stop to call out his name or identify himself. "You could have gotten seriously hurt," Big Jimmie said, then walked away.

Pierre and his roommates were in trouble. How in the world would they explain to the missionaries who broke the door or how it got broken? Pierre had to think of a way out of this one. Probably his mission school days were numbered. Who was going to be the snitch? Not him, he thought to himself.

The next afternoon, Headmaster John Kingston accompanied by Pilot Donnie Corlleon, and Teacher Davies Daniels went over to the boys' dormitory to investigate the incident involving the door. The boys were called into the Mess Hall. Mr. Kingston started the interrogation. "Boys you know who broke the door down. Just come out right now and call his name or identify him. If not, everyone will be punished." The boys just looked at each other without saying a word.

"Maybe you did not hear me. This time I will call each boy by name." "Pierre Nah, do you know who broke the door? Don't tell me you don't know because you live in that building." "Yes, Sir, but I was deeply asleep. When I woke up everyone had left," Pierre replied. "Jay Glew," "I don't know, Sir." "Harry Tay," "I don't know, Sir. I sleep in different building." "Joe Boy Kollie!" He was a terrible stutterer. "I I I I don't, don't know, Sir." "Lester Tay," "I was studying and fell asleep and didn't wake up until this morning, Sir."

"J.D. Dean, you are one of the oldest boys in the dormitory. Tell us exactly what happened here last night," Mr. Kingston said. "I am in charge of a different building. I don't know, Sir," J.D. said. "All right Pete Lorlu, what about you do you know who broke the door?" He pretended as if he did not hear Mr. Kingston. "Pete, you heard me," Mr. Kingston repeated. "I don't know, Sir," Pete replied.

Pete Lorlue knew who broke the door. He did not want to be a good mission boy and admit his guilt. He was searching for a snitcher to keep grudges. Pierre wanted to shout at him. "Admit your guilt, you jive maroon. Don't just sit there and lie." Pete was one of the meanest boys on the mission. He never smiled at anyone, but always ready to fight any of the younger boys. He did not pick on any boy his age or size. He survived the dreaded and deadly viral disease, smallpox when he was young. The disease scarred him so bad that he appeared much older than his age. Pete must have been in his late twenties. Without the missionaries, Pete would have probably taken out another boy's teeth. But his little plan was not going to work.

Pierre was the newest student, the new kid on the mission, and had not formed bounds with all the boys, except Jay Glew. He had stepped forward as a big brother on the day Sam Barker was expelled for showing up late for school.

Pierre was vulnerable. He seemed to be easily intimated so the Headmaster picked on him. Pierre was later sent to Mr. Kingston's office for further interrogation. Jay had advised Pierre to be consistent in his answer. "Everyone said they did not know. So, stick with 'no' for an answer. You do not want to be a snitch on this mission. The boys will hate you forever."

As Pierre left that afternoon for his interrogation, the boys were standing by an old foundation near the Mess Hall. Today would be Pierre's first trip to the Headmaster's office since he entered the mission in early March.

The school house was a singlestory building with several classrooms and offices. Kindergarten and first graders met in one classroom, second and third graders met another, and fourth, fifth and sixth graders met together in the same room. At the end of the hall were two offices, one on the right, and the other on the left. The one on the left was used by Mr. Davies Daniels and Missy Corlleon. The one on the right was Mr. Kingston's office. It had a bookshelf with a few books, and four chairs. The interior was painted white. Mr. Kingston sat behind a heavy wooden table. In the middle of it was a wood carved nametag that read, Headmaster. He must had brought it with him from England when he came as a missionary.

Pierre was shocked to see other pastors on the mission in the Headmaster's office. There was no lady among the men. Daddy Marv was there. That was how he was known by everyone, including students on the mission. He was a fair skin well-built man with squint eyes. A stern man who never took "no" for an answer. He was known for slapping students in church services when he caught them sleeping rather than listening to the gospel. And when he preached, no one dared to leave the church to use the restroom, or get outside. He was married, and had no children. But his nephew Zahn Marv and his wife's niece, Jessica Karntay lived with them. Both were students in the mission school.

Of course, Mr. Davies Daniels, was present. A self-proclaimed religious zealot, a real latter-day Pharisee who labeled anything sinful that did not have God written on it. He would suspend or expel a student caught playing ball or carrying a load on Sundays on mission grounds. But his characters, conduct, activities and attitudes somewhat indicated, "Do what I say, but don't do what I do." The man was a walking Torah, the first five books of the Old Testament. He lived and taught in the mission Bible school. He was married and had five children. Don't ask for his wife's name because every woman in the denomination, except a female student was called "Mommy." All of them, four boys and one girl attended the mission school.

Donnie Corlleon was also present. He had been called to the mission field as an aviation pilot. He stood six feet and five inches tall and had a receding frontal hairline. Without hair transplant, he would be completely bald in less than five years. He had a knack for laughing when something terrible happened to others. He talked or spoke the same way he took off and landed his small plane, fast. He never spoke to boys who worked in their home as maids when he came home. He and his wife Charlene had two teenage children, a boy and a girl that were homeschooled on the mission by Mrs. Corlleon.

Big Jimmie was not invited because he had testified at the initial hearing that he only saw a figure running from the aircraft-hanger and gave chase. When he got to the dormitory, all the boys were standing up and did not identify who was responsible. Big Jimmie was a resident of the big city down the hill. Though a Christian, he did not live on the mission station. He only worked on the mission as a security guard or watchman. He spent nearly all of his time on the mission. There were rumors that he was married, but Big Jimmie never talked about his wife or children; at least not to the boys.

These people were not kidding. Pierre was about to face the mission tribunal. Pierre's heart began racing just as it did when he and his teammates faced the government school soccer team a few weeks earlier. He thought about Uncle J.K. Nah and his mother at home. What would they say if he got suspended or expelled? Pierre was determined never to be suspended or expelled. And he was not going to be a snitch either. Pierre wished he had sent a message by someone from Yeatown to have Uncle J.K. Nah come to this trial. It seemed like a trial and it was a trial, except that Pierre was not represented by a lawyer. Whatever the case may be, he was going to stick with, "I don't know."

Pierre was not really worried about the men that had gathered in the room. There was no way on earth they could know that he knew the student who broke the door. They would bring some of the boys back to the Headmaster's office, but that was of no use to them. Every boy had sworn that he did not know the culprit.

The afternoon belonged to Headmaster Kingston. As a single English missionary, he had been sent to this rural mission station in northeastern Liberia to oversee the activities of the boys. He had served as a teacher in a small English community in England before his call to the mission field. He wore a wire framed spectacles when teaching or reading. Even in the midst of the tropical heat, he had a knack for wearing a white T-shirt and a black jacket on top. He always wore a pair of black pants as if there no other color in the world of pants. He also had a passion for wearing leather sandals or white tennis shoes. His deep English accent was slippery to understand, especially for a first-year student.

He plunged into the issue of Christian children obeying their parents and doing what is right to guarantee a long life on this earth. Then, he watched as the men nodded their heads in agreement with him. "Since we know this biblical truth, can we say that a child who disobeys parents and lies ought to be punished?" Daddy Marv answered the loudest. "Yes, Sir, Mr. Kingston, a child should never lie to the parents." Most of Mr. Kingston's questions only provoked a "yes" or "no" answered.

The Headmaster started the interrogation by asking; "What is your name, and how long have you been a student on the mission, and do you know that it is a sin for a Christian to lie?" Pierre answered the second part of the question first. "Yes, I know. My name is Pierre Nah, and this is my first year on the mission."

Never answer a missionary's questions with phrases. They have to be a complete sentence or sentences. If not, he or she would ask the same question over and over until the answer was given in a complete sentence. "Did anyone tell you to lie when you came here," Mr. Kingston continued. That was a trick question, and he knew it. But Pierre was not intimidated by it. "No, Sir, no one told me to lie," Pierre replied.

The men took turns asking Pierre questions about his Christian background, and how he had come to know Jesus Christ as his personal Savior. Daddy Marv was particularly curious to know why Pierre could not identify the wrongdoer knowing everyone would get a whipping if no one was found.

Daddy Marv, then rose to his feet and cleared his throat. "Men of God, Jesus Christ said in His teaching that a Christian's yes should be yes and his no should be no. We have been in this room for almost two hours, and this boy had maintained that he did not know the boy that broke the door. Just announce a corporate punishment so we can go home."

It was approaching two o'clock, and soon the boys would be at work. Donnie Corlleon, the mission pilot added "Since no boy was willing to identify the person who broke the door, each boy will receive ten lashes in his hands and the door will not be repaired for a year. They must suffer the consequences of lying." He also promised to tell his wife to demote Pierre from working at their home. Pierre did not mind going back to **cut grass**. He had been working on the farm since he was ten years old. In fact, he had assumed responsibility for farming following the death of his father.

Mr. Daniels weighed in with his own advice. "Pierre, remember this, a child who lies will never be trusted even when he tells the truth." Court adjourned. Mr. Kingston followed Pierre to the dormitory to announce the verdict. The boys knew Mr. Kingston was bearing bad news when they saw him with Pierre. "Every boy in the dormitory will receive ten lashes for failing to give the name of the boy who broke the door.

The door will not be repaired for a year. You know what that means. Everyone, go to work," Mr. Kingston announced. He then, turned around and walked to his office.

That night the boys met in the Mess Hall to pray and ask God to help them withstand the ten lashes. Pete Lorlue led the prayer meeting. He had to because he brought this curse on the boys. He was like the bad man Achan in the group. The man, whose sin caused Israelites their first defeat at Ai. In that second battle for the Promised Land, the Israelites lost thirty-six soldiers. The boys would not stone Pete to death as God commanded the Israelites to do to Achan and his family. But the boys' eyes, twenty-four of them were focused on Pete. Pierre and some of the older boys, J.D. Dean and Jay Glew did not close their eyes or bow their heads when Pete offered the closing prayer.

Pierre wanted to ask Pete if he really knew God, but that was too much to ask. They had done this together to protect Pete from being expelled. After all, he was one of their own. They had already lost two men to expulsion, and were not willing to let go of another boy.

It was a somber prayer meeting. Ten lashes were nothing to anticipate with joy. "Let us go to bed and tomorrow we shall be whipped," Jay said as the boys went to their rooms.

The following day, the boys were sent to Headmaster Kingston's office one by one to receive their ten lashes. Donnie Corlleon was waiting in the office with his two refined whipping switches. There was no MP's or whipping table on the mission station. Each student had a choice to make; receive the ten lashes or get expelled. They all agreed to receive the lashes, 130 of them painfully gladly that one of them would not be expelled, at least that semester.

Joe Boy Kollie was the first in line. He came out crying like a baby wanting to be fed. J.D. Dean stood there with two palms opened; five lashes in the left hand, and the last five lashes in the right hand. He did not even wink his eyes. Loud-Mouth Harry Tay got four lashes and began to jump or hop around like a chicken with the head cut off. He finally settled down and received the last six. Headmaster Kingston had time for him to settle down. Pierre tried to be brave, but the thought of suffering for someone else's error made him to cry. After the first five lashes, he put his right hand between his legs for comfort for at least two minutes, but he would not let the Headmaster wait all day.

As he left, Pierre looked at Pete again, and stepped outside the school building heading to the dormitory. "Never, never again will this happen to me," Pierre cried as he changed into his working clothes. "Never." Well, Jesus died for the sins of others. But was this the boys' idea of everyone suffering for the sake of one student? Pierre hoped there was no next time, because Pete Lorlue would pay for his own sin.

The next day after school, Pierre and the boys went down to play soccer. It seemed things were back as usual. But everyone surrounded Pete Lorlue to hear what he had to say. "I swear on the Holy Bible from now on, I will treat everyone nice, I mean every boy in the dormitory." He looked mean as usual with solemn emphasis on his face. The idea of Pete being nice to everyone was like a myth. Loud-Mouth Harry Tay said, "We will see tomorrow when I cook dinner." All the boys laughed, including Pete.

ONCE UPON THE TIME IN LIBERIA, a young boy called Pierre Nah and his friends on a small rural mission station manned by missionaries stood their mendacious grounds to protect one of their own from being expelled from school. They paid for their loyalty with lashes in the hands of their choices and lived and went to school together until the end of the year.

CHAPTER 3

NOT GUILTY AS CHARGED

"You have been able to cross a river with a female tiger,
but here is an angry male tiger."
Meaning: You were given a lesser task, and you
completed it in no time, but let's see if you complete
a bigger task as you did with a lesser task.
Or you escaped a smaller a trouble, but let's see if you can escape a bigger one.

This small rural city of less than two thousand people had seen its share of strange, sometimes bizarre or weird events. From the sighting of an Unidentified Foreign Object (UFO) to the vision of the Virgin Mary in the night sky by a father last Dry Season.

But this was the weirdest and strangest of them all. A landmark trial involving a Station Director of a mission station accused of being a Christian, but he must prove his guilt rather than his innocence. A man's reputation and faith as a Christian were at stake. On both sides of the bench, the lawyers were worried that the case would set a bad precedent in the city. Would they find impartial jurors to find Simon Sarpley guilty of being a Christian?

The selection of jurors lasted three days. To find impartial jurors in this city was the most difficult task the Sawdust and Drinkwater Law Firm had to face. The firm had to send out their jury consultant Josiah

Gonwoe to interview prospective jurors. For the next three days, Consultant Gonwoe's work was cut out for him. And he was prepared for it. When it came to litigation in religion matters, Josiah Gonwoe was an expert. He had studied the faces of the prospective jurors until he did not want to look into their faces anymore. The District Attorney Jake Cassell (DA) and his lawyers were also busy working just as hard.

Josiah Gonwoe was no novice. He was a graduate of Tchien Theological Seminary, a renowned seminary in the southeast. After graduation, he had thought about going into the pastoral ministry, but his wife Gertrude Gonwoe had convinced him that pastoral ministry was a poor man's profession. In fact, she put it bluntly to him that she was not cut out to be the wife of a pastor. Josiah had had to readjust his life and find additional money for law school. For the last three years, he had worked at Sawdust and Drinkwater Law Firm as a jury consultant. He had built a reputation for himself at the law firm.

There were about twenty prospective jurors, fourteen men and six women. There were also seven alternate prospective jurors. The trial required eight jurors. Juror number one was Dahnvah Duzer, a resident of Ziantown and self-made thousandnaire who had made his money through *Cane Juice*. He and his wife had later abandoned their brewery and accepted Jesus Christ as their Savior. Since their conversion, they had never attended church services. Mr. Duzer maintained that since the Bible says no one knows when Jesus will come, there was no rush to go to church every Sunday.

Their only daughter Venacious Duzer had been courted and engaged by Konah Sarpley, Simon's mother. Simon had disappointed everyone by getting engaged to Winifred McCoy, a schoolmate from college. Mr. Duzer had been previously listed as a potential character witness, but had instead showed up for jury duty. He was automatically disqualified as a man after personal vendetta. Mr. Duzer was a short-tempered man with chip on his shoulders. He was known for filing frivolous lawsuits against many residents of his town for reasons, sometimes better known to himself. He had acquired a nickname, "Mr. Litigious." The man slept with his temper right under his pillow.

Juror number two was Milton Leeway, a high school dropout who had made a reputation for himself as a traditional singer and dancer. He led a group of men who followed him from towns to towns, and had lots of fans. Never pick a singer and a dancer in an African courtroom. He would turn the courtroom into a circus. He was better known than the president of the country. His mere presence in the courtyard attracted people from all over Zama City. He was turned down on the ground that his followers and fans would disrupt the trial.

Juror number three was a tiny man, barely three feet and four inches tall. He had made thousands of dollars as an herbalist all over the district. Though a high school graduate, he was known for making special protective dashikis or African shirts that supposedly walled-off witchcraft. Cooper "Smallman" Tommie was turned down by Judge Brownkai Garwin. "Mr. Tommie, please stand up. This courtroom required that jurors be seen and heard. Your statue posed a problem for the court," said Judge Garwin. "Your honor, I have no disability or handicap. That is discrimination against short people. **Men like me** cannot be dismissed because of my height. If I am dismissed, I will sue the court for discrimination. What judge in his or her right mind would want to be sued in his or her courtroom? Judge Garwin would not risk his own reputation and career by turning down a known voodoo chief in the district. "Mr. Tommie, you are selected as juror number three and the juror's foreman," Judge Garwin announced to the applause of the audience. "Thank you, Sir," Mr. Tommie replied as he took his seat in the jury box.

Juror number one was replaced with Borbor "Oldman Baker" Kittens, a local bakery shop owner. He had been a pipe smoker all his life. He was married and had three grown daughters. He was a Jehovah Witness, but his business kept him away from the Kingdom Hall. His wife refused to go without him. He was granted special permission to smoke his pipe when court was in recess.

Juror number two was replaced with Mary Richards-Doorman, an English teacher at the local government high school in Zama City. She was a devoted prayer warrior who never missed
Sunday worship services. Judge Garwin wanted to know if Mrs. Richards-Doorman had known Mr. Sarpley personally as a Christian prior to his arrest. But she was of a different denomination. Mr. Sarpley's denomination did not practice or believe in cross-denominational fellowship or association. His missionary upbringing asserted that no other denominations possessed the truth besides his denomination. Mrs. Richards-Doorman was a patient educator who wished Bible was taught in public schools. She had often stood and prayed for students in her classroom. Her husband Gollie Doorman was a carpenter. He was known for his woodworks throughout the city.

Juror number four did not fit Josiah Gonwoe's profile of a perfect juror, but he was willing to take a chance on Prince Torwah. Mr. Torwah was a former amateur footballer in his late forties. He had abandoned football in his senior year in high school due to a terrible knee injury. He had almost dislocated his right knee cap when he was deliberately kicked by another player. He had graduated from high school and gone on to work at a local rubber company as a recording clerk before going to college. He had studied agriculture in college and had returned to the city to help local farmers with modern techniques in planting rice, especially in the swamp. He was not a Christian, but did not drink or smoke.

He was health conscious to the point of being a hypochondriac. He was not a vegetarian, but he preferred fish to meat. In spite of his work in the swamp, Mr. Torwah was a sharp dresser.

Judge Brownkai Garwin knew somehow that the selection of juror number five may be longer than usual so he recessed the court for an hour. Court would resume immediately after lunch. There were several cookshops and restaurants in the proximities of the courthouse.

Prospective jurors were given straight orders by Judge Garwin not to discuss the case at lunch or anywhere. That was automatic dismissal. The lunch was the compliments of the court.

Judge Brownkai Garwin was brought from the west coast specifically for this case. Most local judges were either members of Simon Sarpley's church or associated with his denomination. Some had attended the mission station school before going on to law school.

His Honorable Judgeship had been a presiding judge over Criminal Court F in the Sonehwein District where he grew up. He was not a religious man and had no sympathy for criminals. He was known for handling down some of the stiffest prison sentences in the country. When it came to sentencing, Judge Garwin did not mince his words. He had acquired the nickname "Criminal Disgracer." At age forty-four, he was always cleaned-shaven, tall, dark-skin and wore no corrective lenses. His hair was always neatly combed. He had a deep voice that reminded one of a bass singer in a church choir. He was married, and he and his wife Francine Garwin had three adult children, two boys and a girl.

The jurors went to lunch at Ma Fatta's Home Cooking Restaurant about five blocks across the street from the courthouse. A commotion almost broke out at lunch after the jurors took their seats at a long table designated for a large group of diners. Borbor Kittens, the baker wanted cassava leaf or potato green soup so everyone can get to court promptly.

When he made the suggestion to Foreman Cooper "Smallman" Tommie, Mr. Torwah felt offended that someone else would tell him what to eat. He rose to his feet and **bounced grumble**. He wanted jollof rice with fried fish, and not oily fried potato green soup. He insisted that he did not know who or where the greens were planted. "Were the greens properly washed and caterpillars removed before cooking?" He asked. He was not sure about that so he would not eat it.

Ma Fatta did not hear him because she was in the kitchen. Lord, Ma Fatta did not know anything about customers' care. She had always said, "If you are really hungry, you will eat no matter what is set before you."

The situation would had gotten out of control without the presence and intervention of Mrs. Mary Richards-Doorman. Lord, Mrs. Richards-Doorman had words to calm nerves and settle disputes. She calmly asked for a vote of hands. "All in favor of cassava leaf soup, please raise your left hands." Nine left hands went out. "And all in favor of potato green, please raise your right hands." Ten right hands went up. Mr. Torwah abstained. Potato green won by one vote. Potato green always won when it was pitted against cassava leaf. Cassava leaf had gotten bad raps over the years as being responsible for making people susceptible to Hepatitis A (though never medically proven), or sticking to one's teeth and gum after ingestion. After a dinner of cassava leaf soup, no one readily smiled in public. Oh Lord, the latter would reveal immediately that this person has had a cassava leaf soup and failed to rinse and brush his or her teeth thereafter. Therefore, cassava leaf had been relegated to expecting and nursing mothers to increase breast milk (again never medically proven).

Since Mr. Torwah abstained, he would have his jollof rice and fried fish and the nineteen jurors would have their potato green soup. Let the jurors eat!

The jury selection process resumed immediately after lunch. The prosecutor objected to the selection of juror number five, Mr. Obadiah Mento. He wore a thick pair of lenses. It was so thick one had to stand in his face to see his eyes. Mr. Mento has had bilateral cataract operations two years earlier. According to him, he had never been declared legally blind by his eye physician. He further declined to reveal the physician's name. He pleaded physician-patient privacy. Lord, the man would only see objects within the distance of his lenses. He threatened to personally take the DA to the highest court of the land if he were turned down. Mr. Mento was a widower whose wife had died of ovarian cancer three years earlier. He was now living with the oldest of his two daughters and her husband. He was a moderate stutterer. His selection was followed by "Thanks-thanks-thanks, your honor."

Time was running out. It had taken nearly six hours to select five jurors with only two more days to go. Judge Garwin was running out of patience, especially in dealing with Jury's consultants on both sides of the aisle. He asked Currie Sawdust with her team, and DA Jake Cassell and his lawyers to approach the bench. He warned them that it was getting late. Therefore, they needed to speed up the selection of juror number six. After that he would adjourn his court until eight o'clock in the morning.

Juror number six was Yarwolo Kakata, a transplant from Margibi and Bong Counties who had lived in the city for nearly fifteen years. He had met his wife while working at a sawmill in Kakata. Both had fallen in loved and gotten married. Two years after the wedding, his wife had persuaded him to move and resettle in this big rural city in Nimba County.

Ten years later, he abandoned Mrs. Rebecca Kakata and moved in with another woman. On the educational section of the juror's questionnaire, he had written, "I don't know." Mr. Gonwoe wanted to know why a forty-nine years old man would not know about school.

During crossed examination, it was revealed that he had abandoned school in grade six to work in order to help his ill and aging parents. The reasons he was living with Gorlon Gayetay now as his common law's wife was no one's business. "Your Honor, my personal life and myself are not on trial in this court," he told the judge. The audience broke out into laughter. Judge Garwin shouted for order in the courtroom and had to warn the audience of being in content of court that would result in a fine of fifty dollars or go to prison for five days. That had quieted the courtroom.

Both sides were not willing to take a chance on Mr. Kakata. He looked and appeared unpredictable. If he failed to appear in court when the trial began, it would drag the case on forever. "Mr. Kakata, you are free to go. It is correct that you are not on trial in this court," Judge Garwin said as he adjourned the court until eight o'clock Tuesday morning.

After the dismissal of Yarwolo Kakata, Judge Garwin would ask for an alternate juror as the first order of the day in the morning when the court resumed. Judge Garwin exited the courtroom through the rear door, and was met by Foreman Cooper "Smallman" Tommie. "Yes, your Honor, how much do we get paid for this job?" He asked the judge. He would be making more money treating people and selling his supposedly witchcraft-walled-off African shirts rather than being a juror. He had only come to experience what it was like being a juror. "Two dollars a day, and is more than what people earned in this country working regular jobs," the judge replied. "Thank you, your Judgeship," Mr. Tommie said to the judge as he [Mr. Tommie] headed home.

Mrs. Richards-Doorman and Prince Torwah headed to the south side of Zama City together. She was curious to know if Prince believed in God, the Creator of the universe. He was too busy doing good works helping others and wished God would see his good works and reward him. He was not interested in organized religion. He had seen it all, church folks gossiping about each other, backbiting and hatred for each other rather than loving each other. If God was good as Mrs. Richards-Doorman claimed, why did He allow locusts to destroy the last rice farms he and his farmers planted? "Why did God allow such a terrible thing to happen to poor farmers who were struggling to raise their families on less than a dollar a day?" He asked Mrs. Richards-Doorman. "Our Mighty God is not the author of evil. But He allows the evil one, the devil to bring events into our lives to determine if we actually love Him," she replied. They parted ways to see each other Tuesday morning at eight o'clock.

The court began at eight o'clock on Tuesday morning as announced by the judge on Monday. The first order of the day was the selection of an alternate juror to replace juror number six, Mr. Yarwolo Kakata. The alternate juror was Moses Karnwein. Mr. Karnwein prided himself on traveling in the West African sub-region. He had traveled to Guinea, Ivory Coast and Sierra Leone in search of diamonds to buy. He was a broker and had his own Honda Motorcycle.

He had a soccer team in Zama City called "Smell No Taste." He was known for spending hundreds of dollars on players on the team. When it came to spending money on football, Moses Karnwein was the man. Mr. Karwein was a member of the Free Mormon Church in Zama City. Based on Mrs. Richards-Doorman's answer earlier, the judge and jury's consultants would not question him on Simon Sarpley's faith and denomination. Moses had two wives and seven children. His church did not forbid or condemn polygamy. His doctrinal teachings required him to have as many wives as he desired. He boasted that he would only enjoy his wealth by marrying multiple wives, and he was happily married in that state. This was not a divorce case; therefore, it would not possibly influence the jurors in any way.

Midway through the process it was discovered that an alternate juror, Mr. Sekou Kromah was absent. Mr Kromah had not returned to the courtroom Tuesday morning as required. He had to rush his sick child to the clinic. He was a resident of Zama City. Judge Garwin abruptly ordered a fifteen minutes' recess to inquire about the whereabouts of Mr. Kromah. Mr. Kromah was a Muslim, thoroughly schooled in the Koran. He had traveled to Saudi Arabia twice to attend the Hajj, the Muslims Annual Pilgrimage. He was the head of the School of Imam in the city. How and why the court did not discover his absence during roll call was a mystery to everyone.

Lord, this was Liberia where anything would happen in a given day, even in a courtroom. The clerk of court, the bailiff, jury consultants and lawyers on both sides were immediately summoned to Judge Garwin's chamber. He demanded to know how the error or omission occurred. While they were in the chamber, Mr. Kromah arrived at the courthouse. A sheriff deputy informed the judge that he had arrived.

When Judge Garwin returned, he delivered a strong lecture on civic responsibility and challenged anyone to be absent without prior authorization from the court. He also dared jurors to try to Liberianize the court proceedings. In other words, he would not tolerate jurors coming and going as they wished, or arriving late at the courthouse, then taking extended breaks for hours. He would not tolerate family members meeting with jurors, or taking them to lunch and handling out gifts or money to the jurors.

No member of the legal team on both sides or member of the juror would accept gifts of live animals or meat; chickens, ducks, Guinea fowls, sheep, goats, cows, monkey meat, deer meat, chopped lamb, or porcupine meat. Under no circumstance would he allow family members and friends of the defendant to bring or carry live animals in the courtyard.

The clerk of court and the bailiff were also warned that a repeat of such incident in the future would lead to immediate termination. Mr. Kromah was excused to return home to take care of his sick child. He was replaced by another person.

By four thirty in the afternoon, two more people had been excused and three others had been told to refill their applications or questionnaires. The clerk of court, Miss Esther Woodens handed out another applications and asked them to stay behind after the court was adjourned to help them in completing the forms. The court was adjourned at five thirty p.m.

The application forms or questionnaires contained questions like, Are you a Christian? Do you believe in God? What is your denomination? Is any member of your family a Christian? Do you believe in the Bible? Did you or any member of your family attend a Christian school? What is your opinion about organized religion? Do you believe in the freedom of religion? Do you believe in the Bible accounts of creation? Who is or was Jesus Christ?

Page two had the most important questions: State your opinion about religious persecution. State your opinion about forced conversion. State your opinion about removing the Bible from the curricular of all public and private schools. There had never been such a case as this one, so jurors had nothing to use as precedents. But if they wanted to serve as jurors in this case, they had to answer all the questions completely with the help of the clerk of court.

Judge Garwin told both sides of the bench that the jury selection should be completed by Wednesday. By then, Jake Cassell and his prosecutorial team would be ready to present their opening statements on Thursday morning. He did not intend to drag this unusual case forever. He was brought into Zama City for this case, and he would do everything in his judicial power to render his decision within four to five days.

Court returned to order Wednesday morning an hour late at nine o'clock. A deputy announced, "All rise, the Honorable Judge Brownkai Garwin in the court!" Seventy-five people jumped to their feet as the Honorable Judge Brownkai Garwin stepped up to the bench and asked everyone to take his or her seat. He cleared his throat and asked the lawyers to proceed with the selection of the final two jurors.

Juror number seven was Miss Marie Dainnuan, age forty-seven and a divorced mother of two sons who owned a clothing business. She rarely attended church services unless they were held at her home. She was always busy in the market square selling clothes to send her boys to school. She was of medium height and build, a nonsmoker, and a member of the Baha'i Faith.

They met in the homes of members. She had never heard of the case and was not familiar with Simon Sarpley's denomination. According to her, she practiced her faith in the privacy of her home. At the end of the examination, lawyers on both sides were cautiously pleased with Miss Marie Dainnuan.

The eighth and final juror was Mrs. Cecelia "CC" Kartoe, a thirty-two years old former Jehovah witness. She had left the church after her marriage to a Lebanese Merchant, Mr. Mahmoud Nabil in Zama City. She felt members of the church did not approve of her marriage. Mr. Nabil had divorced her after two years of marriage on the grounds that she was unable to bear a child or children for him within those two years.

Mrs. Kartoe had filed a lawsuit against him asking for $500.00 a month alimony payment.

The case had been dismissed and judgment granted to Mr. Nabil by the Divorce Court on technicality that Mrs. Kartoe and her lawyer did not present sufficient evidence to substantiate the claim of hardships following the divorce. The court had ruled that she would suffer no hardships because she was a resident of the city and had families, relatives and friends who would lend her helping hands if and when she needed them. There had been rumors and suspicion that Mr. Nabil may had bribed Judge Johnnie Yangar of the Divorce Court to dismiss the case. Cecelia had remarried Darius Kartoe, a principal of Saint Judas Iscariot Elementary School in the city.

Mrs. Kartoe was a home economist by profession. She taught Home Economics classes at various high schools within the city. She was known by her student as Teacher "CC" Kartoe. She loved the color red. She had on a red dress and wore red matching shoes. She and Mr. Kartoe had been married for one year and had no children.

After three grueling days on the selection, jury consultants on both sides thanked themselves on picking a group of impartial jurors. They felt the days and hours on selection were both worth the time and money. Jake Cassell had seen some hostile jurors, and some cheerful ones in his career as a prosecutor.

Josiah Gonwoe was glad, though that did not stop his suspicion that this city was trying to declare war on Christianity. But he was guardedly optimistic that Judge Garwin was a neutral man brought in to render a fair and an impartial decision. No religious zealot, or an outright atheist had been selected as a juror. All five men and three women had certain levels of education. One was a college graduate and three were teachers.

The main courtroom of the city was half a mile from the city center on Main Street. It was a singlestory building with several courtrooms. Every morning people with cases lined up in the hallways leading to those various courtrooms. It was not unusual to see lawyers consulting with their clients in the hallways.

Thursday morning at sharp nine o'clock, Judge Garwin looked over the packed courtroom and decided that everything and everyone were in place. He lightly knocked his gavel on the table and the court became dead silent. He asked Mr. Alieu Donzo, his bailiff to bring in the jurors. The eyes of the audience were focused on the jury Box. Cooper "Smallman Tommie appeared first, leading his pack of jurors. They all came in and took their seats according to the seating arrangements. The two remaining alternates sat in plastic chairs next to the jurors.

"Good morning everyone," His Judgeship said in his deep bass voice and bright smile. Everyone smiled back in agreement. "We do have a foreman, right?" He asked. All eight nodded their heads in unison. "Wonderful," who is he?" "I am the one, Your Judgeship," Cooper "Smallman" Tommie said from his first-row seat. He sat in the front row to be seen and heard. Judge Garwin was satisfied that everything had gone as anticipated. There was no objections or quarrels arising from the selection of Mr. Tommie as the jury foreman.

On the front row sat DA Jake Cassell and his team of three lawyers. And directly behind them sat defense lawyer Currie Sawdust and her two lawyers. Miss Sawdust was the youngest and brightest lawyer in the district. Her father, Mr. Titus Sawdust had been a supervisor at a sawmill at the Craneshaw-Nehemiah Company (CNC) in central Liberia. He had acquired the nickname "Mr. Sawdust" because he was always covered with sawdust at the end of the day. His nickname had stuck on him to the point that he had to change his name from Titus to Johannes T. Sawdust.

At age thirty and single, Miss Sawdust stood almost five feet and seven inches tall with dark-curly hair. It was hard to tell whether they were her own hair. She was dressed in all white business suit with matching white shoes. She even wore white earrings. Her assistants were two sharply dressed men that appeared like identical twins.

Judge Garwin stopped going through his files and pointed to DA Jake Cassell, who stood up quickly, straightened his tie and buttoned his black jacket. He smiled at the jurors and turned around to make his opening statement. He would tell the jurors exactly the nature of the case and why Mr. Simon Sarpley was on trial. The courtroom became so quiet that one would hear, if a pin was dropped.

The jurors would determine that Simon did not walk, talk and imitate the Person of Jesus Christ he professed as Savior and Lord. They would determine that his conduct and activities in his communities did not prove that he was indeed a Christian. Then, they would prove that he was a selfish and compassionless man bent on making name and money for himself and his immediate family. A man who showed no pity and mercy on the countless souls who visited his mission station on a daily basis. He was only concerned about meeting the spiritual needs rather than physical needs of people he encountered. Jake Cassell would present to the jurors, people who had come across Station Director Simon Sarpley and found him wanting as a Christian.

But how would they prove that Simon Sarpley was not really a Christian, and that he was hiding behind Christianity to carry out other dubious activities in the communities? There would be many character witnesses. First, they would bring Venacious Duzer, the young woman from Ziantown he disappointed when he got engaged to Winifred McCoy. In his attempt to convince the jurors, DA Cassell took three days to narrate the life story of Simon Sarpley.

Simon encountered missionaries at an early age. The folks in his hometown called missionaries "the white people who brought the good news of Jesus Christ." They visited Simon hometown every third Sunday of each month. On one those Sundays, at age ten, Simon accepted Jesus Christ as his Savior and Lord.

The missionaries, Jess and Cathy Abraham were sent to rural northeastern Liberia in the late 1960's. In addition to spreading the gospel of Christ, Jess Abraham was a handyman who fixed anything that was broken. They have three grown children, two girls and a boy back in the United States. Mrs. Cathy Abraham was a practical nurse for several years before she and her husband were sent on the mission field. The couple met in high school when they were young. Lord, they were inseparable. Mrs. Abraham ran the small clinic on the mission station. They had lovely voices when they sang, with Jess playing the guitar and Cathy playing the accordion. They had lived on the mission station for five years. There were other missionaries on the mission.

Simon was a bookworm. For that, the missionaries loved and admired him. They had big plans for him. Upon graduation the following year, he would be given a scholarship to study in the county capital. After completion, he would return to serve as Station Director of the mission. Lord, the thought of Simon Sarpley as the director of the mission station was too lofty for Simon Sarpley to fathom. Heaven would not wait!

The missionaries followed through with their plans. Following graduation from Ziantown Public School, Simon was given scholarship and sent to the county capital to attend a prestigious government high school in that city. Simon did not care about social activities for the first two years. He was not anti-social. He just did not have time to fool around with his scholarship. He had to maintain 3.5 grade point average to keep the scholarship. Lord, other students in the school considered Simon Sarpley a genuine because he maintained 4.0 grade point average.

Wherever he was, Simon always took his parents' advice. Mr. & Mrs. Sarpley had advised their son to go to church every Sunday and read his Bible. He heeded the advice and followed through Sundays after Sundays. He became a member of Saint James Covenant Church in Seingbein City. Saint James' doctrine was the same as his home church. They followed the letter of the Bible; no work on Sundays, no fornication, and always keep the Ten Commandments. It did not take too long for Simon to become one of the Sunday school teachers.

The first two years in the city were challenging. He had to get used to city life and blend in with city boys. For the first time in his life, Simon had to rent a room from an older couple with no children of their own. They treated Simon like a son they did not have.

In two years, Simon was promoted four times; two times in each semester. He graduated in his third year at the top of his class, and was accepted at Maryland Teacher's College (MTC) in the southeast of the country. MTC had a reputation for putting out the best teachers in the country. Simon Sarpley became an instant standout student at MTC.

In his senior year, Simon found a transferred student from the northeast and fell in love with her. Miss Winifred McCoy had been a student at another teacher's college in the northeast of the country. She did not like it there. The meals were terrible, and everyone seemed judgmental about anything she did. She had always given them a piece of her mind, reminding them that the teacher's college was not a convent or a religious school. If she wanted a life of celibacy, she would have given herself up to nunnery.

Winifred was a beautiful lady who stood five feet and nine inches tall. There was not a single gap in her teeth. Her dark gum made her smiles even prettier when she opened her mouth. She always dressed to impress.

Every man at MTC attempted to have a date with her and failed until she met Simon Sarpley.

What Winifred McCoy was searching for in a man, she found it in Simon. She had always envisioned a quiet religious man who would love her for what she was and nothing more. She had a past that she was not proud of, but had moved on to make something better of her life. Lord, she was proud of the changes she made in her life!

Her Daddy, Benson McCoy, a product of missionary training had abandoned his family as soon as the missionaries left. He was disillusioned with the church for judging him and later dismissing him for financial impropriety. He did everything humanly possible to clear his name, but failed. He had later come to find out that one of the deacons in the church was having an affair with his wife. Mrs. Jennifer McCoy had even testified against her husband during the hearings before the church council.

On the day of his final hearing and dismissal, Mr. McCoy had lashed out at the church council, calling them a bunch of Pharisees and Sanhedrins deliberately bent on destroying his life and family. He had sarcastically referred to members of the United Fellowship International (UFI) as Ananias Imitators. He felt bruised by people he trusted and believed.

Winifred McCoy, the only child then, was thirteen years old when her father left home. She had cried herself to sleep on the night her father left home in tears, vowing never to return. Mrs. Jennifer McCoy later remarried Deacon Pee-wee Peabody and had two boys by him. Being an African child, Winifred stayed clear of the conflict between her parents. Lord, she wished to have left that fateful night with her father. Thereafter, she attended churches on New Year's Sunday, Easter Sunday, and Christmas. Her mother did not pressure her when it came to church attendance.

But Winifred was a fighter. She did everything, with the help of her mother to acquire an education. She had to sell boiled eggs and cold water to pay her tuition. She possessed the same spirit that her father had. She was a good student, but became sexually active at age fifteen. She would cry when she told the story of her life. She was told by relatives and friends that her father went to Monrovia, the nation's capital.

Simon Sarpley did not care about Winifred's previous lifestyle. He was a deeply religious man who believed that his God would change or redeem anyone. He loved everything about Winifred. He had always wanted a perfect Christian girl, but he was willing to settle for an imperfect Miss Winifred McCoy. He began preparation to take Winifred home to introduce her to his parents and to the Abrahams who were responsible for his educational success. They planned on going during the Easter Vacation in early April of that year.

April arrived quickly! In the second week of April, they set out to see Simon's parents and sponsors. They arrived in the Zama City on a Friday night. It was a pleasant Friday night with the moon and stars visible in the sky. A night when one would be at an Easter revival. There was no revival going on. They had to sleep and, in the morning, and then visit Mr. Jess and Mrs. Cathy Abraham. Simon had been gone for nearly five years without visiting home, though he had written often to check on his parents and the Abrahams. The missionaries were the line of communication to his parents.

They found a motel and spent a restful night. Simon and Winifred talked about their future life together, and how wonderful it would be to raise their children on the mission compound with Simon as the Station Direction. The thoughts of it all sent her into a dreamland filled with angels at their wedding and Simon's father officiating at the ceremony. Her father was in the service, but he was seated all the way in the back corner of the church and was silent throughout the service without saying a word.

She woke up that morning not knowing what to make of the dream. When she told Simon about the dream, he replied, "Dreams are just dreams unless you wanted to make something out of them."

They got up, took showers and went to a cookshop next to the motel and had boiled cassava and yams with scrambled eggs for breakfast. By ten in the morning they set out to see the Abrahams. They were not married, but they had met and fallen in love. They have had premarital sex, and now they were going to see his missionary friends. Lord, Simon was smart, but he did not think like a man who had been around missionaries for years.

They arrived at the Abraham's home by eleven thirty. It would have taken them at least forty-five minutes to walk to the mission. The mission and missionaries were going nowhere. So, they took their own time to walk. Simon rang the doorbell when they arrived. Winifred stood ten feet behind him. Mrs. Abraham opened the door and embraced Simon like his mother would have done. She was glad to see Simon. "You are a grown man now, Simon," she said as she called her husband. "Dear, guess who's here, our son Simon!"

As Jess raced to the front door, Mrs. Abraham wanted to know the young woman that was with Simon. Mr. and Mrs. Abraham, this is Winifred McCoy, my fiancé. We met at MTC," Simon said. "You are engaged? Have you told your parents?" Mrs. Abraham shouted. "Dear, allow the children to come inside the house before you interrogate them," Mr. Abraham interrupted.

Winifred was taken aback by the question. Simon Sarpley was a grown man. Within a month he would turn thirty-six years old. And the missionaries were treating him like a kid? The missionaries who trained Winifred's father had left before she was born. So, she had no experience in dealing with missionaries except stories from Mr. McCoy about how nice the missionaries were to him.

Simon and Winifred followed the missionaries into the dining room and sat around the table. Again, Simon introduced Winifred as his fiancé, and how they had met at school and fallen in love. Mr. Abraham was impressed with the young lady. Lord, she was just stunning to behold. "She is very beautiful, Simon," Mr. Abraham said. And he added, "When is the wedding?" That is why we have come to inform you first, then my parents," Simon replied.

"What about . . .?" Mrs. Abraham almost let the bird out of the cage. Winifred wanted to follow-up with "About what?" But she got hold of herself when she glanced at Simon and Mr. Abraham.

The next few minutes the conversation was centered Simon's graduation and his eventual takeover of the mission station. He looked forward to it with anticipation and being able to influence other youngsters in Zama City and beyond. With Winifred on his team, God would archive great things through them for His kingdom here on earth. The thoughts of Winifred McCoy being on his team got him so excited that he began to perspire. Mrs. Abraham interjected again. "If you are planning on getting married to Winifred, consult your parents before the final decision." Yes, I will," Simon answered.

Winifred wanted to get out of her chair and choke Mrs. Abraham into a stupor, but she would not do that on a mission station, and in the home of missionaries. The flashback from the day her father left home when the elders of the church drove him away came back like floods. She began to have a terrible headache. She wanted to get out of there before all hell broke loose. Winifred McCoy did not take mess from anybody. She was beautiful, talented, educated and had class. Simon knew Mrs. Abraham was making Winifred uncomfortable, so they decided to leave.

As they stepped outside the house, Mrs. Abraham turned to her husband and said, "We don't even know her or her background." Mr. Abraham replied with a question of his own. "Are you getting married to her or Simon?" "Honey, we want to leave this mission in good hands when we leave," she replied. "Just leave that to God," her husband angrily responded.

As they walked back to the motel, Winifred wanted to know what Mrs. Abraham was talking about when she said "What about . . .?" But how would Simon know? The man had not been home for nearly five years. Only God knew what was awaiting him at home. He was glad that Mr. Abraham did not have any problem with Winifred. In fact, he seemed to like her very much. They arrived back in the city at three o'clock in the afternoon.

Though Zama City was big, but it had no cabbies or local transportation services. They were glad that they had to walk and talk about their future. Lord, to them the future was theirs.

Simon had been out of this city for quite a while. He and Winifred decided to walk the streets and do window shopping. As they walked down Main Street, onlookers could not keep their eyes off Winifred. A few of the men who knew Simon came and greeted them. They only came because of Winifred. They wanted to get closer and just take a look at her face.

Arthur Suo, a classmate of Simon in grade school came running and hugged him. "My men, whatever happened to you?" "Well, I had to leave home to complete my studies," Simon replied. "My men, your book business is nothing to play with." "Yes, I know," Simon said. "And by the way, Arthur, this is Miss Winifred McCoy, my fiancé." "Nice to meet you, Miss McCoy," Arthur said. He left the couple and promised to visit them on Sunday, the following day in Ziantown. As he left, he could not help, but think about the beauty of Winifred. "Simon is getting ready to marry a **Mommywater**," he said to himself.

Simon decided to pick up a few things for his parents; bath soaps, laundry soap, bug sprays, candles and some clothes for his mother. He also bought a fine African shirt for his father. They visited the market square and bought fresh fruits, oranges, mangoes and tangerines to eat at the motel when they return.

He visited the market several times as a kid. He accompanied his mother on weekends when she came to the market to sell her produce. He always wanted to leave early because he could not stand the flies. Lord, Simon hated flies.

They decided to leave for Ziantown during the evening hours when it was cooler. Simon had already sent words to his parents that he was on his way home, and that he was bringing a special guest without giving further details. About six o'clock in the evening they found a lorry going their direction and got on board. Within twenty-five minutes, they would be home. The lorry would drop them off on the main road, then they would walk the rest of the way.

When words got home that Simon Sarpley was coming, nearly every citizen of Ziantown remained to see him. Very few farmers with urgent works on the farms left. However, they left representatives of their families behind to greet Simon on their behalf. This was the most wonderful thing to ever happen to this town. The constant fighting among men when they went to work on someone's farm has given this farming town a bad name.

In one of the fights a year ago, David Firemen had nearly killed Tapper Moneysweet. These men who got their names from working on various rubber farms in the country always fought each other as if they were strangers. They have resorted to drinking **Cane Juice** during working hours. And when they got drunk, all hell broke loose. The younger generations were right behind them, fighting on the soccer field during practices and games. Every moment, Ziantown seemed to be on the edge.

Today's edge was different. Simon, one of their own was coming to town. Everyone was proud of him and his achievement. The fact that he would take over the mission station in the big city gave them an added advantage. Simon would make ways for their kids to enter the mission school and be educated like himself.

Ziantown sent out three lookout kids to watch the road. They would run back and inform everyone that Simon and his guest were arriving. That was exactly what they did. As soon as they spotted Simon and Winifred, they ran back and told the crowd that had gathered in front of Rev. Gideon Sarpley's house. The crowd broke into spontaneous singing and dancing. *"Kwi* had taken our child for a long time, but he is back. *Kwi* women thought the child was theirs and proud of
it, but he is back home." Rev. Gideon, usually a reserved and quiet man, joined the crowd as soon as his wife joined in the singing and dancing.

The women took one look at Winifred and immediately spread their lappas or fabrics on the ground for her to walk on. When they saw him, Simon's parents ran and embraced him. Mrs. Sarpley held her son so tight, almost choking breath out of him. Rev. Sarpley had to tell his wife to let go of their son before he passed out from lack of oxygen to his brain. Karlie and Albert also ran and greeted their brother. They were glad he was back home. Karlie and Albert have had to endure ridicule from some of the young men of the town that they were high school dropouts stuck in Ziantown with no future. But they had boasted of their brother's achievement as if it was theirs.

Winifred was no stranger to crowds welcoming government officials to their towns and villages. It was an obligation that got the towns' folks into trouble if they did not do it. The fines ranges from twenty-five dollars to three goats, two sheep or a cow, or a combination of all the fines. But for a kid who grew up in the town with them, it was a shock to her. She gloried in every moment of it. She felt comfortable immediately as if she had lived in Ziantown before.

Winifred and Simon took their seats in front of Rev. Sarpley's home. He had brought out two of his best chairs in the house for his son and his guest. The crowd continued to sing and dance. They would go around the town and come back to the Sarpley's house. After about forty-five minutes, Rev. Sarpley stopped the crowd and handed them five dollars. "I have postponed the singing and the dancing. We will continue it throughout the week. For now, let the strangers eat and rest."

When everyone had left, Winifred was curious to know the meaning of the song the crowd was singing. "Nothing really, just that I have been away for a long time and they are glad I am back," Simon answered. "Are you sure about that?" Winifred wanted more details. "Yes, I am sure," he replied.

Mrs. Sarpley went into the house and brought out dinner. For a very long time the Sarpleys have never had dinner together. This was wonderful to have the boys, all three of them with their parents at the same dinner table together. Rev. Sarpley and his wife were glad that their advice to Simon did not fall on death ears like with Karlie and Albert. He had taken their advice and gone on to get a quality education to improve the lives of his family. Simon was glad too, that he had listened to his parents and followed his dream.

Though Simon was educated, he had never forgotten his home training. No too much talking at dinner table. There was a time to eat, and a time to talk. Whatever he had to say to his family about Winifred would wait until after dinner. During dinner, Karlie and Albert would look at

Winifred and smiled without saying anything. She knew something was up in the air with the two men, but she would keep her eyes on Simon rather than worry about the unknown.

After dinner, Karlie and Albert helped to clear the table. Winifred wanted to help, but Mrs. Sarpley told her everything was under control. After all, she was a stranger, and in Ziantown a stranger did not work on his or her first visit. After three days, she would fit in to work. Winifred was never afraid of work. She grew up working. In fact, she worked to put herself through school.

Everyone gathered in the living room to hear from Simon. He had been away for five years on studies and had returned home. His parents, even his brothers were anxious to hear from him. Simon gave everyone presents. He gave his mother and father the African attires he bought for them. To his brothers, he gave them nice red T-shirts with the inscriptions, "As long as there are studies, there will be prayers in schools." His brothers were happy. These were their first new clothes in a long time.

Simon pushed his chair closer to Winifred's and said, "This is the moment we have been waiting for. Mother, Father, Karlie and Albert, this is Winifred McCoy, my fiancé. As soon as I get your approval, we will get married." Karlie and Albert began to laugh, but their mother was not amused by the announcement. This was no laughing matter. Rev. Sarpley wanted to clap his hands, but the look on his wife's face said it all; don't do it.

When it came to marriage, Rev. Sarpley was biblically liberal. He was willing to give chances to his boys to choose their own wives, but not with Konah Sarpley. She knew the women that were best for her boys. She wanted them to choose their wives among their own people. She had always stressed to them, "Make sure to marry locally. I would love for my grandchildren to grow up right under my arms."

She said to Simon, "I want to meet with you privately before I give my opinion to you." After the meeting, Simon and his mother took a long walk around the neighborhood. When Mrs. Konah Sarpley knew that they were far away from her home, she said to her son, **"You boy**, what's wrong with you, bringing that kind of fine woman in this town? You know the witches in this town. That woman that **Mamiewatta**. I can see it right in her face."

"Mother I thought we were Christians, and we were not to believe in such a thing as witchcraft," Simon said. "Even in the Bible, there were witches," Mrs. Sarpley countered without going into details or specifics. "Your father and I will meet and discuss the matter," she concluded.

While Simon was away, his mother had engaged a bride for him in his absence. Venacious Duzer was the only daughter of the assistant chief of Ziantown. She was five feet and four inches tall with fair skin and Brown eyes. She also had a wonderful smile. A dancing sensation, Venacious would dance any style of music, African as well as Western. Lord, the young woman could even "moonwalk." But her parents did not want her to go to school. Beatrice and Dahnvah Duzer did not want their daughter to leave home. They needed her and she needed them.

Mrs. Konah Sarpley had gone through a lot of troubles watching and coaching Venacious since she was ten years old. She had always said to herself, "This is Simon's future wife."

At this point, Miss Sawdust interrupted, "Objection, Your Honor, the prosecutor is attempting to prejudice the jurors against my client unduly influencing them. Simon had the right to pick his own wife." "Overruled; you may continue Counsel," His Judgeship replied.

Simon and his mother headed back to the house. As they began walking back home, Konah said to her son, "I have engaged a very fine young woman here for you. She is only nineteen years old. All the men in this town wanted her, but she turned them down and kept herself just for you. She will make a wonderful wife." And she added, "Remember in the Bible parents chose wives for their children." Simon felt irritated, but he did not want his mother to know.

They arrived home and took their seats. Winifred asked Mrs. Sarpley if she would retire for the night. She was shown her room just opposite Simon's room. His mother had always kept his room in order. She knew Simon would come anytime, and he would sleep in his own bed. Winifred did not mind or object to sleeping by herself. After all, they were in Simon's home, and she was willing to go out of her way to respect the Sarpley's house rules.

Early in the morning the next day, Rev. Sarpley and his wife met with their son. The Reverend was in disagreement with his wife choosing a bride for their son. "The man is educated, for Christ's sake. He knows what he wants in a woman." He stressed that to his wife. "I am the head of this house. Leave the boy alone so he can choose his woman, even if it is Winifred, that would be his choice," he concluded. Mrs. Sarpley sat there with tears in her eyes looking at her husband. She rose to her feet, "My people, what did I do wrong in this house, will anyone ever listen to me?" she lamented. Her husband had to respond. He knew his wife was about to start playing the blame game. "Well, the last time I listened to you, Karlie and Albert did not complete high school," he said. And he added "Let's treat this young woman nice because she is a stranger in this house."

On the second day, Venacious Duzer showed up at the home of the Sarpleys. She had been away visiting her aunt when Simon and Winifred arrived. She entered and ran straight to Mrs. Sarpley and hugged her. Then she came back and said, "Hello, Pastor, hello Simon, and hello my friend." She just called Winifred her friend as if they had met before. Simon and his father responded, but Winifred did not. From the look on her face, Winifred knew the young woman had something other than hello on her mind. "She better not start anything in the Pastor's house," Winifred said to herself. "Simon won't you introduce your friend to me?" She asked Simon. "She is a stranger. You introduce yourself first," Simon responded. "OK, my name is Venacious Duzer, and you?" "Miss Winifred McCoy, in case, you have any other idea."

Rev. Sarpley knew the conversation would progress into a shouting match if he did not interrupt. "All right, Venacious, Winifred is our stranger. Please be nice to her." Venacious turned to Simon and said to him, "Simon, I am your future wife. I know your mother had told you." "Venacious that is not true," Simon responded. And with emphasis on his face, he added, "My mother cannot pick a wife for me."

Venacious wished the ground she was standing on would open and swallow her up. She did not hear Simon right. For the last five years she had been groomed, fashioned, refined and polished to be an uneducated wife to an educated man. And now this? This was no dancing matter. She felt betrayed and let down. She would be the laughingstock of Ziantown. What would her friends say to her? She wished her parents had attended church services more often. Venacious ran out of the Sarpley's house in tears.

Rev. Sarpley had never been a fan of the Duzer family. Since their conversion, they had never attended any church service. He thought they did it to impress the missionaries, but were never interested in the things of God. Occasionally he had seen Dahnvah Duzer in a *Cane Juice* shop drinking. Mrs. Sarpley had always maintained that the Duzers were testing God's water before committing. "My dear, the people want to know and see that God is good before they become serious Christians." "Well, when will that be," her husband had always demanded.

Simon knew that it was time to begin preparation to leave. He and Winifred would spend the rest of the vacation days in Zama City. This had the potential to ruin his future with Winifred. He did not want to even think about it. Disappointing Winifred would be the biggest mistake of his teacher's college life. And he was not willing to take that risk. Lord, Simon was getting nervous about everything around him.

After dinner that night, Simon told his parents that he and Winifred would leave in the morning. They would spend the rest of their vacation days in Zama City. "You mean, you came to tell us hello after five years, and you will leave after two days?" Simon's mother asked with sternness he had never seen in her face before. "Mother, I hope you understand. I have got a stranger with me. I don't want her to feel uncomfortable here," Simon responded. Rev. Sarpley did not have any problem with Simon and Winifred leaving the next day. He felt his son's sympathy and dilemma. "I would do the same thing, too," he said to himself.

Simon's brothers were not around. The boys did not sleep at home last night. Since his arrival, the boys had never sat down with him to discuss anything after the first night when he introduced Winifred McCoy. They were out there somewhere having fun.

This was the first day of the hearing. When DA Cassell got to this point, it was already five o'clock in the afternoon. Judge Garwin decided he had heard enough about Simon Sarpley for the day. He adjourned the court to resume in the morning at nine o'clock.

Friday morning, at sharp nine o'clock, the usual court rituals resumed. Bailiff Alieu Donzo cried out, "All rise, Honorable Judge Brownkai Garwin in the court!" "You may take your seats," His Judgeship said as he took his bench, followed by "Good morning everyone! DA Jake Cassell, are you ready? Begin where you left off yesterday."

Again, this Friday morning was in the grip of DA Cassell's fingers. He seemed as dramatic as ever in an attempt to convince the jurors of the charges against Simon Sarpley. He began in a slow methodic voice.

The next morning by nine o'clock, Simon and Winifred were on their way to Zama City. They did not bother to wait on a lorry to catch a ride. Simon loved Winifred too much to subject her to anything that would make her feel unpleasant. They walked as fast as they could in the cool of the morning hours and arrived in Zama City within two hours. There was no conversation, not one word from Simon or Winifred. Both were too numb to talk.

On arrival back in Zama City, Simon and Winifred put their suitcases away and sat on the bed by each other. There were no words to describe what just happened to them. They looked at each other and smiled, and then laid down across the bed. During the conversations at the home of the Sarpley, Winifred did not make any comments. She felt this was a family matter that did not involve her. She was never rejected or accepted by Mrs. Sarpley. In her own right,
Mrs. Sarpley did what a mother in her ethnic group would do for her son. But Winifred knew Simon would do the right thing. He had always done it since they met a year ago.

Meanwhile in Ziantown, Venacious and her parents were preparing to go to Rev. Sarpley's house to confront his son about his choice of a future wife. It was because of Simon that Venacious was still single. After all, in this culture marriage or wedding ceremony was money and other festivities. Dahnvah did not really care if Simon loved his daughter. There were plenty of strong men in Ziantowm, or other towns that may make great sons-in-laws.

He did not think an educated man was good for his daughter. He was searching for a son-in-law who would help him on his sugarcane farm, and not one who was far away.

Mrs. Duzer knew that it would come down this, Simon showing up in Ziantown with another woman. She had repeatedly told Konah, "I know your son will not marry my daughter. He knows too much book, and my daughter did not go to school." But Konah Sarpley had always rebutted her by saying, "You don't have to go to school to be a good wife. Look at us, we are good wives, and we never completed high school."

To Mrs. Sarpley, a good wife respected and honored her husband. She cooked and raised the children with his help. And she took good care of her home. She had been teaching Venacious all these manners when she visited the Sarpleys at home or on the farm. To her Venacious Duzer would make a very fine wife for her son. She was not as pretty as a **Mamiewatta**, but she would be a good wife to any man. And she was a terrific dancer, too.

In the evening, the Duzer's family came to see the Sarpley's family. It was just after dinner when they arrived. It was a pleasant evening to sit outdoor. The Reverend invited his guests outside to sit and talk. Dahnvah started with an apology about not attending church services. He had pressing issues that demanded his undivided attention than church services. After all, he knew that Jesus was not coming anytime soon. So he and his family had ample time to come back when they were ready.

If God was not complaining about the Duzers being absence in church services, why would the Reverend care so much about it? Mr. Duzer had always maintained that going to church didn't make anybody a Christian. And there was no way that the merciful God of heaven would keep his family out of heaven on church attendance technicality.

In spite of not being a fan of the Duzers, the Reverend assured his guests that he would not make this an ecclesiastical matter or meeting. Somehow, he knew the reason the Duzers made this important courtesy call on his family.

Dahnvah cleared his throat and said, "Pastor, I just want to know if your son Simon will marry my daughter?" "But Dahnvah, you and I have never discussed anything about your daughter and my son getting married. Why today?" Rev. Sarpley asked. "Your wife Konah didn't tell you?" Mr. Dahnvah responded. "Tell me what? Ask her if she told me anything."

The two women interrupted simultaneously. Mrs. Sarpley said, "This was a secret between us. We didn't want the husbands to know." Mrs. Duzer added, "We are very sorry." "Apology accepted, but I cannot choose a wife for my son," Rev. Sarpley responded.

Mr. Duzer rose to his feet and angrily said, "Well, that's it. Venacious you and your mother get up, let's go home! There are many men in this town and the surrounding towns. Simon is too educated for you anyway. You, your church and your God can go throw yourself into the Lee River right now." Mr. Duzer was angry that his wife had secretly engaged their daughter to a man who did not love her.

As they left the Sarpley's home, Mr. Duzer felt like a fool. How in the world could his wife do such a thing without his permission? He was the head and sole decision maker in the home. He felt disrespected. Mrs. Beatrice Duzer would only manage profuse apologies. She had no words to explain herself. She was deeply sorry for keeping the matter away from her husband. But they would sleep on it and live with it happily ever after.

Venacious was disappointed, but she was willing to live with it. As long as her feet would dance, she would find a man to marry her. Of course, Karlie and Albert were automatically eliminated by their last name.

Easter Vacation was ten days. They were over quickly. Simon left Winifred at the motel and went to bid farewell to the Abrahams on the mission station. Mr. Abraham was home when he arrived. Mrs. Abraham was away visiting Paul and Jackie Sanderson, another missionary couple on the mission station. Mr. Abraham was glad to see Simon back. Simon did not spend much time to explain the event that took place when he and Winifred went home. That was a conversation for another time. They said their goodbyes, and Simon left for Zama City to join Winifred for the trip back to MTC.

They left early the next morning heading back to MTC. The Raining Season was just beginning. The roads were still in better conditions. Good thing the dust was not as bad as during the Dry Season. Winifred needed a piece of cloth to cover her hair. Simon handed her a large red handkerchief, a perfect match for the dust. Within six hours, they were back at MTC. There was no stopping. All passengers on the lorry headed to cities in the southeast around MTC.

They had a restful night at their respective residents. Both lived in a residential housing complex just a few blocks from MTC. They were glad to be away from the drama that unfolded in Ziantown. Simon and Winifred wondered what was happening behind them. But for now, they were focused on their studies.

Graduation was seven months away and they had papers to write. Fellow students who had often seen the two together on campus began to ask questions. Monday morning while waiting for Winifred to join him before walking to class, Habakkuk Zorhu, a fellow student from Zama City met him. "Hey Preacher, waiting for Winifred?" Habakkuk asked. He had always called Simon a preacher. "Yes, Habakkuk," Simon answered. "You are the luckiest Preacher alive in this country. Every man on this ground tried to date Winifred McCoy, and failed, and you got her just like that,"

Habakkuk added. Simon responded, "My God is a good God." As Habakkuk left, he shouted again, "By the way, when is the wedding?" "I will let you know," Simon answered. By this time Winifred was closer and heard Habakkuk. "These guys will never give up teasing you," Winifred said. "And it would never bother me at all," Simon said as they walked to class.

Winifred told Simon that she planned to visit her mother in September of that year. Mom was still living in Zorzor City with her husband Deacon Pee-wee Peabody. The thought of going home to see Deacon Peabody with her mother made Winifred angry. "How could a deacon in a church do such a thing, driving her father away from home?" She had often asked herself that question repeatedly.

She did not really trust or believe in Deacon Peabody's God until she met Simon. "Maybe Simon worshipped a different God," she had often wondered. But for the love of her mother, she would go and sit down with the Deacon and her half-brothers. She had never blamed her mother for being the reason behind her father leaving home. She laid the blame at the doorsteps of the Zorzor United Fellowship International. Like her father, she had always considered them a bunch of hypocrites.

One morning in September, she set out to visit her mother. After nearly six months of relentless tropical rains, the roads were in terrible conditions. The Department of Public Works had slowly begun to regrade the roads as usual. The roads were regraded every year after the Raining Season to prepare for Christmas's travelers. This was the time of the year when villages, towns, and cities had soccer games across the country. It was a long and difficult ride, but it was worth it. Winifred McCoy would do anything on the face of the earth to please her mother.

She arrived late Friday night after the Peabody family have already had their dinner. Mrs. Peabody spotted her daughter one hundred yards away, rose to her feet and ran to meet her. Both women were in tears when they embraced. Winifred had not been home for almost a year.

"Mother, I missed you so much," Winifred said. "Me too, I thought you would not come home again," her mother replied. "But mother, this is my home, and there is no place like home," Winifred added. Her half-brothers, Borbor and John Peabody came and embraced their sister. They were glad she was home, or were they? Yes, they were glad.

Borbor and John were born after Mr. Benson McCoy had already left home and their mother had remarried. "You guys are grown men now, and hope you are in school," said Winifred. "Yes, we are Sister Winifred. We are both in the tenth grade now. Within two years we will be out of high school,'" Borbor replied. "And then what?" Winifred inquired. "I want to attend MTC just like you," John answered. "Well, everyone in the family cannot be a teacher. Try medicine, law, or business," Winifred told her brothers.

When they entered the house, Deacon Peabody was outside the backdoor watching some seasonal geese go by. He wished they had flown over him two days ago outside when he had his doubled-barrel shot gun. The family would have had a goose or geese stew for dinner tomorrow. Too bad, he could not shoot his gun inside the city. He would be arrested and fined or go to prison.

Mrs. Peabody shouted to her husband, "Dear, I know you are back there. Winifred is here to visit us." The Deacon came running from the backdoor and hugged Winifred. "Good to see you. The college had made you into a fine young woman," the Deacon said. "Thank you, father. I would had come in July if the roads were not bad. Even now, they are still bad though the Department of Public Works is doing the usual annual regrading." "No big deal. We all know the road conditions in Liberia when the rains come," her father added.

Mrs. Peabody was already in the kitchen preparing food for her daughter. "I hope you have something for Winifred to eat," the Deacon shouted across the living room. "Yes, the rice is cooking already. She will eat it with sardines, then tomorrow, I will prepare a special welcome meal for her," his wife replied. She told her boys to go to the nearest shop to buy a can of sardines for their sister. The boys darted around the street corner and within fifteen minutes, they were back with a can of sardines.

Winifred hated sardines. To her they tasted somewhat mushy in her mouth. She was not a great fan of eating white rice with sardines. She would rather have the rice cooked with Maggi Cube seasoning, mixed with grounded dried fish and sprinkled with a little hot pepper. But she was home and would not make her mother to feel bad. After the long ride, she needed something in her stomach immediately. She enjoyed the rice, every bit of it. She always like her mother's cooking.

For the next three days, the conversations within the family were centered on graduation, and her engagement to Simon Sarpley. She told her family everything about Simon, including the incident in Ziantown when they went to visit his parents.

She urged her family to attend. "Father, I know you are busy with the church, but I hope you and mother can make it to the graduation, and get to meet Simon. He could not come because he is busy preparing for graduation, too," she stressed to her parents. "The boys can stay behind and take care of the house," she added."

Sunday morning while the family was preparing for church, Winifred was packing her suitcase to catch the earliest lorry for the southeast. They embraced each other in tears and promised to meet again at graduation. The Deacon and his wife would not miss this graduation for anything in the world. The boys would like to go, but they must remain behind and take care of the properties. John was the youngest of the three so, he accompanied his sister to the lorry station. He carried his sister's suitcase. "John, do you have a girlfriend?" Winifred asked her brother. "Yes, but she hardly comes around. She is shy and seemed to be afraid of our father," John replied. "Well, she will get over it and come around, believe me," Winifred concluded.

They were already at the lorry station. John had to hurry back to be in time for church service. The Deacon did not take it lightly when his boys showed up late for church services. They had to give tangible reasons for being late or else they would fast for two days. Deacon Peabody's God did not have rooms for tardiness. John and his brother knew it.

Winifred was fortunate to find one of the early birds heading for the southeast. She boarded the lorry and waited inside for additional passengers before the lorry would take off. She began to read "Murder in the Cassava Path," written by a Liberian author way back. The book was older than Winifred. She enjoyed reading all kinds of books. Reading had become her hobby at MTC since she was alone majority of the time before she met Simon.

"Love must be blind," she said to herself. She was thinking about the love between her mother and step-father. How could her mother love a man who was responsible for the dismissal of her husband, her first love, and then turned around and married him? How could she in good conscience actually love Pee-wee Peabody? Maybe love was blind and it did not possess the feeling of guilt either. Anyway, that was her mother's life and not hers. If she ever had a chance. . .! No, she did not want to go there at all.

She abruptly changed her focus to Simon Sarpley and their future life together on the mission station raising beautiful children. Yes, that was pleasant and refreshing. The thought almost put her to sleep. When she opened her eyes, they were already on their way. Lord, she was thankful that the weekend lasted only two and half days. She felt embarrassed looking at her step-father all the time.

After several stops and goes because of potholes and muds, they arrived safely at MTC late Sunday evening. She went over to Simon's to inform him that she was back. As usual, he was in the books again. "Does this man ever stop reading books?" Winifred said to herself. He opened the door and let her inside the house.

"How are your mother and your step-father?" Simon asked. "I am glad it lasted only two and half days. I don't think I would live with my mother and her husband. Good to be back at MTC," Winifred answered. She was not judging Deacon Peabody. The real reason for her anger was that she missed her father; the father she knew as a child; Mr. Benson McCoy, a loving man driven nearly insane by a perfect church that harbored the likes of Deacon Pee-wee Peabody, her step-father.

They sat down and had cups of tea together. Winifred was tired from her long rough ride and wanted to retire and get ready for school in the morning. They kissed goodnight and Winifred left for her house. She took a warm shower and went straight on to bed.

Meanwhile Simon completed his reading assignment and went to bed. He woke up earlier than usual because he had to get ready and wait for Winifred to walk to school. Lord, both loved walking together to school. It had become a routine for them, walking to school together. It was not strange to anyone on campus at MTC.

It was getting late and the jurors had heard enough about Simon Sarpley. Everyone in the courtroom was beginning to murmur. The jurors also seemed restless. Judge Garwin was willing to grant everyone two hour-lunch period today. Again, he warned the jurors against discussing the case with each other, with family members, relatives and friends. He would had loved or wanted the jurors to be sequestrated, but the city had two motels that were already booked beyond normal occupancies. And more importantly, the court did not have funding for sequestration. The jurors were already being paid sixteen dollars per day, except on weekends when the court was not in session. The jurors were permitted to reside in their own homes with straight orders and restrictions on where they would go or not go.

After lunch, Judge Garwin requested that the prosecutorial and the defense teams meet with him in his chamber. He asked that the court be adjourned to resume Monday morning at the same time. This would give each team the chance to collect more evidences and retool their arguments. They accepted his request and the court was adjourned at five o'clock p.m.

On Saturday, there were rumors that Venacious Duzer was spotted in Zama City in the market with juror number four, Mr. Prince Torwah. But investigation into the matter revealed that it was simply a mistaken identity or *they say* that could not be substantiated.

On Saturday afternoon, defense jury consultant Josiah Gonwoe visited the mission station to interview another missionary couple. The Abrahams were back in the United States on furlough. They would return within a year to bid farewell to everyone and go into permanent retirement.

With the arrest of Station Director Sarpley, Paul Sanderson was acting until after the trial. They had written back to the states informing Jess and Cathy Abraham about the situation. They had requested prayers for Miss Currie Sawdust and her team of lawyers and for Simon. They had expressed confidence that their God would see Simon through the trial.

When Mr. Gonwoe rang the doorbell, the houseboy opened the door and told him that Paul and Jackie Sanderson were not home. They had gone to visit friends on another mission station seven miles away. But they would be back later that same day. Josiah left a message with the houseboy that he would return on Sunday after church.

When Mr. Gonwoe returned to the home of the missionaries on Sunday after church, the houseboy told him that Missy and her husband were resting and would not be disturbed. But he insisted that the houseboy woke them up. And when he did, the missionaries were not pleased. This was the Lord's Day, the day of rest from all activities, except worshipping God. But they had to come out because this was about their Station Director. The Sanderson declined to be interviewed on Sunday, but agreed to testify on behalf of Simon as character witnesses.

Paul and Jackie Sanderson were in their late sixties when they heard and accepted the "Macedonia Call" to come to Liberia. In their retirement years, they had come with the hope of managing the mission station when the Abrahams left the country. That was what they were told before leaving the United States. Instead, it was handed down to an indigenous Liberian in broad daylight. They had never gotten over the feeling of betrayal by their mission organization. He and his wife had boycotted the dedication ceremony. They had cooked up a frivolous emergency that Paul was sick and needed a doctor's attention in Monrovia. Lord, Mr. Sanderson desired the Station Director's title to the point of testifying against Simon Sarpley. In Paul Sanderson's view, no indigenous Liberian was capable of managing a mission station. He had been a managing director at a lucrative manufacturing company in the United States for nearly forty years. He and Jackie had met at the company and gotten married. Thereafter, Jackie had served the company in various capacities for nearly thirty-five years before her retirement. They would take over the mission station immediately no matter what happened at Mr. Sarpley's trial.

The court resumed Monday morning at nine o'clock as expected. This was the third day of the trial. Judge Garwin asked the defense team not to interrupt unless they needed specific clarifications, or find compelling reasons to raise objections. The prosecution had to complete Simon's background story today and begin calling witnesses to the stand. Counselor Jake Cassell picked up where he left off on Friday.

Early October Simon and Winfred had to meet with their advisor to make sure everything was on course for graduation in December. They met with Professor Nathaniel Samuelson early Tuesday morning. Professor Nat Sam as he was known by everyone on campus, was an American educated Liberian. His great grandparents were Americo-Liberians. Indigenous Liberians called them the "Congo People." He was a tall medium-bill man in his early fifties. Professor Samuelson wore no corrective lenses, unusual for a man his age on MTC campus. He was a nice and quiet man who kept to himself. He never gave make-up examinations. If a student failed his class, he or she flunk the course. He never minced his words when he advised students.

Simon and Winifred were two of his favorite students on campus. He designated himself as their advisor. Lord, he treated them like his own children. He was married, but had no children. His wife Julianna Bowen-Samuelson was an English teacher at one of the local public high schools. She always wore pants, and would be caught dead in a dress.

As far as Professor Nat Sam was concerned, Simon and Winifred would graduate tomorrow if he controlled everything at MTC. He was proud to be their advisor. The President of MTC, Dr. Jeffrey Easter kept his academic calendar intact. Nothing on this earth would change anything on his calendar. He always wanted everyone to know that he was in charge at MTC. When it came to the academic calendar, Dr. Easter kept his eyes on it like a hawk watching its prey before diving for it.

Professor Samuelson told the couple that everything was on course for graduation. He had already gone over their dissertations twice. All they needed to do was finalize the necessary corrections before final submission. Simon had written on the Roles of Christianity on Early Childhood Education in Liberia, placing emphasis on the arrival of missionaries in the 1930's and 1940's respectively. And Winifred had written on Public School Education versus Private School Education placing emphasis on the advantages and disadvantages of each system. Their dissertations were brilliantly written. Professor Samuelson was so impressed that he invited all educators at MTC to be present at the final presentations.

Simon Sarpley and Winifred McCoy presented their dissertations the first week of December. They were well received with standing ovation by the Graduation Committee (GC). This was the most notorious committee at MTC. Two years earlier the committee had disqualified a dissertation written by Garrison Lehleh, a graduating senior. Mr. Lehleh and his student supporters had almost rioted on campus. The situation was brought under control only by the intervention of the local police force. Garrison Lehleh was later given a second chance by the President of MTC, Dr. Jeffrey Easter before he would graduate.

Meanwhile on the mission station, the Abrahams were getting ready to attend Simon's graduation. During their last visit to Ziantown, they had informed the Sarpley's family that they would come to pick them up for the trip to MTC for the graduation. Graduation was scheduled for the second Friday in December.

Early Thursday morning, the missionaries arrived to pick up the Sarpleys. They were ready, everyone, including Karlie and Albert. They had promised Simon that they would attend the graduation. If they reneged on their promise, Simon would be disappointed in them. Venacious Duzer wanted to go, but her father vowed, "Over my dead body." Mr. Duzer was right because she would not fit in the picture at MTC on graduation day. Though it would had been nice for students at MTC to see Venacious Duzer do the "moonwalks" at the graduation reception.

The missionaries filled up the tank on the late model Land Rover Jeep and left Zama City about nine o'clock in the morning. They would drive all day and arrive there late at night. Jess Abraham was on the wheel. Cathy Abraham was not cut out for driving on rough roads in rural Liberia. She drove from the mission station to Zama City and to Ziantown, and no more.

Riding along with missionaries was fun. Mrs. Abraham would interrupt the conversations with choruses like, "Are you sleeping, are you sleeping, Brother John, Brother John, morning bell is ringing, morning bell is ringing, ding, ding, dong, ding, ding dong." Or "Everywhere He went, He was doing good, He's a mighty healer, He cleansed the lepers, when the cripples saw Him, they started walking, everywhere He went, my Lord was doing good." She had a pretty voice. Lord, the woman could sing all tunes, alto, soprano, bass, and tenor. A yodeler, yes, she was, too.

Every now and then, Rev. Sarpley would come in with one of his favorites from Bible school days, "I want to be ready; I want to be ready; I want to be ready, to walk in Jerusalem just like John." He sang this chorus at work and at his leisure times. If you woke him up in the morning, Rev. Sarpley would sing, "I want to be ready to walk in Jerusalem just like John." Lord, Rev. Sarpley, did not consider the readiness of Christians lightly. He lived and preached it. "Be ready because Jesus would come anytime," he had always said.

He and his wife also enjoyed Mrs. Abraham's singing. They were used to it in Sunday school and church services. Lord, the Reverend and his wife were fond of the missionaries. Karlie and Albert were the wild bunch. They kept quiet most of the ride. Their parents were in the car, and they would not do or say anything to **embarrass** them. They knew that and tried to keep the conversations civil. They were grown men, though they behaved otherwise. Their parents had always advised them, "It was time you two got married and settled down." But those words had always fallen on death ears.

They arrived late evening on Thursday in Maryland City, home of Maryland Teacher's College (MTC). There were some students standing around and talking. Fortunate for them, one of the students was Habakkuk Zorhu, a resident and friend of Simon Sarpley. He also knew the missionaries from the mission station. He greeted and took them to Simon's apartment. Lord, Simon was overwhelmed to see the Abrahams and his own family. He was almost in tears, tears of joy to see his entire family and sponsors at his graduation. It has been three long years, but the missionaries stuck with him until this day.

He tried to whip up some cassava dough for dinner, but his mother took over. Within one hour and thirty minutes, dinner was ready, almost a pre-graduation reception feast. Mrs. Simon knew her son lived alone, so she came prepared; dried fish, dried monkey meat, seasonings, grounded peanut, yes, she brought them all. The missionary also brought their own rations, though they had accepted Liberian delicacies and eaten them often. But when they traveled, they avoided spicy foods to prevent diarrheas.

After dinner, Simon told his parents that Winifred McCoy's parents had also arrived to attend her graduation. He asked if they would be willing to meet them. Rev. Sarpley and Mr. Abraham did not have any problem meeting them. In fact, they were delighted. And Mrs. Sarpley was also willing, though she wanted Cathy Abraham's opinion on the matter. Jess looked at his wife and nodded his head. "All right, we will meet them.

It won't hurt anything. After all, this is Simon's day, and we would not want him to feel bad," Mrs. Cathy Abraham responded.

Early Friday morning at ten o'clock, Simon's party went to meet Winifred's party. They shook hands and introduced themselves to each other. Winifred's mother was delighted to meet Simon for the first time. Winifred had told her mother so much about Simon it seemed like they already knew each other before this encounter. Jess was also glad to meet Winifred's mother. He had come to like Winifred since they met her when she and Simon visited the mission station. But Mrs. Cathy Abraham still had doubts about a girl who practically raised herself with the help of her mother, and later went to be a scholar.

Rev. Sarpley was Winifred's number one fan. He just loved her the first time he laid eyes on her. He felt Winifred would make a terrific wife for his son. He hugged her and said he was glad to meet her again. All this time Deacon Pee-wee Peabody had not spoken a word. Winifred led them into the living room of her apartment. Both Simon and Winifred made official introduction of their parents.

Simon rose to his feet and began the introduction first. Deacon and Mrs. Peabody, these are my parents, "Rev. Gideon Sarpley my father, Mrs. Konah Sarpley my mother, and my brothers Karlie and Albert Sarpley. And the missionaries are Mr. Jess and Mrs. Cathy Abraham. They are responsible for my educational success."

Now it was Winifred's turn. "This is Deacon Pee-wee Peabody, my step-father, and Mrs. Jennifer Peabody my mother. I have two step-brothers, Borbor and John Peabody, but they had to remain behind and take care of the properties." When Winifred said, "step-father," Mrs. Abraham rose to her feet. Jess looked hard at his wife, and she sat right back down. "Simon and I are special friends, and I have met his family, including his sponsors. At the appropriate time we will let you all know our intentions," Winifred concluded and took her seat beside her mother.

Winifred offered everyone tea and they accepted. Karlie and Albert took theirs and stepped outside the door as everyone stayed indoor to get acquainted with each other. The boys were never interested in anything in life other than drinking and partying. They were somehow restricted in Maryland City because they did not know their ways around.

The women sat and talked. Mrs. Abraham was interested in knowing what happened to Jennifer's first husband, Mr. Benson McCoy. She said nothing was working between them, and everything became a distraction in the church so she decided to file for divorce. Lord, she would not have the audacity to mention her affairs with Deacon Pee-wee Peabody before Mr. McCoy left home.

Winifred knew that her mother would never tell the truth about her relationship with her first husband. It was painful so Winifred walked into the kitchen while her mother was being an Ananias' Imitator. Lord, she also hated when her mother fabricated stories about Mr. Benson McCoy.

Mrs. Konah Sarpley did not say much. She was glad to finally meet Winifred's parents. From the looks of Winifred, she knew her mother was a beautiful woman. Mrs. Sarpley was not actually interested in anything at this moment. She had traveled to Maryland City to attend her son's graduation. She was focused on having a great time with him. Until then, everything else would wait.

Jess Abraham and Rev. Sarpley got to know little about Deacon Peabody and the Zorzor United Fellowship International. The Deacon was not willing to go into further details about his personal life and what had happened to Mr. Benson McCoy. Deacon Pee-wee Peabody was a walking Ananias Imitator. On the other hand, Jess Abraham was a man who had always pleaded "Thomas" the first day he landed in Liberia as a missionary.

He had to see it to believe it. This had been his missionary philosophy since he accepted the call and came to Africa. Today he believed that Simon Sarpley was a student at MTC, and he would graduate as an honor student. He was proud of the man and his accomplishments.

Rev. Gideon Sarpley and his wife were in this together. They were focused on their son's graduation, and what it meant to the family and the farming town of Ziantown. He was proud of his son. If he could bring down heaven on this day, he would had done it. He was overwhelmed with joy to see his son graduate on top of his class from a prestigious college as MTC. Lord, only heaven knew what was boiling inside the Reverend. He would kill the biggest goat in Ziantown and have the grandest graduation party on arrival back home. And he had seen and known the likes of Deacon Pee-wee Peabody before in his Christian life. The one who passed judgment on everyone and said, "Do as I say, but don't do as I do."

At the end of what seemed like conversations, the parties went to their respective apartments to get ready for the graduation ceremony at five o'clock in the afternoon. They had to be ready and on time. To Dr. Jeffrey Easter, this was no such a thing as a Liberian Standard Time (LST), where guests and invitees showed up two, three or four hours later than the event time. Lord, when it came to tardiness, the man was intolerable. He had always said, "Five o'clock is five o'clock whether in China, United States, Great Britain or Siberia. Those countries may have different time zones, but five o'clock is still five o'clock in those countries."

This year was MTC's 15th Commencement Convocation. For a graduation speaker this year, and with the recommendation of Dr. Jeffrey Easter, MTC selected Dr. Jeremiah Fickles, an educational historian, the one and only in the country at the government's university in the capital city. He, too had a "Congo," or Americo-Liberian backgrounds. He was a tall and slender man with lots of facial hairs. He wore beard and mustache.

He also wore black framed clear spectacles. Without his facial hairs and spectacles, he would appear to be in his late forties. They had studied together in London, England before Dr. Easter transferred to another university in the United States. They were not personal friends, but both men had deep respect and admiration for each other. So when the invitation arrived from MTC with the President's signature, Dr. Fickles gladly accepted it. He was delighted to meet his former classmate again.

By four forty-five in the afternoon, the graduates were seated. Honored guests, friends, family members and relatives were required to be in their seats at four thirty. Dr. Easter's rules with no exceptions. Those who came after had to wait outside to receive their graduates.

There were 120 graduates including Simon Sarpley and Winifred McCoy. Simon was the top of the class with Winifred coming in closed second.

Faculty members were seated just to the right of Dr. Easter, and Dr. Fickles sat to the left of Dr. Easter. Dr. Easter spoke briefly about the history of MTC and how proud he was as the president. He also outlined his vision for MTC within the next ten years, hoping to expand MTC satellite campuses around the country to enable aspiring teachers to have access to quality education. He did not care if the government had the grant money or not, he would strive to create a culture of quality teachers in the country. He also took the liberty of introducing his former classmate, Dr. Jeremiah Fickles as a man of principle who would sacrifice his life for better colleges in the country. Throughout his life, Dr. Fickles had fought corruption in schools at every level almost to the detriment of his own career. He vowed to keep fighting until death.

In his valedictory speech, Simon Sarpley credited his parents and the missionaries for his educational success. He asked Mr. Jess and Mrs. Cathy Abraham to stand up as he paid tribute to them. To him the

Abrahams possessed true missionary spirit of compassion, not only in words, but also in deeds. He likened them to Aquila and Priscilla of the early church in the New Testament who lent hands to the Apostle Paul and Apollos. And he hoped more missionaries like the Abrahams would come to Liberia. He challenged his fellow students to strive for excellence in education and in whatever they endeavor to do.

Dr. Jeremiah Fickles rose to his feet with a standing ovation from the audience. He put his right hand inside the left chest pocket of his coat and took out a piece of paper and began his speech. After reading the first two paragraphs, he folded the paper and put it back in his coat pocket and raised both hands and asked the audience, "Do you see anything my hands?" The audience responded, "No!"

"That's exactly right because the government of this nation has done nothing to improve education. Therefore, the nation will not get anything substantive out of education. If you don't put anything into it, you will get nothing out of it," he added. For the next twenty-five minutes, he outlined how government had degraded the educational system of the country.

The Liberian elites did not care because they can afford to send their children overseas for quality education. And upon graduation, they would never come back to serve their country.

For a name like "Fickles," one would think that he was one of them, but he set himself apart from the corruption of the elites in the country and lambasted them for raking the coffers of the nation to build mansions for themselves and their relatives. When he called for "an educational revolt," everyone including faculty members and graduates rose to their feet, shouting, "We want educational revolt, Dr. Fickles for president." They shouted for at least five minutes before taking their seats. In closing, he thanked his dear friend Dr. Easter for his wonderful work at MTC and for inviting him to MTC as the convocation speaker. After his speech, graduates were called and handed their diplomas.

When the ceremony was over, Simon and Winfred met and told their families that they had arranged for a hall near campus for the graduation reception. They had also arranged to cater the food for the reception so the women would not cook.

Winifred and Simon did not want their mothers to cook on this historic day. For one hundred dollars, the food was all over the place. The caterer had even prepared a pumpkin pie and grapefruit-orange salads for the Abrahams. When the dinner was over, Simon asked for everyone's attention. While still in his graduation gown, he got down on both knees and asked Winifred McCoy to marry him. Winifred, still in her gown got down on her knees, held Simon's hands and said loudly, "Yes, Simon Sarpley, yes. I will be your wife!" Both mothers broke into spontaneous dancing. Everyone began to hug each other. The graduation party had just turned into an engagement party. And everyone loved it.

Friends who had come to the party were not surprised. They knew it was a matter of time before the two got married. In fact, Habakkuk Zorhu had asked Simon or Winifred on many occasions about the wedding date. He was happy for Simon.

Karlie and Albert took two soft drinks bottles and popped them. They were happy for their brother. They were party animals. They were always at their best when it came to drinking and partying. Though there were no beers or liquors, they were happy to be at any party, even this one without alcohol.

Rev. Sarpley, Mr. Abraham and Deacon Peabody took turns thanking Simon and Winifred for their hard work and achievements in college. They were proud of them. Though the engagement took them by surprise, somehow, they knew something special was in the making when the couple spoke earlier in the morning about their intentions. Mr. and Mrs. Abraham could not wait for Simon to return and take over the mission station as the Station Director. Their missionary furlough was almost overdue. They were anxious to return to the United States to visit their children.

Deacon Peabody did not spend much time with Winifred when she was growing up. But he had confidence in her that she would make the right choice or decision. She was a scholar and knew what was best for her. He did not have a problem with their engagement. He hoped the best for his step-daughter.

By two o'clock in the morning, it was time to stop the party and go to bed. They would meet in the morning and set the wedding date. Everyone went to bed happily.

Early in the morning, they gathered at Simon's apartment to talk about the wedding date. They ate too much last night. Therefore, no one was interested in breakfast. They brought some of the leftovers to be heated in the morning for breakfast, but no one wanted breakfast.

After thanking their respective parents, Simon and Winfred set the wedding date on the second Saturday of March of the following year. They did not want a wedding near the Raining Season. Their parents understood without complaints.

On Saturday, the parents went around Maryland City and got to see the city. Karlie and Albert were interested in going to the beach. Rev. Sarpley warned them strongly to stay away from the Atlantic Ocean.

By five o'clock in the afternoon, Simon's parents and the missionaries were back. Simon accompanied his brothers to the beach to make sure they stayed out of troubles. They walked around the beaches without swimming and came back by six o'clock. After dinner, they agreed to leave early Sunday morning for home. Simon would return home later that week. He had to clean his apartment and turn it over to the landlord. He and Winifred would stay behind for one week. Thereafter, they would communicate through letters and later visit each other in January before the wedding.

Early in the morning everyone got up, ready for the trip back home. The morning devotion was led by Mrs. Abraham. She read the 23rd Psalm and asked her husband to pray. Jess prayed for safe trip back home, for both families and for Simon and Winifred's future. He thanked God for Simon and asked Him to prepare Simon for the tasks ahead in leading the mission station.

They headed to Winifred's apartment after devotion. They had come to bid farewell to Winifred's parents. The Deacon answered and opened the door. Winifred was in the kitchen preparing breakfast for her parents. She asked them to stay for breakfast. They politely refused and said they would eat on the way home. Jess drank a cup of coffee for the road. They all embraced and promised to meet at their children's wedding in March.

After breakfast, Winifred asked her parents what they thought of Simon's parents. The Deacon did not have dislike for the Sarpleys. But he said Mrs. Cathy Abraham was a nosy missionary, and his daughter should watch out for her. Winifred nodded in agreement and narrated her first experience in meeting Mrs. Abraham on the mission station. Winifred understood from Simon's explanation from that day that Mrs. Abraham was trying to protect their investment. They had sponsored Simon from grade school all the way to college. And they wanted to make sure that the mission station was left in good and capable hands.

Mrs. Jennifer Peabody loved Simon's mother. Both women just hit the ground running as if they had met before. She also liked Simon. He seemed like a good and quiet man who would make a good husband for her daughter. They promised to get to know him better on his visit in January.

Simon returned home a week later as promised. At a brief ceremony on the mission station, Simon Sarpley was named the Station Director of the mission station by Mr. Jess Abraham. Within two weeks, Jess and Cathy left Liberia for their furlough. They would return within a year to prepare for permanent retirement.

Winnifred McCoy also went home to be with her family within the same week Simon left MTC. She was unable to attend Simon's program when he was appointed as the Station Director of the mission station.

In late January of the following year, Mrs. Jennifer Peabody began losing weight. It was not serious to alarm her husband. She reported of severe pain in the lower left side of her stomach. She did not think it was serious. But Winifred was home and decided to take her mother to the clinic. After her initial examination by her gynecologist, Dr. Martha Mason, she was referred to Kolahun City Referral Hospital (KCRH). There, they had specialists and equipment to do conclusive diagnosis. Dr. Mason suspected that Mrs. Peabody had a lump growing in her left ovary, but she was not sure.

The following morning, Jennifer took her mother to KCRH. She had heard of Dr. Jacqueline Frankenstein, a visiting gynecologist from the United States. With a name like Frankenstein, one would think that she would be in Hollywood making monster and horror movies, but no, she was a gynecologist, and a pretty good one too. After several hours of examination, Winifred and her mother got the worst news of their lives since Ben McCoy left home several years ago. Mrs. Jennifer Peabody had a stage three ovarian cancer that had already spread to other reproductive organs. Lord, what good news would Winifred and her mother expect from a Dr. Frankenstein? She was given some strong pain killers and told to put her house in order because she had one month to live.

Winifred wanted to cry, but there were no tears. She wanted to shout to God, "Why me again, God?" But she had to be brave and strong for her mother, step-father and her brothers. How could she break the news to the rest of the family? She and her mother sat outside on a park bench in the hospital yard for nearly forty-five minutes. Mrs. Peabody had never been a woman of prayer, but she told her daughter, "Let us pray for God's strength so I can break the news to the family." For the first time in her life Winifred McCoy heard her mother pleading with God for forgiveness. If she was going to die, she wanted to die with a clear conscience. Even now, she was asking God to heal her fast. She promised to change her ways and be a good mother and a wife to her husband and her children. At the end of the prayer, they got up and went home. Winifred insisted on preparing the family dinner that night, but her mother refused. If she were going to die, she would go down fighting until the last breath. She was not dying now so there was no need to turn her wifely responsibilities over to her daughter. This night she went extra miles with the dinner. Deacon Peabody thought they had a guest coming over for dinner.

After Dinner that night, Mrs. Peabody gathered her family in the living room and broke the horrible news to them. Deacon Peabody nearly passed out. He could not believe it. After all, he had been a faithful and dedicated servant in his church for thirty years. He had helped to cleanse God's house just as Jesus Christ drove the money changers and thieves out of His Father's House when He was on earth. He blamed God for his wife's illness no matter what anyone told him. Yes, God was responsible because he had slept with Jennifer while she was still married to Ben McCoy. Now God was judging him through his wife.

Borbor and John Peabody were confused. They could not believe that their loving mother would be dead in a month. Mrs. Peabody reassured her sons that their sister would take care of them after she was dead and gone. "Winifred was a strong woman. She almost raised and sent herself to school." She had told her boys.

Early the next morning, Winifred wrote to Simon that the wedding would be postponed because of her mother's sudden illness and the possibility that she would be dead within a month. Simon received the letter, but he could not leave the mission station immediately because of some pressing budget issues that needed his attention. He would be in prayers daily for Mrs. Peabody. Winifred wished Simon had come to be by her side. The Station Director refused to go and stand by his fiancé when she needed him most. He was busy doing and going about God's business.

"Objection Your Honor," prosecution is trying to blame my client for a situation in which he had no control over," Miss Sawdust shouted to His Judgeship. "Sustained. Counselor stick to the facts of the story," His Honor responded.

Within thirty days, Mrs. Jennifer Peabody was dead. Winifred and her family were devastated. She had to step up and help the family with funeral arrangements. It was not easy, but she did her best with the help of her step-father and her brothers. They had wanted a small church funeral service limited only to the immediate family and closed relatives, but not while Zorzor United Fellowship International (UFI) was still standing. They put up the greatest funeral show Zorzor City had ever seen. UFI had a special budget set aside for the likes of Mrs. Jennifer Peabody and prominent members in the church. Lord, to them, it was not a funeral, but a ***home going celebration***.

This is the time Liberians actually show their love to fellow Liberians. One had to die to be loved and appreciated. When a person is alive or sick, no one cared until death.

UFI spent a whopping $9,000.00 on the funeral services. Mrs. Peabody was the wife of a deacon, therefore, she had to go in style; the best coffin, best bouquet of flowers, and best of everything.

Again, Simon Sarpley got the news about Winifred mother's death. He was the only director and had just assumed the position without an assistant. Therefore, he could not abandon the mission station. He did not want to leave the station in the hands of the Sandersons. He did not like them, and they did not like him. If there was ever a time Winifred wanted Simon to be with her, it was at Mrs. Jennifer Peabody's graveside. She desperately needed Simon, but he could not come because of pressing issues on the mission station.

Winifred also wished her father had come. But she had not heard from him in years. She was not sure if her father was still alive. On the night of the wake, Winifred passed out and was carried away by her brothers. They gave her water to drink, and she was able to return to the wake. Her step-father was crying like a baby. Deacon Peabody couldn't get hold of himself. Members of the Deacon's Ministry sat by him until the service was over.

The funeral was on Saturday, the next day. Rev. Cyrus Korlubie Korlu preached a beautiful eulogy. He reminded his church that they had come to bid farewell to a dear sister who had died in the Lord. And they had not come to judge her. He shouted, "Let our sister go in peace from this wicked world where there is no peace. Let him or her who is without sin be the first to speak up!" Lord, who would dare to speak such a blasphemy at a funeral? Deacon Peabody would lose it, and all hell would break losse. Talking about death at a funeral, yes that too, first in Liberia.

The UFI Senior Choir sang one of Mrs. Peabody's favorite songs; "Fill My Cup Let It Overflow with Joy." The song had caused Deacon Peabody to fall on his wife's coffin lamenting, "Jennifer I will go with you. Please don't leave me behind." The deacons had helped to remove him from the coffin and advised him to get hold of himself.

At the gravesite, all the women in the church had to take hold of Winifred McCoy. She wanted to jump into the grave and be buried alive with her mother. Her brothers were of no help either. Borbor and John Peabody were crying uncontrollably.

If Winifred was going to be a strong person for her family, it was now. She had to take the words of her mother at heart. "Be strong and take care of the family," her mother had said on her deathbed. She was educated and had the talents to work, especially teaching at any high school within the country.

Three days after the burial, Winifred wrote and told Simon that she was postponing the wedding indefinitely. Now was not the time because she had to find a teaching position at a local high school in order to earn money and take care of her family. Her step-father was in no emotional condition to return to his work as a security guard at the county offices.

At this juncture, DA Cassell turned around and pointed to Simon Sarpley, and said sarcastically, "That is the man sitting there, a man who called himself a Christian, but had no love and compassion for his own fiancé when she needed him most." And he added, "Honorable men and women of the jury, find this man not guilty as charged. He is not a Christian." The court became dead silent.

"Your Honor, I will now present my witnesses," said DA Cassell. It was already three-thirty in the afternoon and His Judgeship needed a break, so he recessed the court for fifteen minutes. The court would resume at four o'clock in the afternoon.

When the court resumed, prosecution's first witness was Venacious Duzer, the woman from Ziantown whom Simon had turned down. She came in wearing a white satin blouse and a dark blue skirt. She also wore a black low heel shoes.

She shared her biography, beginning with her birth. Her parents did not send her to school, being the only child in the home, her friends, engagement to Simon through his mother and her future aspiration to be a professional dancer. Lord, watching a beautiful young uneducated woman turned down by an educated man was compelling at first, but the jurors soon learned that Simon had never met her personally, or had any relationship with her. Her secret engagement was the making of Mrs. Konah Sarpley and Mrs. Beatrice Duzer.

The recess was not long enough. His Judgeship was beginning to grow weary and restless, and Borbor Kittens needed a pipe smoking break. After thirty minutes, the judge adjourned the court.

When the court resumed Tuesday morning, Venacious Duzer was called back to the witness stand. She had nothing else to add to her previous testimony, except she loved Simon very much though they never met personally until he visited his home with Winifred McCoy. "Your witness, Counselor," Mr. Cassell said as he took his seat.

"What is your name again?" Miss Sawdust asked Venacious. "I am Venacious Duzer," she replied. "How old are you now?" Miss Sawdust continued. "Objection "Your Honor, the DA interrupted. "Overruled. Answer the question young lady," His Judgeship said. "What does that have to do with anything?" Venacious wanted to know. "Anyway, I am nineteen years old," Venacious replied. Miss Sawdust continued; "You are nineteen years old and you were willing to get married to a man twice your age?" "Yes, it did not matter to me," Miss Duzer answered. "No further questionsYour Honor," Miss Sawdust concluded and took her seat.

DA Cassell had a reputation for not losing cases. He and his team had resorted to all sorts of underhanded tricks to win the case by all means necessary. They had offered money to family and friends of the jurors to spread false rumors about Simon throughout Zama City and the surrounding towns and villages that he had several girlfriends, and this was the reason he had refused to be by his fiancé's side when her mother died. Simon was not actually a Christian, but a sheep in wolf's clothing who went to church only on Easter Sundays and at Christmas, and had been spotted in several bars and clubs in Zama City drinking beers.

These things happened in Liberia in all court cases. Judges are bribed to dismiss or throw out court cases. Lawyers are bribed to drag cases until the plaintiff or defendants run out of money or options to pursue a case. When it came to court cases, Liberia was like a rawhide city where the slowest man to draw had the shortest lifespan. In other words, the poorest man or woman did not stand a chance of winning any court case in the country. Rather, the richest person with the money to bribe lawyers and judges always won his or her case. It had come to be accepted as part of the legal and judicial systems in the country with no qualms. A poor man or woman always lost a court case, and a rich man or woman always won. That was the mother of all Liberianizations.

For the next seven days, prosecution and defense teams paraded a slew of witnesses, including ordinary citizens, the parents of Simon, missionaries, Muslims, non-Christians and Christians alike. The prosecution even brought in a religious expert to testify on what he referred to as the "good deeds or "fruits of the Spirit" in the life of a Christian. A Father Clarence Masterson, a Liberian ordained Catholic priest who specialized in Christian Charitable deeds. But his expert testimony did not hurt or advance the case of either the prosecution or the defense.

Miss Sawdust thought that putting Simon Sarpley on the witness stand would hurt his case. He did not testify on his own behalf. But a letter from Simon's missionary sponsors, Jess and Cathy Abraham was read in court. In the letter they pleaded for the court to have mercy on Simon because he was new in his position and had lots to do, and they wished they had adequately trained, precepted and prepared him before leaving for the United States.

On day seven, Judge Garwin did not appear until ten o'clock in the morning. And when he stepped up to the bench, he noticed that his courtroom was unusually packed. News had spread around the city and the surrounding towns and villages that the end of the trial was closer.

Bailiff Alieu Donzo opened the door and the jurors filed in to hear the closing arguments of both legal teams. When everyone sat down and the court became quiet, His Judgeship instructed DA Jake Cassell to begin his closing statement. "Keep it to at least thirty minutes and don't bother going over the life story of Simon Sarpley again," he demanded.

DA Cassell wearing his favorite black suit with a gray speckles necktie launched into a description of Simon Sarpley as the epitome of all Christian pretenders. There are hundred more Simon Sarpleys out there, pretending to be Christians, but they are not. At the end of the day one thing stands out, they got into it for the money. It was time ordinary citizens expose these mendacities so the true Christians can do their job in serving their true God.

Then he talked about the hundreds of people who visited the mission station in search of help, but were repeatedly turned down by Director Simon Sarpley. He also talked about Miss Winifred McCoy, a beautiful young lady, Simon met in college who believed that Simon was a compassionate and merciful man, but it turned out that he would rather win the whole world and lose his family.

He made a sketch of Zama City and drew a draw bridge between the city and the mission station. He then explained that when people attempted to go to the mission station, Mr. Sarpley Simon would withdraw the bridge. This case was not about sending a Christian to jail, but to expose fake Christianity at its very core. How does a court punish a Christian? No, it was between him and his God whom he misrepresents.

Judge Brownkai Garwin could hardly hear as Currie Sawdust, Mr. Sarpley's lawyer began her closing arguments. Despite the Judge Garwin's stern warning of, "Order in the court," everyone heeded the warning except for an old man standing in the corner in the back of the courtroom. He shouted at the top of his lungs, "He's not guilty as charged. Mr. Simon used to pass me all the time on his way to work. Your honor, he does not possess the characters of a Christian."

Simon looked to the direction of Miss Sawdust for reassurance. He had a look of sadness on his face. He whispered to her, "I did not know." Miss Sawdust asked Judge Garwin if she would approach the bench. When the judge refused, she asked for one-hour recess. That, too was denied.

Mr. Sarpley again whispered to Miss Sawdust. This time it was a question. "What did I do wrong?" She turned her head and looked straight in his eyes and said, the primary charge against you is, "You did not live and walk the Life and Person you professed and proclaimed."

It took Miss Sawdust half the time it took the DA to present his closing arguments in an attempt to shoot down the veracity of the witnesses who testified against Simon Sarpley. She impressed on the minds of the jurors that this was purely a vendetta to discredit a man who rose from a humble beginning to become the best, and returned to help his own people. And doing so, he had to be not only a Christian, but a professional and trained teacher who had a job to do to keep his mission station viably afloat.

What she resented most was the vilification of Mr. Sarpley as a compassionless man who embraced Christianity as a for-profit-religion. Miss Sawdust drew near the jurors' box looked straight into their eyes and repeated slowly, "Even the Bible asserts that lazy people who do not want to work should not eat. I saw the emotion of Venacious Duzer and her crocodile tears, and her desperate attempt to marry an educated man to prop herself up, and use Simon Sarpley's resources to seek after her professional dancing career."

As Miss Sawdust took her seat, Judge Garwin thanked both legal teams and said to the jurors, "Ladies and gentlemen, the case is now yours. Do your job and do it timely. The instructions for you will be handed to you in the jury room. Wish all of you well in your deliberations."

The jurors deliberated for two hours, then went to lunch. After lunch Cooper "Smallman" Tommie stood up said, "We were here for two hours before going out to lunch. Based on the various arguments, there is no doubt that Simon Sarpley accepted Jesus Christ at an early age. The question before us is, whether he did what a Christian ought to do." "I have a plan that would cut our stay here in half if we all were willing to try it," Prince Torwah said. "Did everyone believe that Mr. Sarpley was a Christian?" Eight hands went up. After going over the fruits of the Spirit in Galatians 5.22-26, do you believe that Mr. Sarpley exhibited these evidences?" No hands went up. It was unanimous.

Mr. Tommie took over the rest of the deliberations. "We will now take the final vote so we can get out of here. All those who believe that Mr. Simon Sarplay is not guilty as charged, raise your right hands." All eight right hands went up. "Not guilty as charged," Mr. Tommie said. The jurors returned to their seats and became quiet.

Mr. Tommie stood up and said to Judge Garwin, "Your Judgeship we the men and women of the jury have reached a unanimous verdict." He handed the verdict to the Bailiff, and he gave it to Judge Garwin. It read, **"We the honorable men and women of the jury found the defendant, Mr. Simon Sarpley not guilty as charged."** The court became dead still as everyone began to exit the courtroom one by one after His Honorable Judge Garwin and the jurors had left.

Following the verdict, Simon Sarpley resigned his position as the Station Director of the mission station. He left for Zorzor City in search of the love of his life, Miss Winifred McCoy. The mission station was happily turned over to Paul and Jackie Sanderson to run. Lord, the missionaries were overwhelmed with joy and gladness.

Judge Brownkai Garwin returned home to preside over Criminal Court F as the usual "Criminal Disgracer." DA Jake Cassell was reassigned as a DA in Yekepa in a magistrate court. Miss Currie Sawdust was later elected as a superior court judge in Monrovia, the nation's capital. She severed her tie with Drinkwater Law Firm following her election to the highest court. The Drinkwater brothers, Adamson and Jeremy Drinkwater took full control of the law firm, and changed its name to Drinkwater and Drinkwater Law Group.

Miss Venacious Duzer returned home to help her parents. She later married Saturday Deesee and they had four boys. And she kept on dancing as usual.

ONCE UPON THE TIME IN LIBERIA, a young and brilliant Director of a mission station was arrested and charged to prove his guilt beyond all reasonable doubts as a Christian. But he failed because in the eyes of the jurors of his day, he did not live a life of the Jesus Christ he proclaimed and professed. *He was found not guilty as charged.*

CHAPTER 4

THE DAY TONY SAID DIED ON THE FOOTBALL FIELD

"There is only a one-time warning for an ear that will heed advice."
Meaning: You only warn an obedience child once, and he or she will listen.

"Hey Nell, pass the ball, man. You like to hug the football. Football is not one man's game, and you know that!" Tony shouted to his cousin. This was the first week of December, and the boys of Yiplay were practicing hard for the Christmas Day game. This year's game featured Beipea against Tony's hometown of Yiplay. The rivalry between these two towns went way back, at least three generations before Tony was born.

Today, the practice lasted at least two hours. There was no referee so the practice went on until it was pitch dark. They quit because they could not see the football anymore. It was the usual practice; eleven men against eleven men, and the winner was the side that scored the most goals. In those days, Yiplay did not have a coach. In fact, no town had one. Boys from the various towns and villages who had gone to other schools throughout the country came back home for Christmas and led practices. Even the high school dropouts who were in Monrovia roaming the streets, or rubber plantations came home for Christmas. Lord, towns and villages were packed with men and women who had never been home for months, perhaps years.

Tony could still recall the day football as he knew it changed forever in the district with the arrival of two men; Jake Frog and Mahmoud. No one knew the second or last name of the latter man. Both were older men, probably in their early forties. No one knew where, and how they came, and to this day, no one knows how they left and where they went.

They were so good that the cheerleaders in the district made up a song with their names. Lord, do not ask what was the song? The words were so complicated in the local dialect to the point that only the cheerleaders would sing it perfectly. They made it up so they knew how to sing it. In the days of the diamond rush in the district, many men (just like Jake and Mahmoud), and women came in search of fortunes. And when they found them, they vanished mysteriously just as they had come.

Jake played the central defense position and Mahmoud played the left or right forward position. Tony recalled when Yiplay played Zalestown when Jake and Mahmoud had just arrived in Zalestown. Yiplay did not know that Zalestown had secret weapons in their arsenal in the persons of Jake and Mahmoud. It was a horrible game that Yiplay had tried so hard to forget. Zalestown defeated Yiplay seven goals to one. Mahmoud would receive the ball in the midfield and dribble the entire team from Yiplay, including the goalkeeper. Lord, in those days, it was a disgrace for anyone to dribble a team's goalkeeper. That was by far worse than *dirtying another player's news.*

Yiplay could not get any closer than fifteen yards from Zalestown's goalposts. Yiplay's single goal was deliberately or intentionally allowed by the goalkeeper and Jake for Yiplay players to save faces. Yiplay boys and girls came rejoicing, but they left in disgrace, totally despondent. Yiplay was accompanied by their powerful football medicine man, Dre Zogo, but he was powerless to stop the influx of goals from Mahmoud. He alone scored five goals. In the end, Mr. Zogo blamed it on Yiplay players. They should not had stepped in the creek near Zalestown before arrival. That violation had caused the voodoo not to work on Mahmoud.

Yiplay players returned home one by one so the town's folks would not know that they were defeated. But that was a wishful thinking. Some of the men who accompanied Yiplay players had already returned and told the horrible news about their home team.

As the years went by, and the two men became known in the district. They were known as "football "**whorepoejoe**." In other words, they would play for any town or team that got to them first. So, it was not unusual to see Jake Frog and Mahmoud played for Zalestown against Yiplay, and then the following day played for Kpatown against Zalestown. It did not matter where they resided. It caught up with them one day when Zalestown played against Doantown. Though they were temporarily residing in Zalestown, the men went to visit some friends in Doantown. When the people of Doantown saw their skills, they immediately asked Jake and Mahmoud to play for them against Zalestown. And they gladly accepted to play against their hosts.

Midway through the second half, when Mahmoud scored the first goal against Zalestown, fights broke out. Mahmoud was chased by the men of Zalestown around the field until he ran into the bushes. And that was the end of the game. And that was how he and Jake left Zalestown forever, never to return.

In those days, there were no police officers in towns and villages like Zalestown or Yiplay. Lord, no one was held accountant for anything done on the football field; beatings, rioting, or injuries. And when a fight broke out, the men on the field playing would stop the play, and say, "You all leave them, let them do it." Lord, lazy men did not pick fights on football field.

Tony grew up in Yiplay and watched grownup men fight each on the field. Towns and villages also fought against each other during football games. Tony was always told by his older brother Obe Said to stay home and not accompany them when they went to play. When fighting broke out, the fastest men saved themselves from severe beatings and crippling injuries. At that time, Obe Said was the goalkeeper for Yiplay. But Tony was never afraid. His passion and love for the game of football grew and he became one of the standout players in Yiplay.

One thing though, he was afraid to fight on the football field. He avoided that at all cost. When he was fouled, he complained to the referee. He knew how and where to pick his fights.

When Tony was thirteen years old, he went out hunting with cousin Leviticus Gaye. They were hunting lizards with rubber slingshots. Leviticus tried to shoot a lizard on a kola tree and missed. The stone from the slingshot hit Tony in the head and he began to bleed. Leviticus ran as fast as he would go with Tony in pursue. Leviticus ran into the arms of his grandfather Sahngbey.

When Tony arrived and explained what had happened, Grandpa Sahngbey was mad because Leviticus had run away from a fight. Anyway, Tony left after Grandpa Sahngbey begged him. Later on, that evening, rumors spread that Leviticus had run away from a fight with Tony. Lord, Leviticus and Tony were second cousins. How could they fight each other publicly without being ridiculed by the town's folks? Their mothers would have also punished them for fighting. Back then, family did not fight each other, except a husband and his wife.

In Yiplay, husbands and wives fought all the time. In a case where the wife was stronger than the husband, the football field rule was invoked; "You all leave them, let them do it." A husband beaten by his wife never picked a fight with her or with anybody for the rest of his life. If a man got dropped by his wife, another man would never attempt to pick a fight with him.

One day at home during practice, Tony was forced to fight a kid who was always bullying him on the field. Tony was only five feet and six inches tall, and weighed less than 150 pounds. But he would dribble any man on the face of this earth if he got the ball first.

Every time Peter Gunday came at him, Tony would **dirty his news**. He got upset because everyone laughed. He turned around and deliberately kicked Tony in the rear. A fight broke out between both men. Everyone followed the rule, stop the practice, "You all leave them, let them do it." Tony did not only play, but he could also fight. Every time Peter Gunday threw a punch at him, he would dodge and nail him on his chin or his face.

When they finally stopped, Peter Gunday had so much swelling on his face that he and Tony became best of friends. Lord, that was the rationale behind "You all leave them, let them do it." When a bully got beaten, he would never pick another fight for the rest of his bullying days. He would become friends with the boy who beat him up.

Hunting was part of Tony's childhood. Oldman Said had hunting dogs. After school Tony and some of the boys of Yiplay would go hunting for squirrels, opossums, chipmunks, groundhogs, deer or birds. It was fun when Tony's teacher would abruptly shut down the school and join the hunting party if the hunting was closer to town and the animal being hunted entered the school campus. Imagine fifty to sixty kids chasing one groundhog around with a pack of dogs. Lord, who got what piece when the animal was killed? Please do not ask!

Tony was the middle child of three children born unto the union of Oldman Said and Mrs. Mordea Said. He had an older brother and a younger sister. Tony was born premature. And when the empirical or traditional midwives decided to bury him alive, his maternal grandmother, **Oldma** Nan Kongor Menwood told the midwives, "Give him to me. He is my grandson. I will take care of him." The midwives handed Tony quietly to his grandmother without the four chanting calls traditionally associated with the birth of a male child. A female child got three chanting calls.

Grandma Nan Kongor did so well caring for Tony until he grew up and became a man. When one looked at Tony, he or she could tell that Tony was a special fragile child. His skin was real light and it peeled easily. His hairs were nappy. He would bruise easily on his head if and when he bumped into an object.

Tony had one uncle and two aunts. Like Tony's mother, Aunt Leah and Aunt Yarwoan were given into marriages in Yiplay. Aunt Leah was given to Chief Koon of Yiplay as his wife. Aunt Yarwoan married Oldman Whimp, a cousin of Oldman Said. In those days, parents gave their daughters into arranged marriages. It did not matter if the groom was much older than the bride.

If he had the bride's price or dowry ($140.00), and expressed the desire to the parents, he would be given the daughter as his bride.

Tony's Uncle Bullbear Menwood was a traveler. He traveled to Firestone, Monrovia and various rubber plantations on the west coast of the country. He believed in voodoo.

He always believed that there were witches after him to take his life and money. He wore all kinds of charms around his waist, neck, ankles and wrists, and made strange sacrifices daily to his unknown gods. Many people in Yiplay were afraid of him. It was rumored that Uncle Menwood was a voodoo priest and used other people's children as sacrifices to appease his voodoo gods. He died before his three sisters and his parents, barely forty years old. He left behind three wives and two sons. Lord, a complicated and brittle family, but one would not dare to call them cursed or jinxed.

Uncle Menwood's parents also died years later. Unlike their children, Oldman Menwood and Nan Kongor Menwood died in their good old ages. *Oldman* Menwood was an unusual man. He would laugh when something terrible such as a death, an injury, or a disaster occurred in another family. He was sad when others rejoiced. *Oldma* Nan Kongor Menwood was a tiny woman with a pretty smile. She was dark in complexion with lots of hairs. She wore nothing on her feet until her death. Except for Aunt Yarwoan, three of their children predeceased them.

Aunt Leah, the chief's wife also died early before her parents. She did not have children. Aunt Yarwoan Whimp and her husband had five children. Lord, the children had some of the funniest names in Yiplay. No parents would dare to name a girl "Shorty," or "Dwarf," but they did.

Oldman Said had four wives. His beloved wife was Mordea Said, Tony's mother. She died when Tony was a teenager. The family was heartbroken. Oldman Said would not take care of three children and work on his farm at the same time. The oldest wife, Sisaw Said had four children, the next older wife, Mengor Said had a girl, and the youngest wife Monday Yongor Said had a boy. There were terrible sibling rivalries within the family that nearly tore them apart. Lord, it was almost like Jacob's family (Joseph and his brothers) in the Bible.

The oldest son left home and did not return until the death of his parents. Mother Sisaw Said died before her husband. Then, all her children also died. Then, Mengor Said divorced Oldman Said before his death and went to her hometown. She left her daughter behind. She was an epileptic who was treated cruelly by Tony all her life until her death. He would beat her all day for no reason. She was misunderstood because of her illness.

In the early 1970's when record players and Kenya vinyl albums or music reigned supreme, Tony returned home from Monrovia with one of those to the delight of Yiplay and the surrounding towns and villages. Following a football game, he would stage a dance concert all night. He would go around the various towns and villages staging dance concerts.

Back then, the man with a record player with Kenyan Music, got all the girls. Yes, even boys from Yiplay who accompanied Tony on those weekends got girls because of him. Lord, every boy in Yiplay wanted to be a friend of Tony, and every girl wanted to sleep with Tony Said. Lord, the boy did not care. He slept with some of the ugliest girls and women in his days. Some were old enough to be his mother, and others were two or three feet taller than he was.

Tony, his older brother, younger sister and the son of the youngest wife were the only ones left within the family. They had to provide for Monday Yongor Said, the mother of their half-brother. There is no such a thing as a half relationship in the Liberian society. Children born out of wedlock are still considered brothers and sisters with no "half" attached to them.

Tony was the favorite child. His mother, father and even his step-mother loved him more than all the children. He was the only one in the family who completed high school and became a teacher in one of the big city's private schools. He became the breadwinner of the family. He took care of everyone, including his wife, five children and his legally blind step-mother. She did not fully recover her vision following a bilateral cataract operation.

The odds were stacked against Tony, but he failed to live wisely. He was born a premature baby. His mother died young of an unknown disease. His father died following a massive stroke. All his siblings from his oldest step-mother also died of heart failure or stroke. Yet, Tony became an active cigarette smoker and drinker of **Cane Juice** in his late thirties. By age forty, he had graduated to marijuana. Again, the odds kept stacking up against him. He had five growing children to feed, including his wife and step-mother. As a teacher, he had to develop lesson plans and teach.

One day at football practice, a goalkeeper fell on Tony's right leg and broke it. He had beaten the central defender and attempted to score a goal. Lord, the boy was a football wizard. He would handle the football like a clown juggling at a circus. The injury sidelined Tony for several months. At middle age, he would had retired, but his love and passion for the game were greater than the desire to retire. An aging and wise footballer would hang up his jersey and boots following a terrible injury. But that was not Tony Said. He was treated by a traditional bone specialist. Within three months, Tony was back on the football field, even better than before the injury. Football was his life, and football would one day take his life away from him. When Tony was in his late fifties, he was still actively playing football.

When the Liberian Civil War broke out Christmas Eve of 1989, Tony became a commander in Yiplay. That called for heavy drinking, smoking and womanizing. Lord, Tony had so many girls he could not even count them, though he was married with children. Lord, some Liberian women would tolerate that for the sake of their children.

Many commandos brought home wives from warfronts. Tony was one of the commandos. He brought a woman, though his wife and kids were home. His wife did not mind or care. Yes, it was part of her culture and upbringing. Her own father had two wives. And she married into a family where the husband's father had four wives, not counting concubines and insignificant others. Lord, breakups must be good medicines to some relationships. Without breakups, Tony would have been in a lot of troubles with many women.

In spite of the history of Tony's fragile childhood, he was strong as a player. He led other boys in Yiplay. They depended on him to win every game Yiplay played. Of course, there were both younger and older boys who played alongside him, and they were good, too. Cousin Nell Young, Fazzah Wonpoe, C.Q. Mao, Fred Quigley, Pete Wantoe and others were his teammates in Yiplay.

Many of these men left football, except for Pete Wantoe. He died from Meningitis when he was just seventeen years old.

At Wisdom High School in the big city, Tony became the Vice Principal of the school. The position came with influence and possibility of more girlfriends. Lord, a welcome addition for Tony. The man did not sleep alone when his wife was out of town on business. Mrs. Marian Said would go back home to visit her parents, or go to the big city to sell her produce and used clothes.

In the late 1970's, Tony and the Yiplay boys went to the borders of Liberia and Cote D'Ivoire and began playing various towns and villages along the borders coming all the way down to Yiplay. They would walk several miles, stop in one town, play and, then leave for another town. By the time they arrived back in Yiplay, they had played five games in ten days. They won three games and drew two. The sixth game with Lehglay **ended in confusion**. Yiplay boys scored a goal first, and, then the referee from Lehglay started to cheat. Tony and the boys walked off the field due to bad officiating by the referee.

Every town they played, Tony and the boys were so confident that they asked the host team to pick a referee from the town. They saw cheating or poor officiating, but the referee in Lehglay topped them all. This town was notorious for fighting on the football field, so Yiplay boys did not want to take any chances. When Tony and the boys played in Sandtown, he got a girl, even as a stranger in another town. Lord, the boy was pretty good to the point that girls practically threw themselves at him after a game.

In those days, Tony and the boys thought they were invincible. They were in good physical conditions because they trained at all times. They did not visit doctors or the nearest clinic. Their parents did not have the money to take them to the clinic to see a doctor. The boys who were brave stuck around and got vaccinated against Polio, Measles, Smallpox or Whooping Cough. Those who got sick with Whooping Cough were treated with boiled toad frog. After cooking it, the skin was removed and the toad frog was eaten. It worked like magic. One time, Tony was sick with Whooping Cough and had to eat a skinless boiled toad frog. He said it tasted like real edible frog and it was delicious.

To Tony, hunting was an adventure to be had. On a Saturday, he and his friends, accompanied by Oldman Said's pack of hunting dogs, would hunt all day. They would return home with fifteen to twenty squirrels, five opossums and seven chipmunks. Depending on the number of boys on the hunt, everything would be divided equally. If there were more boys than animals, the boys would stay in the town and cook a large pot of hot pepper soup. Everyone would be eating, sneezing, and sniffing at the same time. Lord, the rice was never properly cooked, but the boys enjoyed it anyway.

When Pete Wantoe, one of the boys died, Tony and the other boys were out hunting. They came running to town when they heard people crying in the town. It was a dark day for the boys of Yiplay. The town stood still for a day, except the mourners. A young man so brilliant and full of life was taken away suddenly by the cold hands of death! Tony and the boys had to watch his lifeless body being bathed and wrapped in a white sheet. Tony and the boys had to escort Pete's coffin to his grave. The day Pete was buried; no one left Yiplay to go anywhere. Tony and the boys wore their football jerseys and sang, "Never Disappointed One Day Since I joined the Army of the Lord."

For the first time in Tony's life, he realized that, even with all his football skills, he was on borrowed time. It could had been him who was being led to his grave. The death of Pete was painful, and his memories left Tony and his friends with many unanswered questions about life and death. Why did Pete die so young? What killed him, witchcraft or voodoo? If yes, who was responsible? What happened when people died? Is it true that the dead are with us, and others with special power can see them regularly carrying out their usual activities they were involved in prior to their deaths? Why did a grave cave in several weeks after burial? Was it true that the grave caved in because the dead person rose up and left the grave? Back then in Yiplay, concretes were never laid on graves.

C.Q. Mao, a cousin of Pete claimed one day that he saw Pete while he was on his way to his parents' farm. Pete too was going to his parents' farm. That had caused fear and panic among the boys. Pete was a very close friend. What if C.Q. actually saw Pete Wantoe? Tony and the boys had to suspend hunting for a while for fear of running into Pete Wantoe while hunting. Lord, those were scary days for Tony and his friends.

Meanwhile, Tony's cousin Leviticus Gaye had a girlfriend from one of the surrounding towns. Martina Jensen was a beautiful young girl with pretty smile and a nice gap in her upper teeth. She always wanted to be with Leviticus, but he had to be away at school. He promised to return home when school was out. That he did on Easter, midyear and Christmas vacations.

The one Easter Vacation he did not come, Leviticus lost Martina. Tony was sleeping with her, though they [Matina and Tony] were distant cousins. Tony did that a lot, stealing friends' girlfriends. No one blamed Tony. He was not particularly handsome, but he had scandalous ways of persuading girls. He told Martina that Leviticus did not want her anymore. He was busy with school and did not have time for a girl. Martina did not wait to hear from Leviticus himself before making her decision. She believed Tony. That was Tony all right, at his best. He even slept with closed cousins and distant nieces.

One year, Tony got the run for his money when it came to girlfriends. Chief Koon's long-lost son showed up. His father found and brought him home to Yiplay. The man was light in complexion and stood five feet and eight inches tall with an Afro hairdo. All the girls in Yiplay wanted a piece of Frank Koon, except those who were related to the chief. Frank Koon took every boy's girl away, including Tony's. When it came to stealing other boys' girls, Tony was no match for Frank Koon. Tony would have fought another boy for taking his girl, but not Frank. Frank was bigger and stronger than Tony. Unfortunately, Frank's luck finally ran out when he became a thief and a petty criminal. Chief Koon was a no-nonsense man who took pride in his position in the town and would not stand by a son who was a criminal. After several brushes with the law, Frank Koon disappeared. No one knew where he went until the death of Chief Koon several years later.

It was on a Saturday, three weeks before the Christmas Day. Practice began as usual; eleven men against eleven men, and the winner scored the most goals. This was a practice for the Christmas Day game. That year Christmas Day fell on Sunday. Perfect, just perfect! That meant everyone in Yiplay would stay in the town to watch the game. Many girls would come, too from the surrounding towns to the dlight of tony.

All day Tony had been smoking cigarettes and drinking *Cane Juice* before practice. He was in a good mood as usual when he drank. Midway through the practice, Tony collapsed in the middle of the field and could not breathe. None of the boys knew Cardio Pulmonary Resuscitation (CPR), or they would had helped to save his life.

Cousin Nell's younger brother ran to town to get help. He was crying as he ran, and people could not understand him because he was out of breath. Many of the older men of the town ran back to the football field with him. It was too late to help. Tony Said was dead.

If there was any day that the people of Yiplay would wish the ground had opened and swallowed the town, it was that day. It was tragic beyond grief. Residents of Yiplay were shocked! The best player they birthed and raised from premature birth laid dead in the center of the field. Lord, there was no word to describe the atmosphere. He was not only the best player, but he was also the Vice Principal of Wisdom High School in the big city. The town folks were proud of him. And his last surviving siblings, Obe Said, Cornelius Said and Selena Said-Noah were proud of him, too.

His wife Marian and their kids were devastated. How could she explain it to the children that their father fought and survived the Liberian Civil War, but died on the football field? Will his two boys ever be brave to play football? Or will they stay away from it, somehow believing that football killed their father? Their mother would probably impress the fear of football upon them on a daily basis.

Now came the daunting question. Who was responsible for the death of Tony, especially on the football field? He was not a stranger to football. He had played this sport all his life until he was over fifty years old. Somebody, somewhere put a voodoo curse on him. This is the first of its kind in Yiplay and the surrounding towns and villages, and perhaps in Liberia.

In Yiplay no one died from diseases. The town's folks always claimed that those who died were killed in animals. In other words, they turned into raccoons, deer, antelopes, elephants or buffalos and were killed by hunters. Before Tony's burial people were pointing their fingers at J.G. Glow, a cousin of Tony who had a land dispute with him. The shock of Tony's death gave way to anger directed at J.G. Glow. He wanted Tony off the land, so he killed him on the football field with witchcraft.

The day Tony died on the football field, J.G. Glow was out of town, yet he was accused of Tony's death. Shortly after Tony's death, J.G. Glow also died. No one actually pointed finger at anybody because everyone believed that Tony came back and took J.G. Glow with him, so he too could experience how painful death was.

The day Tony was buried, Yiplay stood still just like the day Pete Wantoe died and was buried. The football team stayed up all night during the wake, singing and dancing. The next day, the team accompanied Tony to his grave on the football field where his life ended. Friends, former teammates and schoolmates from surrounding towns and villages also came to pay their last respects. The entire town escorted him to the ball field to say their final goodbyes. This was where the greatest football wizard of Yiplay took his last breath. Yes, Tony the boy who would dribble any man on the face of this earth if he got the ball first would lie there forever. And his mesmerizing displays of football skills and the memories of stunning goals scored on this football field would live on forever, too.

It was not easy saying goodbye to Pete Wantoe. It was even more difficult saying goodbye to a man like Tony Said. Lord, how would the men of his generation come up with words to do that? It was impossible to say goodbye to a man like Tony Said. The man who did everything unimaginable for a boy born and raised in a small rural town. He was born premature and nursed back to life by a grandmother. He danced, womanized, drank, and smoked both Marlboro and marijuana. He eventually became a father and a husband of one wife; became the best football player among the men of his generation in his hometown; got education when no one in his family dared to; taught other kids how to read and write, and finally became an administrator. They all felt a vacuum that this town had never felt before.

The man woke up Saturday morning. The town folks saw him playing with his kids in his yard. But within eight hours Tony was dead, gone forever. Football as Yiplay knew it changed forever with the passing of Tony Said. Lord, the football wizard of Yiplay was gone! To this day, Yiplay keeps asking the Creator this daunting question, "Will there ever be another Tony M. Said to be born or to rise up in Yiplay?"

Footballers from towns and villages around Yiplay also came to say their final goodbyes. They too, would remember Tony Said forever. He played for their teams when they **borrowed** him on numerous occasions. For the sake of girls, Tony would play for any team, town or village.

In Yiplay death is celebrated in many ways. Tony's death was no exception. After four days, a feast was held in his memory. Obe Said, the older brother came back home to take care of the family. His brother Cornelius also came back to help. Tony's death was celebrated for several days thereafter.

A celebration of the dead for a deceased male family member centered on his life's accomplishments, events and activities he was known for while alive. If he were a noted farmer, other men who are also noted farmers will gather to portray his skills and talents. If he were a known singer or dancer, other singers and dancers from other towns and villages would be invited to come to sing and dance. Depending on the wishes of the family, this may last several days or weeks.

Yiplay had several football games to mark Tony's death. These games were simply exhibitions and nothing serious, but to remember Yiplay's greatest player to ever touch the leather.

The primary goal or objective of death's celebration was that as time passed with the celebration, healing would take place. Celebration would take the family's focus away from their pain and grief due to the loss of the loved one. It is fascinating to note that the literal interpretation of the celebration of the dead is "driving death far away."

So, Tony Said's death was driven far away. But his grave remains a permanent landmark on Yiplay ballfield. Though his grave had no marble headstone or special marking, residents of Yiplay know where Tony Said lies. No one enters the football field without first seeing his grave, just right to the entrance. And during a football game, the residents would call on the spirit of Tony Said to come and take control over the game and grant them victory.

Shortly after Tony's death and burial, his step-mother Monday Yongor Said died. Another sad day in the family. Years after her death, Selena Said-Noah's husband, Mr. Jacob Noah also died following a protracted illness. He was highly educated just as Tony. Lord, the man was a college graduate, for Christ's sake!

He was one of the most educated residents of Yiplay. He left behind a wife and five children. Lord, if heaven would open for families to ask the Creator a question, the Said Family would be the first in line.

ONCE UPON THE TIME IN LIBERIA, Tony Said, a little-known kid born prematurely unto an impoverished family in a small town in northeastern Liberia survived against all odds to become one of the best football players in his hometown, and perhaps the entire district. His skills surpassed men of his generation in Yiplay. He went on to become the Vice Principal of a local high school.

On one infamy December day in Yiplay, he met his untimely death on the same ballfield where he dazzled fans and disgraced many goalkeepers for several decades. May the soul of Tony M. Said rest in peace. His memory remains in Yiplay forever.

CHAPTER 5

THE MEN OF THE MIANTOWN MAGNIFICENT NINE

"The kwi (a law enforcement officer) who arrests you has a kwi
that can also arrest him." Meaning: No matter how powerful
a person may be in his or her position,
there is another person who may be more powerful than he or she is."

"Who is the commander in this town, and where is he?" The fearsome rebel commando inquired from the town folks. The town folks feared for their lives, so they pointed to Johannes Nunn. He was immediately arrested and duck-tied; the rebels called it tie-bay. He sat in the one hundred twenty degrees heat all day waiting to have his throat cut like a lamb.

Miantown was a small farming town approximately thirty miles from the Ivorian border. Residents were predominantly farmers who survived by horticultural farming. Annually, farmers planted rice, cassava, corns, sweet potatoes and varieties of green leafy vegetables. The farming season lasted from March to November each year. Those farmers who planted first were done with harvesting their crops by mid-November. The late ones kept harvesting until Christmas.

The origin and history of Miantown were as strange as the events that took place in the town. It was best told by Miantown Historian, Oldman White Bear. He was the oldest man to ever live in Miantown. He lived to be 113 years before he died. Oldman White Bear was so old that he told stories of World War I & II. He told a story of World I in which Miantown Warriors marched against a town called Sugarville five miles northeast and captured it. In the decisive battle, Miantown captured a male Caucasian Commander (probably an albino) who was leading Sugarville. He was killed and eaten, and that was the end of the war between both towns to this day. And when he was in good mood after drinking a cup of palm wine, he narrated stories about World War II. He always referred to it as the Hitler's War.

According to him, a group of migrants came from the Cote D'Ivoire (formerly the Ivory Coast) came and resettled there. They were led by a man called Tutu Mian for whom the town is named. He became the first chief of the town before others migrated and joined them. He had several wives. Lord, his wives were too many to count.

Meanwhile, one of the men of the town was sleeping with one of the chief's wives. The man who was having an affair with Chief Mian's wife was a traditional masked dancer. While the chief was away, the lappas (West African fabrics) he had purchased for this particular wife, she had taken and given them to the followers of the masked dancer. They had used the lappas to dress him up for dancing on that day. When the chief returned to town, he saw the masked dancer dancing in the lappas he had purchased for his wife. He called his wife from the dance and inquired about the lappas on the masked dancer. Lord, she admitted to the disbelief of Chief Tutu Mian. The chief took his machete and went to the dance. While the masked dancer was dancing and spinning, Chief Mian cut off the masked dancer's left arm with his machete. Lord, blood was all over the place! The masked dancer ran into the bushes and was never found to this day. Thereafter, Chief Tutu Mian issued a decree that no masked dancer would set feet on the grounds of Miantown as long as the town existed whether a short one, or a long one.

Chief Tutu Mian was a generous and compassionate man. He shared his meals and wealth, but not his wives. His wives were off limit to all men of Miantown, including his own children. Residents who were unwilling to share their meals and wealth with their neighbors were expelled or kicked out. They left and resettled in a town called Bonaville three miles away.

One day a long-masked dancer called "Long Devil," was invited to town to perform. There had been no visible and recorded diabolical or devilish acts attributed or associated with him. He was given that name because his followers claimed that all women, including his wife did not know his identity. Uncircumcised males were also forbidden from knowing his identity. When he was being dressed, only his closed followers and circumcised elders of the town were permitted into the camp. The dancer was also forbidden to make his identity known to his own wife though somehow, she knew because he was the only man missing in the town when "Long Devil" came to dance.

Some diehard liberals and skeptics of Miantown defiled the longstanding decree and invited Mr. "Long Devil" to dance. He came and danced for fifteen minutes and had to be hurriedly taken away because he developed an acute diarrhea. The last thing the diehards, skeptics and the town needed on their hands was a "Long Devil" with diarrhea. Lord, who would dare to get him down, undress him before he would use the toilet? And when he left, he vowed thereafter never to return to Miantown.

Miantown also had a fertility tree called Tutoah that was fed annually at a special festival organized by the residents of the town after the harvest season. It was believed in Miantown that no woman ever remained childless in the town. Seasonally when Tutoah was fed, women from all over the district and from neighboring Cote D'Ivoire and Guinea, West Africa came to carry pieces of the tree. Women who wanted to get pregnant and have children would take little branches of the tree and tie them behind their backs. They would leave without looking behind until they reach their homes (for fear of the curse of Lot's wife, though they did not admit). And when they entered, they would then, take off the branches and lay them on the mud beds and covered them up with blankets or sheets. Within seven days, they would become pregnant. It was believed that a woman who went through the ritual without getting pregnant had more than an infertility problem. She probably sold her womb to a voodoo priest or priestess.

Harvest season was the best time to be alive in Miantown. A chief harvester by the name of Harvest King Walkerson, was a delight to all farmers harvesting rice. He and his followers, including men and women would be asked to help with harvesting. It was a sight to behold! King Walkerson with a white furry headdress would be shaking his head and dancing as he cut the rice into bundles. His followers would be right behind him collecting the bundles of rice. Lord, he and his followers would harvest an entire rice farm in a single day. At the end of the day, his followers would return to town, and danced way into the night or until the wee hours of the morning. And the Miantown Magnificent Nine (MMN) were always part of every celebration in the town

After the harvest season, no one left town, especially if the chief had a visitor or visitors. The epitome of it all was if the visitors were singers, dancers or special performers. Lord, many visiting singers and dancers came through Miantown in those days. It seemed as if Miantown was on their radar screen or map. One day after the harvest season, three men from the Kpelle ethnic group took Miantown by stormed with their shakers and singing. For three weeks, the young and old people of the town did not sleep. They joined the men and danced day and night for seven days. On the seventh day, the singers made up a song with the name of the chief. When they started to sing, the entire town went crazy because a song had been written and dedicated exclusively to their chief. Lord, if the singers had not begged the chief to leave, they would had become citizens of Miantown. In a matter of days, the men had girlfriends.

The Magnificent Nine were Miantown born and Miantown bred. Their wives and children were also Miantown born and Miantown bred. Every citizen knew the Magnificent Nine. They too knew every citizen of Miantown, from the least to the greatest. They were men that Miantown turned to in time of crisis. When a farmer was struggling because he did not start early before the rains came, the Magnificent Nine rose up to the occasion and helped the farmer to complete his farming. When death occurred, they became grave diggers. When there was a fight, whether between two men, or between a husband and his wife, the Magnificent Nine stepped in to bring about peace. Of course, they too had bad days and fought each other, especially the younger ones. In that case the older ones would step in to settle the matter and bring about peace.

One day during the Dry Season, two strangers came and went through Miantown without saying a word or greeting anyone. Lord, in those days, no strangers went through the town without greeting somebody, whether a child or an adult. Such a conduct or behavior was thoroughly investigated and reasons established why the stranger did not greet the Miantown folks.

When the men entered the town, two women attempted to greet them in their local dialect, but the men did not understand the local dialect, so they did not answer the women. The women ran to town and informed the chief that two strangers had just gone through the town without greeting anyone.

The chief immediately assembled the Magnificent Nine and other men of the town. Words were sent out by runners to farms to alert every citizen of Miantown in the bushes to return home. Words were even sent to surrounding towns and villages to be on the lookout for two strange men.

Miantown Magnificent Nine sprang into actions. They grabbed their single-barrel shotguns, muskets and their bows and arrows. Within two hours, the two men were brought back to town. Everyone citizen of Miantown assembled before the chief's compound to take a look at the strangers. One was slim and cleaned shaven. He wore a white round hat made out of cloth. He stood almost six feet tall. He also wore a blue gown commonly worn by Muslims in Liberia. He appeared to be the older of the two men. The younger man was shorter, dark, medium built, and about five feet and four inches tall. He, too was cleaned shaven, and wore a light brown gown, but no hat.

Both men were asked to sit down. They took their seats and were given cold water to drink. Lord, no one mistreated a stranger in Miantown. They were then interrogated through an interpreter about where they were heading and why they refused to answer when two women from the town greeted them. After thorough interrogation, it was revealed that the men were of the Mendi Tribe, one of the sixteen ethnic groups in the country. They did not answer because they did not understand the women. They had come to the diamond rush and were on their way to Doantown seven miles away.

The chief of Miantown extended an apology to the men on behalf of the town for the inconvenient caused to them by the town folks. They were fed and later escorted by the Magnificent Nine as an assurance that no one would harass them on their journey. It was getting dark, the two men had seven miles to walk to Doantown.

Back then during the diamond rush, a town such as Miantown did not take chances with strangers. The diamond rush brought thieves, petty criminals and murderers. Lord, the diamond rush brought the good, the bad and the ugly. Those who were not fortunate to find diamonds turned to thieveries, stealing cattle, livestock, and breaking into rice barns on various farms. Town folks who raised their livestock on the farms had to sleep on their farms to prevent diamond rushers from stealing them.

One day, two thieves who had come because of the diamond rush were caught by the Magnificent Nine and beaten almost to death. They stole a goat. When the men stole the goat, they killed and prepared it to be taken home for consumption. Those who had cattle in the town branded them with special marks. Each family had different marks that were peculiar only to their family. No two families had the same or identical branding marks. And in the evening when the animals came to eat dinner, they were counted to make sure none was missing.

On this particular day, when Mr. Greystone Payne's goats came to feed, one was missing; a big nanny goat that was pregnant was nowhere to be found. Mr. Payne went to the chief and reported that his pregnant nanny goat was missing. Immediately the chief summoned the town crier or announcer to cry that Mr. Payne's pregnant nanny goat was missing.

As soon as the Miantown Magnificent Nine heard the announcement, they sprang into action again. Five of them grabbed their usual weapons and went into the bushes in search of Mr. Payne's pregnant nanny goat. Four men were left behind to observe any strangers entering the town on that day. These men were skillful hunters too, and knew how to trace the blood of wounded animals, domestic and wild.

When the diamond rushers stole the goat and slaughtered it, they were sloppy in handling the blood. They spilled the blood on leaves around where they killed the animal. After killing the goat, they came to Miantown pretending to be visitors. As usual, Miantown was singing and dancing. The men joined the celebration. But they looked and smelled different. When the Magnificent Nine suspected that, they slipped away from the dance and joined their comrades in search of the location where the goat was killed. When they found it, they set an ambush.

At midnight, the diamond rushes came back with flashlights to retrieve their meat from its hiding place and head home. The Miantown Magnificent Nine jumped on the men and overpowered them. They tied their hands behind their backs and brought them to town. When they arrived at the chief's compound, the town crier went into action again to announce that the men who stole and killed Mr. Payne's pregnant nanny goat had been caught. Without inquiry into the identities of both men, the residents of Miantown gave the two men names that matched or rhymed with their crime. They called them "Nanny Goat Head-splitters." Lord, if human beings would die easily from beating, the men would had died. They were beaten until no one would see their eyes. Lord, they looked pitiful, but it was how rogues or thieves were treated in those days in Liberia. It did not matter if the thieves were citizens of Miantown. A rogue was nothing, but a rogue and deserved no sympathy or empathy.

At the crack of dawn, the men were taken to the big city and handed over to law enforcement officers. There, they were put in prison and beaten some more, this time in the market square.

The same fate that befell the diamond rushers befell two Miantown elementary school dropouts who had turned to stealing cattle in the town. One day, they stole the wrong pig; Miss Nancy Zola's pig. Lord, no one messed with Miss Zola's animals and got away with it. She was a single mother of two boys and a girl. She stood almost six feet tall and weighed over two hundred pounds. She made her farm without the help of any man. When Miss Zola got mad, Miantown was set on edge.

Words had spread around town that Andre Doe and J. Stuffbottle Gbaar were stealing chickens and frying them when the town was quiet. In the evening, Miantown would smell like fried chicken joint because the men had been frying chickens all day. During the farming season, nearly everyone went on or to the farm. And Miantown became a ghost town, except for those who were into committing petty crimes like Andre Doe and his buddy J. Stuffbottle Gbaar.

In the evening Miss Zola went to the chief and reported her pig missing. The chief told her to remain calm and silent because men of the Magnificent Nine were already working on a lead. The next day, the Magnificent Nine pretended as if they were leaving for their farms. When they had gone at least a mile from the town, they turned around and came very close to the town and hid themselves.

About ten in the morning, the two men took out the dead pig and began preparing it to be cooked. With no refrigeration, the meat was beginning to smell. Lord, men of the Miantown Magnificent Nine would also smell rotten meat miles away like bloodhounds. Andre Doe and J. Stuffbottle Gbaar were caught right-handed with the evidence in their hands. There was no way of denying the crime. Both men were tied up and given fifty lashes on their bare backs. They were also made to swim on the ground for one mile. They were also made to eat the uncooked intestines of the rotten pig. Lord, it was a disgrace for both men to be treated like that in the presence of their girlfriends. J. Stuffbottle Gbaar was one of the most popular guys in Miantown. His parents were disappointed in him, especially for dropping out of school to follow another school dropout like Andre Doe, a known petty criminal.

The men were transferred to the big city just as the diamond rushers. They too were put in prison and beaten in the market square as deterrent. When everyone saw a thief being beaten in the market square, he was ridiculed to the point of saying "no" to stealing. But for men like Andre Doe and J. Stuffbotle Gbaar, beating them in the market square did not deter them. They went on stealing and they got beaten up in the market square every time they were caught. A man can only take so much beating without developing some type of illness. Yes, Andre Doe developed a crippling bone disease that later led to his early death.

In Miantown, everyone knew each other. It was a town where everyone raised a child. Lord, in Miantown it took the entire town to raise a kid. The people of the town took pride in being each other's keepers.

Since the eruption of the war, Moe Leigh and the men of Miantown anticipated that one day they would be on the frontline, but they did not know it would be so soon. The rebels had not advanced to the middle of the country, but had turned and were marching on every town and village in and out of its path to the nation's capital, the seat of the national government. They had to recruit to replace men who had been injured or killed. It was not a voluntary recruitment. Anyone afraid to go to the battlefront did not deserve to live. He or she was shot pointblank by a designated commando.

So, the recruitment went on for several months. When Moe and the men of Miantown heard about the forced recruitment, they decided to volunteer many of their sons and daughters. Some were glad to leave home and fight, though they did not know the reasons for fighting, or know the enemies they were being recruited to fight. Some were glad because going to war meant bringing home the spoils of war home; wives, cars, bikes, household goods and money. The reluctant ones ran away and hid themselves on farms and in the bushes.

Recruitment initiation was bizarre and dramatic. An enemy soldier captured at the battlefront would be brought before the recruits and his head chopped off his shoulders with a sickle in their presence. This was a demonstration of what they would do on the battlefront. No prisoners kept for exchanges, or to be freed after the war. The recruits had to be careful not to be captured by the enemy. The same fate awaited any recruit who was captured by the enemy.

Moe Leigh and the men of Miantown decided to organize themselves into a special militia group called, "The Miantown Militias" (TMM). Moe Leigh became the commanding general with core of officers. Johannes Nunn, one of the Miantown Magnificent Nine became his deputy commander. Powder Peaye, another MMN member became the messenger. He would carry messages from Miantown to other towns and villages in case of troubles. All the men were armed with single-barrel shotguns, muskets and with bows and arrows. Powder was not armed because he had to be mobile to run as quickly as possible in case of an emergency. Lord, who ever heard of fighting modern warfare with men bearing shotguns, with muskets, and with bows and arrows?

There were shifting loyalties within the ranks of the fighters. One day they would be fighting for General Mosquito and the next day, they would be fighting for General Lysol against general Mosquito, or fighting for General Scorpion J against General Lysol. Lord, they had to assume these names to instill fears in the hearts of the populace. That they did, accompanied by bizarre headdresses and fearsome attires. Men dressed up as women and women dressed up as men. Some fighters even wore traditional masks sacredly reserved for the traditional mask dancers of the country. And some wore wedding gowns, too.

The rebels methodically marched on each town and village burning down homes, raping women and carrying some with them as bush wives and cooks. They had to eat and fight, and someone had to do the cooking, so they took many women. In fact, a song was written by one of their singers that "In times of war no man searched for girlfriends. They were readily available."

When they entered Liberia on December 24, 1989, Miantown residents and residents of other towns and villages thought they would hear and read about the war without firsthand experience. As they [civilians] went about their normal businesses, some were cut unaware, and killed as in the massacre in Miantown.

Six months into the war, terrible news reached Miantown that two of her volunteer recruits had been killed in an ambushed. Walter Pee and Yancy Neilson were killed in an ambush between Gompa and Gbarnga Cities. Those were the first two casualties from Miantown, but more would follow in the center of town within a few weeks.

TMM posted capable militia men at every entry into Miantown. Except for residents who had voluntarily gone into hiding, no one was allowed to enter or leave the town. A dust to dawn curfew was imposed on week days, and on weekends, Christians were allowed to go to church. They had to go to church and pray for the country, and the safety of their boys fighting on the fronts.

Meanwhile, on one of the farms used as hiding place, a terrible news reached the families assembled there that Nartine Gladine's only son living in North America had been killed in a firefight between two rebel groups in Gbarnga, Bong County. The man who brought the news, Mr. Danny Wonka told them that Nartine's son had entered Liberia through

Guinea, West Africa leading another rebel group he had organized in North America to overthrow General McRambo and his rebel group. Nartine passed out and almost had a heart attack. But some wise men and women within the group cautioned her that she needed to ascertain the facts about her son before she would start mourning. Mr. Wonka was a notorious story teller, worse than an Ananias Imitator. And it turned out that he was lying after he had a lot of **Cane Juice** to drink.

During the civil war, news was not hard to come by. People who went to Miantown and returned, always had news to share with those in hiding. There was news about how far the rebels had gone or how close they were to overthrowing the government. And there was news about a mysterious commando who would vanish or become airborne in the heat of the battle. Some were purported to be bulletproof who would only die by being stabbed to death.

According to Moe Leigh, the Commanding General of TMM, when the war entered the country on December 24, 1989, Miantown suddenly became a frontline town. The war had begun in Butuo at the Liberian-Ivorian border. From the onset of the war, General McRambo Forces and General Scorpio J Forces fought alongside each other. They came as a combined force to overthrow the government. They split into two groups before they would march on Miantown.

On March 12, 1990, General Scorpio J and his men forced their way into Miantown. Lord, TMM men armed with shotguns and muskets were no match for men carrying sub-machine guns and AK47 Rifles. General Scorpio J's men were accommodated and fed. The next morning, the general and his men woke up early and headed to the next town two miles away. The general and his men did not harass or mistreat anyone in the town. But troubles began when the deputy commanding officer of TMM, Mr. Johannes Nunn met with the men of General Scorpio J secretly and pledged his loyalty to them. He also pledged the loyalties of TMM and MMN men to them.

Three days later, General McRambo Forces arrived with Commanding Generals Peanut Butter Pizzarah and Hellfire Mouse. Moe Leigh was arrested and duck-tied. And they began interrogating him about the whereabouts of General Scorpio J and his men. He told General McRambo men that General Scorpio J and his men had left for the next town two miles away. While the interrogation was going on, deputy commander Johannes Nunn wrote a note and sent it by Powder Peaye informing General Scorpio J and his men that General McRambo's men were right on their heels.

When General Scorpio J received the message, he and his men set an ambush between the two towns. When General McRambo's men arrived at the site, General Scorpio J and his men opened fire with automatic weapons. Many of General McRambo's men were killed and injured. They had to retreat in the midst of the firefight. When General McRambo's men arrived back in Miantown, they branded all citizens of Miantown as collaborators. And then the massacre of the Miantown Magnificent Nine began.

Men of the Miantown Magnificent Nine came from different backgrounds and every walk of life. They were from the same town, but had special diverse skills. There were things about them that stood out. Miantown was never the same again following their deaths. Miantown changed forever, even to this day. They were ordinary men who did extraordinary deeds in their town that would live on forever. Yes, even in the end, the Miantown Magnificent Nine met other men who outmatched their audacities, hunting skills, bows and arrows, muskets, and single-barrel shut guns. As we come to a close, we meet the nine men so named; Miantown Magnificent Nine, and their deeds in Miantown.

Mr. Warsaw "Big-money" Sixty-Six, stood over six feet tall and weighed over two hundred pounds. He was the millionaire of Miantown. He had five wives and ten children. His beloved wife did not have children. A tall beautiful woman with a pretty smile. Rumors had it that Mr. Sixty-Six sold her womb to a voodoo priestess for money, and that was the reason for his wealth. He always paid men of the town to work on his wives' farms.

He was an intriguing man, always the first in Miantown to complete farming and harvesting his rice farms. He always said, "When he talked, money talked." A light skin man, who hated his wives' cooking. As long as he had breath, he cooked his own meals.

He did that three times a day. All his life, he worked as a store manager for a Lebanese merchant in the big city. The people of Miantown believed that a man who cooked for himself would grow breasts like a woman. But all those years Mr. Sixty-six cooked for himself, he never grew breasts. He was not educated, but he was no fool.

Every time he opened his mouth, people listened and learned. Of course, he sounded like an Ananias Imitator when he told some stories. There was something strange about this man. He did not have any siblings, and no one knew his parents. One day, and out of nowhere, *Kalaaa-Walaaa,* Mr. Warsaw Big-money Sixty-six came into being, and became a citizen of Miantown.

After him was Mr. Morris Kenneth, a self-styled former footballer. He was the first man to ever perform goalkeeping duty for Miantown. He was not a good one, but his size and height intimated opposing players. He was a terrible stutterer with quick temper. When he attempted to finish his statements, he fought anyone who jumped in or cut him off. He weighed over two hundred and fifty pounds, unusual for a farmer who worked on his farm throughout the year. He walked the same way he talked, fast. He was the older of two boys, and his father was one of the first chiefs of Miantown. He was married and he and his wife Annie Kenneth had one daughter. He had many halfsiblings because the chief had five wives.

Immediately following him was Mr. Robertson "Widemouth" Boom. He too was a player- goalkeeper. He did everything with his right hand, but he kicked the football with his left foot. He was a peculiar man. The funny joke on Mr. Boom in Miantown was that his mouth was so wide he looked like a young hippopotamus. When he smiled, one would think that he was crying. He had two older sisters who were married in Miantown. He was a distant cousin of Mr. Sixty-Six. When his playing days were over, he became a builder, bricklayer and a carpenter. Before tin roof came into being, he was one of the men who gathered special weeds for roofing in Miantown. He and his wife Wanda had seven children. His wife died before him due to complication from child birth. He was an elementary school dropout.

Joe Kenneth was another member of MMN. He was a nephew of Morris Kenneth. Joe Kenneth was born a comedian. He would make any man or woman laugh no matter how angry he or she was. Joe was a high school dropout who thought life was all about having fun. When he played football with others, no one was able to kick the ball. He would be cracking jokes throughout until others got tired of laughing at him and give up playing. He was single, and in his late thirties. He was the oldest of five children. His mother suffered a heart attack and died after hearing of hedr son's death. The men who killed her son were from her hometown of Siantown.

Dagon Wanderer was the older of two boys. He was born and raised on a rubber plantation twenty-five miles away. He refused to go to school as a kid. His parents did all they could, but he refused, even on the plantation. When he returned home with his parents, he became a good hunter. He alone would kill five to ten squirrels or opossums in a day. Dagon never wore a shirt unless he was going to the big city to sell his meat.

Mr. Sam Whimper was the oldest of the group. Mr. Whimper was a family man; a husband, a father, an uncle and a prominent member of Miantown elders. He served in various capacities such as a co-chief, farm brigade leader, and a messenger. He had two wives and seven children. He was always in a hurry when he walked. He was not an angry man, but he did not smile or laugh often. What made other men to laugh did not amuse him a bit.

Johannes Nunn was a people person and every kid in Miantown called him Uncle J. He was a motivational speaker though he was not educated. He was also an awesome traditional singer. He wrote many songs that he and his group sang all over the district. When his active singing days were over, he taught himself how to do circumcision and give injectable medications. He became a bag doctor or quack. He went all over the district circumcising boys.

He once played central defense position for Miantown Football Team. He smiled always. When one met Uncle J, the first thing he did was to smile. He was a compassionate man who would help anyone in trouble. He later became a marijuana grower. He sold it to those who were willing to smoke it. He never personally encouraged anyone to smoke it. He grew it on his farm for personal consumption. He had three wives, and when his cousin died, he took his wife to care for her. In spite of the many wives, he had only two children, a boy and a girl by two of his wives.

The boys of Miantown enjoyed working on Uncle J's farms. They were always anxious to go and work on his farm. He treated them nicely every time they worked for him. His daddy, Mr. Nunn was the wickedest man to ever live in Miantown. No one ate his food, including his own children. His head wife, Uncle J's mother divorced him because of his wickedness.

The eighth MMN member was Powder Peaye, the messenger. He was the first transgender man to ever be born in Miantown. He walked and talked like a woman. He never had a girlfriend. News like that would not be hidden in Miantown. Everyone knew everybody's secret. When he put on pants, he looked like a woman. The man even laughed or sang like a woman. He became the joke of the town. One thing stood out about Powder. He never let anyone down when he was asked. No matter where anyone wanted to send him, Powder would gladly go, no matter how far the distance. And he would also work for anyone who asked him. Powder only said, "First come, first served." In school, he never got beyond the first grade. He spent three amazing years in the first grade and finally quit. The man could not recite the two times table.

The ninth and final man was Mr. Gleason Zuahn. He was one of the strongest men in the district. He was reported to have had voodoo to repel bullets. In other words, he was a Big Zoe. Mr. Zuahn was a fantastic defender when he played football. No matter how hard the football was kicked, he would head-butt it away from his goal. In spite of his strength, he was nice and gentle, always joking and laughing. He was a wanderer who never settled down to raise a family. He was the second born of four men. He smoked tobacco and drank palm wine.

The following morning after the incident, the elders, and Christian leaders led by an audacious Chief Komminie Luoway of Miantown went with chickens, sheep, and kola nuts in the tradition of Liberian goodwill to appeal to General McRambo's Forces. Through the mediation of Commander Rusty Nails, McRambo's Forces agreed to leave Miantown residents alone.

Commander Rusty Nails warned his forces that killing innocent people would not be in the best interest of the revolution. "We came to save these people, and not to kill them. We need to move on to our target which is Monrovia," the general said to his forces.

McRambo's men accepted the apologies from the chief and elders of Miantown. Thereafter, Miantown volunteered many of its young men to McRambo to replace those killed when they were ambushed by General Scorpio J and his men.

One of the boys, Owusu Lawlay, worked his way up and became a tactical general to General McRambo himself. And then, six years later, he was implicated in a coup attempt against General McRambo. He and his alleged co-conspirators were captured and killed in Gompa City.

To this day, Commander Moe Leigh does not believe that his life was spared after being duck-tied for nearly six hours. He remained fearful just thinking about his ordeal. And survivors' guilty has never left him to this day.

ONCE UPON THE TIME IN LIBERIA, nine innocent fathers, uncles, nephews, cousins and friends lost their lives in a small rural farming town of Miantown after they had been branded as enemy sympathizers. The men were known as the Miantown Magnificent Nine (MMN).

CHAPTER 6

THE RESURRECTION OF MOTHER GRUKERN WEHTAY (MOTHER G)

"Why is my child's skin so hot (running a fever), and I am seeing
dead people in my dream?"
Meaning: Why am I dreaming of the dead while my child
is sick or running a fever? Or you are trying to make
progress, but someone is trying to sabotage your efforts.

It was the Dry Season when Christmas had just passed and the residents of Glayville were getting ready for the next planting season. It was the second conservative year of bad planting season because the last Raining Season did not see much rains. It was not really a drought, but it was bad enough to cause some crops failure. In those days, residents were desperate for food. They would go into the bushes for hours searching for wild cassavas and yams.

Early in the morning, Mother G got up and prepared for her usual two miles walk to her farm. Her husband, Mr. Oscar Wehtay had already gone ahead with son Karntay Wehtay to check on their traps they had set the day before. Mother G and her daughter, Teresa Wehtay would join the family later. She had to go to her neighbors to borrow three cups of rice to be repaid during the harvest season.

Soon it would be time for Karntay and his sister to go back to school. Karntay was turning sixteen next month and was a fifth grader. Teresa was nine and was a first grader. The couple loved their kids more than anything in the world. They were not educated, but they had promised to do everything to educate their children. The meager harvest from last year's farming was sold and the money used to buy uniforms for Karntay and his sister.

Teacher Canker Matson had vowed that no students would step on Glayville Elementary School grounds without uniforms unless over his dead body. That had gotten to Mr. Matt Leahdo
so bad that he had threatened to kill Teacher Matson so his son Francis Leahdo, Jr. would walk over the teacher's body to go to school. He promised to meet Teacher Matson on the football field at practice. There, no one would hold him accountable for anything. The elders of Glayville had intervened and some had volunteered to help pay for Leahdo, Jr.'s uniforms.

That day, Mother G and her family returned safely home in the evening. They had to watch out for rattlesnakes and cobras when walking in the dark on the road, especially when it was raining. Last Raining Season a neighbor's dog was bitten by a rattlesnake during a rainstorm when the family was returning home. The dog had a seizure and died on the spot. Rattlesnakes usually followed running rainwater and laid just beneath it until someone or an animal stepped on it, and then it would strike at its victim.

The Wehtay family's farm this year was smaller than last year's. They were afraid that another drought would cause the crops to fail again. This year they would plant more cassava and sweet potatoes than rice and corns. Cassava and sweet potatoes required less rain than rice and corns.

Mother G and her family were not Christians. Mr. Wehtay was the chief musician to the traditional masked dancer in Glayville. This masked dancer was exclusively a male societal thing. Women were not allowed to see him in person. When he got ready to come to town, an announcer went before him and informed all women, kids and uncircumcised males to lock themselves behind closed doors with no exceptions! Violators paid lavish fines for months, perhaps years. And a woman who saw him in person became his wife, even if she was married to another man.

The first husband and the masked dancer would become her husbands, giving priority to the masked dancer. That was acceptable in Glayville with no qualms. The men loved the masked dancer because he brought unity among the men of Glayville, and served to prevent crimes. Men of Glayville with discipline problems were sent to the masked dancer to be disciplined. Lord, he straightened them out all right. One would tell the differences in their behaviors before and after.

Mr. Oscar Wehtay was highly respected in Glayville. He was a family man, and the chief musician to the masked dancer. But there were other men who were after his position. His position was a lifelong career like a Supreme Court Judge. He would only be replaced upon his death. Of course, there were men waiting for Mr. Wehtay to die, so one of them would take his place.

Mr. Wehtay was a smart man, though he lived in Glayville where everyone had steam mill breweries to make **Cane Juice**, he did not drink **Cane Juice** or dip tobacco. He loved hunting and setting traps for small animals like groundhogs, antelopes, opossums and rats. He also built a small damp near a creek by his farm. During the Raining Season, he would catch many fish to sell in Glayville. He would sometimes exchange some of the fish for cups of rice or a bag of cassava. Though Karntay was in school, he was learning everything his father did. But, Mr. Wehtay always said to son, "I want you to go to school and know your book. I don't want you to suffer, making farms like me."

The year's end harvest was moderate. The family did not have a large farm, but they were somehow pleased with the harvest. They were able to complete their harvest in time to get ready for Christmas and New Year's Days. On these days, residents of Glayville would make big feasts to celebrate. Everyone would begin singing and dancing from Christmas' Eve until three days into the New Year. In those days in Glaville, the residents would say they were whipping the old or previous year into oblivion.

This was real old time Christmas at its best where residents celebrated as families. They did not have Christmas trees, ornaments, lights, or rein deer, but they sure had a good time.

Christmas clothes purchased at the beginning of the year were kept in a large black wooden suitcase and sprinkled with mothballs. Every now and then, one would open the suitcase and smell the mothballs. On Christmas' eve, everyone would stay up all night and take a hot bath at the break of day. Then, they would open the wooden suitcase and get dressed up. Lord, everyone smelled like mothballs. That was real oldtime mothballs Christmas in Glayville!

One year after Christmas, Mr. Whehtay accompanied the masked dancer to Danville. He was away for at least two weeks. The masked dancer in Danville had a case against one Mr. Monger Saabiah. Mr Saabiah had violated the taboo of the masked dancer when he wore a red T-shirt on the day the masked dancer came to town. Mr. Saabiah had claimed that he was innocent of the taboo because he had lived nearly thirty years on Morris' Farm down in the southwest of the country.

He did not know anything about a ban against wearing a red T-shirt when the masked dancer came to town. The masked dancer in Glayville was the chief investigator into such matter, so he was invited.

Some of the men in Danville had sided with Monger to reduce his fines. Because of the intervention of his friends, he was asked to pay seven dollars, along with a ram and five ducks. He had just returned home and had the money to pay. But Mr. Saabiah was mad about the whole matter, the unfairness of it all. How could they charge him for something he did not have the slightest idea or knowledge? He had threatened to take the masked dancer to court, but his friends had advised him that no one knew the identity of the masked dancer.

Even those who knew it, kept it as a secret to themselves. Violating the taboo was one thing, but bringing the wrath of the masked dancer on oneself was the most dreadful thing to do. Lord, he was the chief of all the medicine men in his town. No man messed with him and lived to tell the story.

Mother G was the oldest of three sisters. They had a younger brother called Duoteegbe Duotay Vayetay Vaye. He was named in the honors and memories of his maternal grandfather, Duotee Vaye and great grandfather Vayetay respectively. The family had to cover all the naming grounds on the mother side of the family. He was away working on a rubber farm in Suakoko in Bong County. Lord, if the people of Glayville had hard times calling his names, what did the people in Suakoko, Bong County do? They thought the man was not from the planet earth. Only a man from another world would have names like Duoteegbe Duotay Vayetay Vaye.

Mother G was in her early forties. She had been given into an arranged marriage by her parents to Mr. Oscar Wehtay as his wife when she was just eighteen years old. Her parents, Tiatum and Wonseh Vaye were also residents of Glayville. Mr. Vaye and his wife were in their early seventies respectively. His right eye vision was failing due to a cataract. In spite of that, he was one of the inner circle men of the masked dancer.

Mrs. Vaye was in good condition for a woman her age. She was still actively farming. She was beautiful and all her hairs were completely grey, but she still had all her teeth in her mouth. She and Mother G were almost exact replica of each other. Mother G stood two inches taller than her mother at five feet and five inches tall. Except for a few countable grays in the middle of her scalp, Mother G had beautiful dark hair. Even in her forties, she looked fabulous and went about her chores as if she were in her thirties. She, her sisters, brother and parents were closed-knit family. They would not dare to disobey their parents. So when her parents said to her, "Mr. Oscar Wehtay is your husband," she gladly accepted the offer.

Her parents were always proud of her. Among her sisters, she was the only one still married to her first husband. Her sisters Marleay and Vayelue Vaye had to divorce their husbands because of spousal abuses. Marleay was given to Sonkarely Duopue of Glayville as a wife. From the first day of the arranged wedding, Sonkarley consistently treated Marleay as his personal property. Two years ago, he beat Marleay and nearly broken her right arm.

When Marleay returned home with her injuries, Oldma Vaye collected his bow and arrows and went to meet Mr. Duopue. The oldman shot and narrowly missed Mr. Duopue with an arrow. Before he would reload, the men in the quarter or neighborhood wrestled him to ground and disarmed him. Thereafter, he and his wife returned the bride's price of $140.00 to Sonkarley Duopue, vowing never to allow him anywhere near their daughter.

Being an inner circle man of the masked dancer granted Oldman Vaye certain privileges and prestige that would never be challenged by a man in Glayville. No man alive or dead would dare to mistreat any of his children. In fact, after the incident with Marleay, Sonkarley Duopue was investigated and made to present two Billy goats and seven ducks and one Guinea fowl as fine payments.

Vayelue Vaye had also been given into an arranged marriage to Saye Glaaglagbey in Yenville, a town five miles southeast of Glayville. Vayelue was Daan or Gio, and Saye was Mano, two of the ethnic groups in Liberia. Vayelue had spoiled or messed up family dinners on many occasions due to dialect or language barrier. When Saye asked for pepper soup, Vayelue had prepared palm-butter or Cassava dough soup. After several attempts, Saye had tried to beat his wife into learning his dialect rather than waiting on his wife to learn the dialect at her own pace. He had vowed never to allow his wife to **embarrass** him again before his friends. He had angrily brought Vayelue home and given her back to her parents saying, "Your daughter cannot cook. Give me my money so I can go." Mr. Vaye and his wife had asked for three weeks, and had repaid the bride's price thereafter.

Lord, it was a relief for Vayelue because she just could not grasp the dialect despite trying so hard. Both Marleay and Vayelue were now at home awaiting the next arranged weddings or marriages. They too were proud of Mother G and her family.

Despite the fact that their marriage was arranged, Mother G loved her husband dearly. Mother G was highly respected and admired by her peers. Lord, the man she married was the chief musician to the secret masked dancer of Glayville. She was a role model to her sisters, and to many younger women in Glayville. She was making the best of her marriage despite the fact that her husband was twenty years older than she was. She had always told her sisters, "Whatever situation you find yourself in, do your best so that when you leave, you would never look back with regrets. But don't let any man take advantage of you."

She lived by her philosophy to the letter. In her own ways and tradition, she honored her husband, and he respected her. Of course, the chief musician to the secret masked dancer would not dare to lay his hands on his wife publicly. That would automatically disqualify him. Lord, he would not, knowing that there were other men lying in wait for his position.

When she travelled or appeared with her husband, she always looked good. She would braid her hair into large beautiful corn-rolls. And when she went by, men would be drooling after her. She did not see herself as the wife of an oldman, but a woman married to the most popular man in Glayville, and perhaps in the district. Lord, being married to a singer, she had a reputation to keep. Mr. Wehtay did not only sing in secrecy, but he would also do so publicly on special occasions when a government official visited Glayville, or on Christmas or New Year's Day.

The next Christmas arrived quickly, but it did not take Mother G by surprise. With her sisters' help, she organized the women of Glayville, and they had the grandest Christmas Day celebration ever recorded in the history of Glayville. It was the greatest show on earth by Glayville standard. Women from the surrounding towns and villages were invited. And they came happily in large numbers. The women of Glayville had special attires called *suitoos;* meaning, the women were dressed in identical colors of clothes, headdresses, etc. Whatever they wore, including footwear, were identical in colors.

Of course, food was all over the place, and everyone had enough to eat and to take home. After dinner, Mother G and the women danced into the wee hours of the morning. With her husband leading the song, and the "Glayville Conga Crew" (GCC) of six men with white furry headdresses, under the leadership of a man known only as Glorwoah (pronounced Glug-wide), Mother G showed to the women of Galyville and the visitors that she could dance. One of the women from Yenville where Vaylue Vaye had been married challenged Mother G to a dance contest.

Manpue Yeanay was the best dancer to ever walk the streets of Yenville. This was not her original plan, but when she saw how good Mother G was on her feet, she decided to challenge her. Both women were given the dance circle to showcase their dancing skills. Lord, Mother G would dance and spin like a top on a smooth surface. And Manpue Yeanay had dance tricks of her own, too. When she took the circle, she came out with a special dance called "Yenville Deer Glide." She would pretend to be a deer, and then she would glide like a deer coming down a hill or slope. That had even brought the hometown crowds up to their feet. But in the end, Mother G won the contest. As long as the secret masked dancer was alive and breathing, no stranger ever won a contest in Glayville. Even in a football game, it was either a tie game or Glayville won.

The winner was presented with a beautiful headdress or a head-tie to be worn at next year's Christmas Dance Contest. So Mother G got the first-place prize and the second-place prize was presented to Manpue Yeanay, a beautiful hand-crafted sandals to also be worn at next year's Christmas Dance Contest. She was extended another invitation to participate in the next dance competition. This day became the birth of Glayville Christmas Dance Contest which would continue for decades with Mother G being the winner for five conservative years. But she lost to Manpue Yeanay in the sixth year when the venue was changed to Yenville. Mother G made name for herself in Yenville and became known to Yenville residents as the "Woman with the spinning feet."

As years passed, walking back and forth to her farm and the burdens of horticultural farming slowed her feet down. But Mother G would dazzle the hometown crowds in Glayville when the right occasion arose. Her sisters would dance, but they were not good enough to take her place. Marleay and Vayelue were anxiously waiting the next right men to come along and ask their parents for their hands in marriages. Dancing would had helped in the process, but they were not very good at it. Being a fantastic dancer like their sister was one thing, but being a bad dancer actually drove men away from a woman. Lord, the epitome was a woman with a bad singing voice. That repelled men like insect repellant repelling insects!

On the morning of Mother G's fifty-seventh birthday, she did not feel good. She woke up with a dull headache. She told her husband about it, but he brushed it aside and said it may had been the hard work on the farm the last couple of weeks. Mr. Oscar Wehtay was a traditional herbalist in his spare time. He had learned some of the stuff from singing for the masked dancer. He went into the bushes, and brought back a few leaves, boiled them and told his wife to drink the liquid. He grinded some and rubbed it on her forehead. By evening around six, Mother G felt better, but she was not out of the woods yet. She was still having low-grade fever and by midnight she was shivering like a child. She was immediately covered with blanket to sweat out the fever. That she did until the morning. She felt good enough to go to her farm.

On the farm that day, she hardly worked. She had begun to feel nauseated, though she had not vomited. She thought about enema, but she was too weak to be running to the toilet every five minutes. Her husband attempted a second remedy, but that too did not help. The couple had to return to Glayville earlier than usual.

Her son Karntay had grown and moved away to a high school in the big city in the district. Within two years, Teresa would join her brother. They were proud of their kids. And their kids were proud of them too. Mr. Wehtay sent a message to their son that his mother was sick, and he needed to come home.

By weekend, Karntay Wehtay was back in Glayville. He took one look at his mother and said to his father, "I will take my Mom to the big city tomorrow to see the doctor." Early the next morning, Karntay and his father took Mother G to the big city to a clinician called Baryon Philips; a Sierra Leonean native who had called this big city in rural northeastern Liberia his home for more than twenty years. He was actually a druggist and had no formal medical training as a doctor. Because he gave penicillin injection and anti-Malaria pills, everyone called him a doctor. He gladly accepted the title, and behaved like one, too. He looked at Mother G's face and said, "That's Malaria." He immediately injected her with two cc of penicillin, including two Quinine pills to swallow. He gave her two additional Quinine pills to take one in the morning and last one the following day. The fees for the clinic visit was two dollars. Lord, back then, it was difficult to raise that kind of money.

By midafternoon, Mother G's fever began to break. She started to sweat and her temperature drop to normal. The family rested until in the evening before they began the two and a half miles walk to Glayville. The walk also did her some good. She was able to prepare the family dinner that night. Lord, they were glad that Mother G was feeling better.

Mother G fully recovered her fever and went about her normal activities. By the end of November that year, she and her family were getting ready for harvest. Other residents were way ahead of them. They were behind in everything this farming season because of her sudden illness. Soon, Glayville residents would start preparations for Christmas and the dance contest.

Mother G had begun to train one of the older girls in Glayville to represent the town. She would not teach her own daughter because she was in school and was not interested. Tina Yanzee was doing just terrific under Mother G's tutorship. She would dance just like Mother G in her blazing dancing days. Tina had just turned thirty years old and was in the prime of her dancing life. With the rumors of Yenville Deer Glide, Manpue Yeanay retiring, there would be no contest between Glayville and Yenville.

By mid-December, Mother G's illness had returned, this time with vengeance. Early one Friday morning, she woke up with a pounding frontal headache. She began running a fever of over 103F.

By late afternoon, she began to vomit. The news of Mother G's sudden illness spread in Glayville like wildfire. Her parents were now old and weak to walk, but they took their thousand steps to be there by her side. School was out and Karntay was home by his mother's side. And Marleay and Vayelue were also there by their sister's mud bed side.

All the traditional medicine men and women in Glayville sprang into actions. By nightfall, they had come with millions of leaves to be boiled and drunk. Some brought enema for Mother G while others brought special rice cooked with spice and herbs. The masked dancer prepared a special hot lavender liquid bath for Mother G and sent it by her husband. That medicine was given a special priority. Marleay and Vayelu went and gave their sister a thorough hot bath. Lord, the people in Glayville did not know that no one ever treated fever with hot water. But this was a special prescription from the masked dancer. Who would dare to challenge it? Mother G's temperature shot up nearly 107F. She was about to go into seizure when her son said to his father, "Let's try cold water." They did that for a while and her temperature began to drop. Karntay Wehtay saved his mother and the day.

The next Saturday morning, Karntay insisted on taking his mother to Dr. Baryon Phillips. When words got out that Karntay was about to take his mother to the clinic, the people of Glayville descended on the home of the Wehtays like swarm of bees. The special assistant to the masked dancer, Mr Dehpue Zeaytay was infuriated. He began to shout, "How dared young man like you want to disobey the entire town? What do you know about medicine? Your mother will remain here and we will make the medicine." Karntay looked at his father with tears in his eyes.

He desperately wanted some type of reassurance from his father that their mother was in good hands. Mr. Wehtay calmly said to his son, "The elders of the town have spoken, and we cannot disobey them or go against their will."

For the next seven days, Mother G, was given various types of enemas until she could take it no more. She drank more than twenty-five different liquids. Her neighbors from Yenville brought herbs to try and make her well. Manpue Yeanay and her husband, Mr. Walakehwon Yeanay brought special kola nuts that Mother G ate at bedtime. Lord, that had made it difficult for her to fall asleep because the nuts were rich in caffeine. But she could not make her dancing best friend shame by refusing her medicine. When they left for Yenville, her son took the kola nuts and threw them away to the delight of his mother. The following night she managed some sleep.

The illness had reduced Mother G to a mere 120 pounds. She normally weighed between 160 and 180 pounds. As she ate the different herbal meals, took various colored baths, and rubbed on thousands different kinds of topical medicines, her skin began to peel like someone with some type of skin disease or dermatitis. Her skin also began to itch. Her son went to the big city and explained his mother's skin condition to Dr. Phillips, and was given a Calamine Lotion to apply at night before bedtime. That helped to stop the itch. But, in the morning before the medicine men and women could make their daily rounds, Mother G took a quick bath to remove the lotion.

By nightfall on the ninth day on Christmas' eve, Mother G's illness took a ninety-degree turn for the worse. By eight o'clock that night,

Mother G was dead. Lord, Glayville was turned upside down with the news of Mother G's death.

Back then, a typical hut or house in Glayville had two doors, one in the front and another one straightway in the back. Then, a fireplace was built in the middle with a square hanging grill made with pieces of sticks hung over it. As Karntay and Teresa cried uncontrollably, Mr. Wehtay gently removed his wife's lifeless body with her sisters' help and placed her on a mat by the rear door and covered her with a blanket and left the door opened so Mother G's spirit could easily escape.

It was the custom of Glayville to place a dead body at the rear door. That would allow the spirit of the deceased to flee or escape through the rear door. If the body was placed at the front door, the spirit would remain in the house, hovering over the front door or standing there for the life of that house.

The house was suddenly packed with mourners. It was total chaos! The chief musician's wife, the lady with the spinning feet was dead. Lord, the mourners came from every corner of Glayville. When the house was full, the spilled overs sat outside the front door. Glayville chief, Mr. Dankuahn Karkuahn declared Glayville-wide period of mourning for three days through the town crier or announcer.

While everyone was crying and wailing, Mother G suddenly began to breathe, and her fingers and toes began to wiggle. And then, she lifted her head and laid it back down. Where she was laid by the rear door was dark enough to conceal her from the mourners. She rose up slowly and sat up, looked around and stood up. She wrapped herself in the blanket used to cover her body. She tiptoed and went out quietly without the mourners noticing her. All of a sudden, she regained her strength, and walked at least a mile towards the road leading to Yenville. By then, it was ten at night and the place was pitch dark. She sat on a tree trump to catch her breath for at least fifteen minutes. When she knew that she had regained sufficient strength, she rose up, stood on her feet and shouted on the top of her

voice, "Help, someone please help me!" Her voice reverberated throughout the smelly and smoke-filled air of Glayville like thunder. A group of men standing thirty yards from the Wehtay's house hastily ran around putting a rescue team together.

All of a sudden, an unusual quietness hung over Glayville as the men of the town raced towards Mother G's voice. Every man had his weapon in hand; single-barrel shotguns, muskets, and bows and arrows. Of course, those without weapons brought their machetes. Men bearing touches made out of bamboo sticks tied together went ahead. Even with touches, one would barely see ten feet ahead, especially when the touches were carried overhead.

When they arrived on the scene, they could not see anyone because Mother G was sitting on a tree trump below them. One of the men bearing a touch shouted at the top of his voice; "Who is it? We are here to help!" Mother G replied, "It is I, Grukern!" No, it was not! Mother G was dead and the body was still lying at the rear door of her house. It must be her ghost. Lord, if only the grounds would open and swallow those men! There were no brave men in Glayville who would dare to stare the ghost of a dead woman in the face. They all panicked, and there was a great stampede as the men struggled to escape what they thought was the ghost of Mother G. In the chaos, the men dropped their touches and left their weapons behind as they ran. One of the men sustained head injury when another man climbed on his shoulder and stepped on his head. Another man had superficial burns in his chest when a touch landed on him while he was on the ground.

Some of the men ran breathlessly straight to Mother G's house. When they arrived, they told the news of what had just happened. When everyone heard it, they went helter-skelter all over Glayville, except for the families of Mother G. When everyone had left, Oscar went to the rear door to check on his wife's body, but she was nowhere to be found. He and his son hurriedly went to the road leading to Yenville. Oscar called out to his wife, "Grukern, are you here?" "Yes Oscar, I am here. Thank God I am alive," she answered. When Mother G saw her husband, she collapsed into his arms. She was exhausted and needed a good hot bath and a meal to regain her strength.

In the midst of the chaos of the night, she had attempted to grab onto one of the men, but he had escaped her grasps, almost dragging her and leaving his shirt in her hands. She then, handed the torn shirt to her son.

Oscar and his son helped Mother G home. Her sisters and parents were waiting at the house. When her parents saw her, they passed out. The sisters could not believe their eyes that their sister had died and resurrected. Marleay and Vayelue got hot water readied within minutes for her bath, and within one hour and thirty minutes, they had prepared hot meals for Mother G to eat. She took a hot bath, and as she ate, her parents were resting to regain their strengths from the shock of her resurrection. Lord, for the first time in the lives of the residents of Glayville, heaven shut its gate and refused to accept one of their own. They could not imagine a Glayville without Mother G. Glayville would had changed forever!

Throughout that night, Oscar kept waking up and looking at his wife to make sure she was still there. Another disappearing and resurrection of Mother G would give him a fatal heart attack. Karntay and Teresa also slept near their aunts. They too were afraid and though they were sleeping with their mother's ghost.

Meanwhile, families and residents of Glayville would sleep over this one and search for answers and meanings in the morning. Lord, thank you that the next day was Christmas Day. The Whehtay and Vaye families got the best Christmas gift any family could ever wish. Karntay and Teresa just sat there in the morning looking at their mother. At first, they were afraid to touch her. But they finally mounted courage, reached out and touched her. Yes, indeed she was real, and not a ghost. She was the same mother who gave birth to them.

Early the next morning, the men of Glayville went to the scene to retrieve their weapons, except for the man who left his shirt with mother G. He did not dare to be heard, noticed, seen and branded as the scariest man to ever walk the streets of Glayville. Mother G kept the shirt as memorabilia to the timidity of the men of Glayville.

Some residents came in the morning to make sure that Mother G was truly alive. Yes, she was alive! After morning breakfast, and about ten o'clock, Oscar brought out a chair for his wife. She sat down and waited for her husband to introduce her to the residents of Glayville again. Over the night, Marleay and Vayelue had braided her hair into several tiny corn-rolls from front to back. She looked thinner, but she looked beautiful as a Mother G had always looked.

Oscar had a wonderful task to perform. He had to showcase his resurrected wife. He told the crowds that had gathered before his house, "This is my brand-new resurrected wife, Grukern 'Miracle Woman' Wehtay." The crowds spontaneously broke into dancing. Lord, please someone had to give some money to Tina Yanzee to rest from the dance! The young woman was just phenomenon. She was just awesome on her feet. Even a young Manpue Yeanay of Yenville at her very best would not had stood a chance against her in the dance circle.

Suddenly Glayville came alive again as residents descended on Mr. Wehtay's house! After all, Mother G, the lady with the spinning feet was alive again. They sent words to Yenville quickly that the contest was cancelled, but the celebrations were on and would last until way into the New Year. The chief assistant to the masked dancer offered one of his biggest pigs to be slaughtered for the feast. Others brought goats, sheep, chickens, ducks, and Guinea fowls. This was a celebration of resurrection from the dead, a celebration of new life. Therefore, Glayville would spare no animals, not even the best.

Mrs. Manpue Yeanay and many residents from Yenville came and joined the celebrations. By midday, lunch, dinner, and whatever anyone called it was ready.

After the dinner feast, Mother G and her husband were dressed up in all over white apparels as signs of purity and new life. Oscar was dressed up in a white African gown with a matching hat and sandals. Mother G was also dressed in a white lappa or fabrics suit with matching head-tie and sandals. And another greatest show on earth in Glayville began this time for a new and resurrected life. Midway through the dance when her husband began to sing, Mother G jumped into the dance circle. Lord, the people of Glayville went mad, shouting, "Miracle Woman Grukern!" This went on almost for thirty minutes. Of course, she had to take her seat by her husband and rest while the celebrations continued way into the night.

But there were skeptics in Glayville who just could not believe that this woman was the same Mother G they had known all their lives. They thought to themselves, "This is the Ghost of Mother G. We saw her body lying at the rear door of her home. There was no way on earth she would be alive today and dancing." But the skeptics were wrong because they did not accompany Mother G's body to her grave. They would not prove that she was dead and buried. Though she was dead, she was never buried.

Those who believed otherwise thought that when Mother G died and went to the spirit town of Glayville, she met her grandparents, Mr. Duotee Vaye and his wife Nahtay. They told her to return home because it was not her time to die. But when Mother G tried to persuade them, they shut the gate in her face and would not allow her to enter the spirit town. When the gate was shut, Mother G began to breathe again, and came back alive. And then, when she came back to life, she wanted to test the bravery of the men of Glayville. And this saying spread throughout Glayville and it was believed to this day.

Three years after the resurrection of Mother G, her parents died. Glayville fearing another phenomenon of fearsome resurrection within the family, Oldman Vaye and his wife Wonseh were quickly buried far away from the town. After the deaths of their parents, Marleay and Vayelue finally found their own husbands and remarried respectively. Marleay remarried Mr. Joshua Gonsahn, and Vayelue remarried Mr. Freeman Mentee. And their brother, Duoteegbe Duotay Vayetay Vaye also returned home with his own family. Both women, their husbands and their brother's family lived happily ever after.

Mother G lived long enough to see her grand and great grandchildren. Oscar continued to sing for the masked dancer until he voluntarily retired. Mother G would no longer spin, but she continued dancing all the remaining resurrected days of her life.

ONCE UPON THE TIME IN LIBERIA, a woman called Mrs. Grukern Wehtay; Mother G for short, died and resurrected in a rural town called Glayville. After her resurrection, she tested the wills and braveries of the men of Glayville and found them wanting. Fearing they had come across her ghost, the men who had gone or come to her call to rescue her, scattered in fear when she said, "It is I, Grukern!" One of the men left behind his shirt when Mother G got hold of him for help. She kept the shirt as memorabilia to the timidity and wanted-ness of that generation. The identity of the man who left his shirt with Mother G remained a mystery in Glayville to this day.

CHAPTER 7

THE REJECTION OF WILLIE WILLIAMS BADEH AT HIS DEATH

A child who does not accompany his parents to the farm,
but remains in the town is likely to shake hands with a soldier."
Meaning: A child who does not listen to his parents is likely to fall into troubles.

"I will raze you. **My men** if you mess with me, I will raze you, **Men move from here men**," Willie Williams Badeh said angrily to Jerome Yoomie. These angry outbursts were followed by several "F" words that cannot be written down in a fictional book. Willie Williams never fought a man his age, height and size. He stood barely five feet and two inches tall, but his words outweighed his height and strength. If words were indications of a man's strength or fought for a man, Willie Williams would be crowned as the champion of the world.

When Willie Williams fought, he was always, always beaten. But fighting Willie Williams was not a one-day affair. It was an everyday affair that never ended unless the other man moved away or died. He would jump on the man to fight everywhere, and anywhere they met. And he would rise up early in the morning and set an ambush by the door of any man who fought him. When his fighting spirit came over him, Willie

Williams did not listen to anybody, not even his parents.

He was always a loner. His friendship with anyone lasted a maximum of three days. The next thing Willie Williams would be shouting to his friend, *"**Men, move from here, men**! I will raze you just now!"* Those statements were always followed by epitaphs. Lord, the boy knew every "F" word under heaven.

Though, he later got married after enlistment in the Armed Forces of Liberia (AFL), Willie Williams did not have a girlfriend. He did not possess the temperament to keep a girl.

With his sharp tongue wrapped up in those "F" words, no girl or woman under heaven stood a chance with him. When he was in a terrible mood, Willie Williams would hit or fight a girl. Lord, this little man thought the world was too small for him and another person.

When Willie Williams was a teenager, the extended family ate together in one bowl. Men and boys ate together at Grandpa Walpole's house. And the women ate at Grandma Gormein's house (Willie Williams' grandmother). All the wives and mothers would prepare rice and cassava dough (dumboy, gaingbah, or GB) dinners and the boys would bring them to Grandpa Walpole's house. In those days, mothers and wives prepared all kinds of delicacies. The favorite ones were cassava leaf, or palava sauce with fresh or dried snails soup for rice, and dried green or black mamba, opossum, groundhog or palm worms soup for cassava dough.

During the meals, no one ate the meat until after dinner, then, it was divided by Grandpa Walpole among those who came to dinner. If a mother or wife did not send a dinner, her boys or husband did not come to dinner. If she was noted for bad cooking like she made the cassava dough (dumboy, gaingbah or GB) soup real slimy, or slippery, and cooked the rice soup, normally cassava leaf, real hot with pepper, her husband and boys were reprimanded or ridiculed before they ate. And after dinner, they were given a stern message by Grandpa Walpole to be delivered to her. "Tell your wife to cook decent food; less spicy and not so slimy, or else, do not come to dinner. It was wrong for you and your boys to come here and eat dinner when your wife did not cook." And if the message was delivered, her next meals were her character witnesses.

During dinners, the boys would be watched closely so they would not steal the meat from the soup. When a boy dipped the cassava dough into the slimy soup (not slimy in the sense of being disgusting, but it was slippery), he would open his palm for Grandpa Walpole's inspection before the dough landed on the boy's tongue. There were no exceptions. It did not matter if a boy's mother was the beloved wife in the family.

One night the extended family came to dinner at Grandpa Walpole's house as usual. That night Mrs. Badeh prepared a slimy bow frogs dough soup and sent it by Mr. Badeh and his son. Lord, the bow frog legs and thighs were all over in the soup.

Grandpa Walpole decided to test the honesty of the boys. Instead of removing the frog legs and thighs from the soup and inspecting every boy's palm after his cassava dough-slimy-dipping, he left everything as is. But he added several boiled pepper-balls on the sides where the boys were doing their dipping. The pepper-balls were so soft and felt like bow frog legs and thighs in the dark. Everyone sat by a fireplace and ate in those days. One would barely see the next person sitting close by.

Midway through the dinner, Willie Williams picked one of those soft-boiled pepper-balls, mistaken it for a bow frog thigh. When he bit it, the pepper burst in his mouth and he shouted for water. Right then and there, Grandpa Walpole knew Willie Williams was trying to steal the bow frog legs and thighs in the slimy soup.

Willie Williams had to go and roast his tongue on the fire. In those days, fire was the remedy for spicy food. It was believed by residents of

Claysville that one only fought fire with fire. Anyone who ate hot pepper was made to either show his or her tongue to blazing flames or to drink a tablespoon full of red palm oil. The fire or flames increased circulation to the tongue and sensitize or deaden the taste buds. And the palm oil would sooth the tongue and the throat.

Normally, no one drank water while eating cassava dough because of the sliminess. Lord, it was a taboo for some men or women to see anyone drink water while swallowing cassava dough. If someone did, they would angrily quit the dinner and leave.

Willie Williams Badeh was the only boy of four siblings. At his birth the four traditional chanting calls made by midwives at the birth of a male child was never made. They did not believe that he would survive outside of his mother's womb for a long time because of the size of his head. But with Grandma Gormein's help, Willie Williams Badeh grew up to be an adult, barely taller than five feet. But she raised Willie Williams to be a tough man and never to bow down to any man no matter how big or small. She always told her grandson, "Never run away from a fight. You may be beaten, but in the end, everyone would respect you."

Willie Williams Badeh followed his grandma's philosophy to the letter because he was always beaten, but he never stopped, gave up fighting, or got the respect. When he fought, Willie Williams never threw punches. He always went under his opponent and try to knock him to the ground as his father would knock his opponents to the ground in his wrestling days. Grandma Gormein died at a good old age when Willie Williams was a teenager.

As the only boy in the family, Willie Williams was the designated pigs' feeder. Early in the morning at the crack of dawn, the pigs came to breakfast and he got out of his mud bed and fed them. And in the evening, the pigs also came to dinner. If they were late coming to breakfast or d inner, Willie Williams went into the neighborhood or bushes and called them. He had a special pig call that was recognized by all of Mr. Badeh's pigs.

One morning while feeding the pigs, a rather aggressive male pig grabbed Willie Williams' right hand when he presented a piece of raw cassava without paying close attention to its mouth. He had gotten so used to feeding the pigs that it became a no brainer for him.

He would look another direction while presenting pieces of cassava to them. When Willie Williams cried for help, Mr. Badeh ran out, got hold of the pig and cut its throat to save his son's right hand from being amputated by the pig. From that day onward, Willie Williams never fed any pig for the rest of his life.

Willie Williams had three sisters, one directly from his mother and father, and the other two from another wife of Mr. Badeh. Mrs. Karpoleh Badeh was the mother to Willie and his sister Zayetee. Karpoleh died shortly after the birth of Zayetee. She was breastfed by her paternal grandmother, **Oldma** Gormein. Grandma Gormein stood almost six feet tall, and she always had her hair in ponytail. As she aged, it became difficult for her to stand up straight. She was a disciplinarian.

Grandma Gormein first instilled such rigidity and discipline in her own son, Mr. Kerhu Badeh, Sr. Mr. Badeh was also the first man to ever be volunteered for school as was the requirement of each household when he was a young man. He spent several years and came back not knowing a single word in English.

Upon his return, Mr. Badeh took up wrestling as a profession. He took his mother's advice and rose up to become the most recognizable and contentious wrestler in the entire district. He was a champion wrestler until he was nearly a hundred years old. No man ever dropped Mr. Badeh's knees on the ground until he was 100 years old. And then, he lost to a younger man because he refused to listen to the men of his generation that he was too old to challenge a younger wrestler. For the first time in his life, Mr. Kerhu Badeh was dropped on both knees. He got up and ran straight into the bushes and was never seen or heard from for seven days. And when he returned, Mr. Badeh kept a low profile, rising up early in the morning, going to his farm and returning late at night when everyone was asleep.

Mr. Badeh also had an unorthodox way of giving gifts to people. He would give a gift to a man or woman, but return to demand it if and when he had a fight with any of the family members of the gift receiver. He would go like this: "The other day I gave you a gift, but after the fight with you or your family member, I have changed my mind. I want my gift back." He would insist until his gift was physically returned to him. If the gift was a food item that had already been eaten, he would demand cash payment and accept it.

Mrs. Deidor Badeh was the mother to Willie Williams' sisters Nainyoun Zaygoah and Pillar B. Both women were married to two cousins in Zuoville, and their houses were just a few blocks apart. The older sister was married to Mr. Moneyman Zainbor and her younger sister was married to Sinkala Jim. Both women were very pretty. They appeared almost like twins, though Pillar was younger than her sister was.

During the diamond rush in the late 1960's, Mr. Moneyman Zainbor and his wife were millionaires by Liberian standard in those days. They were the first couple to ever buy one of those spinning record players that played vinyl records. They later built a five bed-room house in his wife's hometown. Mr. Zainbor was so rich that he used dollar bills as toilet tissues. When he ran out of cigarette papers, he would use dollar bills to roll up his tobacco and smoke it. Lord, the man was so rich that he lost his mind.

Mrs. Zainbor's sister Pillar B and her husband Sinkala Jim were not rich, though they acted like rich folks. Mr. Sinkala was a tall light skin man with slender built. He was notorious for filing lawsuits against people from all walks of life. He even filed a law against his father-in-law, Mr. Badeh while he was still married to the man's daughter. Lord, the man picked fights with anything that would move, walk and talk. He wanted to possess all the farmlands from Mr. Badeh and his family. He forced Pillar B to testify against her own father in several courts. The bitterness exists up to this day.

Both women had beautiful children by their husbands. Before her death, Mrs. Nainyoun Zaygoah had two girls and four boys, but only one of the boys survived. Her husband also died years later of heart disease and diabetes.

Pillar B and her husband Mr. Sinkala had five girls with no boy. Mr. Sinkala also died years later from heart disease.

Back then, and with chaos within both families caused by Pillar B and her husband, Willie Williams would go to both sisters and spent quality time with their families to the dislike of his father. Willie did not care. He loved his family no matter what was happening within the family. He refused to fight his father's bitterness battle, or other relatives within both families.

Like his father, Willie Williams was sent to school, but never got beyond the first grade until he dropped out. On his way to school, Willie Williams would deliberately fall in a river near the town, and return home complaining that he fell into the river and his uniforms got wet. Lord, the boy hated school until he would pull any tricks in his arsenal not to go. And he succeeded every time!

Willie William had an unusually large head. Do not ask about the diameter because back then, no one had a measuring tape. The only man who did was a tailor, and he was always busy sewing clothes and did not care about the size of anybody's head.

Willie Williams' hometown Claysville Elementary School had a student doctor. He was not a real medical doctor. He was appointed by the principal because he always looked neat and kept himself cleaned. And his hair was always cut short and neatly combed. My Lord, Steve Gahn was the cutest and handsomest kid in the entire school. If he wanted girls, he would had gotten them.

Steve's job was to inspect each student during devotion in the morning when the Liberian Flag was hoisted. He inspected every student from the top of the head to the sole of the feet. If a student did not comb his hair before coming to school, Steve and the principal would comb it for him in front all the students. Then, at the end of the combing, all students would be asked to boo him for at least five minutes. Booing was a form of ridicule and deterrent. It let the student know that he needed to take good care of himself in the morning before coming to school. Lord, Steve took his job seriously. He would comb a female student's hair if it was not braided neatly for school.

If Steve found a piece of cassava leaf stuck to a student's tooth, he would take the student to the nearby creek and brush the student's teeth with wet sand.

Steve Gahn was a distant cousin of Willie Williams. He had warned Willie Williams on numerous occasions to properly brush his teeth before coming to school. One day, Willie Williams ate cold rice in the morning with cassava leaf and came to school. When Steve got to him, he asked Willie Williams to open his mouth. He hesitated at first, but he had to comply because the principal was standing right there watching them. When Willie Williams finally did, the cassava leaf was all over in his mouth, and on his teeth. He must had eaten it on his feet while running to school.

Steve and the principal asked Willie Williams to smile for all the students with the cassava leaf on his teeth. The cassava leaf was transient, but all the tartars and plaques of the world somehow found their ways into Willie Williams Badeh's teeth. A maximum brand of any toothpaste would not had done a thing to those tartars and plaques. The students were asked to boo him every time he smiled. As a male student, he had to smile four times, and the students had to also boo him four times. At the end, he was taken to the nearby creek and his teeth brushed with wet sand. And he gladly returned to class.

It did not bother Willie Williams at all. He was one of those kids who did not know or care about anything or situation that was **embarrassing** or shameful. Willie Williams went home jumping up and down singing happily after school as if nothing happened that day. And he came back to school the next morning happily. Of course, there was no cassava leaf on his teeth this time.

In the first grade, Willie Williams shared a desk with another cousin called Alfred Mangle. He was smarter than Willie Williams. When he knew that he was unable to do his own work, Willie Williams began ripping Alfred's note book pages and giving them to the teacher as his own. But he would not trick the teacher. The teacher knew the kind of student he was. He brought him before the students in the auditorium and gave him fifteen lashes in both hands. Willie Williams would always be Willie Williams no matter what happened to him at school.

At the end of the year during graduation, the principal praised the students who were promoted to next grade levels. He would say nice things about them and how good their parents were in making sure that they learned their lessons and did their homework. Students who failed got the wrath of the principal. They were brought before the entire townand the student assembly and ridiculed for at least thirty minutes before the final death sentence; "They will not be promoted to the next grades."

The principal would bring Willie Williams before the audience and say, "This boy with his head as big as Mount Kilimanjaro, did not do his homework, or listen to the teachers. He will grow up to be like his father because the man went to school as a kid and ran away. He came back not knowing a single English word. Willie Williams failed the first grade again." Lord, Mr. Kerhu Badeh would be sitting right there in the audience, but the principal would ignore his presence and say what he had to say.

After the graduation program, Willie Williams would leave the school campus singing and jumping up and down. His favorite song was, "Come and buy my opossum. I am selling my opossum. If you want to go and play, come and buy my opossum." Lord, do not ask about the meaning of the song. No one in Claysville knew the meaning, except Willie Williams Badeh.

Midway through elementary school, Willie Williams dropped out and went to Monrovia. He had to quit first grade after three years without, even a social promotion. No one heard from him for nearly five years. One day, Willie Williams showed up in Claysville in military uniforms. He had enlisted in the Armed Forces of Liberia (AFL). Residents of Claysville were shock. Lord, everyone was curious as to how on earth Willie Williams Badeh was able to enlist in the army? Who did the interview, and who took his enlistment tests? Lord, what language was spoken at the interview? Willie Williams did not even speak English like a man who dropped out of school.

The only distinctive thing Claysville residents knew about Willie Williams was that he could outrun any man his age. Sometimes when he was badly beaten, he ran away and went to his father. From Claysville to the big district capital, Barnesville, Willie Williams would cover the two and a half mile-distance, going and coming within fifteen minutes. Lord, if Willie Williams had been fast at everything else, he would had been considered the genius of Claysville.

As the custom was with all soldiers, he asked for Claysville chief and demanded to be fed. As usual he threatened to raze Chief Edwin Dahntee if his demands were not met. Lord, Claysville had to assemble rice, chickens and dried monkey meat to feed Willie Williams. That was the accepted practice throughout Liberia back in those days.

Soldiers went around towns and villages to be fed. Those who refused to feed them were severely beaten or threatened to be shot. In worst scenario, the soldiers would call for backup, and they would march on the town or village. And when they did, every resident ran into the bushes and left the town to the soldiers. The soldiers would catch any animal, kill it and commandeer a woman in the town to prepare a dinner for them. Lord, Willie Williams was afraid of soldiers when he was a kid, but he was now one of them.

Millville was another town about five miles northeast of Claysville. Its residents paid a heavy price when soldiers marched on the town. One of the residents of Millville had slept with a soldier's wife bringing a curse on the town. Every soldier in the country at that time marched on the town. Every time they came, they would remain for several days to be fed. And when one group was leading, another group was entering the town. It came to a point when soldiers were asked where they were going, they would answer, "To Millville." Lord, it got so bad that everyone left Millville and the soldiers took over the town. They had their ways with everything in the town and finally left.

Again, this was Liberia where anything, everything, and everybody went where they were not qualified to go or be. In those days, there were government officials, senators and representatives who did not speak or write the English language. They did not know how to write their own local dialects. But yes, they were in both houses making laws for the country.

When the Liberian Civil War broke out, Willie Williams survived as a soldier by shifting loyalty. He continued that until the war ended. When the rebels were doing well on the battlefront, he was a rebel. And when the government soldiers were doing well on the battlefront, he was one of them. His father, Mr. Kerhu Badeh died shortly before the war ended. The cause of his death was never established. After the war, Willie Williams was transferred to the Liberian-Guinean border. There, he made some money from Guinean traders who came through the border.

And then came his first marriage. Willie Williams got married when he enlisted in the AFL. He was being paid by the government and was also making money at the border, so he would take care of a woman. The marriage did not last. Willie Williams Badeh declared war on his wife the first time she cooked a salty potato green soup. They fought over the salty potato green soup.

No matter how hard she tried, Willie Williams always criticized her cooking in front of his friends and her friends. She either cooked the green with too much or little oil, or there was no pepper or too much pepper. Sometimes Willie Williams just took the food and wasted it outside for the animals to feed on. When Mrs. Martha Kwikerwon Badeh was razed five times by her husband because of her cooking, she packed up her belongings and left while he was at work.

After the war, the national government decided to upgrade the armed forces by recruiting men and women who were at least high school graduates. Willie Williams and the old AFL were honorably discharged.

A one-time lump sum of money was given to Willie Williams and his friends to either invest, or start businesses. Do not ask about the exact amount because he would not disclose it to anyone even if a millstone was tied around his neck and thrown into the ocean.

One day Willie Williams took his lump sum of money and gave it to a politician who was running for the presidency for the country for safe keeping. He did not trust the banks in the country to safeguard his money. From the day he gave the money to the presidential candidate, it was the last time Willie Williams saw him. Again, he invested his money in a politician and lost.

Early December 2013, Ebola entered West Africa. It was a hemorrhagic or bloody feverish viral disease that grinded every organ in the body and spat it out. It was highly contagious and would be spread easily by coming in contact with bodily fluids of the victim whether dead or alive. Very few people miraculously survived Ebola. Scientist believed that the viral lived in hanging bats. It was thought to have started in Guinea, West Africa when a thirteen-year boy killed a bat and ate it. When he got sick and died, those who came in contact with him contracted the disease. Some of the contacts came to Liberia, West Africa and later died at a local hospital.

At first, Liberians did not believe in the fatality of Ebola. They attributed the viral to a genie brought into the country by its leaders. Some claimed that it was a **Mommywater** brought into the country by government officials to collect human blood. Others went as far as believing that the water supplies of the nation were poisoned with formaldehyde leading to massive deaths, and that Ebola had nothing to do with it. Another strange phenomenon Liberians believed at the time was that Ebola came about because the so-called industrialized nations of the world were experimenting with germ warfare in the affected countries when something went terribly wrong. That had caused the viral to escape from the laboratories, causing deaths. Whatever it may had been, one thing was sure. It was deadly! It killed people, and fast.

The traditional practices of washing dead bodies and dressing them up, spread the disease in Liberia, Guinea and Sierra Leon like widefire. Cote D'Ivoire next door to Liberia did not report a single case. Cases reported in Nigeria were allegedly carried over by a Liberian government official. A Liberian also brought a case to the United States and later died in the country.

The disease spread and killed people by the thousands. The inner cities and the slumps of Monrovia were hit the hardest. Liberians were banned from hugging, kissing, shaking each other's hands, or washing dead bodies. Sanitary measures such as washing of hands, and burning of Ebola deaths were instituted. Schools and some public offices were shut down to prevent the spread of the disease. Towns and villages within rural Liberia would not allow any visitors to enter or leave. Lord, Liberians of all walks of life were beginning to wonder if this was a latter-day plague.

As the death tolls mounted in the city, many city dwellers scattered throughout the country in search of safe haven. But no one could hide from the viral. The disease killed the young and the old. It killed the good, the bad and the ugly. It killed ministers' families, and in some communities wiped out an entire family. The medical community was also hit hard because they were directly on the frontline fighting the disease. Many doctors, nurses, nurse assistants and medical personnel lost their lives. Their families, relatives, and friends who came in contact with them also died.

Several months into the epidemic, words reached Sister Pillar B that Willie Williams was sick in Monrovia. No one knew the nature of his illness. In those days, some relatives did not visit a sick family member for fear of contracting the disease. Every disease was attributed to Ebola. Patients were left on stretchers in hospital parking lots until they died because they were rejected by medical personnel. Hospital staff too, began to be afraid of patients when their colleagues who handled Ebola patients got sick and died.

There were reports coming from Monrovia and the surrounding cities that visiting Liberians from the West were also dying of the disease on arrival. They had come from the West, and were not afraid of any viral disease. Those who frequented bars and night clubs paid a heavy price with their lives.

Lord, those were difficult days in Liberia. Families living in the West were fearful of answering phone calls from Liberia. They did not want to receive or hear a terrible news about a relative or friend who had died of Ebola.

In the midst of the chaos of deaths and dying, Willie Williams became a **grownaman.** In other words, he became homeless and began roaming the city streets. With death hovering over the city, everyone was afraid of everybody. Willie Williams roamed the streets in the day and slept in the graveyard at night.

Liberian cities, whether large or small, had never had homeless shelters. Homeless children and men roaming the streets were **grownaboys or growngirls**; the latter word being designated for street girls or women. Liberians believed that these people just chose to be this way in life. They wanted to be tough, so they chose the streets. No person was an island. After all, they had families. If they wanted to go home, they would do so anytime without being rejected or thrown out in the streets. They survived by pick pockets, stealing and committing burglaries. If they found a person talking on a cellphone, they would jerk it from the person and run.

They operated in groups of three, four, five or six men and women. One of them was always used as a decoy. He or she would be the one to engage a potential victim in conversation while the rest went to work. He or she would even **bounce grumble** or start a fight for no reason with a total stranger he or she just met on the streets. These men and women were the ugliest of all large urban cities. Ebola would had wiped them out if it were not for their mobility. Sometimes the viral was three or four steps ahead of them, but many survived.

Willie Williams became one of them. He came from being an honorably discharged veteran of the AFL with lots of money in his pocket to a **grownaman,** a homeless man.

A **grownagirl** or a **grownawoman** would stand around a street corner pretending to be sick, and in need of an urgent medical attention while the rest of the gangs lie in wait. As soon as a motorist or motorcyclist stopped, they would all jump out and overpower him or her and take the car or motorcycle away. Of course, some **grownagirls** or **grownawomen** survived by prostitution rather than crimes.

No one dared to search for Willie Williams. There were many citizens from Claysville who lived in the city, but they did not care. Some were cousins and nieces to him. As always, Willie Williams Badeh was a loner who kept to himself unless he desperately needed an assistant. And after he got the assistance, he verbally abused the provider and left. Lord, the words, "Thank you" were never a part of Willie Williams' vocabulary. He always felt anyone or everyone, whether a citizen of Claysville or not, owned him a gratuity. It was a matter of time, and he would receive what was owned to him.

When everyone deserted him, including the politician who took the only possession he ever had in this world; his money, a **grownagirl** called Feona Swein befriended Willie Williams. She was in her late thirties and stood five inches taller than Willie Williams at five feet and seven inches. Her eyes were unusually yellow (a sure visible sign of infection with

Hepatitis A), and her lips were cracked from smoking street tobacco and occasional boo. She also drank **Cane Juice**. When she was desperate for cash and meals, she slept with men from all walks of life.

But Willie William needed a companion in these dark days in the history of his country. He was not searching for a Mother Teresa. He just needed a friend, and that he found in Feona Swein. Lord, these terrible times must had changed Willie Williams's perspective on life, death, and dying. When Willie Williams Badeh was on top of his mean game-self, no one would catch him alive or dead with a Feona Swein. He would had called or labeled her a **whorepojoe** in a matter of seconds and threatened to raze her.

Time was running out on Willie Williams and Feona. One morning he woke up first and tried to wake Feona up. But Feona was dead. She had drunk **Cane Juice** heavily and smoke some boo on top of it before falling asleep that night. Her liver gave up in the night, and by morning, she was dead. Willie Williams tried desperately to get Feona to wake up. When he rolled her over and realized that she was dead, Willie Williams ran as fast as he could run in those days when he was a young man.

With Feona gone, Willie Williams had nowhere to turn. He wondered if his number would be up too any time. He slept by a dead woman all night and did not know. Where would he turn now with Feona gone? He was losing weight fast, too. Ordinarily he would weigh around 130 pounds, but he just weighed a hundred pounds. And his eyes were getting yellower by the minutes. The thought of dying on the streets with no relatives or friends around him weighed heavily on mind. That night he found a grave site north of the city and tried to sleep, but could not.

Meanwhile his sister Pillar B Sinkala was worried about him. She was desperate to know his whereabouts in a city gone mad with deaths and dying. How could she get words to him to come home, so she would take him to a traditional herbalist? After all, they were the only two surviving siblings still alive. Zayetee Badeh had died in child birth just like her mother before her twenty-fifth birthday. Zayetee was shorter than Willie Williams. Lord, imagine Zayetee trying to have a baby in the midst of traditional or empirical midwives!

One day while walking down Center Street near the graveyard, a Claysville resident Alphonso Menwon ran into Willie Williams. Alphonso was shock! He thought Willie Williams was dead and gone; at least that was the news they and other Claysville residents in their community had heard. Willie Williams did not have to tell Alphonso anything about himself. Alphonso would tell that the man was sick and dying. If nothing was done to save his life, Willie Williams would be dead within a week.

In spite of the precautions people had to take when they traveled, there were some die-hards business men and women who took chances and risks their lives to travel. They avoided shaking hands or hugging other people. When they got off at any checkpoint, they washed their hands before boarding a lorry again.

Alphonso promised Willie Williams that he would get in touch with his sister Pillar B Sinkala. The following day, Alphonso did just what he promised. He met some women down Waterside Market Square and sent a message to Willie Williams' sister that he was alive, but sick and in need of urgent medical care. Within three days, Mrs. Pillar B. Sinkala had Willie Williams removed from the city streets of Monrovia heading home to Claysville. He was being escorted by two men, Robert James Sinkala, his nephew (Mrs. Sinkala's son) and David Bookie, a close relative of her late husband, Mr. Sinkala Jim.

They arrived in Gompa City about two o'clock in the afternoon. They had to hurry up because it was getting late, and they had at least fifteen miles to cover. They met several residents from Claysville who had come to the market to purchase food items. They sent words to inform Willie Williams's extended family in Claysville that they needed to get ready to receive him because he was on his way.

When the women arrived back in Claysville, one of them who saw Willie Williams went to Co-chief Eastman Norgon and told him that Willie Williams was infected with the Ebola viral and he was being brought home to die. When Chief Norgon heard it, he informed the Claysville Informer, Mr. Austin Gruel to announce that Willie Williams Badeh was dying of Ebola and he was on his way to the town. And that he needed every resident of Claysville to assemble over the bridge linking Claysville to the outside world to form a human blockade.

All the residents of Claysville went to the bridge and formed a human blockade over the bridge as instructed by the co-chief. There was no way under heaven would they allow Willie Williams to bring Ebola into Claysville. They sent two men across the bridge as lookouts.

When Willie Williams and his escorts arrived in the big city, Barnesville, they were left off by the lorry driver. The two men hastily put a makeshift hammock together made out of lappas or fabrics so they would carry him on their shoulders to Claysville. Normally, Willie Williams barely weighed 130 pounds. With this illness, he had lost weight, was down to only ninety pounds.

The lookout men spotted Willie Williams and his escorts first, and ran back to inform the people of Claysville. When they arrived about thirty yards from the bridge, Chief Norgon shouted to the men, "Hey you men carrying Willie Williams, stop right there!" They stopped and slowly lowered Willie Williams to the grounds and waited for the next action or move by the chief. "What's wrong with him?" The chief asked the men. "We don't know. We know it is not Ebola, or he would had died ever since," the men replied. "How do you know it is not Ebola, and do you have a medical certificate of clearance from a doctor that he is not sick with Ebola?" The chief asked again. "Well, chief, Ebola would had killed him a long time ago. Look at his eyes, I think he had Yellow Jaundice," one of the men responded. "I don't want to look at anybody's eyes. I am not a doctor," Chief Norgon replied angrily.

At the end of the exchanges, the chief went back to the residents to inquire if they would allow Willie Williams into the town. The residents responded in unison, "No! We do not want that man in this town. He may be carrying Ebola. If we take the chance, everyone in this town will die."

Other extended relatives tried to negotiate with the town by suggesting to build a tin roof shack outside the town to accommodate Willie Williams, but the elders, the chief and the residents of Claysville shouted in unison, "Over our dead bodies."

After what seemed like an eternity during the standoff, Willie Williams Badeh was finally rejected by Claysville; a town where he was born, bred and raised. The town folks allowed the two men to cross the bridge, but to walk in the bushes on the peripheries of the town with the human chain and blockade following a few yards behind to make sure that the men did not enter the town. That they did and took Willie Williams to Naperville a farming village almost fifteen miles away from Claysville. This was the farming village of Pillar B and her late husband Mr. Sinkala.

Three days after they arrived in Naperville, Willie Williams Badeh died of liver failure due to chronic Hepatitis A at age sixty-nine. Following a quiet funeral service attended only by the men who escorted him, his sister Pillar B, and her very few friends, he was buried in an unmarked grave in the village. There in Naperville lies Willie Williams Badeh, a man who dared to raze any man on the face of this earth no matter how tall, fat, skinny or short the man was.

ONCE UPON THE TIME IN LIBERIA, Willie Williams Badeh, raised by an audacious grandmother and a hardened-father wrestler, rose up to become a soldier, and was later honorably discharged with a lot of money. In his own ways, he battled whatever life threw at him, including beatings, education, friendships, marriage, the Liberian Civil War and Ebola.

He finally lost the battle to a chronic liver disease that had been with mankind for centuries. He razed every man he encountered in life, but Willie Williams Badeh was razed by a viral disease and lowered into the very bottom of an unmarked pit because his own folks rejected him at his death. May the soul of Willie Williams Badeh rest in his own peace.

CHAPTER 8

THE STORY OF A LIBERIAN KARATE KID WHOSE DREAM OF A BLACKBELT DIED IN A TRAINING CAMP

"When you are bitten by a dog on the nose, you do not
present a single white kola nut to the healer if you want to be healed.
Meaning: Some issues in this life do not require simplistic solutions or answers.

Ha, Ha, Ha, yaaaaa, ha! The martial arts instructor, Mekong Timbuktu shouted to his students as he led them in the martial arts drills on the first day of the training camp. There were about fifteen students most of them from the same high school. Nearly all the men played on the high school football team, except for maybe four or five students. Some of the men were in their early thirties and already married with children. But they wanted to get in shape and also learn to defend themselves.

In those days being a footballer would automatically put a boy or a man on any event on campus. Since Mr. Timbuktu was already the football coach of the high school, the football team became part of his martial arts training camp without registration. Of course, all the footballers did not enroll. Some felt that they did not have bones to pick with anybody, so there was no need to learn self-defense.

Sanniquellie is a large metropolis by Liberia standard. In those days, the city never slept on weekends. With several mining towns just seven miles away, there were always events in the city. If a band was not playing, one of several elementary and high schools in the city was having Some types of sporting events. Lord, men and women from the mining towns would come every weekend to drink. And when they did, the men womanized, while the women manized.

Sanniquellie also had a large market hall beside a lake called, "Lake Tarawa. The market hall opened six days a week, and closed on Sundays. Back in those days, no one opened or did business on Sundays. Anyone who dared was arrested and fined or sent to prison. Whether a person was religious or nonreligious, no one did business on a sacred day reserved, or set aside only for God.

But Sanniquellie was a tough city, a real Liberian survival of the fittest. At the beginning of each school year, the population of the city jumped to nearly ten thousand people. By July, hunger had driven half of the student population back to their homes. No strangers helped anybody. The original inhabitants of the city were nowhere to be found. Most people on the streets were either visitors or travelers. Or they did not claim their citizenship of Sanniquellie for fear of students asking them for food.

Hunger in Sanniquellie set it apart from all rural cities in Liberia. Lord, the hunger that caused a student on the campus of a big government high school to pass out during a morning devotion, and was taken to a hospital nearby and given glucose drips. Students had scattered all over the campus when the boy collapsed on the ground, some of them shouting, "Vietnam, Vietnam has come to Liberia!" My God, there was no mendacity about the hunger of Sanniquellie. The city was the hunger capital of Liberia. It was unrealistically palpable!

Incidents that took place in Sanniquellie were as difficult, strange and sometimes bizarre as life itself in the city. One day, a boy went to do his laundry at a creek two miles from the city center. Though he did not know how to swim, he decided to swim in the deep waters of the creek. Some parts were very rapid, even for a good and experienced swimmer. When he plunged into the water, the rapid stream took him down in the drainage system of the creek. He got caught in the large cement pipe used as drain, and got drowned. It was a sad and difficult day when the news of his drowning death reached his school campus.

Another boy who had come to school from a town far away fell in love with an elderly lady and left school. He and the woman lived on her farm for several years. Through her influence, Jackson Zoovaar became a seasoned farmer. She was with him one day when Jackson was cutting down a large cotton tree. Please do not ask about a cotton tree because that was how Liberians from all walks of life called that particular tree. When she shouted, *"T-i-m-b-e-r,"* while the tree was going down, Jackson did not know which way to run. He ran into the path of the tree and was crushed to death instantly. The accident may have occurred due to language barrier between Jackson Zoovaar and his **oldma** or **god-ma** because they were from two different ethnic groups.

The following incident was the strangest and most difficult. One evening, a humpback student called Johnny Knell from one of the private schools in the city was cooking his rice outdoor in the cool of the evening. While the rice was boiling, a hot pot rice thief was lying in wait watching every move Johnny made in and out of the house. When the rice was cooked, Johnny went inside again to wash plates to dish up the rice. When he returned, the hot pot rice thief had struck; taking Johnny's hot pot of rice away. Johnny Knell almost had a heart attack. He had to regroup and cook another pot of rice, but this time inside his bed room.

For months, Johnny kept reading the book of Psalms chapter 109, hoping that God would punish the thief that stole his hot pot of rice. Every time he went to school, he cautioned other students never to cook their rice outdoor. He became an expert adviser to students at school on how to protect their hot pot cooked rice from being stolen. At recess hours, students would gather around to hear him lecture on the prevention of hot pot rice theft, and how not to become a victim of the hot pot rice thief.

The following story was the most bizarre, or the mother all unbelievable incidences that took place in the city. One day a seventh grader from one of the high schools was caught with a hen he had stolen. Where Kelson Yealuo lived, another woman lived there. She raised her livestock in the yard, including several hens and roosters. Kelson stole one of the hens sitting on her eggs. The hen would had fled, but it could not do so and leave her eggs behind.

He killed the hen, and while he was preparing to cook it, he was arrested. Following his arrest, the feathers of the dead hen were made into a head-dress and placed on his head. He was marched down Main Street to the police station, just three blocks from the big government high School. Lord, as he was led, women were shouting, "Young man, why you did you steal a chicken? If you had come to ask me, I would had made you a delicious okra gravy!"

In those days, nothing in the life of a student was ever hidden from other students, especially students at the government high school. Kelson spent seven days in jail, and was later tried and acquitted of theft and burglary of a chicken. Lord, why under heaven would Kelson Yealuo bother to return to school? He tried to, but other students made him miserable on campus until he quit school. Every time, he stepped on campus, the students would shout, "Chicken Thief, Chicken Thief!" And when he heard that phrase, he ran for his chicken-killer life.

The population of students at the big government high school at the beginning of each school year was staggering. It grew year after year. As usual, hunger in the city would send them home packing by July when all roads leading to the city were cut off by torrential tropical rains.

Lord, no student at the government high school would dare to do anything stupid, but some always did. Like the boy who went on Easter vacation to his hometown and slept with the wife of an oldman.

When school resumed following the vacation, the oldman came to the campus and marched to Principal Marias Duluth's office and reported the case. Principal Duluth stood barely five feet and seven inches tall, but the man did not take "no" for an answer. He whipped any student who misbehaved, whether a boy or a girl. When he told a student, "My man run man," the student ran as fast as he could run. No ifs or buts! He walked as fast as he talked or spoke. My Lord, Principal Duluth spoke good English and was also a very good teacher.

The next morning during the devotion, the oldman was brought before the student body; over a thousand of them and introduced. Principal Duluth began slowly, "Good morning, students! This oldman is Paye Dologbian from Tonglaywein. Though, he is standing right here before you all today, yet he is dying slowly because one of our students is sleeping with the oldman's wife." And all of a sudden, it became dead silent as if all the students were dead. Quietly, they began looking at each other and whispering, "Who is he, or who is it?" The atmosphere was like the one at Jesus' Last Supper with His disciples when He said, "I tell you the truth, one of you is going to betray me" (John13.21b).

And then Principal Duluth dropped the bomb that the students had been waiting for; the student's name is Nyan Quoibiah Doma. When the cat was let out of the bag, everyone breathed a collective sigh of relief. And then he added, "Mr. Doma, will you please step forward."

Then out of the thousands of students gathered that morning, came out a six-foot dark-skin slender fellow wearing a white T-shirt, kakis pants, and black dress shoes, with a flat-top haircut. Principal Duluth told him, "Mr. Doma, this high school has more than two hundred women on this campus. You would have approached at least one of them to sleep with, but no, you went after this poor oldman's wife. You have no conscience. I will give you fifty lashes on your back. After that you will get on your knees and say to Oldman Dologbian that you are very sorry, and you would never sleep with his wife again."

At the end of the principal's speech, Nyan Quoibiah Doma was pinned down by a group of students and given fifty lashes as the oldman looked on and smiled with every lash. Oh yes, fifty lashes, fifty smiles! My God, Oldman Dologbian enjoyed every moment of it. He was still smiling as he left the campus. When he was let go, the principal also asked the students to boo Nyan for at least five minutes. Lord, students at the school lived and died for such a moment as that! It was more than a swarm of bees!

Again, the city of Sanniquellie was full of some of the strangest events Liberia ever saw, like a contemporary biblical healer who showed up one day and took the city by storm, healing anything that had breath; the cripples, the lames, the blinds, the death mutes and the lepers. But when he left town, they all went back as they were. Lord, city accommodated the best, the worst and the ugliest.

And there was another man who walked the streets of the city all day and night singing only one song. The song became his name; "Mr. Follow me." He only sang, "Young girls follow me. If you think I am not man, follow me. If I finish with you, you will know. If you think I am not man, bring your mother. If I finish with her, she will know." Lord, he did not talk about someone's mother! Of course, for heaven's sake, he did.

The man was a beggar and homeless. And all the **grownaboys** followed him when he went around singing in the streets.

Meanwhile, Melvin Hansen enrolled at the big government high school as a transferred student from a private religious school about seven blocks away. The school was a prestigious government high school that offered free education. Students were only required to pay registration and activities fees at the beginning of each school year. Back in those days, the fees were referred to as sports fees. Whether a student played any type of sports or not, he or she was required to pay a one-time fee of one dollar. The registration fees went up every year by fifty cents or a dollar. Lord, some students and their parents could not afford to pay a measly two dollars and fifty cents for registration and sports.

Melvin was born and raised in a rural farming town called Mianplae about twenty miles from Sanniquellie. He was one of two children. His only younger sister was at home with their mother. Their father, Mr. Wonpoe Zoedahn died several years earlier. Melvin attended grade school in his hometown and later a religious school. He was a timid kid who shied away from fights. He was not particularly strong, but he tried fighting once and almost lost two of his front teeth. Thereafter, he came to rely heavily on his feet to get away from any fight as fast and as far as possible.

He became an instant standout footballer when he transferred to the government high school after his graduation from the religious school. He also became the top student in his class. By the end of the first semester, Melvin had been promoted to the eighth grade. By the end of the year, Melvin was promoted again to the ninth grade. He was not a genius, but he was a smart kid. Lord, Melvin would memorize an entire book and spit it out. He passed the ninth-grade government administered National Examination, now known as the West African Examination

Council (WAEC) administered tests with no sweat. Lord, the boy scored a perfect mark on the science examination.

In spite of the city's reputation as the city of hunger, it was a paradise for footballers. Men who played football in the city were well known and got girls. They were recognized everywhere they went. Men from towns and villages around city would **borrow** footballers on weekends to play for their hometown teams. In the end, the hosts would provide food items and cash to the footballers.

Lord, Melvin was glad to be a footballer because he made friends quickly at the high school. One of his best friends was a boy named Abdulla Konni. He never answered if the "B" sound in Abdulla's first name was never heard. If he did not hear it, he would repeat it at least two or three times slowly with emphasis; **Ab-dulla.** He was a terrific footballer, a brilliant defender!

Another boy called Pat Sammy would **borrow** Melvin, Abdulla and other boys and take them to his hometown about six miles away to play for his hometown. After the game, Melvin and the boys would eat until they could not eat anymore. Melvin was not particularly interested in girls. He was always interested in having decent meals to eat in order to study his lessons. He felt school was his only hope out of poverty from his small farming town of Mianplae

During his first year in Sanniquellie when he attended the religious school, five men came with him from his hometown to attend the same religious school. By July that year, hunger had driven them back home. But Melvin Jansen refused to be defeated by hunger. When everyone left, he bounced from one home to another until the end of the year.
The last home Melvin stayed until graduation, he met a single older lady who was staying in a rooming house where he, too lived. She had a five years old daughter called Princess Layee. She carried her father's first

name rather than the family name. The house belonged to a clan within a particular district in the county. The lady liked Melvin, though she was older than he was. Melvin also liked her. This was the trend with younger men in the city. They slept with older women who had wealthy boyfriends. When the wealthy boyfriends supported the women, younger men like Melvin Jansen and his friends got pieces of the pies. Younger men who did it survived the hunger of city and eventually went on to graduate from high school.

In those days, the younger men referred to those older women as **god-mas**. When it involved older men with younger women, the younger women referred to the older men as **god-pas**.

Melvin's **god-ma** Yealeay Barleay had an older boyfriend about her age. Layee Mamadee was a truck driver who hardly slept at home. When she and Layee met, he decided to rent a room for her almost a quarter of a mile away from the rooming house. There were too many men in the rooming house including Melvin. Therefore, Layee wanted to protect his wife from the hungry students in the house while he was away. Lord, when the men were hungry, they would say anything to a woman. Fortunately for Melvin, Yealeay introduced him to Layee as her only brother who was away at school. And he believed her. Layee also came to like and love Melvin as a brother to Yealeay.

One night while Layee was away on the road again, Yealeay invited Melvin for a sleepover. Unfortunately for Yealeay and Melvin, Layee's truck broke down, and he had to return home that night around three in the morning. Melvin and Yealeay were getting ready to make love when Layee knocked at the door. If the ground in the room would open, Melvin Jansen would had jumped into it. Yealeay had to employ all the tricks in her womanly cheating arsenals to stall her boyfriend while Melvin tried to get dressed up. While he was dressing, the knock on the door grew louder and louder and turned into Layee yelling, "Woman, are you stupid, what's wrong with you? Open the crazy door before I break it down!"

It was so dark that one could hardly see the palm of his or her hand. When Yealeay finally opened the door, Melvin Jansen dashed out under Layee's arms without being noticed and without his slippers into the dark night with dogs barking after him. He ran as fast as he had never run in his life, even on the football field. He could hear Layee shouting at Yealeay, "What took you so long to open the door, eh?" Lord, what if Melvin had been seen and caught by Layee? Just what if, Melvin had been caught in bed with his sister Yealeay, Lord? When Layee inquired about the slippers the next morning, Yealeay told him that they belonged to one of her friends, and he believed her.

After three days, Yealeay brought Melvin's slippers to the rooming house. She and Melvin just looked at each other and began to laugh. After the laughs, Yealeay told Melvin "My womanly gut instincts told me Layee was coming back that night. That was the reason I told you to leave early, but you refused and wanted to stay until in the morning. The next time I tell you something like that, you should believe me."

Two months after the incident, Layee Mamadee accepted a driving job in the city of Monrovia and left Yealeay with her insignificant brother Melvin Jansen from Mianplae. With Layee gone, Melvin and Yealeay were absolutely free to do with each other as they pleased. When Melvin returned home from school, his food was ready. If he wanted water to bathe, Yealeay prepared it without complaints. Lord, she was like a mother away from home.

During Easter vacation that year, Yealeay accompanied Melvin to his hometown. Lord, Melvin's buddies in Mianplae did not play to laugh at him for bringing a girlfriend at home that was closed to his mother's age. Melvin did not mind the jokes. They would had done exactly the same thing if they have had the opportunity. Melvin and his buddies knew each well for doing things like that; sleeping with older women. As long as the end justified the means, he did not have a problem with it. After all, Yealeay was good to him and treated him like her own son rather than a boyfriend. In return Melvin highly respected and admired her, and would not do anything in the world to hurt her feelings. He did not call Yealeay "Mom," but he called her by her daughter's name; "Princess' Mother" until he graduated from high school while his friends were sitting back in Mianplae drinking palm wine. He did all that with Yealeay Barleay's help. Lord, Melvin Jansen appreciated Yealeay Barleay more than anything in the city. Yealeay if you are out there, Melvin is searching for you to say he is really sorry for that fateful night when he had to run when your husband came home.

One day Melvin was waiting around a lorry parking station. He was on his way to D. Q. Barnabas's farm about four miles away from the city. D.Q Barnabas was a mentor to him. He was a tall middle age man who worked for the county government as a clerk of court. He sat and typed on a manual typewriter eight to nine hours a day, and five days a week. Lord, Melvin never met any man who would type faster than Mr. Barnabas. It was unbelievable!

When Melvin boarded the lorry around five thirty in the afternoon, he sat close to a gentleman who was reading a leaflet. He must had been in his early thirties and spoke French fluently. The leaflet had pictures of several male martial artists practicing their arts in a variety of positions. He asked the gentleman if he could take a look at the leaflet.

The gentleman gladly handed it to Melvin. He [Melvin] just sat there with his mouth wide opened without saying a word. He immediately folded the leaflet and handed it back to the gentleman. After a while when they left the parking station, and on their way, Melvin asked the gentleman again if he could have the leaflet this time and keep it? The gentleman said, "Yes," and handed the leaflet back to Melvin. He could not find words to thank the gentleman. After seeing several Chinese martial arts movies, he wanted to learn the arts by all means, and this would be a great beginning for him.

During the weekend on Mr. Barnabas' farm, Melvin began practicing the various positions whenever he had breaks from the work on the farm. Mr. Barnabas' parents were curious to know what was going on with Melvin shouting, punching and kicking the air.

He told them that he was learning a self-defense style called karate. Mr. Barnabas Senior told Melvin, "Boy you better learn to wrestle people to the ground than learning to shout and kick. The time you would take to position yourself for kicking, someone would have already knocked you to the ground."

But Melvin Jansen was not convinced or persuaded. He would dare to teach himself just from that leaflet to become the most-deadly human weapon to ever walk the streets of Sanniquellie. Melvin returned to the rooming house after the weekend confident that he would learn martial arts. In the evening after football practice, he would go out in front of the rooming house and practice his martial arts for hours and hours, way into the dark night. When the moon was up, he practiced until twelve mid-night.

Gradually Melvin's joints began to be flexible, and his wrists would stiffen easily to throw a karate punch. This was the year that Mr. Mekong Timbuktu came to the city for a visit. One evening the goalkeeper for the big government high school invited him to watch the football team's practice. After the practice he was impressed with the team, and told Sport Director Jeff Wilkerson that he would love to coach the football team. The school had a Sport Director, but no coach. And with that request the director gladly accepted him.

But Mr. Timbuktu had a problem; he did not speak or understand English. He had only spoken French throughout his life where he was born and raised in Guinea, West Africa. Until now, he had never encountered English speaking people. The little French the goalkeeper knew he would help Mr. Timbuktu to translate during coaching. Mr. Timbuktu was a very handsome man, well-built with nice teeth. His teeth were small and evenly matched with no gap between, above or below. He stood over six feet and two inches tall, and had a nice closed cut hair. He spoke in a very soft voice unusual for a man of his height and size.

He did not play football well, but he knew a lot about coaching a football team. He had been a goalkeeper throughout his life. And being a former goalkeeper, Mr. Timbuktu knew so much about taking shots at the goal, including taking free or set kicks. My God, he would tell a player, "When you kick, you got have to bend over the ball." Those who did, always scored goals. Lord, the man was a walking genius on free kicks. He was later brought on the campus and introduced as the coach of the football team. If he was paid a salary, no one, including the football team knew.

Midway through the school year, it became known to the entire school that Mr. Timbuktu also knew martial arts, and was willing to start a training camp for students, or players who were interested in learning the art. This was the news Melvin Jansen had been waiting for all his Minaplae village farming life. He wanted to jump up and touch the sky upon hearing the news. Now his dream of acquiring a black belt in karate was a reality.

While a student like Melvin Jansen and others were desperate to obtain a black belt in martial arts, or graduate to the next class, some students would not just stay out of trouble. And for that, there was never a dull moment at the government high school. Students were always doing the dumbest things on campus and getting caught all of the time.

One of the most beautiful young ladies on campus, Miss Fannie Landan was being courted by a boy. She was in the eighth grade. The boy courting her, Dave Jonah was in the tenth grade. He wrote a nice letter and sent it to Miss Landan. Yes, Lord, in those days when a letter from a boy to a girl meant something special! Rather than keeping the letter to herself and reading it at home, she brought it to class. She tried to read it under her desk while the English Teacher, Mr. Job Dodo was trying to teach his class. When he noticed that Miss Landan was not paying attention to his teaching, he called her to the front of the class. Lord, she had the audacity to bring the letter with her too. Mr. Dodo took the letter away from her and marched to Principal Duluth's office and filed a complaint that Miss Landan was disrupting his class reading her boyfriend's letter while he, Mr. Dodo was trying to teach.

Principal Duluth took the letter and brought it in the morning during devotion, and called Fannie Landan and Dave Jonah in front of the student body as usual. Again, Principal Duluth plunged into his usual speech. "Good morning ladies and gentlemen. Here again we have a love affair on campus, this time in our very classroom when a poor teacher was trying his very best to teach. In that same class, Miss Fannie Landan was disrupting the classroom reading a letter she received from her boyfriend. Since Miss Landan felt that this letter was important to be read in class rather than paying attention to her English Teacher, I will read the letter so everyone would hear it." Lord, there was never dull moments on the grounds of the high school during devotions.

The letter read:

"My Dearest Miss Landan, you are the most beautiful woman in the whole wide world. I love you like fish loves water. The first time I kissed you, you tasted just like sweet apples and bananas.

And chills went through my spine! When I see you, I see the stars in the heavenly places, and I can hear my own heart beat in my chest. Oh, if only I could just hold you in my hands over my heart, then, and only then, will my heart beats go down. Sometimes I lay in my bed all night thinking about you because I am afraid. Most beautiful women are like cassava sticks, they have many eyes."

When Principal Duluth read the last sentence, the entire student body went crazy. Everyone, including Principal Duluth was on the ground laughing. Lord, why do students do the dumbest things in the world, thinking that they would get away with them? He did not read the rest of the letter thereafter.

Both Dave and Fannie were suspended for three days. Dave Jonah never returned to Sani-Quentin after the incident. Fannie Landan returned, but she did not last because every time students saw her, they would shout, "Women are like cassava sticks with many eyes."

That same year Jay Vin, one of the best footballers at the high school played Russian-Roulette with twelve bottles of poisonous liquor and lost. He accepted another student's challenge to drink twelve bottles of **Cane Juice**. One would call it a suicide because each of those bottles contained at least twelve ounces of that poisonous liquor. He dropped on the floor of the liquor store as soon as he drank the tenth bottle. He was rushed to the nearby hospital by his buddies and the same friend who had challenged him to drink the liquor. He was pronounced dead on arrival (DOA) by the medical staff at the hospital. The football team led the funeral procession all the way to the grave. The big government high school still feels the loss of Jay Vin to this day.

On top of all the bizarreness on the campus of the high school, two teachers stood out as the epitome of high school insanity. Mr. Hosea

McDougal, the Physical Education (PE) teacher and Mr. Jason Kumis, the Agricultural teacher were two bizarre educators to ever step feet on the campus of the high school. How these two men got into the school as teachers remained a mysterious to this day.

Mr. McDougal was a self-styled longdistance marathoner who never ran five miles in his entire boring life. He was reported to have represented Liberia at a marathon in the Democratic Republic of Congo (DRC) in the 1960's. He did not know how to read, and never taught from a text book. He gave tests on subjects he never taught. If students wrote two to three pages on his tests, they got "A's". Those who wrote just two or three paragraphs got "F's".

During the long jump practical test on the field, students got above or below averages. Lord, only Mr. McDougal knew what those two words meant. But at the end of the semester, the students he knew well, got passing grades on their report cards for the long jump. Those he did not know, got failing grades on their report cards. And of course, girls who walked with him side by side daily after school got passing grades, too. Men on the football team were always fortunate because they were known. Lord, a PE teacher would not dare to fail a footballer at the school if he wanted to keep his job and be in a good book with the team.

On the other hand, Mr. Jason Kumis was a self-proclaimed agriculturalist who knew everything there was to know about planting rice in the swamp. Everywhere he went, he had on Wellington's boots (Liberians called it rain boots). The man even slept with his Wellington's boots on. He taught on planting, but he had a **Cane Juice** shop that would kill people when they drank it in excess just as Jay Vin did and took his own life. He never taught a class in any of the buildings on campus. Students met with him at his house or in the swamp where he stood on the edge, and pushed them into the waist deep swamp. And then at the end of the semester, he too, would record passing grades in the report cards of students who went to his **Cane Juice** shop and bought bottles of the poisonous liquor. Those who did not go there to buy liquor had failing grades recorded in their report cards.

One semester Mr. Kumis pushed Melvin Jansen into the swamp for one of his special classes on planting rice. Melvin worked from sunup to sundown. Some of his team mates saw him standing in the waist-deep swam all day. At the end of the semester, Mr. Kumis recorded a failing grade in his report card. Melvin confronted him about the grade, but he refused to change it. That morning Melvin's blood was boiling as he ran to Principal Marias Duluth's office. At that very moment, Mr. Kumis was walking down the hall of the main school building in his Wellington's boots as usual. Principal Duluth shouted to him, "Mr. Kumis, please come!" Lord, when Principal Duluth called, every teacher, including Agriculturalist Kumis moved fast. Principal Duluth looked at Melvin's grade, and they were all "A's," except for Mr. Kumis' grade. Principal Duluth told him, "Change the boy's grade right now to a "B." He wanted to explain, but Lord, no one did that to Principal Duluth, no not even Mr. Kumis. He stuck the report card in Mr. Kumis' chest until he got hold of it and changed Melvin's grade to a "B."

From that day on, Mr. Kumis never messed with Melvin again. Every time he saw Melvin, he would say, "Oh yes, the principal's son." Melvin Jansen gladly accepted the name and behaved like it in dealing with Mr. Kumis, the agriculturalist.

Yes, that was the big government high school all right, where students who were police officers came to school every morning dressed up in their police uniforms, fully armed to the teeth, and ready for any eventual shootouts with nobody. Soldiers came too, but they did not bear arms like police officers, except for high ranking officers who wore their revolvers around their waists. They, too came prepared for a war that did not exist at that time.

Melvin narrowly missed being expelled on one occasion when students, led by some hooligans at the school rioted over students' meals almost killing the cooks. The chief lady cook was thrown into a large pan full of hot cooking oil. She had to be taken to the nearest hospital with first and second degree burns on her face, hands, and feet. She would have been burned all over her body if she had not been fully dressed. The assistant male cook, Mr. Brown was knocked out cold and unconscious.

The food riot took place during recess hours when students went to the Mess Hall to eat lunch. Melvin returned to campus in the middle of the chaos when student leaders were helping Principal Duluth to identify those responsible for the riot. Oh yes, they had cooking oil all over their uniforms, and that was how they were easily identified. Lord, that was a no brainer for a man like Principal Marias Duluth who was never proud of his high school's reputation as breeding grounds for the rudest students in the country. Lord, some students, both male and female transferred to the high school just for that bad reputation.

Fifteen students were immediately expelled and twenty more suspended for at least two weeks that day. My Lord, it seemed like fate was always on the side of Melvin Jansen. With his martial arts skills coupled with the hunger of city, he would have been in the middle of the riot just to get some food into his belly.

Meanwhile, Mr. Timbuktu decided to use the Mess Hall as his martial arts training room. The building was constructed in the early 1960's as students' dining room. It was never used for that purpose because it could not hold the number of students on campus. The interior was no more than 3,000 square feet with two doors, one in the front and the other one directly in the rear. It also had several windows, but had no restrooms. There were no chairs, so students stood up on the inside and ate when the food was distributed. Sometimes when the student population was unusually large, it was used as classroom. But students had to carry their own chairs if they wanted to sit down.

The martial arts training would be three days a week following football practices; Mondays, Wednesdays and Fridays. Saturdays were optional for students who were interested in taking extra lessons for faster progress. A lot of students showed up on the first day of training camp. Mr. Timbuktu had to turn down some students to make rooms for the players. They were top priorities. Goalkeeper Oleseh Kamara and his brother Molehseh Kamara did not want to participate in any martial arts. They were afraid of being injured. For some strange reasons, Goalkeeper Oleseh thought Mr. Timbuktu did not know martial arts well enough to teach others. But Melvin and the other footballers were willing to take a chance.

Two months after the training began, the government high school had a game with its arch rival high school across town. They were always afraid to challenge the government high school in any sporting events. Lord, in those days, no school officials in their right minds would dare to challenge the government high school. But on this particular occasion, the Catholic High School challenged public school in volleyball, basketball and football. The government high school won the first two games in volleyball and basketball.

Mid way through the second half a fight broke out during the football game when the central defender fouled Melvin Jansen nearly breaking his right leg. It was deliberate, and he knew it. His school was losing badly, so he decided to hurt someone. When they got up, Melvin shouted, *heeee-haaa* and flew in midair with a karate kick and hit him in the chest. He landed on his back, and by the time he would get up, the referee and the line judges were all over them. T Boys from Melvin's high school also came, ready to fight. Lord, that was one of the reasons they never challenged the public school to any sporting events because the government school boys enjoyed fighting on the football field. Lord, the **game ended in confusion**. The referee would not bring both teams back on the field without starting another fight.

From that day onward, Melvin Jansen became known as the Liberian Karate Kid in the city. He cherished the name for a long time because it made other men to think twice before picking a fight with him. He was born lazy and ran away from many fights, but now he would stand his karate grounds and challenge any man to a duel of hands to hands combat.

In spite of the incident on the ballfield, Melvin was never cocky. He did not boast to anybody that he knew a little bit of martial arts. As usual, he kept a low profile throughout until the end of the school year. He knew there were still a lot more things to learn in martial arts. In fact, Mr. Timbuktu told him never to be cocky because he nearly won a fight. He always stressed to Melvin and the other students that a martial artist did not pick a fight, but only used his or her skills when forced to defend himself or herself.

The year ended on good note, and Melvin Jansen was promoted to the tenth grade. He was happy because he only had two more years to complete high school. That summer Melvin went home rejoicing that he passed his class and had learned some basic skills in self-defense. That meant no boy in Mianplae would mess with him anymore. Except for his closed-friends, most boys avoided him when they learned that he was promoted to the tenth grade. Those who counted him out, including the boys who ran away from the hunger of the city were surprised that Melvin would hang in there and endure the hunger until tenth grade.

Lord, they were wondering what was his secret? He did not tell them, but he knew his secrets were **god-ma** Yealeay and football.

Leaving school at the end of the year and going home was fun, but returning to school after summer vacation was the most difficult thing for Melvin. Vacation always seemed shorter and was over faster than school days. School days always seemed forever. But he vowed to hang in there until the end no matter what the city threw at him, including involuntary hunger strike.

The following year began great as usual with inter-classes football league. This was the time high school picked or selected its new players to add or replace the ones that had either transferred to other high schools or graduated. In spite of its love for the game of football, the high school did not take academia lightly. It had almost ninety-five percent graduation rate. Principal Duluth at one time banned footballers whose grade point averages were below 2.0 from playing on the football team. That year school only played a single football game the entire year.

Yet the inter-classes football league that year was nothing short of remarkable. The high school added enough new players to organize two football teams; one called Team A and other called Team B. Students from across the nation would transfer to the high school every year because of its reputation as a prestigious government high school in rural Liberia. The rivalry was tough at times because men were doing their best to move from Team B to Team A. Lazy men would lose their starting positions if they did not do well in practices. Lord in those days, men played football for the love of the game, and not for money. They only got preferential treatment on matters like wearing uniforms, showing up late for school, physical education classes, or leaving school early.

Following the league, Mr. Timbuktu resumed his classes in martial arts. At the very beginning of the school year, he did not teach classes because he had to observe or scout new student players to select his starting eleven men team. That year he added three new students to the class. He refused to overload the class. He kept the number of students at twenty-two, and no more. If a student dropped out, he would be replaced.

It was about early May when martial arts resumed at the high school. After Melvin's fight with another player on the Catholic High School ballfield, words began to spread around the city that the big government high school was training all members of its football team in martial arts so they would always be prepared to fight on the field during football games. Surrounding towns, including mining towns or camps began to fear the school. The high school already had a reputation for harboring some of the most outlaw students in the country.

The likes of goalkeeper Roy Matthias, Tupac Kington, Craig Kumolo, Samson Nokia, Benedict Donaldson, George Kibble, Ham "Karate" Jethro, Jimmy Bartee and the late Jay Vin were feared in the city. On weekends, these men would drink **Cane Juice** and danced in the streets morning and night until the weekends were over. No man crossed their paths when they were drunk. And they always got all A's in Mr. Kumis' agricultural class because they were his regular customers.

Some of these outlaw students were also in the martial arts training camp. Goalkeeper Roy Matthias, Tupac Kington and Ham "Karate" Jethro were members of the martial arts team. As his name implied, Ham "Karate" Jethro was a man who said to any other man he met, "You venture, you get it wrong." He got his nickname from fighting a man in Monrovia when he resided there several years earlier before transferring to the high school. He stood five feet and eight inches tall. If it were not for his bow-legged, he would have easily been six feet tall. He was a slender man and had the best Afro hairdo on campus. When he walked by, all the girls on campus drooled after him. But they would not venture, or else they would had gotten it wrong.

It was one Friday evening when Mr. Timbuktu and his students met after football practice. They had sweated all afternoon and evening and were exhausted, but they reported for martial arts practice anyway. Lord, the drops of sweats from their body were all over on the hard cement floor. There was nothing, absolutely nothing to wipe the sweat off the floor. The boys lined up for the routine step and punch drill. Melvin Jansen was in the middle with at least nine students on either side of him.

This night was not a good night. Mr. Timbuktu was not in a good mood, even during football practice. He would have easily cancelled practice that night without any student complaining. After the step and punch drill, the students moved to flying board kick. He would hold a piece of wood board at his chest level, and each student would fly and kick it.

All was going well until it was Melvin Jansen's turn to kick the board. Melvin had been practicing since he took the leaflet from the gentleman, months back when he was on his way to Mr. Barnabas's farm. When he came running and flew to kick the board, Mr. Timbuktu deliberately lowered the board to his waist level fearing that Melvin would step in his chest. When Melvin's right foot went over the board, Mr. Timbuktu swung the board around throwing Melvin into the air coming face down on the cement floor.

To protect his teeth and his face from smashing on that hard floor, Melvin maneuvered and landed on his big toes. He had learned to do push-ups on his fingertips and on his toes. But he was almost six feet in the air when he crash-landed. He broke all the bones in his big toes on both feet. It was an excruciating injury.

Mr. Timbuktu stood there looking all sorry as if he did not mean to do it. He meant it because the other students saw it coming. It was the end of martial arts practice that night. Melvin sat there on the cold and sweaty floor with members of the football team around him, not knowing what to do next. The first thought that crossed his mind was that his dream of a black belt in martial arts just died. Lord, would he even be able to play football again? He was afraid to go to the hospital for fear of someone amputating his bid toes. That night his friends, Carlos Nehemiah and Abdulla Konni helped him to walk home. Walking home was easier, but would he be able to walk to school next Monday morning?

As soon as Melvin arrived at home, he heated some water and applied hot pads to his big toes. Lord, that was a wrong remedy. He could had applied ice first, then hot pads three or four days later. But obtaining or getting ice was not a luxury for the poor and less fortunate students of the city.

When Goalkeeper Oliseh Kamara heard about Melvin's injury, he was mad. Melvin was one of his best defenders. He would not do without his skills. Melvin was replaceable, but it would take some time to train and get used to a new defender. When Oliseh saw Melvin on campus that Monday, he said to him, "I told you so. This man did not know much about martial arts to teach. He had learned some judo in high school when he was a young man. And that was it." Melvin accepted Oliseh's invitation to go and live at his house until his toes were healed. Lord, friendships in football those days were just plain magical.

The next Tuesday morning, Oliseh went to Principal Duluth's office and convinced him to abolish the voluntary martial arts program. Oliseh was highly respected and admired by school officials unlike no other student on campus at the school.

The next Wednesday morning during devotion, Melvin Jansen and other hundreds of students heard the dreaded news they did not want to hear from Principal Duluth. "Ladies and gentlemen, unfortunately, we had to abolish the martial arts program. One of our best players and brightest students almost got crippled on the hard cement floor of the Mess Hall last Friday night. It is good for self-defense, but karate is equally bad when people get hurt. No more martial arts at this high school." He concluded and walked away leaving martial arts students speechless. Lord, what would they say? When Principal Duluth spoke, the case was closed. And it did!

That Wednesday morning with every student's eyes focused on him, and with tears welling in his own eyes, the dream of the Liberian Karate Kid, Melvin Manuel Jansen, obtaining a black belt in martial arts died. Yes, dead, shot pointblank to death face-down by Mr. Timbuktu. Lord, would the Liberian Karate Kid find grace in his heart to forgive Mr. Timbuktu? Walking away from martial arts was one the hardest decisions Melvin Manuel Jansen ever made in his life.

Melvin could not wait for the next weekend when he would go home and consult Uncle Eddie Noble, a traditional bone specialist in Mianplae. The weekend came quickly, and by Friday evening, Melvin was on his way to Mianplae. He arrived that night and before the cock would crow, Uncle Eddie Noble was waiting outside the door to pull on his broken toes. That was a morning Melvin Jansen would never forget. It was horrible to bear. He nearly passed out. The same thing was repeated Sunday morning. By the following Monday morning, Melvin would walk on his feet, and not on his heels.

Uncle Eddie Noble gave a chunk of the medicine to Melvin to take with him. He would apply it twice a day, one application in the morning before school and another one at bedtime. Within two months Melvin Jansen was back on his feet as new on the football field. His friends, especially Abdulla Konni and Goalkeeper Oliseh Kamara were glad to see him back.

It took weeks, perhaps months for Melvin to get the thoughts of the night of the injury off his mind. He had nightmares about it on several nights. In his dreams, he would see himself practicing with Mr. Timbuktu, and then all of a sudden, he would see himself in midair coming down and crashing on the hard cement floor. In one of those dreams, he had lost all his teeth when he fell face-down. He woke up that night sweating, and thanking God that it was only a dream. Melvin Jansen would have never returned home to Mianplae without his teeth. He would have remained a toothless permanent citizen of Sanniquellie City where he lost his teeth, or move to another town where no one knew him.

ONCE UPON THE TIME IN LIBERIA, a young man called Melvin Jansen who later became known as the Liberian Karate Kid lost his dream of obtaining a black belt in martial arts when he got badly injured in training camp. The injury was ruled a fault of the instructor, Mr. Mekong Timbuktu. Thereafter, the martial arts program was abolished.

His dream of a black belt died that fateful night on the cement floor of his high school Mess Hall. The dream died, but Melvin Manuel Jansen lived on and graduated as one of the top students in his class. His parents were proud of him on graduation day. After graduation, Melvin and his parents returned home and celebrated for weeks to the amazement of many men and women of Mianplae. He did not obtain his black belt, but Melvin Manuel Jansen surely got his high school diploma.

CHAPTER 9

THE WOMAN WHO FAILED TO DISCIPLINE HER ONLY SON AND LIVED TO REGRET IT

"A thing that dances fast does not have the best dancing feet."
Meaning: Those who desire to succeed quickly in
life are likely to be disappointed, or to fail miserably.

The procession to the hangman's gallows began about ten in the morning. Angry crowds followed the procession, shouting, "Down with that boy! He does not deserve to live. Hang him so our community can rest in peace!" As they drew closer to the gallows, Philemon Bundor turned around to look at his mother for the last time. Mrs. Gracie Bundor had her hands over her stomach. She would raise her hands towards heaven and bring them down over her stomach. Lord, a mother's cry for mercy for her only son, but no one was listening.

Davidson and Gracie met in high school. Both were students at Mount Zion Multilateral High School in Elizabeth City in the southeast of the country. They had fallen in love in their senior year in high school when Davidson Bundor served as the president of the student council with Gracie Theophilus as his vice president. Both graduated on top of their class and got engaged immediately after graduation. Davidson had studied masonry while Gracie had majored in bookkeeping and accountant. Lord, Gracie was a genius with numbers!

The Theophiluses had pressured Davidson into getting married in Elizabeth City. They had always been busy with plantation work and unable to attend any of their children's weddings. And this was a chance for them to lavish real money on their last child. Lord, Davidson would had been a fool to refuse such an offer when the parents of the bride were willing to spend a whopping $15,000 for the ceremony in rural Liberia.

Gracie Theophilus came from a Liberian middleclass family in Elizabeth City. Her family history went far back as the early settlers in Liberia. Her father, Mr. Marvelous Theophilus owned and operated a rubber plantation near Elizabeth City. Marvelous T. Rubber Plantation was five miles south of the city. He and his wife, Mrs. Drusilla Theophilus had five grown children with Gracie being the youngest. Except for Gracie, the rest of their children, three boys and another girl, Gracelyn were living with their families in the United States of America. Mr. Theophilus and his family were very religious people. They were members of the Ebenezer Cathedral of the Holy Trinity (ECHT) in Elizabeth City, a local nondenominational church.

The wedding ceremony was the greatest show on earth that Elizabeth City had ever seen since its origin. The guests came from as far as Monrovia. Auntie Minnie, cousin Lydia, Grandmas Seraphina and Norcia, Uncles Jared, Jeffrey and Jessy, including hosts of other relatives from Atherton, Brewerville, Caresburg, Congo-Town, Franklinville, Francisburg, Gettysburg, Johnsonville, Taylorsburg, Taylorville, Tolbertsburg, and Tubmanburg came. Lord, Elizabeth City suddenly became another Monrovia outside of the capital city, Monrovia. Strangers and visitors came from all over Liberia to attend the wedding. Lord, even the workers on the rubber plantation were given two days off to attend the wedding ceremony.

Ebenezer Cathedral members lived for moments like baby-showers, birthday parties, funerals and weddings. They always went out of their way to make such occasions memorable. That was exactly what they did when Davidson Bundor and Gracie Theophilus got married. After all, Mr. Marvelous T (as he was popularly known in the church) had single handedly paid for the construction of the Fellowship Hall. His daughter's wedding was an opportune time for payback.

It was an extraordinary ceremony that left indelible memories in the minds and hearts of the people of Elizabeth City. Rev. Dr. Josiah Petticoats, the founding bishop was the officiating minister as usual. Rev. Dr. Petticoats never allowed any other minister to stand in his place on such occasions. He preached a brilliant message on the benefits of marriage versus the perils of co-habitation or shacking up. It was a message aimed at the young men and women of the church. He reminded them to do what is right in the sight of God just as Davidson and Gracie were doing. The message had gotten a standing ovation before the exchange of rings and vows.

After the wedding, Davidson Bundor and his wife moved home to Summerville to find employment and to later start their own company after earning some money. Davidson found an employment with Richard Batt Construction Company and rose quickly to the position of supervisor of construction just after two years. Gracie decided to stay home and help tutor kids in mathematics in the neighborhood to the delight of her husband. She would start her own consulting company when the funds were available. She would not do it with her parents' money. Gracie hated to depend on her parents, even before her husband found a job. She felt that they had already done enough by underwriting their wedding.

In the seventh year of their marriage, Gracie got pregnant with their son. Lord, Davidson and Gracie were excited beyond words. Prior to her pregnancy, the people of Summerville had begun to gossip about Davidson Bundor that he had married a barren woman from the southeast and brought her to the city. Gracie had almost come to believe that she would not have children. But her husband had always reassured her that the people of the city were not gods and had no control over anything, including their ability to have a child or children. "Don't listen to their gossips," Mr. Bundor had always told his wife.

Summerville would have easily been called Gossipville. Summervillians talked about anything that moved. It was so bad that residents referred to their city as rumors mill. There was a Mrs. Gossip Rueben at Summerville United Lutheran Fellowship (SULF), who lived up to her name. If there was anything in Summerville that Mrs. Gossip Rueben did not know about, then, it did not happen in the city. She had a peculiar name for every woman in the church, including the Pastor's wife. Mrs. Rueben referred to her as the "Palm Worm" because Mrs. Wendy Garfield looked short and chubby. Living in Summerville was like living in a glasshouse. Everyone stood outside and watch everything that was happening on inside of the house. In spite of its reputation for gossips, Mr. and Mrs. Bundor loved Summerville and would not exchange it for any city in rural Liberia. They were proud to be its residents, and would not mind raising their children in the city.

Philemon Bundor's birth was normal. His mother had no complications during pregnancy. He came out crying with his fists clinched, ready to take on the world. The couple put all their love into raising their son. As a child, he lacked nothing. With the birth of Philemon, Davidson and Gracie felt that they were on top of the world. Gracie had always vowed that she would love her children to death if she ever had them. Lord, she sure followed her words to the letter. As long as Gracie was alive, Philemon did nothing wrong under the heavens. To Gracie, Philemon was a perfect child who was always right no matter what the case or situation. She always said to her friends at church, "I am proud to be the mother of a Philemon. If you don't know what I am talking about, go and check in the Holy Bible in the New Testament."

Mother Gracie would not even give her husband a chance to discipline their son. When Davidson felt that Philemon had done something wrong and needed to be disciplined, Gracie had always stood between her husband and son, vowing that no person alive or dead would touch her son with a ten-foot pole. By his tenth birthday, Philemon was completely out of control. He got into trouble at school, after school, on the playgrounds, and in other public places.

One day at school, Philemon Bundor spat in the face of the reading teacher, Miss Leona Henderson when she corrected him for mispronouncing the word "phase." Philemon had pronounced the word with the "P" sound rather than the "F" sound. He had also stood on top of his desk and verbally insulted Miss Leona Henderson, calling her "bat face." When Miss Henderson invited Mr. and Mrs. Bundor to a conference with their son, Mrs. Gracie Bundor swore upon the name of the God of the Holy Bible that her son had never done anything wrong in his life, and would not have done such a thing, especially to a teacher. She would not give her husband a chance to say a word. At the end of the conference, Mr. Bundor warned her about raising their son to be an outlaw and a rebel. "Do not spoil this boy. If you continue, you will turn the city against this family," he had concluded. But his wife countered, "If they messed with with me and my son, I would stop tutoring their dumb children."

Philemon misbehaved everywhere he and his parents went, even at church. The Bundors were members of Summerville United Lutheran

Fellowship (SULF). Mr. Davidson Bundor was a layleader and Mrs. Gracie Bundor served on the Finance Committee of the church. Both were in good standing until Philemon began getting into fights at Sunday school. During the Pastor's Appreciation Day Dinner, a month earlier, Philemon threw a piece of chocolate cake at Mrs. Wendy Garfield, the wife of Rev. Marshall Garfield, the senior pastor of SULF. Lord, Mrs. Garfield was **embarrassed** and did not know how to respond. Thank God for His grace because the dress she had on that day was her special occasion dress purchased by her husband on his many trips to the United States of America.

Without God's grace, all hell would have broken loose at the church fellowship. Lord, Mrs. Garfield was one of those pastor's wife who did not take anything from a church member lying down. She had always said to other women in the church, "We will spoil it down here, and when we get to heaven, Jesus will fix it." She had even gotten the nickname, "Jesus will fix it." Immediately after the incident she told her husband to place the Bundors on probation until they learn to discipline their son. Rev. Garfield gladly did as his wife demanded.

As a young man, Mr. Davidson Bundor had worked with his father, Mr. Romeo Bundor in construction before going to trade high school. He learned bricklaying at an early age. So when he started working with Richard Batt Construction Company, he already had several years of experience.

On Philemon's eleventh birthday, Mr. Davidson had a terrible accident at work when he fell to his death from the third floor of a building while doing his regular general inspection. He slipped and fell through a cracked in the unfinished part of the floor. He was pronounced dead on the scene. Gracie Bundor nearly died from grief following the tragic death of her husband.

After her husband's death, Gracie and her son went to spend some time with her parents. Grandpa Marvelous Theophilus and Philemon Bundor could not get along. The boy went around the plantation destroying the newly planted rubber tree crops, and chopping some of the older trees down. When Gracie's father confronted his daughter about her son's behavior, she angrily responded, "I will take my only son and get off your farm." Mrs. Drusilla Theophilus got angry at her daughter, almost throwing her out along with her son. Mrs. Theophilus was angry to the point of referring to her grandson as "a heathenish child." Her daughter responded by calling her mother "a witch who only loved her own children." Within three weeks, Gracie and Philemon were back home in Summerville.

Mr. Bundor was the oldest of three children; two boys and a girl. His sister Susanna Bundor was now residing in Summerville after spending nearly fifteen years in Monrovia. She had returned home following the death of her brother to assist her sister-in-law Gracie Bundror. She had never been married and had no children.

Susanna Bundor was the middle child of the three siblings, but she was the most outspoken. She had completed high school in the city with the goal of going to college to get a law degree. But she had become disillusioned after three failed relationships. The last man she dated had promised to marry her. But after one and a half years, Domingo Daniels had broken their engagement citing unexplainable reasons. After that incident, Susanna returned home vowing never to try marriage again. She had always said, "If God wanted me to get married, I would have gotten married a long time ago."

Upon her return from Monrovia, she filed a wrongful death Lawsuit against Richard Batt Construction Company winning thousands of dollars. In spite of what the likes of Domingo Daniels and other men had thrown at her, Susanna was a beautiful woman who believed that she had every right under heaven just like any other man.

But the youngest of the sibling, Matt Bundor was a different case. He was a walking Ananias Imitator. After his brother's tragic death, Matt Bundor became an instant role model to his nephew Philemon Bundor. Philemon believed every story he heard from Uncle Matt (that was how Philemon called him). Everything about Uncle Matt was pure and simple mendacity.

He stood five feet and four inches tall. Uncle Matt was a real dark skin man whose eyes were way back in his head. He seldom smiled at anyone. He would not be described as a bow-legged man, but he walked like one. Even in his late forties, Uncle Matt would outrun any man his age. And he still actively played football. Without formal education, or being a student of any school in his life, Uncle Matt knew about all races and nationalities of the world, their customs, cultures and their very ways of life. He spoke of them as if he lived, played and ate with them in the same house. Lord, how did the man know all these facts if he could not even understand, write, or speak the English language?

Philemon was required by his upbringing to believe Uncle Matt because kids were supposed to believe whatever adults told them. It was an insult to tell a grown man or woman that he or she was lying. If and when the kid's parents heard it, he or she would be spanked on returning home.

Uncle Matt had an opportunity to travel to the southwest of the country to work on a rubber plantation. He barely spent a year on the plantation. When he returned, Uncle Matt had stories of his dramatic escapes from murderers, and his narrow escapes from fatal car crashes where he was the only survivor. And how on some occasions, he and his buddy would beat fifteen men, taking out all their teeth.

He once told a story of one of his fights where he and his buddy were surrounded by a group of angry and drunken men. And their only way out of there alive was to throw a cocktail bomb at the men. One of them mistaken the bottle for a cigarette lighter, picked it up and attempted to examine it. The bottle blew his face off causing his friends to scatter. That cocktail bomb saved Uncle Matt and his friend's lives. Philemon and his friends believed him because he was alive sitting right there and telling them the story.

Many Ananias Imitators told strange and sometimes unbelievable stories in the city of Summerville. One day, Uncle Matt told Philemon that white people do not die. A white person who died in Liberia, or elsewhere would be alive within days again in his or her country in the West. And when they are old, they simply shed their old skins for new ones, then, *walaa,* they are young again! And in the white people's countries, money grew on trees. There were no poor people. When people were broke and needed money, they just went to the nearest dollar-tree and picked as many dollar bills as possible. By the next morning, the dollar-tree had grown the dollar bills back.

Philemon and his friends were always surrounded by Ananias Imitators who repeatedly told them these strange stories about white people. Ananias Imitators also told Philemon and his friends that white people did not eat rice, or any other foods, except bread. Their skins were always soft because they only eat bread. Bread in the morning, bread in the afternoon, bread in evening and bread in the night just as God fed the Israelites with manna during their wilderness journeys in the Bible. A kid who grew up hearing such stories would grow up with the same mendacity, coupled with the audacity and then become another Ananias Imitator.

Young Philemon Bundor was more than an Ananias Imitator. He became a cheater, a liar and a thief. And when he was caught, he denied it. Of course, Mrs. Gracie Bundor was always there to plead for her only son or bail him out when he went to prison. Lord, she loved her boy to death. The residents of Summerville had and felt sympathies for Gracie for the sudden violent death of her husband and her tireless work in tutoring their kids. But their patience was wearing thin by the weeks, days, hours, minutes and seconds.

Three months after they had returned from his grandparents in Elizabeth City, Philemon broke into the home of his aunt. Susanna Bundor was away visiting another city when Philemon and two of his buddies broke into her house and ransacked it in search of cash and valuables. Philemon had previously commented to her aunt that he would make sure that she returned every penny she had won from Richard Batt Construction Company following his father's death. Aunt Susanna had brushed it aside as a childish talk, but Philemon was not kidding.

When Susanna arrived home, she was shock to see her entire house upside down. She broke down and cried. While she was crying, some of her neighbors came and told her that Philemon and two of his friends had been around her house two days earlier. Early the next morning, Susanna went to Gracie to inquire about Philemon. Mrs. Bundor said that her son was in school and could help her sister-in-law if she needed anything. "Someone broke into my house and ransacked it while I was away. My neighbors said Philemon and two of his friends were around the house two days earlier," Susanna explained to Gracie. "For the last five days, my son had not left this house. He had lots of school works, so I told him not to leave the house," Gracie responded. "But my neighbors said that they saw Philemon at my house," Susanna countered again.

"Well, your neighbors must be blind because I know the identity of my son, and I have told you that he was here all of the time," Gracie concluded.

The city of Summerville was not equipped to fight crimes. It had a small police station in the middle of town. The building had three rooms and the fourth and smallest one was used as a jail. There were only four police officers in the city of nearly 2,000 people. One police chief, one desk sergeant, one traffic cop and one crime fighter. No criminal spent no more than two days in jail. Prisoners whose parents had money spent only a few hours in jail and, then they were out. All they had to do was to pay ransom to the police chief, and then, their criminal family member was set free.

Susanna felt it was no use going to the police. She would not dare to take her nephew and his mother to the police. She would not proof that Philemon broke into her house since she did not physically see him at the time of the break-in. She had no evidence to submit to the police. But if this happened again, she would take the law into her own hands. She told her brother Matt Bundor about the incident, but he had nothing to say. He was Philemon's mentor and hero. Lord, what bad would Uncle Matt say about his nephew Philemon Bundor?

Uncle Matt did not steal, but he had taught every conceivable trick in Ananias Imitator's manual on lying to his nephew. Philemon was now better at telling lies and stories than Uncle Matt. When he and his mother returned home from his grandparents, he told his friends that he fought Grandpa Theophilus and broke one of his teeth, and that was why they returned sooner than anticipated. His friends were now beginning to listen to him more than Uncle Matt. Philemon was turning eighteen and had begun to attract his own followers.

By eleventh grade, Philemon had dropped out of high school. When the Principal, Mrs. Amanda Floods contacted Gracie to inquire about Philemon Bundor's possible return to school, she told the principal, "Look, school is not for everyone. Look at Uncle Matt Bundror, he did not go to school and he is doing all right." Mrs. Floods felt disappointed, but she could not do a thing about it. This was Liberia, where every family did as it wished or pleased.

Summerville Elementary, Junior and High Schools were just half a mile north of the city. There was no bus or any type of transportation for students to get to and from schools. A few residents owned automobiles. There were several commercial drivers in the city, but they worked for other car owners. At the end of the day, the cars were brought home and parked in the yards of their owners.

One night, Philemon and a friend broke into Mr. Sekou Konneh's Peugeot 504 taxicab and shattered the driver's side window. Mr. Konneh was faster than Philemon's friend, Paul Hector. He helped to identify Philemon the next morning. Mr. Konneh went to Gracie Bundror and the parents of Paul Hector and threatened to take the case to the magistrate judge in Summerville. For the first time in her life, Gracie was afraid of what was going to happen to her son. Both families agreed to pay for the damage to Mr. Konneh's car. He did not go to court when the parents paid for the damage as promised.

That night Gracie scolded her son gently fearing she would hurt his feeling. Philemon was the only thing she had in this wicked and unfriendly world. She was not planning on getting married again. She had enough money to take care of her son and herself. Though she had not officially launched her bookkeeping and accountant business, she was helping business owners in the city to keep their books and prepare payrolls. And she was being compensated handily.

One Friday afternoon, Philemon broke into his mother's personal safe and stole $600.00 while she was away from home. She had gone to meet with one of her clients when Philemon broke into her safe. It took twenty-four hours for Gracie to discover that someone had broken into her personal safe. When she noticed that a large sum of money was missing from her safe, she called her son to inquire. But Philemon swore on the Holy Bible that he did not know who stole the money. When she threatened to take him to the police station to be jailed, he confessed to taking the money. He told his mother that Paul Hector had pressured him into stealing the money so they could travel to Monrovia to visit Paul's grandparents. He knew that Paul Hector had been sent to Monrovia to live with his grandparents for a while following the incident with Mr. Konneh's taxicab. After the confession, Gracie told her son, "I hope you don't do that again. If you need money, just say so, and you will get it."

The following week, words reached Gracie that her mother was sick and had been admitted at Elizabeth City Medical Center (ECMC). Gracie did not want to take her son along for fear of him getting into trouble with Grandpa Theophilus at the time when Mrs. Theophilus was sick. Her siblings were in the United States, so she had to be at her mother's bedside. Mrs. Drusilla Theophilus had a case of chronic bronchitis, and was later discharged after one week in the hospital.

While Gracie was gone, Philemon turned the family house into a party center. He invited all the **grownaboys** in Summerville to his parents' house to party. For three nights straight, they partied until in the morning. Some of the boys brought their girlfriends, and they slept in Mrs. Gracie Bundor's bed. They drank beers and broke bottles in the kitchen. When one of the girls, Lisa "Sugar-Girl "Franklin began to break-dance half-naked, Philemon broke into his mother's safe again and brought out dollar bills to be thrown at her feet. Lisa was the attraction that night, and Philemon threw almost two hundred dollars at her.

On the fourth night, words got to Susanna Bundor that her nephew had turned his parents' home into house-party central. At nine o'clock at night she brought her brother Matt Bundor along with police crime fighter Officer Billy Wilson. When they arrived, Philemon was on the floor flipping dollar bills at Lisa "Sugar-Girl" Franklin. It was not an appropriate scene for church folks to walk in on, except for Uncle Matt. He could not spell the word "Bible," and had never been to a church throughout his life. But Susanna was infuriated that this young man would go this far in turning his parents' house into a nightclub. She asked Crime Fighter Billy Wilson to arrest Philemon. As soon as she said that, the other kids ran, leaving Philemon and Lisa there on the floor. But Officer Billy Wilson refused, saying "Susie, the last thing I want in this city is to get into a bad book with Mrs. Gracie Bundor." When she turned to her brother Matt Bundor, he, too replied, "This is his parents' house, and he can do whatever he desires in here."

Susanna Bundor angrily left the premises with nowhere else to turn. She did not sleep well that night. She kept rolling in her bed not knowing what she would do about her nephew. She was frustrated, but she would not dare to take on Gracie Bundor and her son. After all, her older brother Davidson Bundor had died tragically on the job, and his death had brought her home to be an assistant to her sister-in-law. But Lord, she did not anticipate what was going on with her nephew, and how his mother was responding or handling it.

The next morning around eleven, Susanna went to see Rev. Marshall Garfield about what had transpired the night before. Susanna was a member of Summerville United Lutheran Fellowship (SULF). She served as an assistant chairlady of the Usher Board to Mrs. Darling Martinson. When she got through explaining the previous night's incident to Rev. Garfield, he replied, "My Sister Susanna, I know a criminal when I see one. Philemon's mother is leading him to his grave, and nothing anyone can do until he goes to his grave."

As Susanna left on her way home, she thought about what the Man of God had just said to her, "Philemon's mother is leading him to his grave, and nothing anyone can do until he goes to his grave." Those were some tough words coming from a prophet of God. She said to herself, "maybe Rev. Garfield would be the right person to talk to Gracie." But she was not willing to make such a suggestion to Gracie knowing that her sister-in-law would react angrily. For the next few days, she thought about leaving town. If anything would happen to her nephew, she did not want to be in Summerville to see it. That would resurrect her grief for her brother, and she was not willing to go there.

When Gracie returned from Elizabeth City, she met her house in a mess. Philemon had tried to clean up, but he made more mess of the house rather than cleaning it. He swept the broken pieces of bottle under the kitchen counter and covered them with a piece of newspaper. The house smelled like a tobacco factory. One of the boys who slept in Gracie's bed, burned a hole in the bedsheet with a lit cigarette. Oh yes, there were empty beer bottles in the front yard, back yard, and in the house.

Gracie called her only son in the dining room. Philemon came and sat in a chair across from his mother. She calmly asked him what happened in the house while she was away. Her only son Philemon Bundor replied, "Mother, me and my friends just wanted to have a good time, so I threw a little party for them. I am sorry if I messed up the house." Gracie did not have words to address her son. She sat there with tears in her eyes not knowing whether to grief for her husband or for her son. She calmly got up and went out the backdoor and sat on the porch for a few minutes. She wanted to pray, but Gracie Bundor had never been a woman of prayer. She had always stayed clear of the Women's Prayer Ministry at SULF.

She had always called them a bunch of jive old-time religious zealots and gossipers.

After a while she went back inside the house. Her son was still sitting at the dining room table. She asked him to help her prepare dinner for the evening. That night Gracie prepared dried chicken gravy with her son's help. Philemon was getting to be a good cook. With all the time in the world on his hands and getting into trouble, he was learning fast to cook. His mother had at one time told him, "If you become a good cook, we will open a restaurant."

After dinner that night, Susanna asked her son to pray with her. "But mother, we never prayed at bedtime before," Philemon replied. "Grandma said, sometimes you have to pray when things get rough," she concluded as she began to pray. Gracie did not know where to begin since prayer was not a regular part of her Christian life. She found words to thank God for her mother's recovery and the strength of her father. And for her only son, she asked God to have mercy on him. She pleaded with God to look at a mother's heart, and hear her cry for mercy on her son. By the time she would say, "Amen," Philemon was already asleep on the dining room table. After several nights of partying, he could not keep his eyes open for a prayer. His mother woke him up, and he went to bed.

Early in the morning while her son was still in bed, Gracie decided to do a thorough inspection of the house, including her personal safe. When she opened the safe, Gracie discovered again that hundreds of dollars were missing. She took a pillow and quietly walked into her son's room. Philemon was deeply asleep. She stood over him trembling. She wanted to suffocate him to death, but that was her only son, the joy of her life. She went back into her room and dropped the pillow on the bed. She ran into the kitchen, grabbed an ax and came in her son's room again. She wanted to split his head in bed and end it all, but she thought about her husband and said to herself, "Davidson Bundor would never forgive me for killing his only son." She went into the kitchen and put the ax away. She sat in one of the dining room's chair at the table and began to sob uncontrollably.

Gracie wanted to go to Rev. Garfield, but her family was not in good standing with the church. Rev. Garfield still remembered when Philemon threw a piece of chocolate cake at his wife's favorite dress. Lord, how could he forget when he himself bought the dress at Bloomingdale in New York? The Man of God still had the receipt for the dress in his desk draw at church. She wanted to talk to her sister-in-law Susanna Bundor, but Gracie's relationship with her had gotten sour on the day Gracie denied that Philemon broke into Susanna's house. Uncle Matt was of no help. He was always busy imitating Ananias.

Meanwhile, Summerville was changing rapidly. There was a new police chief in town, including four additional officers, and one detective (Liberians called the latter Criminal Investigation Division or CID Officer for short). And a new criminal court judge was also brought to the city. Judge Bobby Dickerson was a short middle age man who wore spectacles. He had gray hairline and weighed over two hundred pounds. He stood only five feet and four inches tall and always wore a white shirt with a black bowtie. He was a fast walker. He had been a criminal court judge in Mexico City in the northeast before being reassigned in Summerville. He was widely known in the northeast as "Maximum Bob." His minimum sentence for any crime, no matter what the nature of the crime was seven years. He always, said, "Seven represents a completion."

Judge Dickerson had been sent to Summerville because the city was acquiring a reputation as a safe haven for marauding and hooligan young people, including the likes of Philemon Bundor, Paul Hector, Levi Richardson and others. He was sent to Summerville to clean it up, get rid of the all the criminals. My God, his work was cut out for him. Summerville was growing fast, becoming a major city in rural Liberia.

Three weeks after his arrival, he organized a town hall meeting. He wanted the residents of Summerville to take ownership of their crime problem and find solutions. He was standing by to render any help to the city's new police chief, Captain Dianna Dooley, the first female police chief in any city in rural Liberia. Captain Dooley had been on the police for only two years, but she was a brilliant crime solver. A beautiful fair-skin woman who stood five feet and nine inches tall with dark pretty hair. She had a nice precision gap in her upper teeth. Oh Lord, when Captain Dianna Dooley got dressed up in her police uniforms, every man wanted to see her walk. She walked with her head and upper body raised up, and when she entered a room or a building, her presence was felt. She had a soft voice with a gliding Liberian accent, but placed emphasis on every word to make sure that her listeners got her loud and clear. She was in her late twenties, single and had no children.

The town hall meeting took place in Summerville High School gymnasium. It was a nice facility that seated a minimum of two hundred people. But Summerville would pack and stack it on special occasions like basketball games, Parents-Teachers Association (PTA) meetings, graduations and town hall meetings. The meeting was chaired by Mayor Gibson Newton. He was popularly known in Summerville as Mayor G.N. Mayor Newton was the longest serving mayor in the history of the city. This year would be his twenty-seventh year in officer. He was a distant cousin of the president of the country. Therefore, his appointment was lifetime as long as the president was alive.

He began by introducing Judge Bobby Dickerson, and police Chief Captain Dianna Dooley. Captain Dooley, then introduced her officers. The officials took their seats to the thunderous applause of the crowd.

Residents were glad that they would now sleep at night without worrying about someone breaking into their homes. And then, when the criminal was arrested, he never spent twenty-four hours in jail. A new sheriff was in town, and they were glad she would put the criminal out of business.

After the crowd had taken their seats, Judge Dickerson stood up and cleared his throat and addressed the crowd. "People of Summerville, I have made crime fighting my number one priority since I became a judge. I did it in the northeast, and I am ready and prepared to do the same here in Summerville. I believe law-abiding citizens should be able to enjoy the fruits of their labors, and to live daily without looking over their shoulders that they would be victims of crimes. I promised you, any crime committed by any resident of this city, no matter how young or old, I will make a state crime out of it. This means a minimum sentence of seven years. Every year, month, week, hour, minute, and second of the seven years will be served without any chance of parole," the judge said.

After he had spoken lengthily, Judge Dickerson paused to take suggestions from the audience. He wanted some deterrent measures that would teach criminals lessons to make them think twice before committing crimes in Summerville.

Many made several suggestions, but the suggestion by Mayor Gibson Newton stood out. He suggested to the residents that a hangman's gallows be built within the city as deterrent. Judge Dickerson's court would suspend sending murderers to Monrovia. Rather, convicted criminals would serve their sentences in Summerville. Those who commit a capital offense in the city, especially murder would pay for their crimes in Summerville. When Mayor Newton asked for a vote, it was unanimous. The death penalty was the law of the land, though never carried out in rural cities. That was about to change with Summerville setting the trend.

At the end of the meeting, everyone came to meet and greet Judge Dickerson, Chief Dooley and Mayor Newton. The Mayor became an instant celebrity that night following the meeting. The arrival of Judge Dickerson and Police Chief Dooley suddenly brought out the tiger in Mayor Newton.

Former Police Chief Sergeant Clement Debbeh was corrupt beyond words. He and Mayor Newton did not get alone, especially his handling of criminal defendants. Police Chief Debbeh had a terrible itch of releasing prisoners before and without trials. If relatives of the criminals had money, they were set freed within a matter of hours. Before his reassignment, Chief Debbeh acquired a nickname, "Sergeant Quick." Every resident hated him, but no one dared to challenge him. He was the brother-in-law of the superintendent of the county.

It was irony that Gracie Bundor and Philemon did not attend the meeting. She did not want any undue attention focused on her during the meeting. But Susanna and Matt Bundor attended the meeting and were not thrilled with the mayor's suggestion. Lord, they would not dare to raise any opposition fearing the wrath of the residents of the city.

That year in November, Philemon was celebrating his twentieth birthday. He wanted to throw the grandest birthday party Summerville had ever seen. He felt that his mother had the money to spend on his birthday. After all, he was the only son, and the joy of her life. She had never said "no" to him on anything since his birth. In spite of the troubles he had been throughout his life, and what he had put his mother through, he had managed to survived, and was about to celebrate his twentieth birthday. To Philemon, twenty was a special milestone, a magic number.

At the end of the week, Philemon told his mother that he needed some money to celebrate his birthday. He did not have definite figure yet, but he and his buddies were working on the budget. Levi Richardson and

"Sugar-Girl" Franklin were helping him to come up with some numbers that Gracie Bundor would not refuse. They still had at least nine days to work on the budget because Philemon's birthday was on the twenty-ninth of the month.

The budget included bringing Miss Sono Stewart, a loud-mouth stripper he had met when he visited Elizabeth City with Levi Richardson. Gracie was never informed until Uncle Matt Bundor told her that Philemon had gone to Elizabeth City. While, he was there, Philemon did not visit his grandparents. Lord, Mr. and Mrs. Theophilus would not have allowed him to enter their home. The boy was a thief and they knew it.

Saturday evening after dinner, Philemon presented the budget for his birthday party to his mother. He did not spare any expense. He covered every ground there was to cover in celebrating a man's twentieth birthday according to Philemon. Budget for the party was a $3,000.00. When he presented it, his mother was shocked. Gracie Bundor thought the president of Liberia was coming. She said to her son, "There is no way on this earth I will let you spend such amount of money on your birthday party." Philemon was taken aback by his mother's remarks. "You had secretly stolen all my money I have worked and saved in this house over the years," She concluded. "But mother you have never refused to do anything for me before, Philemon said to his mother. "I will get the money by any means necessary, even if I die in the process," he added.

Mr. Methuselah Gunlee was a divorced man in his late sixties who lived by himself about half a mile from Summerville High School. His wife Linda Gunlee had divorced him twenty years earlier on the grounds of infidelity. The church had tried to intervene, but Linda had maintained that Jesus Christ Himself had said infidelity was the only reason for divorce. And she did not want her Good Lord to bar her from entering heaven on such technicality as being married to an adulterous husband.

Mr. Gunlee was a terrific cabinet maker and had a cabinet store attached to his house. He worked hard to educate his boys when Linda Gunlee left. After the divorce, he had vowed never to get married again though he had one or two lady customers in the city who stopped by every now and then at night to pick up a chair or a kitchen cabinet. And when they did, he had what he called the "avenue conversation" with them and the prices of those items were reduced to one third or donated Liberian style.

Their two boys, Methuselah Gunlee, Jr., and his brother Reginald Gunlee were in Monrovia working for the government. Gunlee Jr., a lawyer was the District Attorney (DA) for the county of Montserrado, and his brother Reginald Gunlee, an economist was the Minister of Labor. Strange for an accountant, but this was Liberia. Anyone who could speak and write a little bit of English, got hired to do anything. In fact, a Liberian in search of a job will always say, "I can do anything."

At the beginning of the week on Sunday night, Philemon Bundor and Levi Richardson decided to rob Mr. Methuselah Gunlee's cabinet store. They planned to enter the store through the backdoor when Mr. Gunlee was gone to bed. Philemon would put Mr. Gunlee in choke-hold while Levi collect the money from the cash draw. They had been in the store several times the previous days mapping out their escape plan, and how they would rob the store and get away quickly.

That Sunday night, he and Levi entered the cabinet store a little after twelve midnight when the city lights were turned off. Mr. Gunlee had just gone to bed when the two men broke into the store through the backdoor as planned. Mr. Gunlee heard the sound and ran into the store with a flashlight to investigate unaware that Philemon was standing behind the door. As soon as he passed the door, Philemon grabbed him from behind, shouting to Levi, "Get the money, I got him!"

Mr. Genlee from behind, shouting to Levi, "Get the money, I got him!" Mr. Gunlee dropped the flashlight when he was grabbed from behind.

When Levi picked the flashlight up and flashed it in Mr. Gunlee's face, he shouted back at Philemon, "Let the man go. You are going to kill him," as he ran out. Philemon strangled Mr. Gunlee to death. He, then reached into the cash draw and took all the money out of it. By the time he would exit the back door, Mr. Gunlee's neighbors were already out. When Levi fled, he banked the door so hard that Mr. Gunlee's neighbors ran out to see what was happening. Two men whose houses were on either side of Mr. Gunlee's gave chase, shouting "Rogue! Rogue! Rogue!" Lord, no one ever remained indoor in Liberia when someone shouted "Rogue!"

Philemon Bundor was caught two miles down the street by the men with the cash in his hands. Crowds gathered quickly and began to take swings at Philemon before the police would arrive on the scene. The crowd recognized immediately that it was Philemon Bundor again. With former Police Chief Clement Debbeh gone, Philemon Bundor days of two-hour prison terms were over. My God, only police would stop anyone from beating up a thief in Liberia. As he was being led to the police station, the crowd followed, shouting, "Rogue! Rogue! Rogue! Some tried repeatedly to touch him, but he was shielded from them by the police until they arrived at the station.

Meanwhile the families of Gary Samuel and Aaron Sehas who captured Philemon, descended on Mr. Methuselah Gunlee's home and tried desperately to revive him, but it was too late. They put him into a cab and took him to the city's hospital where he was pronounced dead on arrival.

Words of Philemon Bundor's arrest spread like wildfire in Summerville. Further interrogation of Philemon that night revealed that he had an accomplice. Levi Richardson was with him when he broke into Mr. Gunlee's store. His accomplice Levi was nowhere to be found. He had run into the bushes behind the city high school and was hiding there. But, he was later arrested at his parents' home following a tip-off, and charged with first degree homicide along with Philemon Bundor. He was brought to the police station and put in prison.

Uncle Matt Bundor and his sister Susanna Bundor were the first relatives to reach the station. When they arrived Philemon was already behind bars. Uncle Matt ran home to inform Gracie that Philemon had been arrested, and his possible charge would include robbery and homicide.

Gracie got dressed up quickly and followed Uncle Matt to the police station. When they arrived, Chief Dooley was sitting at her desk, though it was pretty late at night for a Liberian Police Chief to be at work. Gracie inquired if she would bail her son out and take him home.

Chief Dooley calmly refused, telling Gracie Bundor that her son's crime was not billable at this time of the night until he shall had appeared before Judge Bobby Dickerson in the morning at nine.

Gracie left the station for home accompanied by Susanna and Uncle Matt. They walked the three miles-journey in silence. Susanna wanted to shout at her sister-in-law and say, "I told you so, but you never listened." But, then she remembered the words of Rev. Garfield, "Philemon is on his way to the grave . . ." Uncle Matt wanted to blame himself for being a lousy mentor, but he did not have the courage to say that to Gracie. She was too distraught to make sense out of anything.

They sat with her on her dining room table and tried to pray. Uncle Matt wanted to walk out when his sister said, "Let us pray." For the first time in his life, Uncle Matt Bundor was afraid to walk away from his sister. Susanna Bundor was a powerful woman of prayer. Without prayers, she would not have made it this far. She had been through a lot with men who preyed on her good looks, generosity and kindness, and in the end disappointed her.

She prayed for Philemon and his mother. She pleaded with God to give Gracie strength to endure whatever lay ahead. She also prayed for her brother that God himself would change and mold him into an instrument to glorify His name. At the end of the prayer, Uncle Matt and Susanna said their goodbyes and left around five thirty in the morning.

Gracie went to bed, but she could not fall asleep. How could she? After all, her only son, the joy of her life was in jail facing a capital offence punishable by death. She blamed herself for not giving the money to her son when he asked that Saturday night. She had thought that her son was bluffing when he threatened to get the money by any means necessary. She could not control her emotion. She began to cry for her son. She wished her husband was alive to stand by or hold her in these difficult hours. Gracie finally cried herself to sleep in the early hours of the morning.

She woke up at eight-thirty in the morning and hurriedly got dressed up to be in the court at nine. She was fortunate to find a cab. She arrived at the courthouse at exactly nine
o'clock. She was not late because Judge Bobby Dickerson had not arrived at the courthouse. Susanna and Uncle Matt Bundor were already in the courtroom sitting in the back.

Gracie entered and took her seat between them. She looked into the eyes of Susanna and whispered, "I am sorry. I wished I had listened to you." Susanna replied, "Be strong and trust in the Lord. With Him, all things possible." Uncle Matt looked the other way. He had nothing to say.

At nine forty-five, Bailiff Uriah Brownell called everyone's attention. "All rise, the Honorable Judge Bobby Dickerson in the courtroom!" Everyone stood up and sat back down at the judge's command to take their seats.

While in police custody during the night, Philemon Bundor and Levi Richardson were given special prison haircuts to set them apart from other residents in Summerville. "Zig-Zag Crossed-over" was invented by a notorious prison warden called Corporal Andrew "Lucifer" Zillah of Monrovia Central Prison in the 1950's. The man was reported to have carried out his own executions when the sentences were handed down and there was no one willing to carry them out. For a middle name like "Lucifer," no one expected anything, but the worst from him.

The haircut spread to all prisons in the country like wildfire. It was bad, it was ugly and was detested by all prisoners. Prisoners with lots of hairs looked ridiculous after "Zig-Zag Crossed-over." It was also meant as a deterrent. No man or woman ever saw himself or herself in the mirror with that haircut and went back to commit another crime.

When Philemon and Levi were brought in the courtroom, Philemon's mother nearly passed out. She could not stand to look at her son's hair. He still had the evidence of the cash tied around his waist so there would be no questions in the minds of the residents of Summerville. Everyone was nodding, "Yes he did it. That boy is wicked. Thank God Davidson Bundor is not alive to see this." All of a sudden, the heads in the courtroom turned to the back row where Gracie Bundor was sitting. Lord, people were suckling and biting down on their teeth and lips.

With the evidence around his waist and the body of Mr. Methuselah Gunlee's still lying in the hospital's morgue, Philemon and Levi did not stand a chance in the city. Lord, if the residents were given the chance, they too, would strangle the two men to death right there in the courtroom. Their court appearance was simply a formality for the people of Summerville to see the boys who committed the heinous crime. There was no question asked about their guilt, innocence, or whether they were represented by an attorney or attorneys. There was no need to waste the taxpayers' money to go through such motions.

Judge Dickerson cleared his throat and said in his briskly Liberian accent, "Mr. Philemon Bundor, I am sure you are aware of the charges against you. And you know that the crime of murder in this country is punishable by death through any and all means. Your actions were premeditated and callous. You and Levi planned to kill Mr. Gunlee in cold blood. I know he was afraid and fled the scene, but you remained behind to finish the job." Philemon nodded his head in agreement. The judge asked Sheriff Nicodemus Zachariah to take them back to prison to be brought back in the morning at ten.

It was an unusual Monday morning. The hospital grounds seemed strangely quiet for a hospital. Family members escorting their dead relatives to the hospital morgue were not weeping or crying loudly as they always did. But then, suddenly the crowd began to gather to take a glimpse at the body of Mr. Methuselah Gunlee. The city was shocked that a quiet man like Mr. Methuselah Gunlee would be brutally murdered by a young man. There had been murder cases over the last fifteen years, but the murder of a prominent resident like Mr. Gunlee hit the city hard. Everyone was asking, "Who would dare to do such a terrible thing?"

Words were sent quickly to Gunlee's children in Monrovia that their father had been murdered. Within twenty-four hours of receiving the message, they came with haste to Summerville to investigate. They were accompanied by two detectives from Monrovia, though it was not necessary. The boys came prepared in case of any eventualities. The younger Gunlee had always wanted to remain close to his oldman, but his father had always told him, "Son you have a life to live. Do not worry about me. My God will take care of me." Their mother also came from Mexico City to share their grief.

When the boys had done their investigation, they went to Judge Dickerson and their father's body was turned over to them for burial arrangements. With the assistance of the Summerville United Lutheran Fellowship (SULF), funeral arrangements were made to lay Mr. Gunlee to rest. The wake was on Friday night of that week. It was excellent, and that was how members of SULF described it. It was basically a song service that lasted until three in the morning. SULF Senior Choir sang Mr. Gunlee's favorite hymn, "God Will Take Care of You." Former Mrs. Linda Gunlee, now Mrs. Linda Exodus nearly passed out when the choir began singing the hymn. She remembered the old times with Mr. Gunlee. No SULF member went any closer to her, except her boys. "Maybe if she had not divorced Mr. Gunlee, he would be alive today," SULF members thought to themselves.

My God, it was a beautiful funeral procession from one end of the city to another. It was led by a local band in the city. Liberians loved their dead. Dead loved ones always go home in grand style. Home going was always memorable in the city, and Mr. Gunlee was no exception. Mr. Methuselah Gunlee was the first Liberian man to ever prepare his own coffin and keep it for his own burial. The interior was lined with gold plates and the bottom made so soft like a pillow made of feathers. Outside was so polished that one would see his or her reflection just by looking at it. Lord, it was magnificent!

The eulogy was delivered by Rev. Marshall Garfield of SULF. He talked about the good deeds of a righteous man like Methuselah Gunlee and the wicked deeds of men like Philemon Bundor and Levi Richardson, and how the latter men would end up in hell fire. He spoke as a prophet about what awaited evil doers in this life and thereafter. "Saints of God, those who commit evil acts will never get away with them. Our God will bring them to light. Never forget that God promised to fight our battles for us. Take heart and know that the murderers of our dear father and brother, Mr. Methuselah Gunlee will be punished. In this country, one would think that a man called Methuselah will live to be hundred years old. But we know that his life was abruptly taken away from him. Lord, have mercy, I say, Lord have mercy." When Rev. Garfield completed his sermon, everyone in the church was crying. After the sermon, Mr. Gunlee was taken to his family cemetery and laid to rest.

It was understandable that Gracie Bundor did not attend both the wake and the funeral services. Uncle Matt did not show up either. But Susanna attended both services to represent the Bundor family. The church knew Susanna's reputation and the kind of a person she was as a Christian. She was a woman of prayer, and a compassionate person. The residents of Summerville knew it.

Meanwhile Gracie sent words to her parents that her son had committed a crime. She did not go into details. But she did not have to because rumors and news travel in Liberia at the speed of light. Mr. and Mrs. Theophilus had heard the news about a boy murdering a prominent cabinet maker in Summerville. Mrs. Drusilla Theophilus told her husband, "I told you that boy was a heathenish child. The moment I laid my eyes on him, I knew he was no good." Her husband responded, "My Dear, the Good Book says, 'behold your sins will bring you out."

In spite of their grandson conduct, and what he put them through on his first visit to their farm, they decided to travel to Summerville to see their daughter and be by her side. They arrived a week after Mr. Gunlee had been buried. It was an emotional reunion for the family. Mrs. Theophilus arrived yelling, "I knew it! I knew it! I knew! I knew this child would put you through hell Baby Gracie. The first time this boy stole, he should had been sent to Belleh Yallah and be fed some real white dried salty rice so he would realize that stealing was wrong." "I am sorry Garcie, but I hope they hang him high. I heard Summerville has hangman's gallows. Brilliant, just brilliant," Grandpa Theophilus added.

Gracie understood her parents' position clearly. She could had done a better job raising her son. Her parents did not have the faintest sympathy for their grandson. This boy had almost fought his grandpa when he was barely fifteen years old. And Gracie Bundor had stood by her son, angrily leaving her parents' farm.

In Liberia, there was no sympathy for criminal just as there was no justice for victims. At times vigilante justice was the solution to crimes when perpetrators were caught. When a thief was caught, and before police arrived, victims or ordinary citizens would repeatedly touch him or her with anything at their disposal. They knew when the thief went to jail, he or she would be out within the next few hours or morning.

Criminals whose family members or relatives were in the government were shielded and protected from being punished for their crimes no matter how severe. Those with money had and bought justice, but the poor became victims at the mercies of the rich and the criminals. And when a poor man or woman committed a crime out of desperation, the penalty was swift and severe no matter what the nature of the crime. After all, a poor man or woman was born to suffer until death.

Mr. Marvelous Theophilus would have easily bought justice for his grandson. He had the money and reputation. But sometimes strange coincidences happened in Liberia. Mr. Theophilus did not know Judge Bobby Dickerson and Police Chief Dianna Dooley. These two individuals had been serving on the other side of the Liberian world. To throw a monkey wrench into this particular coincidence, Mr. Gunlee's boys were top government officials in the country. Any attempt by Mr. Marvelous Theophilus to buy life out of his grandson's death penalty would reach the Executive Mansion of the President of Liberia within minutes. And then Judge Dickerson and Chief Dooley would be history. Please do not ask what would happen to them. Only the Lord knows the answers.

This is a country founded on the "Liberian Christian Principles of Who Knows You." A man or woman who knew a lot of important people got away with stuff ordinary citizens would not otherwise get away with. And those who knew important people would be placed into positions in which they were never formally trained or qualified to hold. While on the jobs, they took long hours or repeated breaks, or they would never show up for work, and still get paid a lot of money. Vacations were no brainers. They took them at will, and the durations were up to them. Lord, sometimes strange coincidences did happen in Liberia, and still does.

The reappearance of Philemon Bundor and Levi Richardson were delayed for a week until after Mr. Gunlee's funeral. They had to because emotions were running high with Mr. Gunlee's boys in town. Gracie Bundor did not bother to venture outdoor for fear of retribution by a mob or a vigilante group. The Gunlee's boys were capable of taking the law into their own hands by paying a vigilante group to quickly carry out the death penalty. But they decided to let justice prevail Summerville style.

The two men were brought back to court Monday morning of the third week at nine. Both men were dressed in green jumpsuits and were handcuffed together. The money around Philemon's waist had been collected a week earlier and given to the Gunlee's boys. After all, residents of Summerville had already seen Philemon with the evidence so there was no reason to have the cash strapped to his body anymore.

Today was the date set aside for Judge Dickerson to hand down his death sentence. His Judgeship inquired if the parents of both men were in the courtroom. Lord, they were all in the courtroom not knowing what to expect. His Judgeship first addressed the audience, and then the parents and finally the two men. He told the audience, "To save Liberia and Liberians from criminals, the laws on the book had to be carried out to the letter. When and if there are doubts as to the guilt of the criminal, he or she should be trialed before jurors of his or her peers. But this case was clear-cut because the men were caught in the act and had the evidence to convict them. In fact, Levi testified against Philemon that he had tried to stop his friend from carrying out the plot, but Philemon refused. To celebrate his birthday, Philemon had to kill a man. A birthday is supposed to be a joyous occasion, and not a sad occasion."

Gracie, Susanna, and Uncle Matt Bundor were in the courtroom. As usual, Gracie sat between Matt and Susanna. Grandpa Marvelous Theophilus and Grandma Drusilla Theopphilus were seated directly behind their daughter. Warren and Ruth Richardson, the parents of Levi Richardson, and their other children and relatives were also in the courtroom.

The judge, then turned to the parents and told them to rise as he addressed them in the strongest terms. "Thanks to you for doing a lousy job of raising two criminals. I wished there were laws in the book for punishing bad parents. I would set the examples with you all. But since there are no laws to punish bad parents, I will make sure that these two men never commit any crime in Summerville for the rest of their criminal lives. Liberians must live in peace. The residents of this city must live in peace. Do not, I repeat, do not even think about bribing me or Police Chief Dooley. We will expose you if you make an attempt." When he said that, the courtroom became dead silence because it was strange for a presiding judge to make such a statement in a Liberian courtroom. Everyone breathed a collective sigh of relief and realized again that there was definitely a new police chief and a new judge in the city.

Judge Bobby "Maximum Bob" Dickerson, then turned to Philemon Bundor and Levi Richardson. They were brought closer to his Judgeship so they would hear him loud and clear. "Two of you are a disgrace to your parents and to this country. You have chosen to live a life of crime rather than contribute meaningfully to your families, community, and country. Your lives of crimes stopped here today with me. Levi Richardson, you are hereby sentenced to life in prison without parole. I would have sentenced you to death, but you fled the scene and did not directly participate in the strangling death of Mr. Methuselah Gunlee.

When the judge straightened himself up and called Philemon Bundor's name, everyone held his or her breath. He attempted to rise up, but he was the judge, and did not want to appear awkward in his own courtroom. Mr. Philemon Bundor, you are hereby sentenced to death by hanging for the strangling death of Mr. Methuselah Gunlee. The sentence will be carried out a week from today. Make peace with whatever deity you believed in and served. Court adjourned.

The complete silence in the courtroom was suddenly interrupted by cries from the Bundor and Theophilus families. For the first time in his life, Uncle Matt Bundor openly wept. Lord, the man did not even cry at his brother's funeral until now. Gracie's parents tried to comfort her, but they could not, and no one could. After all, her only son, the joy of her life had been sentenced to die by hanging.

Two days after the sentence, Mr. and Mrs. Theophilus left for their rubber farm. There was nothing they could do for their grandson. They clearly heard the warning from Judge Dickerson on attempting to bribe him or Chief Dooley.

Susanna also left for Elizabeth City to start her life over and again. She thought about going back to Monrovia, but the memories of her ordeals in the city were still fresh in her mind. Uncle Matt Bundor remained behind to be at Gracie's side on the day of the execution.

A week after the death sentence, and on a bright Monday morning two weeks before Christmas, Gracie Bundor was invited to the prison at nine to bid farewell to her son. She was accompanied by Uncle Matt. She could not find words to say to her son, except that she did not do a good job bringing him up, and hoped that Philemon would meet his father Davidson Bundor. At this point, Gracie was not sure if there was any place called heaven, and whether her husband was there.

At exactly ten o'clock in the morning, Philemon Bundor was led to the hangman's gallows south of the city, near the city square. Everyone came to watch the execution. This was the first of its kind in the country outside of Monrovia. History was being made in the country and everyone wanted to be a part of it. Every activity in Summerville abruptly came to a standstill as Philemon was being led.

Just three blocks to the gallows, Philemon called for his mother. He wanted to give her his final words. He would rather whisper it into her ears than say it out loud. The procession stopped and Gracie Bundor came very close to her son so he could whisper in her ears because his hands were handcuffed behind him. When Gracie Bundor put her right ear close to her son's mouth, Philemon Bundor gripped his mother's right ear and bit it off. Gracie withdrew her bloody head from her son's mouth and collapsed on the ground. It was horrifying scene. The crowd drew back, with some of them falling to the ground. Then they began to shout, "The boy is a devil! The boy is a devil! Hang him now!" Immediately, Uncle Matt rushed over and called for a cab. Gracie Bundor was rushed to the city hospital and admitted for traumatic amputation of the right ear lobe.

Philemon was quickly led to the gallows and hanged from sunup to sundown for the brutal strangling death of Mr. Methuselah Gunlee. His body was taken down after sundown and later buried in the city general cemetery the following day. Many people came to see him laid to rest not because they loved him, but because they wanted to make sure that he was dead and buried. His gravestone read, "Here lies Philemon Bundor, a man who took another man's life to celebrate his own. May his soul never find peace and rest wherever it is."

After the event, Uncle Matt Bundor went to Rev. Marshall Garfield and gave his life to Jesus Christ. He was later ordained and became the Minister of Evangelism at SULF. He became a powerful preacher in Summerville to the shock of every resident. He gladly exchanged his Ananias Imitator's manual for the Holy Bible and led many young men and women to Jesus Christ.

Gracie Bundor was discharged after spending two weeks at the city hospital. A week later, she sold her house and returned to her parents' farm and became the bookkeeper and accountant on Marvelous T. Rubber Plantation near Elizabeth City until this day. So if you were to visit Marvelous T. Rubber Plantation outside of Elizabeth City, you will find Gracie Bundor, nicknamed "Lefty" after her right earlobe was amputated or bitten off by her son. She later remarried Mr. Chuck Isaiah and had one daughter in her old age. She named her Gracaiah. She and her family lived happily ever after.

ONCE UPON THE TIME IN LIBERIA, a lady called Mrs. Gracie Bundor did everything imaginable to protect her son Philemon Bundor from being disciplined. He committed every petty crime and was always secretly bailed out by his mother. One night in November, he brutally murdered Mr. Methuselah Gunlee, a cabinet maker in his home outside the city of Summerville. He paid for the crime with his own life. And just before his death by hanging, he bit his mother's right earlobe off for not discipline him during his entire life. Gracie Bundor-Isaiah's one ear remains today a living testimony to any mother who may fail to discipline her child or children.

OTHER BOOKS BY DR. PETER Z.M. NEHSAHN

THE BIBLE'S ANSWERS TO REAL LIFE ISSUES THAT MATTER TO CHRISTIAN: A PRACTICAL GUIDE TO SCRIPTURE MEMORY

WHEN A CHRISTIAN REFUSES TO BE JOYFUL

WHY WORRY WHEN YOU KNOW GOD IS IN CONTROL?

THE POWER OF CARING: AN EVERYDAY DEVOTIONAL for Pastors, Ministry Leaders, Layleaders, Doctors, Nurses, Nurse Assistants, Healthcare Workers, and Christians who desire to Care for God's People

ESTHER: WOMAN THY TIME IS NOW; A PRACTICAL STUDY THROUGH THE BOOK OF ESTHER IN THE CONTEXT OF OUR TIME

SOMEONE SPECIAL DIED AT A CHECKPOINT IN LIBERIA TODAY: THE TRUE MEMOIRS OF THE LIBERIAN CIVIL WAR AS TOLD BY VICTIMS, SURVIVORS AND EX-COMBATANTS

AMAZING ANSWERS TO PRAYERS IN THE BIBLE; THE AWESOME AND UNBELIEVABLE POWER OF GOD

The Power of Worry-Free Living: A Twenty-Week Devotional for Trouble Times